CW00431208

Copyright © Nig

The author would like to stress that this is a work of fiction and no resemblance to any actual individual or institution is intended or implied.

Author's Foreword

I don't really believe in trigger warnings when it comes to books. Life is far more triggering than any words on a page, and a book can be closed and put down, whereas life has to been dealt with, on the fly, when we are unprepared. Those who have read my other books will know what to expect. I don't do sunshine and rainbows. I do violence, criminality, drugs, and other subjects people dare not speak of. However, I will say that there will be scenarios and language within this book that some may find uncomfortable to read. Unfortunately, I'm only the author, and I'm here to document what the characters get up to. Sometimes they're good, sometimes they're bad.

Also, while the murders are fictious, some of the events mentioned throughout the story are real but details have been altered to protect the identity of actual people. I won't say which, I'll leave the assumptions up to you, dear reader. There are also events which were experienced by many people who have lived most of their lives in Milford Haven, like me, and the memories of certain events can vary greatly. If there is a scene within the book that bears no resemblance to your recollection, just go with it, because it has been written how I remember it.

Enjoy.

For my children.
Four beings of unique complexity.
The easy part is loving you all.

For Ange.
You missed this one, and we shall miss you.

By

NIGEL SHINNER

Present Day

Haven. The dictionary defines the word as a safe place or refuge. It also defines the word as a small port or harbour, providing shelter for ships and boats. Both could be used to describe the town by its residents, many of whom had spent every day of their lives waking up to the drone of an oil tanker or fishing boat. Many would also breathe their dying breath just a short walk from the ebbing and flowing body of water which had served the town for more than 200 years. And while the people would come and go, the haven would endure.

The early winter mornings had a malevolence all their own. February had arrived and dawn was breaking earlier, but not so early as to brighten a 6am walk with the dog before work. Steven 'Taff' Davies both relished and hated a bitterly cold walk at the start of a new working week. He relished the walk because it was a positive way to start this week. The effort felt like exercise and the walk helped to clear the mind for whatever was to come in the following days. But he also hated the first day of the working week as he had a twenty-four-hour shift with a sleepover. Working shifts in a residential facility for adults with behavioural issues, he relished and hated the job, too. While rewarding and significant, the job carried risks from difficult to control adults with no presence of mind of their own safety or that of others. It was a tough gig, but someone had to do it.

The opaque grey sky infected the streets with its dull sheen; what was beautiful under sunlight was oppressive under the haze of a new dawn.

Taff kept Lucky on the lead as he paced down to front street, not wanting the excited little mongrel to run off too near to the main road. But once on Hamilton Terrace he was pulled across the road by the dog as it picked up the scent of something interesting.

He wasn't sure of the components Lucky was made from, he guessed some sort of spaniel/terrier mix, floppy ears, thick wavy fur and an excitable attitude. Whatever he was, the dog was a welcome newcomer to the family, loved by Taff's wife and their two young boys. But more so by Taff.

The roads were quiet with only the occasional vehicle passing along the arrow straight Hamilton Terrace. With towering town houses on the north side of the road and sycamore trees and benches along the south, it was the showcase road of the little Welsh town. As peaceful as the day could have been, Milford Haven was never silent, the town or the waterway. There was always a boat with an engine running or generator thrumming, keeping the power flowing for whoever was on board. Whether it was the dead of night or moments before sunrise, there was never a quiet moment.

Walking up to the junction where the Belgian Monument stood, remembering the people of the town for their hospitality to the Belgian exiles during the Great War, Taff took a right and headed down on to The Rath.

If there was any place to show a visitor the best views the town had to offer, The Rath was where you would take them, although, not at just after six on a cloudy winter morning. Any time the sun was in residence it allowed for a spectacular sight of the mile wide waterway, with the evidence of industrial development only vaguely spoiling the scenery. The tankers, the jetties, the Milford Haven docks; all the evidence of a young town with a rapid history which was viewed better under a setting sun casting long shadows.

Taking the walkway past the paddling pool, Taff let Lucky off the lead. The dog was off at a canter, chasing a scent, heading off to the path to Ward's Yard and forcing Taff into a jog when the dog disappeared from view. After a heavy Saturday night at the football club, and two hard sessions of karate in the week, running wasn't beneficial for his forty-six-year-old joints. An early morning jog with a thick head and stiff limbs was the last thing he needed.

Taff spotted Lucky sniffing about in the bushes near a boundary fence on the tarmac path which had replaced the old railway line. He tried to make a grab for the collar, but a rabbit darted from the

2

bush and down the path. Lucky gave chase and was swiftly beyond the grasp of his owner.

Struggling but managing to move his heavy legs enough to keep the dog within sight, he realised the dim morning sky wasn't doing him any favours with barely enough light to define the landscape he was heading into. The rabbit, closely followed by Lucky, dived under the gate of the long-abandoned Ward's Yard. It had been a breakers yard for ships, a century ago, and cars, a few decades ago. Now it was just a fenced off piece of waste ground.

Taff groaned. The gates were padlocked, and warning signs alerted trespassers they could be caught on camera and prosecuted.

But he wasn't one for following the rules and scaled the gate.

Pulling out his mobile phone, he flicked on the flashlight app. It cast shadows were there were none, but it really didn't illuminate anything. Ward's Yard was just a flat piece of grassy land where there used to be scrapped machinery and broken metal. He hadn't walked the area since he was a kid when it had been a dangerous playground for only the brave. He figured he was pretty brave back then.

There was no sign of the dog until he heard a bark beyond the scrub. Carefully picking a path through the unkempt foliage, he headed toward the lock gate between Ward's Yard and the old M.O.D. Mine Depot. The tide was very low, allowing the dog to get down onto the beach. Taff followed, sliding his way through dense seaweed and loose shale, the cloying stench of low tide filling his nostrils. The dog had no such problem. With the rabbit forgotten, he was onto a different scent.

Taff stumbled his way between the lock pits and out onto the beach. In the gloom, he saw the dog scaling the sloping walls of the Mine Depot. Giving chase, calling the dog's name, he was starting to lose patience. The time was running on, and this was supposed to be a short walk. Letting Lucky off his lead had been a bad idea and one that wouldn't be repeated; that is if he didn't kill the dog when he eventually caught it.

Clambering up the rugged concrete slope to a flattened area, Taff stopped for a moment. Three long buildings with curved roofs stood parallel to one another. The air was still, like it hadn't moved in decades, frozen in time.

His voice echoed off the hollow walls as he called after the dog. Somewhere within the derelict buildings a dog's bark pierced the air. The barking intensified yet remaining in the one location. Taff started running toward the sound, feeling apprehensive within the confines of the abandoned, graffiti covered site as though he was caught in some dystopian nightmare and herds of zombies would start crawling from the corners of the long-neglected ruins if he breathed too loudly.

Broken debris littered the ground. Weeds punched holes in the tired tarmac. The once proud factory lay in tatters, and he was intruding on the hallowed ground of the past.

Ducking through an archway, he could just see Lucky yanking at something in the corner of the vast building.

'Come here, you daft sod,' he called after the dog. But Lucky had other ideas, determined to retrieve his prize, ignoring his master's pleas.

The flashlight was on again, searching for whatever had caught the dog's interest.

'What have you got there?' Taff said, shining the light directly into the corner. There was a small room made of the same red bricks as the rest of the depot. The aged door that had once enclosed the room, hung off its hinges, exposing what lay within. The flashlight glare revealed a hole – a recess in the concrete floor – partially covered with sheet metal and some timber boards which had perished over time to nothing more than pieces of sodden, fragmented wood.

Lucky had something in his mouth. It looked like a long white twig. Attached to one end of the twig were several other twigs. They weren't twigs. It was a hand, a human hand, missing a few fingers.

There were more bones in the hole. Maybe more bones than could come from just one human.

Letting the dog off the lead had been a very bad idea.

4

Present Day

For the first time in a long while, I can feel the old me creeping back in. And that's quite a funny thing to say as I wash my face, seeing my reflection staring back as if there's a stranger on the other side of the glass. The young me is the old me and the real old me is the face I stare at every morning when I have a solo team briefing, telling myself to go out there and do my best.

Today, even before I've stepped outside of the house, I'm hearing the rumours. I've heard these rumours before. We all had. Everyone who had spent their entire life living in this little town at the edge of the world had heard the rumours a million times before. They didn't even have to start in our town, but it was in our town where they would finish. And usually, that would be that.

But not today.

In a small town news travels faster than the speed of light – maybe that's an exaggeration – but it does travel faster than the speed of social media, and that's pretty damn quick. In this modern age of technological wonderment, it was possible to video message a friend on the other side of the world, having a sequential conversation, while sitting on the bus if you have the signal and the data. In my teenage years I never had access to a home phone. If you wanted to speak to a friend, you would have two choices; go to their house and call for them or walk to the telephone box and ring them if they were lucky enough to have a house phone. They were simple times, the eighties.

I say simple times but only simple in terms of what we had available to us. In the world of a teenage lad, which I was back then, it was the most complex time of my life. Time has since passed, and the complexities of the old life became part of mundane existence. But some things don't change.

Teenagers were always on the cusp of something exciting; at least they were when I was one of them. The teenagers today have everything delivered in an instant. They hear a piece of music, they like it, they pull out their highly sophisticated mobile phones, tap the Shazam app and it tells them what the piece of music is. Another couple of taps and they've added it to their Spotify playlist or downloaded it using iTunes. Instant results in an instant world. We never had such luxury.

If we liked a song, we had to wait until the DJ on the radio said the name. If we heard the name and the song title, we could go to Woolies and see if it was on the shelves. If it wasn't, we could go to Martin's music shop on Robert Street and see if he had it or could order it. If it was ordered, it could take weeks to be delivered and by then it could have turned up in Woolies at a lesser price. Or even worse, you hear it again and it doesn't sound as good as when you first heard it. That was our reality. Nothing happened in an instant. If you wanted anything, it would take days, weeks, or even months to materialise, and there was always the risk of disappointment when you got what you wished for. It often seemed that way for me.

It still does, even today.

I washed the soap from my face, examining my features more closely than I had in a while. I was in my fiftieth year – not yet fifty – but approaching fifty at breakneck speed and I wasn't strapped in. Where had those years gone?

Patting my face dry, I could see where some of the years had shown themselves. The crow's feet; the receding hairline; the white hairs laced through my beard; the years had attacked my features, attacked my body, attacked the wiry youth I used to be. Age is a game: sometimes you win, sometimes you lose. I think I was doing better than most. I was still alive – not all my friends had been so fortunate. I still looked – or so I was told – younger than my forty-nine years. Again, many of my living friends weren't so fortunate. But then that's how it goes as you get older, we all have a friend who gets old before their time, and we all have a friend who never seems to age. For a long time now, I seemed to be the latter of my friendship group.

'Friendship group.'

6

That was a younger person's term. We were a gang, a crowd, a crew, and one time, we were a posse. We were the guys, even though there were three girls in our crowd. There was none of these gender-neutral terms when we were young. If you brought the sperm to the biology lesson, you were male, and if you brought the eggs, you were female. For the last thirty millennia that's how we identified each other. But somehow, in the last twenty years or so, it all became very complicated. I'm not sure I understood it all. People could identify anyway they wanted; they'd get no judgement from me. But again, it was because I didn't really understand. Maybe it was my age.

Age. There's that word again. For the longest time, I haven't really had the question of my age come up in conversation but, if these rumours were true, that could all change. Not because my age is in anyway criminal, but because I was of an age when things changed. We were all that age. I was a little younger than the rest but still we were bonded by our ages in school and that bond spilled out into the real world when school was done with us. In 1986, the year we left school, that's when life really started. We entered the limbo that most sixteen-year-olds felt back then; old enough to work but not old enough to drink in a pub. My youthful looks worked against me in that respect. I thought I would have to wait until I was eighteen and had some form of identification but, as the old saying goes, fortune favours the brave.

I was brave – more like Dutch courage, bought from the off-licence – but brave all the same. Unfortunately, for some of my friends, they mistook stupidity for courage and paid for it.

I'll have to tell the story of how it all started. I would have liked to have told it before the discovery – before the rumours are confirmed – but I know I've run out of time, and I must come clean about what happened back then. Not just to ease my conscience, but to apologise for the things I did and how responsible I feel. This is where I must justify my part in all that has happened. I hope I can be heard with an open mind.

7

Present Day

Turbulent gusts raced up the Cleddau River, lifting sea water into the air, mixing it with rain to create an icy vortex, penetrating clothing with little effort. Against the skin, the chill would seep its way to the depth of the bones, numbing joints and disabling limbs. It was a version of Hell never imagined but often experienced. There was no escape from the demon which morphed itself into the harsh cold of the winter weather.

Even with the brutal conditions calling the shots, there was another version of Hell being uncovered in the corner of a derelict building. Blue and white police tape stretched across the wide structure, hugging the walls, loose ends dancing for the unrelenting wind whistling its tune through random holes in the aged roof.

Two figures sheltered in a far corner, where the wind couldn't reach them but made itself heard. Two figures dressed the same: bright white Tyvek suits worn over shirts and business trousers. Blue cup face masks hung around their necks like discarded party hats on elastic as they pondered over the discovery made by a local dog walker earlier that day.

'How do you want to play this one?' DC Delgado's Mediterranean features twitched against the occasional spot of moisture which managed to find his face despite the cover taken.

'By the book – but we'll need to throw bodies at this as soon as we have an idea of what we're dealing with.' DCI Brooks was cool under pressure but, as yet, there was no pressure. They had a crime scene, and some human remains, which had been secreted into a concrete hole recently uncovered by the same merciless weather hampering their investigation.

Brooks had moved to the area a few years back. Originally from Bristol, he still had a subtle West Country twang to his voice, even after years of trying to hide it. Regardless of whether he was local or not, he was a good cop who pushed damned hard to get a result from the evidence he was working. Sometimes the weight of the crime hung heavy on his broad shoulders, making him stoop. A grade two haircut and salt and pepper stubble on his hardened, craggy face, made DCI Brooks look completely unapproachable. But that wasn't entirely true. He needed to be approached. He needed to hear what others had to say. He needed to know every detail of every case so that he may apply patterns he had been seen before, solving other cases, especially the crimes that had dragged him to the town of Milford Haven. Every time a body was uncovered, he hoped it was the break to an unresolved crime or

a hot lead to a cold case. Not that many bodies were ever found. If there was a body discovered anywhere within the county, there was usually a missing person's report filed days or weeks before the discovery. Mysteries were few and far between in Pembrokeshire.

'I'll check the missing person's register,' Delgado said as though reading the senior officers mind, his Welsh valley boy accent was completely out of place with his olive skin and Latin heritage.

'You're going to have to go back a few years with that one. That one's been here an age,' Brooks said.

'I know,' Delgado nodded and pulled out his phone.

Brooks left his colleague to call in the instructions.

The wind rushed through the pathways of the disused mine depot, although the rain had given way for the moment. Brooks stepped out of the vast workshop building to gaze at the adjacent structures, long since abandoned; a collection of redbrick buildings, not one with a single window intact. The Ministry of Defence site had been closed since 1990, left to the mercy of the elements, and the curious kids who took thrills from the post-apocalyptic look of the place. No doubt the many spray-painted murals were created under the influence of cheap booze and bravado to impress their peers.

Brooks unzipped his Tyvek suit to rummage for a pack of cigarettes. Sheltering from the wind in an open doorway, he sparked a smoke and wandered towards the edge of the site. The incoming wind was bracing. He resisted its power and gazed across Ward's pier and up the winding length of the Cleddau where river turned to sea, flowing out into St George's Channel. If the river could talk, it could tell some of tales, laying witness to many a dark deed to befall its shores. If only.

He felt a hand on his shoulder. It was Delgado.

'There's been a development,' the Valley man said.

Brooks merely nodded an acknowledgement as he took another drag.

'We've got three skulls.'

July 1986

I can remember that night; not clearly, not one hundred percent but enough to know it was the start of something. There was a change in all of us, our gang, and not necessarily for the better. We had shrugged off the mantle of school life and we were now stepping out into the adult world. That was rich coming from me as I was still two weeks short of my sixteenth birthday.

The plan had been set weeks ago that we would be going out and hitting a nightclub. In Milford Haven there was only one nightclub as such. There were plenty of venues with dancefloors and music but Debrett's – the downtown central of all that was cool and in vogue – was the only place that looked like a nightclub. I mean, who was I kidding, I'd never set foot inside the place, but I'd walked past a few times, and I would often see the local cool people either going in or coming out – usually in the worst possible state. I wasn't sure how cool you had to be to drink so much that you threw-up on the pavement and laughed about it, but it seemed like the thing everyone was doing, so why not me too.

I checked my alarm clock. The hands were at ten to seven, I had about an hour to get ready before I headed over to Dan's house.

Daniel James: if I had to pick one of the gang as my best friend, it would him. We'd grown up together, went to The Meads Infants together and then North Road Boys School. We both failed our eleven plus and so attended The Central School together, too. All that schooling together certainly bonded us. Most people liked Dan. He was funny, real funny. He was the joker of our pack and popular at school because of it. Our friendship was so tight, we always sat next to each other. One time, in a science class, I needed to go for a pee. I always tried to be as funny as Dan but never quite managed it. I held my hand up and without waiting for acknowledgement from the teacher, I blurted out, 'Please, Miss, can I go? I need to siphon the python.'

The glare she gave me was as though I'd asked to take a piss on her desk. Before she could respond, Dan threw his offering into the ring.

'Sorry, Miss, I think he needs to point Percy at the porcelain. Percy being his pet worm.'

There was a titter from a few classmates. Mrs Wallis, a frumpy old lady who had a good nature, softened her features to his remark.

'Shut up, Dan! I really need to go,' I barked. I was annoyed that he had stolen some of my thunder, yet I still found everything he said funny.

'Hey, just cross your legs and hold your breath and you'll be fine,' Dan scrunched his nose up and gave Mrs Wallis a wink.

She burst out laughing, gesturing towards the door because all the words had left her. I walked out to a fanfare of laughter from our classmates. They weren't laughing at me, they were laughing at Dan, as always.

Hopefully that would be the theme of the night. It would be good times with all the gang and Dan constantly throwing in the jokes or taking the piss out of one or all of us.

There was a certain degree of anticipation about the night's events. Firstly, we were all underage, and we were going to be entering licenced premises without any expectation of getting served. A few of the gang had been in the pubs before without a problem; Rob Sherman, the very political and intelligent member of the gang, had been able to grow a full beard since before his fifteenth birthday. We joked that he was actually a forty-five-year-old father of three trying to re-live his youth. He had been into Debrett's before, twice, in fact, and created a Utopian vision of what to expect upon setting forth onto the hallowed ground of the discerning adult.

Jon Samms, the rich kid, had been a regular drinker in the last few months. He was the oldest of our group. Tall and athletically built, he passed for older than his years. Everything about him was just that little bit better than the rest of us. In a larger town or city, his friends

12

would have been the elite in-crowd. In a small town like Milford, he was the big fish in the small pond, and we were all minnows swimming in his privileged wake. If I'm being honest, and I often am, I liked him the least.

And the other one of our gang who liked to partake in a little underage drinking was Jennifer Jones. Just to think of her name makes me take a breath. Jennifer, not Jenny or Jen, always Jennifer; she was everything I was looking for in a girl. She was tall, slim with amazingly long shapely legs, long blonde hair and grey/blue eyes. Other girls had acne. Her skin was flawless. She was flawless. Flawless to look at, flawless to talk to. I only had a problem with one aspect of her being: her taste in men. She liked Jon and she had also lost her virginity to Jon's older brother, Chris. It was another reason for me to like Jon a bit less than the rest of the group. I was fifteen – soon to be sixteen – and I was jealous. It was allowed. I would be mortified if those two – Jon and Jennifer – got into Debrett's and I didn't. That was why I was afraid of not getting in. Those two were constantly on-again-off-again but only in getting off with each other. Snogging and groping when the mood took them.

Jon had said that he had seen her boobs one time, while still on the school grounds, just after last bell. If they were like that sober, in a very public place like the school playground, what were they going to be like after dark with lowered inhibitions because of all the drink? I couldn't bear to think about it. I could take anything in terms of emotional overload. I didn't feel happy or sad in extremes and could tolerate most things with a degree of level-headedness. But there was one thing I wasn't conditioned to deal with – the jealously juggernaut that mowed me down every time I thought of them together.

For now, I would put it to one side and get ready. I'd put the water on to run a bath and prepared my wardrobe. I was going Goth tonight. Black jeans, black grandad shirt, black desert boots; I was hoping that an edgy look would garner the attention I wanted from a certain young lady. Plus, it made me look older.

13

Bath done, clothes on, and a liberal spraying of Insignia, I was ready to go.

It was a short walk from my house on Trafalgar Road to Dan's house on Robert Street; a walk I'd made a million times before. On my way over I noticed a few other revellers, all dressed to the nines, heading into town. They were older, wiser, hitting the pubs early. We couldn't afford to hit the town early. I'd done a few days on the spuds and had managed to earn a meagre twenty quid. I'd taken fifteen with me. At a pound a pint and a pound to get in, that was more than enough.

I knocked at the door. I could see a silhouette approaching the glass panelled front door. It wasn't Dan.

'Hiya, Will.' It was Dan's incredibly attractive mum, Tina. 'Come on in.'

Tina James was the first older woman I ever fancied. She was the first older woman, in real life, we all fancied. As teenage boys we had had our eyes opened to the opposite sex by movie stars like Brooke Shields in the Blue Lagoon and Bo Derek in Ten. Tina stacked up to those women easily. To us, she was an older woman, but she was still only thirty-three. She was short with long chestnut hair and bronze eyes. A dusting of freckles across her nose gave her a youthful look, making her seem more accessible to a younger man. And I couldn't describe her figure without mentioning her gravity defying breasts. I once saw a bra hanging from the washing line – 34D – yet she was about five-two and couldn't weigh more than eight stone. It wasn't a sexist observation. If her womanly charms weren't obvious to you, you had to be blind.

'Is Dan ready?' I said trying to focus on her eyes and not the low neckline she was sporting. At my age, practically anything could set off an unwanted erection and my jeans were already uncomfortably tight.

'He's just brushing his teeth,' she said, looking me up and down. 'My, don't you look smart. You must be on a mission tonight?'

'Mission?' I wasn't following.

14

'Smart clothes; aftershave – you pair must be out chasing the girls tonight.' Her perfect smile drew the eye.

'Er... yeah, something like that.' One question and I had crumbled. How could I possibly cope in a nightclub wall-to-wall with girls and the rush of intoxicants swirling through my immature brain. I was doomed before I'd even had a drink.

'Do you hear what I can hear?' Dan said, standing at the top of the stairs, cupping his hands around his ears. 'I can hear the young women of Milford starting to ovulate, simultaneously, because we have made the effort for them and are hitting the town.'

Tina walked away, shaking her head.

Dan's cheery face was not looking so cheery by the time he'd quickstepped down the stairs.

'Why are you looking so grumpy? I think the young women of Milford will need a smile to go with the effort,' I said, watching his face darken with each word I uttered.

'You'll never guess what I heard today,' he said.

'What?' I can imagine my face had screwed into a scowl at his demeanour.

He told me.

My little world tumbled over the edge of the tiny line I had been toeing for so long. I was crushed. I was devastated. In the grand scheme of my pathetic fifteen, soon-to-be sixteen-year-old existence, this was the worst news imaginable.

Jon and Jennifer were official. They were going out together: boyfriend and girlfriend.

My life was over.

5

1986

I can only imagine what it must have looked like, and it was probably the worst image of a teenage tantrum, ever. I stormed out of Dan's house, slamming the door behind me, not letting my friend follow. I had stomped all the way to the corner by The Manchester Club by the time Dan caught me up.

'Slow down, Will.' Dan gripped me by the shirt, but I tugged myself free, continuing to stamp my feet like a kid who had been refused a new toy. 'Where are you going?'

'I'm going the fuck home!' I bellowed.

Dan raced around in front of me and held me by the shoulders. 'Stop it! This is not how you get the girl.'

'What the fuck do you know?' He knew more than me. He had better social skills, better people skills and was more streetwise than me. If there was anyone I would listen to, it was him. But, right at that moment, I needed to allow the jealously I was infected with to run its course. I couldn't be sure how long it would last – ten minutes – ten days – ten years, but in the grand scheme of my short, shitty life, it felt like an eternity.

'Are you kidding me? Jon isn't going to stay with her forever. He's in it for the sex.' Dan's face crumbled under the blundering of a truly honest remark. I could see he was trying to conjure up an adequate comment to counter his statement.

'And I want to give her more than just sex! I want to be with her – love her – be there for her. How can I be around them now? It's hard enough when she's hanging on his every word and he ignores her when we're all together,' I spat the bitter words at my friend. He didn't deserve it – I knew it, he knew it – but I was hurting and I sure as shit didn't deserve it either.

'You need to be there when he fucks it up – and he *will* fuck it up. You have to be the shoulder for her to cry on.'

He was right, of course. Dan was always right. He had wisdom beyond his years and was the best friend anyone could ask for. He was my friend, and he was giving his best advice to me. And what was I doing? Throwing it back at him like a spoilt little brat.

It took the full length of Robert Street and a chunk of Dartmouth Street for him to convince me to stay out for the night. Dan knew me better than anyone. He knew me better than I knew myself. If there was one person who could deliver a description of the inner workings of my heart and soul, it was him. We had been friends for as long as we could both remember. There was not a time when we weren't in each other's lives, and that's how he knew all my secrets. My soul crushing love for Jennifer; my soul crushing disgust for my mother; my total lack of knowledge of my father, and now, my growing hatred for Jon Samms: every dark moment in my short life could be documented by Daniel James. If I ever needed a biographer, it would be him.

My tortured existence, somewhat calmed, for now, we headed across town toward our safe haven – Rob Sherman's house. Our journey across the criss-crossing roads that lead to his house on Great North Road was made more bearable by the half bottle of vodka Dan had sneaked out of his mother's drinks cabinet and topped it up with some orange squash. I took a long draught from the bottle and immediately choked on it. The mixture still too heavy on vodka. Dan tittered to himself, swigging it easily.

'Screwdrivers are not for you,' he said, pounding the side of his fist against the heavy wooden front door of Rob's house.

I just shook my head.

The door swung open within seconds, as though Rob had been waiting with his fingers on the latch, eager to spill his political opinions at us. As if we cared.

Rob was dressed in typical Rob garb. Black Dr Marten's, skin-tight stonewashed jeans, a German army shirt, buttoned to the neck, and a black military beret. Robert Sherman was almost a

17

caricature of himself. He was a less satirical version of Rick from the Young Ones.

'Greetings, gentlemen,' Rob bowed slightly as he invited us in, 'welcome to Chez Sherman, where we can drink and make merry until such time that we need to flow with the herd and rub shoulders with our oppressed brethren in the catharsis of Thatcher's Britain-'

'Shut up, Robert, where's the fucking booze, my man?' Dan silenced the rambling and got straight to the point.

'Upstairs, gentlemen. Upstairs.' A swoop of the arm directed the way.

We all bundled up to the bedroom we had been into a thousand times. A large cliché poster of Che Guevara hung over our 'Right-on' comrade's bed. A record player crackled away in the corner. The Jam's Going Underground distorted out of the poor-quality speakers propped on top of an antique wardrobe. I perched at the edge of the bed watching the turntable revolve, the vinyl disc rising and falling at every half turn. Dan fell into an old wicker chair, putting his feet up on a battered leather pouffe in the middle of the floor.

Rob walked in with a bottle of red wine and three glasses; only one of which was a wine glass. He kept the wine glass for himself and handed us a tumbler each and proceeded to pour the deep red liquid until they were almost too full to drink from. He filled his own glass and changed the record. There was a brief scratch as he stumbled over lifting the stylus. A new disc was placed onto the turntable and the music started to play immediately as the needle hit the groove.

The dulcet tones of UB40's Ali Campbell reverberated from the sub-par sound system, telling tale of how Red Red Wine helps him forget.

'Gentlemen, I would like to toast to our future, no matter how grim it might be under the current government,' Rob said, holding his glass as though admiring the gloomy liquid in the dust filled air of his stuffy bedroom.

We drank with him. The wine stinging my tongue with its bitter taste in contrast to the sweet orange mixed with vodka still on my taste buds. I downed the rest of the glass, swiftly, imagining my face looked like I'd just licked piss off a nettle leaf. The glass was refilled, and I kept sipping as I allowed the lyrics of the song to ease my pain. I was waiting for the moment the Red Red Wine would help me forget.

If only it was that simple.

Present Day

It was uncomfortable to watch. Only the most experienced of forensics pathologists would have ever had to deal with three bodies in one sitting. But this was something different – something evil – something beyond the realms of normality. Three bodies, one burial site; it smelled of murder. Three murders – one killer? It was too early to tell but initial evidence, coupled with gut feeling, was leading that way.

Brooks and Delgado sat in the corridor of the forensic pathology unit of The School of Medicine at The Heath, Cardiff. Lukewarm coffee from the on-site Costa was not quite hitting the spot for Brooks. He was itching to step outside and spark up another cigarette, but the smoke would have to wait for now.

Through the wired glass panel in the door, they could see a pathologist filling in paperwork for the incoming bodies: three bodies, three sets of paperwork. Just behind the medical professional was another door leading to the examination room. In a moment – any moment now, like any of the many moments they had already been waiting – the police officers would be beckoned through to take a spot next to the pathologist as he carried out a post-mortem on the first body.

Brooks understood there was a procedure to follow but he thought it bizarre that the bodies were to be examined individually. The head honcho at forensic central had given an over-elaborate speech about cross-contamination of the 'victims' and that it was his policy to examine each one in turn. The fact that the victims had spent many years buried in the same hole, on top of each other, seemed of little relevance.

The initial finding was that all the bodies were male adults and had been in situ for many years, possibly decades. Whatever clothing was left was in a very poor state, the majority had completely perished away. The bodies were no more than skeletons; bones barely held together by the remnants of sinew and skin. The pathetic remains of someone's son, someone's brother, someone's father. There was no evidence to those facts, but each collection of bones had a story, had a past, and more importantly, had a person somewhere who knew how they happened to be there.

In police terminology, each crime scene had a 'Golden Hour.' This was the vital sixty minutes from the moment the crime was committed to when the most crucial evidence could be extracted and used to catch the offender. That time had long gone.

One piece of evidence recovered was an old fifty pence piece. Minted in 1982, the coin was larger than the current coin and was found in the remains of a jeans pocket which was believed to be from the body at the bottom of the shallow recess. As an indicator of time, it was pretty thin. Someone could easily be walking around today with a forty-year-old coin in their pocket as a keepsake or good luck charm. But if it was a coin in circulation at the time of death, it would put the crime any time prior to 1998, and put them more than twenty years behind the chase.

That thought sent a shiver through Brooks. Somewhere out in the world there was a family missing a relative who had never come home. Twenty years of waiting for a phone call or a letter or just a word from somewhere or someone to say they were ok. Even worse, there was a killer still walking the streets, as free as a bird, while the victims had been caged in death, waiting to be found.

Brooks was assuming, and that was not part of the police procedure. Every crime should follow the basic ABC – Assume nothing – Believe no one – Check everything. Only go where the evidence leads you. He couldn't help but think of the discarded relics, hidden under cloth on the cold steel examination tables as the living, breathing people he needed to serve justice for. The tragic waste of life left him numb, but it was a numb that he was used to.

1986

I'm not entirely sure how soon after our arrival we left Rob's house but, when I stepped outside, I knew that I was well on my way to being drunk. Not tipsy or squiffy, but completely intoxicated. The summer evening was different: so bright. The sky was so blue; the air was so warm and comforting. The usual street sounds of passing cars and crowing birds became one big batch of white noise: the sounds swirling and mixing, no longer coherent in my drunken mind. In the battle of wills – my will against the will of the booze – I put up a mediocre fight and would suffer for it at some point; hopefully, not with an audience.

We left because some more of the guys had turned up. Rob's place was often the launch pad for our social gatherings. His parents were very easy going and liberal – not in the political sense – and encouraged their son to embrace being the host of the many events we would try to celebrate. Tonight, was the 'End of School' night out, even though we had our last day several weeks ago. The next big event was to be my sixteenth birthday in two weeks' time. I was both excited and nervous about it. But the rest of the guys were just as excited. I was the last of the group to turn sixteen and they didn't let me forget that. I was nicknamed Baby Will by the girls, two of which had joined us at Rob's on the walk – or stagger, for me – into town.

Nikita Brown was walking ahead of me, nattering to Rob and Dan, as I sauntered up the rear. She was a very pretty girl. Some say the prettiest girl in school, but not in my eyes. Nikita's mother was a local girl who had moved to London to work wardrobe on the West End shows, meeting singers, dancers, and even the occasional minor celebrity. The only person she mentioned that I had ever heard of was The Equalizer actor, Edward Woodward. Apparently, he was big in the West End in the late sixties/early seventies.

One of the performers she encountered had managed to capture her heart without much resistance. He was a Russian ballet dancer, called Nikolai Ivankov, who had managed to defect as the wall went up in the early sixties. It was a whirlwind romance which left Nikita's mother, Sandra, pregnant and out of a job while trying to maintain a relationship with a dancer who was constantly on tour. The relationship quickly fizzled out and Sandra returned to Milford Haven to live with her parents. Nikita cannot remember her father at all, but she wasn't sorry about that. Her mother married a good local man who was an excellent stepfather.

Nikita was tall, slim and had dark, exotic looks. She was dressed in a long flowing black skirt, a white frill blouse and wore heeled boots even though she was already taller than most of the other girls. Her raven hair was naturally curled and held in place by more hairspray than was healthy. I thought of her as pretty but not as girlfriend material for me. Whatever I became, it wouldn't be good enough for her. Not because she was picky, but because she excelled at everything, and most boys were intimidated by her. Looks and brains: it was a powerful combination.

As I walked behind everybody else, watching Nikita glide effortlessly along the wide paved walkway of Hamilton Terrace, I was accompanied by Sarah Gardener.

Sarah was my Gal-Pal. If ever I was stuck with homework, or even stuck by other less important things, she was always on hand to help me out of a bind. I considered her my second-best friend. Dan would always be number one, but she was a strong second. In my mind, she was the sister I never had. She was a sweet girl who would do anything for anyone and had such a generous disposition. It had been her birthday just a few days before, but she wouldn't allow herself to hijack our school leaving party with her own sixteenth birthday. Instead, she paid for us all to have cakes at the Welcome Café. But as generous as she was, she often became the figure of fun for some of the guys.

A plain looking girl, carrying a little extra weight, she never got looked at by the boys. I felt kind of sorry for her even though she didn't ask for sympathy. I was very fond of her but had never looked at

23

her as someone I would be romantically involved with. And while I never knew of her having a boyfriend, it was common knowledge that Jon – yes, the very same Jon who had just stolen my Jennifer from me – had snogged Sarah at the school disco last Christmas. Not because he wanted to, but because he had a bet that he could get a snog at the disco. Sarah was the sucker once again.

As we walked together, she linked arms with me to keep me steady and to stop me from falling into the road. Normally we would talk about the same old shit – she would make fun of how skinny I was, and I would make fun of her taste in music. I liked Depeche Mode, Simple Minds, U2: edgy, popular music. She liked Toto, Chicago, Foreigner; basically, any American ballad rock band. The last time I was at her house she insisted on playing Mr Mister and REO Speedwagon at me because she knew I would hate it.

There was no chatting about my xylophone ribs or her weepy music. The only thing my confused brain could focus on was Jennifer and Jon and the injustice of it all. Sarah knew the score and, as always, was there for me. Listening to my unhappy tales, sharing my burden, and offering whatever advice was appropriate. Though I was too young and naïve to understand, Sarah was one of the most critical ingredients in how my life was shaped. She influenced the best of me and overlooked the worst of me. I'm sure I owed her gratitude at many points in those formative years, but I never voiced it openly. There was an understanding in our relationship, and it was one-sided. I benefitted the most. I look back over all the years that passed since that summer, and I was never able to repay all the good she did for me. That's a burden I'd have to carry alone.

1986

For a first night out, it wasn't going too well. The drag along Hamilton Terrace was surreal to say the least. I'd been drunk before, when one of my mother's many boyfriends had handed me some *apple juice* in a pint pot and I had downed it pretty quickly, asking for some more to my regret. I didn't understand the concept of pacing myself. Before I knew it, I was lying on the bathroom floor with the room spinning around me, only lifting my head to vomit apple sweetness into the toilet. I was only twelve years old back then and knew nothing about drinking, other than the fact that I should do it because it's what all the grown-ups did.

Now I was trying to be an *actual* grown-up and it wasn't working out too well. Sarah had bundled me into the poolroom of The Starboard Hotel, keeping me away from the bar.

The Starboard was the place to be if you were young and wanted to be with your own kind – your generation. I had been here before, but again, with my mother and some fella she was seeing at the time. They were doing lunchtime meals and I remember having ham, egg, and chips. I also remember my mother and her current beau getting very drunk and giggling all the way home. On this occasion I was only seven. The giggling continued until there were some very different noises emanating from the bedroom. I was watching cartoons downstairs and playing with my cars. I didn't understand what sex was back then. When my mother came downstairs, much later to see if I was ok, she made up some story about... Dave? Was that his name? Whatever it was, she said that her boyfriend had been jumping on the bed causing the ruckus I was hearing. I didn't care much back then. I was seven.

I was more than twice that age now and, I hoped, a hell of a lot wiser. Although, current conditions were a complete contradiction of that.

Sarah handed me a pint of lager, keeping me away from anything stronger but also trying to increase the volume of the liquid I had been drinking. I suppose it was her logic and I was agreeing with her as I didn't know any different. As she was a little older – two weeks – and wiser, I bowed to her better judgement and sipped on the beer. Slowly.

We huddled together in the corner, trying to talk over the music being played at excessive volume from the jukebox. A-Ha - The Sun Only Shines on TV was distorting through the tiny wooden speaker mounted on the wall, forcing the two men playing pool to shout their conversation. I didn't know them or who they were talking about, but the talk was about the deep meaningful subject young men talked about when there was a need to be philosophical. Shagging.

Sarah shook her head over the occasional overheard portion of conversation and focused her attention on me.

'So why have you got a face like a smacked arse?' she said, swigging on Bacardi and coke.

'Have you heard about Jon and Jennifer?'

She shook her head even more vigorously than when the pool player was talking about getting a blow job in the toilets the previous week. 'Yes,' she said. 'I've heard. Yes, I know you're obsessed with her. It won't last, it's Jon. He'll take advantage, treat her like shit and move on. Do you not know your own friends?'

I often thought about that word. Friends.

Jon was one of the people from school who was ever-present in our lives but did so many things to annoy us collectively and individually. I wondered why we hung out with him at all. That was when the bonus of his rich parents, who like to throw pool parties with expensive food and top buck soft drinks, popped into my head. He liked to use people, so we used him back – for good cake and real Coca-Cola.

'I guess,' I said, feeling silly but still heartbroken.

'Will – you and I and the rest of the guys are out for a good time and we're going to have a good time. You're not going to be sad – I won't allow it. Got it?'

'Yes, Mum.' I cracked a smile, and she mocked a smug grin at me.

With that, the jukebox changed tracks to the crackling sound of Venus by Bananarama. It seemed as good as an excuse to leave the pub as any. Rob stuck his head around the doorway.

'Hey! We're moving on to Debrett's – you guys coming or are you too busy discussing your fate in the jobless wilderness of Tory Britain?'

Sarah and I looked at each other, rolling our eyes in unison and followed the political statesman of our group out onto the street.

As much as I agreed that drinking a lager would counter the effects of the stronger alcohol I'd already consumed, the reality was somewhat different. My head was pretty foggy before, but now, it seemed that all the booze had been concentrated and instantly delivered into the core of my cerebral cortex upon contact with the air. I gripped onto Sarah's arm as though she was the only thing keeping me from falling off the planet.

The walk from the Starboard to Debrett's was an epically long hundred yards or so. My drunken eyes had barely time to adjust to the bright summer evening before I was bundled into the black chasm of the nightclub.

I stood unsteadily next to Sarah as she paid for us both. The pretty girl behind the counter took the money. She was dressed in a black leather skirt, fishnet stockings, and a lace top that exposed the black bra she wore. She looked me up and down – no doubt assessing my age or my ability to walk – and motioned for us to go in.

In my drunken haze, the club looked like someone had attempted to create a chic club noir in the furthest depths of West Wales, and failed. The matt black walls dripped with condensation and the randomly jagged mirrors that adorned the walls were moist with the steam of a hundred revellers. The tune blasting out was not one I

27

recognised but Sarah screamed into my ear from two inches away, informing me that it was called The Walk by The Cure.

The dancefloor was no more than twelve feet square but a crowd of about sixty people bobbed and moved under the hallucination-inducing strobe light. The men were dressed in hard earned finery, strutting like caged beasts, desperate to attract a mate. And the girls – what could I say about the girls – the makeup, the hair and the clothes: it was the uniform of the modern women of 1986. Massive hairspray enhanced styles coloured and crimped to an obsessive level of perfection. The clothing was a mix of high-street and catalogue frilly blouses and long skirts. The signs of occasional rebellion were marked by harsh eyeliner and eyeshadow; bold colours blended across the spectrum until met with a severing black line of finality. Most of these girls were the girls I had spent the last few years hardly noticing. Under my current level of intoxication, and the jarring flicker of the strobe light, they appeared to be a whole other species of woman I had only just become aware of.

Casting my eyes across the many faces hidden within the darkness of the club, I caught sight of another couple who seemed ever present, not only in my consciousness but everyone else's too.

Kath and Stuart were the golden couple of the school. If our school had been an American high school, she would have the homecoming queen and he would have been the quarterback. I couldn't be sure how long they had been 'going out' with each other but for as long as I could remember they had been a couple. It seemed very weird to go from seeing them dressed in the Central School black and blue uniform, hands entwined, lips frequently locked, to seeing them in this very confusing, pantheon of teenage hormones, together, as a couple, while the rest of the patrons were engaged in various courtship rituals.

In my own mind, relationships were cheap and only held significance in the here and now. Tomorrow wasn't promised to anyone, and life should be lived in pursuit of brief hedonistic experiences. What the hell did I know? I wasn't even sixteen yet and here I was failing to grasp the lesson right in front of me. It would only be a lesson I'd learn over the passage of time, when my teenage years were all but forgotten and I was rushing toward the birthday to celebrate my half-century on earth. While some things would change, others would survive the test of time.

In the present, after life had taken its toll on the many, I'd still see Kath and Stuart out and about. They're still a couple. They have a house, children – who were now adults – jobs, happiness, yet no marriage certificate. In the uncertainty of life, where nothing is promised, they had more than many could ever dream of. They had found each other, fusing their lives as one without the necessity for the admin. If only the rest of us could be half as fortunate.

I didn't realise it at the time, but I had tried to create my own good fortune. I had my eyes on the prize. Quite literally.

My blurred vision panned back over the bobbing crowd as the music changed. The Cure gave way to The Cult and She Sells Sanctuary. The patrons on the dancefloor changed too. The edgy electronica crowd stepped off the floor and the contemporary rock crowd stepped on. Through the changing of the guard, I caught sight of Jennifer.

She was sitting alone on one of the long benches, arms folded, no smile. I thought that this could be my moment: the one where I come rushing in to put the smile back on her face.

I made my move and edged past the pogoing on the dancefloor. I was aware that I didn't have a drink in my hand but that didn't matter. Dutch courage was no use here, not when real life was beckoning me toward my destiny. The knowledge that I was already half-cut wasn't even a factor. The parts of my brain that *were* functioning were telling me this was the right thing to do, saving the damsel from sadness.

Her eyes looked up, no longer staring into the dark blue, beer-soaked carpet. She smiled a perfect smile. I'd seen it before, flashing in my direction. My heart danced under my ribcage to the tune of She Sells Sanctuary. Maybe that was what she was doing? Selling me

29

sanctuary? Giving me a place to inhabit that I had always longed for. I could see the joy in her eyes. Oh wow! This was actually happening. I couldn't mess this up.

I kept shouldering through the crowd, smiling back so she could tell it was a mutual feeling, inching my way toward her. So close. Not close enough.

She was still smiling but her eyes were not focused on me. Just ahead of me, in the throng of revellers, was Jon. Her smile became wider, her eyes too. She was looking at him. Not me.

It was time to get lost; to merge with the crowd and become invisible. I couldn't let her see me.

Too late.

Her eyes looked over Jon's shoulder catching me in her gaze, drawing me in. She was still smiling but not with the same intensity as when she had seen him. In fact, it could have been her fake smile. She had one. All girls did. Sarah told me this. Oh no, what could I do. We were friends but this would be awkward. My travel toward the happy couple had slowed to a shuffle. I didn't want to go over but now I was committed to it.

A firm hand gripped me by the upper arm.

It was Rob. He was with another one of the guys, Tom Magee.

I let them lead me away toward the bar, saving me from the ultimate in disappointed meetings.

Dragging me through the crowd, I was pulled into the bar area; the only place with proper lighting and the only place where you could see the flaws often hidden in the darkened corners.

Sarah was standing there; a Bacardi and coke in one hand and a pint of cider in the other.

'I think you're going to need this,' she handed me the pint. It was Sarah selling me sanctuary.

Yet again, I bowed to her better judgement. I'd had four different drinks and the mix was starting to lay heavy in my stomach.

But no matter, the oblivion of drink was salvation, saving me from the crushing of my heart. I couldn't wait to feel nothing at all.

9

Present Day

Approximately a quarter of a million people go missing in the UK every year, and most of those who do, it is usually a voluntary act. When life becomes too tough, a means of escape is often sought. Running away to a different town is an option, and in order to run away successfully, there needs to be a degree of premeditation addressed so a transition can be achieved without issue. Money saved; clothing packed; area recced and researched; cheap, anonymous accommodation acquired. Some runaways don't have the luxury of preparation, and go home, eventually. Though, some don't and the only thing awaiting them in a strange town is a space on the pavement and the potential for exploitation. Every town has characters with no moral compass and a lack of empathy for their fellow human beings.

Brooks stood over the decayed body and wondered if that was how this young man had ended up in a hole, hidden under steel and wood in a derelict building in the arse-end of nowhere with two dead bodies for company.

When looking for a needle in a haystack the most important thing to do was to start looking. Silently, while the pathologist walked around the examination table, methodically noting every mark on every bone, Brooks was trying to figure out the metric; 250,000 people per year, multiplied by the number of years since this individual had last taken a breath – it was a figure he didn't want to contemplate. Most missing persons who are found dead are generally located within a ten-mile radius of their home. He presumed that this was the case this time around. But it was not his business to presume. It was his business to know.

To add to Brooks' frustration, the pathologist had decided to do each body individually. Instead of one collective autopsy, the police officers would have to attend three separate examinations. There were reasons and they were valid. The bodies may have been in the same dump site, but they could have been killed individually at different times. With that in mind, the bodies would be examined in the same manner, individually. It was the pathologist's party, and he was in charge.

'Anything, Doc?' Brooks was impatient.

'Yes,' the pathologist, Dr Mervyn Davenport, looked over his glasses toward the detective, 'I've got the name and address of the killer on a toe tag – didn't you know?'

Brooks rolled his eyes at the doctor's gallows humour. He imagined that a man who dealt in death would have to develop a coping mechanism over time. If tasteless gags at the expense of the dead got this man to the evidence and solved the crime, then so be it.

'But really – what are you finding?' Brooks persevered.

'I can tell you that the wisdom teeth on this body had not fully erupted. I can give you my best estimate on the age of the victim and say that they were between the ages of fifteen and twenty-two.'

'So, this could be a child?' Brooks said.

'Judging by the length of the femur and the ossification – or hardening – at the joints, I'd say it's more likely to be the body of someone in their late teens. But some boys mature faster than others – that's why there's a margin for error.' Davenport was sincere. 'So yes, this could be a child.'

Brooks didn't want to contemplate the possibility of a child murder. When children go missing there is always a public appeal, press conferences, media coverage – the works. He wasn't aware of any ongoing missing children on his patch, and while it was entirely possible that this person had come from somewhere well outside Pembrokeshire, even Wales, the chances of someone of that age just passing through Milford Haven was extremely unlikely. As most of his local colleagues often joked, Milford was somewhere you escaped from, not to.

'Any indication on how long since death occurred?' Brooks was reaching.

Davenport shook his head.

'Judging by the remains being almost completely skeletal with very little soft tissue remaining, even though the body was covered up, I'd say that the body had been in situ for at least twenty years – possibly longer. But that's just off the top of my head because you're asking me for an opinion. Once the other remains have been examined, I may be able to give you a much more accurate estimation.'

'Ok, Doc,' Brooks nodded along. 'Is it not possible that it could have lain in the open and then dumped later?'

'Unlikely.' Davenport dropped his mask for a second so there was no misunderstanding of his words, 'If the body was left elsewhere and moved in this condition, it wouldn't be so complete. I would wager that the body was put in place soon after death and covered up.'

'I'm not a betting man, Doc. I only deal in certainties,' said Brooks.

'Well, I'm certain of one thing: those bodies were not put in the ground at the same time.'

Brooks knew he wasn't looking for evidence for one event. He was looking for the evidence of potentially three separate events added to his list of woes. Three bodies, three murders, one location; 'One killer' screamed in his head but he wasn't about to jump the gun.

10

1986

I peeled my eyes open, disorientated. I knew this wasn't my bedroom. In fact, I wasn't even in a bed, I was on the floor. The carpet I recognised. The posters I recognised. This was Dan's bedroom. In the dim hue of what I assumed was morning, a streak of filtered sunlight crept through a break in the curtains. I thought I must be dreaming or in some kind of alternate reality.

It wasn't an alternate reality. It was the morning after the night before. Two pints of warm cider in Debrett's on top of the lager, the wine and the vodka, had finished me off. I couldn't remember much after that.

I lifted my shoulders, but it was as if someone had had a marathon kick-about and used my head instead of a ball. The throbbing pain above my eyes was only slightly lessened by the ringing in my ears. Music at excess decibels from the previous night was still playing out in my head, chiming on the delicate bones of my ears. And talking of delicate, my stomach was bouncing along to a completely different tune, not one I was familiar with.

My mouth felt like I had licked a sandpit clean. I needed a drink, nothing alcoholic though. I was at the stage that everyone who had ever drunk to excess was at on mornings like this. I would never drink booze again. This was the second time I'd thought it. The first time was when I vomited cider at twelve years old. I didn't learn then and wasn't going to learn now. It would be a situation I would find myself in plenty of times in the future.

Carefully, I lifted my torso up into a sitting position. I was just in my pants. I couldn't remember getting undressed. I couldn't remember anything. Gazing around, I could see my clothing scattered about the room. My stylish threads discarded in heaps. I must have undressed myself. On a chair in the corner of the room I could see Dan's jeans and shirt neatly folded away, his shoes together and tucked underneath. I could only see one of my shoes lying on its side against the Hi-fi unit. I was clueless to the whereabouts of the other one.

I pulled back the duvet of my makeshift bed to assess the damage. There was a mysterious graze on my left knee. I needed to speak to Dan later and have him fill in the blanks. He was zedding away; a subtle snore coming from under the red and blue striped duvet he was wrapped in.

My watch – which I'm lucky I still had on – said it was a little after 7am. If I was lucky, everyone in the house would be asleep and I could sneak down and grab a glass of water before getting dressed and getting the hell out of there. If I was going to suffer a hangover, it was better if I suffered it in the privacy of my own bed.

Easing the door open, I could see Tina's bedroom door was shut, as was Charlotte's, Dan's thirteen-year-old sister. In full-on stealth mode, tip-toing out onto the landing and down the staircase, I made it to the kitchen. So far, so good. I grabbed a glass from the washing up tray, filling it from the mixer tap.

Water had never tasted so good, quenching the thirst and lubricating my arid tongue. I drained the glass and refilled it. I was halfway through my second glass when I was hijacked.

'Somebody had a good night?'

I nearly spat the liquid out. Tina had sneaked up on me. I wiped the back of my hand against my lips, removing the few drips running down my chin.

'Er... yeah... I think,' I smiled an awkward smile as I turned to greet her.

Big mistake.

As I'd said before, Dan's mother was a very attractive woman, a gorgeous face, tight curvy body and the breasts of a goddess. She was now standing before me with just a skimpy Japanese kimono dressing gown. The garment was so short that the hemline stopped halfway between knee and hip, the red patterned material was so sheer that I could not only see her nipples but the outline of her areole, too. The belt that held the whole ensemble together was so loosely tied that more cleavage than I had ever seen before was on view, and less than four feet away from my adolescent eyes.

'You were in quite a state – the first of many?' she laughed as she asked the question, the expanding of her ribcage pushing the faux silk material of her dressing gown further apart.

'I don't think drink agrees with me.' I tried to talk without looking at her, but it was impossible.

'It doesn't agree with any of us. You just have to find your limit and be sensible.' She turned away briefly to grab a mug from the cupboard, 'Coffee?'

I shook my head, holding up the half-empty glass.

'Dan said that you were having a bit of…' I could see the cogs turning as she filled the kettle. 'Girl trouble?'

I shrugged my shoulders. I didn't like talking about my all-consuming love for Jennifer with my best friends, so I wasn't about to open a dialogue with my best friend's scantily clad, hot mother.

'Will, there are going to be a lot of girls out there for a guy like you – prettier than Jennifer Jones – trust me.' Tina's eyes never left mine as she took a seat at the small kitchen table.

'Really?' What was I doing? *Will, for Christ's sake* do *not engage in conversation* – my internal monologue chastised my stupid alcohol addled brain.

'Yeah, really.' Her smile was subtle but powerful; you knew she was working things out that you had not considered. Her focus drifted down my unclad torso and then returned sharpish to my eyes. 'You're a good-looking boy – soon to be a man – and once you put a few pounds on those bones you won't be able to keep the girls away. Trust me – you'll soon forget about Jennifer Jones.'

"Trust me." She'd said that twice now. Maybe I could trust her. Maybe it was the counsel of an older woman I needed. Dan seemed to be doing ok. Maybe that was why.

I nodded at her suggestion.

With that, the kettle clicked off. Tina was on her feet and pouring the boiling liquid into the mug as though it was urgent. It also

37

meant that she was now standing less than a foot away from me. I could smell the sweet scent of her perfume, the same one that she had been wearing the evening before. Maybe that's all she had worn to bed.

'Girls will cause you grief. Never put all your eggs in one basket. Get out there and play the field.' She was so close to me I could feel her breath against my neck as the words left her lips. It was beguiling. She was beguiling. If this was her ruse to get me to stop thinking about Jennifer, it was working. Too well.

I didn't react. I stood still, holding her gaze. An eternity passing before anything else happened. I could feel the hours ticking over between the beats of my heart. I was frozen in time. Stuck in limbo. I didn't want the moment to end because I wasn't prepared for what could come next, but at the same time I needed the world to start spinning again so that I could escape the desire-filled thoughts consuming my young, virgin body.

She broke the moment.

Reaching up, she grabbed my face, and placed a kiss upon my cheek. In a moment of contact, her breasts pressed against my chest. I could feel the warm of her skin against the cold of my ribs. My brain couldn't comprehend the act.

And then it was over.

'You're a great lad, Will. Don't let anyone tell you any different.' Picking up her coffee, she sat back down again, crossing her legs.

Like a British Tommy trapped in the trenches under the sound of a million howitzers, I was rocked to my soul. I didn't know where to go next. I didn't know what to think next.

And suddenly, I was aware of something else. Tina had crossed her legs and the kimono had fallen open slightly, revealing the tops of her legs. In the shadowed area between her thighs, I could see a dark triangle. I couldn't be sure if it was underwear or something else, but I could feel my teenage body reacting. I was shaking with excited

38

anticipation and hyper-aware the material of my underwear wasn't going to be able to hide what nature had on the cards.

I dumped the glass, made my excuses and left, tearing up the stairs to get my clothes. If I was going to recover from this hangover, I didn't need to do it with an uncontrollable erection I couldn't quench. I was going home.

11

1986

'Wake up, sleepy head!'

I peeled my eyes open for the second time that day, not sure if I had skipped over a day and it was Monday already. Although, on this occasion, I was in my own bed instead of bundled on the floor. In the darkness of my room, I could make out three figures milling around. I recognised the voice that had woken me. It was Dan. The last time I had spoken to him I was too drunk to even remember what was said. The Fourth Bridge couldn't span the gaps in my memory.

After my close encounter with Tina, I had grabbed my clothes, got dressed and got the Hell out. I had stumbled back into my house just after eight, climbed into bed and promptly fallen back asleep. Now I was being invaded and rudely awoken.

'What time is it?' I said, sitting up to face the invasion force.

'It's three in the afternoon, Will – time to get up.' Dan placed a mug of tea on my bedside table and ripped open the curtains.

The afternoon sun flooded in. I had to shield my tired eyes but, in the glare, I could see that Rob and Tom were the other two figures.

'What have I done to deserve this intrusion?' I said, not withholding my utter displeasure at their presence.

Rob dropped himself onto the bed with a steaming mug of coffee in his hand. 'As your loyal brethren, we thought it would be prudent to assess your condition and bring you up to speed with the previous night's events.'

'Eh?' I wasn't in the correct frame of mind for Rob's waffling.

'Basically,' Tom interrupted, 'we just came to see if you were still alive – and to tell you how much of a tit you made of yourself last night.'

He was smiling for a change. Tom Magee was one of life's mysteries. He was a smart guy but didn't do too well at school. But that said, he was the first of 'us' to get a fulltime job, working in Woolworths on Charles Street. He was the pick-n-mix king, leaving work every day with a bag of sweets. Tom had loads of vices. He smoked, drank, ate shit food and was even thinner than I was, although a good bit taller. A lanky kid with a massive mop of tangled black hair, he certainly took a lot of stick about how he looked. It didn't bother him, and if it did, we never heard him complain. But Tom had another vice, one that many of us would also indulge in but only at his leisure. Pornography.

Tom was the porn king – Milford's answer to Hugh Hefner, but without the mansion and bunny girls.

If we wanted to see a porno, Tom would charge us a quid, lending out one video tape at a time for one day. He wasn't a business and couldn't enforce any fines like the video store on North Road, but he would stop us from borrowing for a while. Even dropping by his house would be an eye-opener. You dare not look under his bed for the fear of his wank sock or a stray tissue. Tom lived with his mother and younger sister, and very occasionally, his stepfather who was a long-distance lorry driver and the source of all the porn. You could walk into Tom's house at any time, push play on his video player and, more often than not, some badly dubbed, barely comprehensible Swedish or American hard-core would pop up on the screen. Tom never thought to remove the evidence from the player just in case he found himself alone in the house and had the opportunity to 'knock one out.'

'Oh God, what did I do?' sitting up, I feared for the worst. Alcohol was not my friend.

'Danced naked on a table-' Tom said.

'Snogging a bloke-' Dan said.

'Declaring an undying love for Thatcher and the whole of the Tory cabinet-' Rob said.

'Oh, fuck off!' I might have believed the dancing on the table business but the other two were not on my radar. The little bastards just wanted to fuck with my drunken head in its most fragile state.

41

'You have to go too far, don't you?' Dan levelled the question at Rob.

'I thought it was believable…' Rob replied.

I threw back the duvet and pulled on a clean pair of jeans and a black t-shirt. My head was still woozy but sleeping for most of the day seemed to have helped me over the worst of the hangover.

'So,' I said, flicking my eyes between the three invaders of my personal sanctuary, 'what did I actually do?'

'Drank some cider and fell asleep in the toilets,' said Dan, the amusement sparkled in his eyes.

'Oh God!' It was almost worse than doing all the things they had said. The embarrassment of not being able to handle my drink was mortifying. There we were, on the cusp of adulthood, and I was so far behind the rest of my peers.

'Yeah,' Dan chirped, 'I'd get those jeans in the wash. I think you may have been pissed on.'

I can imagine my face was contorted with disgust as I cast a cursory glance toward the pile of discarded clothing heaped in the corner of my room. 'That's grim!'

'Not as grim as Nikita's snogging companion last night,' Rob offered.

My eyes darted between them, and I recognised the slightly smug grin of my best friend.

'Daniel James – you old devil.' While I felt a pang of jealousy for his good fortune, I was genuinely pleased that the coupling stayed within the gang. Nikita was seeing one of the Grammar school boys for a time and we hardly saw her outside of school. We were tight. We were a unit. If we could have shed one of our numbers it could have been Jon, for all I cared, although Nikita and Rob got on very well with him, and Tom did a roaring trade in porn out of him. As for Jennifer's relationship with him, well, I just had to try and forget about that one.

'It was just a snog at the end of the night. No big deal.' Dan stood up and played down his minor conquest. 'Anyway, I had to look after you.'

I gave him a sideways look. 'What you talkin 'bout?'

'We couldn't drag you home in the state you were in. That's why you were at mine.'

Head nodding in agreement, I was grateful not to have been dumped on my doorstep, or shoved through the door, drunk. While my mother was a big drinker herself, and would have no reason to chastise my behaviour, I didn't want to give her any ammunition to start an argument. She had already started giving me the odd dig about not having a fixed job and how I couldn't pick spuds for a living. I didn't want her to harp on about paying my keep before I had a proper job. This was one of the situations where I *would* play the fifteen-year-old kid card.

Selfish thoughts put to one side, I remembered who was looking after me at the start of the night and wondered how her night had gone.

'What about Sarah?' I asked.

'What about her?' Rob answered my question with a question and shrug.

'Did she get off with anyone?' I was always taken aback at how nonchalant the boys were about her. She was our friend and she had always been so good to me, and I assumed she was the same with them.

'I don't think anyone was that drunk…' Rob laughed at his own witticism. 'Well, you were, but you were asleep in the toilets.'

They all had a laugh at my expense, and at Sarah's. You'll often have those days when you don't like your friends very much, and it had been one of those days.

12

1986

It was the day after my sixteenth birthday and the day before me and the gang would go out to celebrate. Almost two weeks had passed since my embarrassing nightclub narcolepsy event. Every time I was with one of the guys, I'd get a dig in the ribs and asked if I was still awake. By now it was an old joke and wearing pretty thin. My time to shine was tomorrow: party on down at Debrett's.

As it goes, I didn't see the guys as much as usual. My days were spent spud picking and my evenings were spent either reading or sleeping. I seemed to be getting better on the farm; my back didn't ache as much, and I was able to pick spuds quicker as the days went on. More spuds meant more money. I had started to understand the importance of a decent work ethic.

I had also taken on another habit to aid my future adventures into the world of alcohol. I had bought a case of lager and tucked it under my bed for the occasional evening tipple. I was working on the principle that regular drinking would add to my tolerance. And when I say I bought a case of lager, I'd asked Tina if she would buy it for me as I didn't want my mother to know. Tina agreed. She wasn't a fan of my mother.

That was how my days passed. Up, dressed, and out the door to catch the minibus to the farm. A morning picking new potatoes in the Pembrokeshire sunshine on a hill overlooking St Brides Bay. The only interruption was a lunch break of eating sandwiches while propped up against a spud crate. I had to make my own packed lunch, otherwise I wouldn't eat at all. The other teenagers on the farm had pretty sandwiches with the crusts cut off, bags of monster munch and a chocolate bar, usually a Penguin. I had a stack of tuna sandwiches, a multi-pack of cheap crisps and a pack of digestives. I was going for the calories. Too long had I been the butt of jokes about my skinny frame, and I was making roads toward changing that.

While the days were filled with constant activity, the evenings were a different matter. I got home from the farm stinking of sweat, covered in mud, and generally exhausted, and wanting sleep. But I knew that if I wanted to be seen as different, I would need to put in the effort to be different. I was sick and tired of being me. Life hadn't dealt me the best cards, but I was playing to win with all I had. If I wanted to win big, I needed to ante up and take the risks. So aside from all the bending and picking and lifting on the farm, I would come home, lift weights and do press-ups. The exercise would be followed by a bath, a mountain of food, and some beer before bed. I'd upped everything; more press-ups, more weights, more bread, more milk; more of everything and anything. I'd also managed to drink four cans of beer one night, without too much of a problem.

The effort was paying off. I looked at myself in my mother's full-length mirror, and I could see there was muscle where there was nothing but skin and bone before. The scales had me weighing in a full stone heavier than when I started work on the farm a month ago. I was hoping for another stone to give me some kind of presence: enough presence that Jennifer might notice me. Fat chance, even with all the weight I'd gained.

Tonight, I was fed, bathed, and huddled into the corner of my bedroom, sitting on a beanbag, James Herbert book in hand, my second can of beer on the bedside table next to me. I was in the house alone as mother was working up at the Manchester Club, serving pints and flirting with men old enough to be her father. She really was a piece of work, and I was the fly in her ointment.

Judy Taylor was a Milford girl, born and bred; a would-be socialite, forever and a day, until she was caught pregnant with me. I'd complete fucked up her twenty-sixth birthday celebrations, me being in my seventh month of gestation and all that. She suffered morning sickness almost every day until I was born, and I think this was the reason why she disliked me so much. Not only that but I also cramped her style when it came to the men in her life. I was the baggage they didn't want to carry. Now, at forty-two her looks were failing her. By

45

all accounts she had been a looker – the girl who turned heads on Charles Street as she walked the pavements to her various jobs. Her looks brought her attention from all the single men of the town – many of the taken ones, too – and this made her unpopular with the womenfolk of the small town perched at the end of Wales. Judy Taylor – the town bike. Everyone has had a go; some more than once.

I could feel the saddened eyes of my neighbours fall upon me as I shuffled past on my various excursions. *"There goes that poor boy – did you hear what his mother did with so-and-so – that's no way to bring up a child."*

I might have been the poor boy, but I wasn't deaf. As much as the gossips were correct, I didn't want to hear the endless rumour mill echoing behind me wherever I went. I knew how much I'd been short-changed in the maternal department – almost as much as I had in the paternal.

I never knew my father. My grandmother had told me, when I was seven, that my daddy was a fisherman from Denmark. She would often call me her little Viking. She died when I was eight. A sixty-a-day habit had eaten her lungs until she could no longer take a breath. That was the last time I had someone who cared deeply for me. I think that's why I was looking so hard to find love.

Maybe I would find it. But not today.

Maybe tomorrow.

Hopefully.

My wistful meanderings were interrupted by a knock on the door.

It was Sarah. I'd not seen her since she was looking after me in Debrett's before alcohol erased my memory and my ability to stay awake.

'Where have you been hiding, stranger?' she barged into my house and immediately made her way to the bedroom. I followed, not knowing what to say to her.

While I had some of the boys turn up on the Sunday after the night of oblivion, I had only seen Dan on his own twice and then again with Rob and Tom last Saturday armed with beer and videos. No porn this time. Highlander and The Terminator were providing the entertainment. It was agreed that we would not drink in the pubs and clubs to save money for my epic birthday bash. *Epic* was not the word I would have used.

Sarah, however, had not called around like she would've normally and it seemed like I hadn't seen her in ages. Somehow, she looked different. I couldn't place my finger on it. Her hair was the same. Her makeup was the same. Her clothes were the same. Maybe it was something on the inside, something I couldn't see.

'How have you been?' I asked, handing her a can of room temperature beer from my secret stash.

Her eyes crossed in confusion at the offer of a drink, but she took it anyway and opened the can. 'I've been good. How were you after Debrett's?'

'Rough!' I rolled my eyes and left it at that.

She giggled her cute girlie giggle and sipped on the beer. I wanted to tell her how mean the guys had been about her. Not because she needed to know but because I didn't want her trying to keep them happy when they really didn't deserve her time. School friends were the people who you spent a massive chunk of your adolescence with. That wasn't to say that once school was over and done with the friendships would be too. In my own mind, I was starting to see that some friendships wouldn't survive, but the best ones would endure the test of time.

Sarah – I believed – would be one of those enduring friendships. She had worked her way into my affections and continued to be the friend I needed.

'So.' I had to ask the million-dollar question. 'Jon and Jennifer: spill the beans.'

Her eyes dropped, breaking her gaze as the words fell from my tongue.

'What?' I wasn't sure what I had said.

'Well...' she hesitated. I could see the cogs turning as her overactive tact drive engaged. She was trying to break it to me easy. 'Jon's parents are away this week...'

'And?'

'She stayed over.'

The burning flush of jealousy in my face must have been obvious. I could see it from Sarah's reaction. The beer was no longer sitting comfortably in my gut. The swirl of rage and hurt twisted my sensitive world into a knotted ball of hatred. I knew what was coming next before she even said it and while it might have been a cruel disclosure, it was something I needed to hear. Not for it to wound me – which it did, mortally – but for it to be over and done with, so I could process it and recover.

'...and they slept together.'

I was done.

13

Present day.

Brooks was looking into the bottom of yet another empty coffee cup. He didn't keep a score on the number, but he knew it was more than was healthy for him. The two trips to the hospital shop for crisps and chocolate were also something he would tell himself was a necessity under the circumstances.

He had just stood up to drop the cup into the metal bin when Delgado came strolling up the corridor, a cardboard file under his arm.

Delgado had driven to the nearest Police station to use the HOLMES database system. Not wishing to wait until they got back to their own station in Haverfordwest, and with plenty of time to kill, Delgado had nipped in to see some of his old colleagues from when he used to be a beat cop in Cardiff and managed to explore the police database for missing persons in the Pembrokeshire area.

'How you doin?' Delgado asked. From the tone in his colleague's voice, Brooks figured he must look ill, hungry, tired, or all of the above.

'I need a shit, shower and a shave, and a pint of Guinness wouldn't go a miss.' Brooks even managed a smile, albeit a painful one. The plastic waiting room chairs were not built for comfort.

Delgado dropped into the seat next to him and pulled a pack of sandwiches from his pocket, dropping them into his superior's lap. 'Tuna mayo was all they had left.'

Before Brooks could state his gratitude, Davenport entered the corridor from his office, a file in his hand.

'What have you got for me, Doc?' Brooks ripped open the plastic packaging, taking a bite before the pathologist had time to answer.

'Well, I would say this person was in a fight just prior to their death or was involved in a fight that caused their death.' Davenport handed over the file.

Brooks pulled out the wedge of papers and started to leaf through them. Without looking up he asked the killer question, 'How did he die?'

'Blunt force injury to the back of the head is the most likely cause of death.'

'How do you know he was in a fight?' Brooks continued to scan the documents.

'Other than the head injury, the nose was broken, and I'd say he punched someone because a knuckle was broken in his dominant hand. Someone hit him – either in retaliation or started a fight and our victim got at least one good punch in,' said Davenport, shaking his right fist in explanation.

'Which was their dominant hand?'

'The right.'

'How can you tell that?' asked Delgado his face contorted in confused admiration.

'Bone density and thickness in the dominant arm,' Brooks said casually, as though it was a common detail to know.

Davenport nodded in acknowledgement. 'What he said.'

Brooks slipped the notes back into the file and stood to bid farewell to the medical professional.

On their way down the corridor Delgado could feel the brooding of his superior officer. After a few years of working together, the younger cop had the measure of his colleague. Tomorrow they would return for another autopsy. Tonight, would be spent in a budget hotel. Delgado would sleep like a baby, while Brooks would deliberate over the printed notes.

Brooks was a damn good police officer but not a great human being. The abundance of intuition for the dead was countered by a lack of empathy for the living. In his head, the dead had already had their judgement. He was there to investigate the living, breathing suspects left behind. Innocent until proven guilty? Bullshit. Everybody was guilty of something, Brooks just had to determine if it was worth reading the caution or not.

14

1986

It was time for my birthday party/drinking session. I hadn't arranged anything. Sarah had done it all for me. I think she was more determined for me to have a good time than I was. I don't know how my life would have been if I hadn't had her looking out for me. When you're a teenager, the friends you keep from school are the ones who add direction to life; sometimes for the good, sometimes for the bad. At the time, I couldn't see much beyond the next morning. Wherever my friends were going I was trying my best to keep up. If it could be classed as progress, I was going to do it.

I decided on a different tactic clothing-wise. Instead of the mock-goth look, I decided to go for blue stonewash jeans, black t-shirt and high-top Puma boots. It was the standard uniform of the lads about town and aiming for the edgy, all-black garb wasn't going to work for me. Jack, the carpenter who lived a few doors up, had given me a bottle of aftershave. He'd said it was too young for him and that he preferred a bit of Old Spice. I wasn't going to look a gift horse in the mouth and took it. It was called Aramis and smelled like carrot juice. I know that it was an aftershave that they keep behind the counter in James the Chemist, so I knew it was an expensive one. It also burned the shit out of my freshly shaved cheeks. I hoped it would be worth the pain.

Preened to perfection, I headed over to Dan's house.

It was a typical August day; blue skies and sunshine, just the way it should be. There were two bits of good fortune about being an August baby. The first was the realistic chance of good weather during any birthday celebration, and the second was to do with school-time birthday traditions.

In our school, Milford Haven Central, if you had the bad luck of having a birthday during term-time, your fellow pupils would often make you a cake. Now, while that sounds a lovely idea, the cake doesn't get baked, instead, the ingredients – eggs and flour – are thrown over your head as you leave school that day, leaving the birthday boy or girl with an uncomfortable walk home to an angry parent with some additional washing to be done. Amen for being an August baby.

I knocked the door and waited for a response. I was determined that I wouldn't let the revelation of Jon and Jennifer's *Carnal Coupling* spoil my evening. It might be a different situation once I saw them, but the knowledge of the act had turned my raging jealousy into a manageable level of indifference. Maybe it wasn't going to be so bad.

The door opened and I forgot myself.

'Fuck!' I said, out loud. I was thinking it, but my brain wasn't acting quickly enough to stop the words from tumbling out.

Tina answered the door. She was obviously going out for the night too. Standing on three-inch black patent stilettos, which really showed of the shape of her legs, and wearing a figure hugging off-the-shoulder red dress. There was very little left to the imagination. Her eternally impressive breasts were held up solely by the straining fabric as I couldn't see a bra. Her gorgeous chestnut hair was curled and held in place by a gallon of hairspray, creating a voluminous mane cascading over her beautifully tanned shoulders.

'Thanks... I think?' She stared at my open-mouthed gaze and then smiled when she realised that all her hard work had had the desired effect.

'Y-you... look... very nice.' *What a fucking bonehead!* I could have said she looked beautiful – gorgeous – pretty, but no, I said *'very nice.'*

She giggled, and I think she may have blushed under her makeup, but she held my gaze and said, 'Thank you, Will. You look... very nice, too.'

I grinned through my embarrassment and stepped into the house. Dan shouted from somewhere upstairs that he would be ready in two minutes. That left me in an awkward silence with Tina.

I couldn't help thinking about her in that tiny dressing gown, two weeks previously. Here I was, stood in the hallway desperately trying to conjure up any words of conversation without achieving an erection. It was proving most difficult.

'So, are you... going anywhere?' Of course, she was. Why did I ask such a stupid question?

'No, I just dress like this to scare the boys.' She held her poker face for a moment before erupting into laughter. She had a sweet laugh, like a schoolgirl's laugh. It suited her. But I couldn't think of anything that wouldn't suit her. 'Yes, I'm going to a wedding party at the Manchester Club.'

'Oh. Good. Enjoy yourself.' Thankfully I managed to reply with something normal.

'Come on, Charlotte.' Her attention turned from me as she shouted into the living room.

Charlotte was Dan's little sister, but there was nothing little about her. She was a carbon copy of Tina and looked much older than her thirteen years. Behind Dan's back, all the boys talked about how '*Smart*' his sister was. *Smart* was the word of choice for good looking girls. It bore no relevance to intelligence.

'Well, have a good night and enjoy your birthday.' Then she leaned in and kissed me.

On the lips.

I'll say that again.

The lips.

Not a long lingering, tongue down my throat kiss like I got from Becky Smith under the mistletoe last Christmas, but a brief placing of her plump red lips against mine.

Then she shouted a goodbye up the stairs and left.

I had been trying to resist my erection but now it overwhelmed me. So much for my inappropriate crush on my best friend's mother. If I fell onto my back in the sun, everyone would be able to tell the time. I was a sexually charged sundial.

53

15

1986

Following the routine of how our nights started off, Dan and I headed to Rob's house where Sarah, Nikita and Tom were already waiting and drinking. I stayed off the drink. If I had learned one thing from my previous drinking escapade, it was to pace myself. There would be no drinking until I was inside licenced premises.

We set off straight away, forming ourselves into pairs, to walk the length of Hamilton Terrace, chatting away and being social. I was paired – as always – with Sarah. She seemed a little different, maybe it was the drink. There was a layer of confidence that I hadn't noticed before or too drunk to notice the last time we were out on the town.

Since leaving school, a couple of months back, a few of us had tried to change who we were. School can be an isolating place when bullies run free and those too scared, or too insignificant to defend themselves, would cower in the shadows until the bell rang each day. If you do that for too long and you'll forget what it is to step into the light. But now, free of school and the domain of the bully, we were emerging from those shadows, testing our own boundaries and flourishing into young adults. Out of our group, Sarah had made the most progress.

In school she was a plain, slightly overweight girl, with mousey brown, shoulder length hair. She would have merged into the background if it hadn't been for her keen brain and endearing personality. In the right situation, she was fearless. She never pandered to the bullies and had taken a beating for it on more than one occasion. I think that's why I liked her so much. She would stand in front of the tormentors, taking the flak, just to allow someone else a little peace. She had done it for me on more than one occasion.

Plain and slightly overweight maybe, but that girl was changing. Makeup transformed her face, showcasing her large green eyes and highlighting her cheeks bones. Also, the mousey brown hair had been cut into a bob and coloured a rich burgundy. Maybe that was the source of this newfound confidence. New look – new Sarah. Whatever it was, I liked it. Not in a romantic sense, but in the way you would always want to see someone living life and living it their way.

We dropped into the Starboard for a single drink and the place seemed completely different from the last time. I think drink was a big factor. The last time I was there, I was shit-faced. This time I was sipping on a pint with more patience. I also felt it as we stepped out into the evening on our way down to Debrett's. Fresh air and alcohol were such a bad combination to my limited experience, but not this time. This time, the effects of the booze flowing through my system were minimal.

Entering Debrett's earlier in the evening, when there were fewer people and less alcohol to alter the perception, the place wasn't as mythical as I recalled. The walls were painted badly in cheap black matt emulsion and the mirrored details were nothing more than mirror tiles cut into squares and glued into random shapes. It wasn't chic – it was shit. And although I could see it, warts and all, I imagined the next few years of Saturday nights would be spent here; many nights merging into one long distant memory once I was old and grey.

With less foot traffic staggering across the sticky blue carpet, it was easy to see how small the venue actually was and how many people there were in total. There was also something else that wasn't obscured by jostling bodies. The lone figure of Jennifer sitting on an empty bench. An empty glass on the low table the subject of her focus.

I could see Jon standing at the bar with a few of his football buddies, laughing and joking and oblivious to his girlfriend's boredom.

While the guys headed to the bar, I walked over to Jennifer and sat down next to her.

'You look like you're having fun,' I bellowed. The music seemed louder without the crowd to absorb it. U2's New Year's Day brought a certain kind of melancholy to the half-filled venue. A few dedicated fans were on the dancefloor shuffling in time to the beat of the drum, raising their arms when the guitar riffs kicked in.

Jennifer's eyes broke from the empty glass and looked into mine. There was a moment – a pause – I wasn't sure what it was. It was like she was seeing my face for the first time, or maybe seeing something in me for the first time. I think it was my heart screaming wishful thoughts at her. Whatever had gone down behind closed doors at Jon's house, I was still looking at her perfect face in the imperfect light and wanted to kiss those beautiful lips. I could feel her breath upon my cheek; the faint scent of vodka lifting from her tongue; the strong scent of perfume on her skin. So close. Too close. I could sense our hearts meeting. I was useless. Powerless. Besotted. All that had come before was just preparation for this moment. The eternal desire I had for her was seeping into every inch of my being, pushing out all the unrequited feelings and replacing them with joy.

No matter how my heart was responding, the real world had other ideas.

'Happy birthday, Dickhead!' A pint was placed in front of me, breaking the moment. Jon stood over me, the mocking smug smile welded to his lips, handing another vodka and Coke to Jennifer.

'Thank you,' I said, graciously.

'Happy birthday, Will,' Jennifer eventually spoke and placed a kiss on my cheek.

I just smiled at her, lost for words. The silence didn't last long. The rest of the gang rocked up, drinks in hand, the air filling with shouted banter and riotous laughter.

Sarah dropped onto the bench; her leg tight to mine.

'Make room for a small one,' she yelled.

'Small one?' Jon said, laughing, 'I can't see a small one.'

There was more laughter, but not from Sarah, and not from me. I think the tone of the night had been set right there and then. It was time for drinking.

16

1986

It was just as Sarah had said. She told me that Jon would be done with Jennifer as soon he had gotten what he wanted. He had conquered her, like he did most people, and now he had cast her aside to pursue other interests, or at least that's how it seemed to me. If she was my girlfriend, or even just the girl I'd had sex with the night before, I'd be trying to keep her interested in me. Maybe that was a confidence thing. Jon was very nonchalant about his connections. He often talked about going to university and how his social circle would change and that we'd never see him again. I longed for that day. As long as I could still see Jennifer, that would be ok with me.

I could see her now, sitting next to Nikita and Dan, sipping on a nearly empty glass. Jon was nowhere to be seen. And it wasn't as if she could engage in conversation with the couple. Dan had his tongue firmly in Nikita's mouth and she was responding by gripping his hair, pulling him closer. If they became an *actual* couple, I know I would see much less of Dan. Life was changing. Moving on, moving forward, moving too fast. I couldn't keep up.

Everyone else's life was a magical rollercoaster, hands in the air, screaming for more. Yet here I was, standing in the spectators' booth without access to the queue because the ride was about to close. I was being left behind.

I wasn't alone in my birthday misery. Tom Magee was helping me through these painful moments with endless talk about his stepfather's new batch of porn. I wasn't interested in watching, or even talking about watching good looking men have sex with good looking women, but that didn't stop him telling me the intricate details of his proposed pirate pornography business; how he could buy six blank tapes for ten quid, copy some choice Swedish or American hardcore erotica on to each and sell them for a tenner a tape. While I could have shown more interest in his golden ticket to the good life, I was still looking over at Jennifer. Jon was still nowhere to be seen.

Rob was staggering his way toward us. I just seen him blown out by some girl he was trying to impress with his over-complicated political ramblings. No doubt he would start to question her sexuality before he would question his own charisma.

'How are we, my oppressed brethren?' His speech was clear even though his pupils weren't pointing in the same direction.

Tom just nodded to indicate he was good.

'Have you seen Jon?' I asked.

'Why?' Rob snapped. 'When have you been interested in him? Why don't you go and tell him that you're in love with his fucking girlfriend – or words to that effect.'

Alcohol had a detrimental effect on Rob. He was an angry drunk and probably made angrier by his lack of success with the local ladies. One day he might learn that women weren't impressed by guys trying to show intellectual superiority over the fairer sex.

I grabbed my glass and left the table. I was done talking about porn and my obsessive love.

The club was getting busy. I had to cut my own path through the throng of people. The air was moist with the condensation of a couple of hundred drunks breathing out their smoke-filled, alcohol-rich breath until it had enough weight and dropped back to the ground, catching heads and glasses on the way.

I wanted to check on Jennifer.

As I pulled level with the end of the bar, I could see Jennifer talking to a random girl. Dan and Nikita had obviously disappeared to be alone. Dan had said that Nikita's parents were away for the weekend, but he had said it with no expectation of what might happen. He wasn't an optimist in such circumstances.

The right move was to go over to Jennifer and see if she was ok, but to my left was the shrill of excited laughter. I could see people rubbernecking out of the open fire exit to see what was happening in the lane that ran parallel to the building. The lane was narrow, leading to the street but was closed off by a gate that was opened at closing time.

I stepped into the lane, pushing my way around a group of lads jeering at whatever was happening. In the dim light I could see

58

what was causing the commotion silhouetted by the streetlight. There was a guy leaning against the wall with a girl, kneeling, sucking on his cock.

I stood watching for a moment. Not for voyeuristic reasons but because something seemed familiar. I couldn't put my finger on it for a moment until the guy turned his head and was caught in the meagre light of the lane.

It was Jon.

'What the fuck?' I yelled. Who the fuck did he think he was? Not content with sleeping with the best-looking girl in town, he also had to get something on the side, and not more than thirty feet from where his lonely girlfriend was. I was raging.

My outburst caused the sex act to cease. The unknown girl, lost in the shadows scurried away out onto the street. Jon hurriedly fastened his jeans.

'Fuck off, Taylor!' Jon was incensed.

I bowled toward him, fury in my heart, venom on my tongue, 'What about Jennifer? You cheating fucking pri-'

My insult was met with indignant hands. Jon pushed me away. He was a good few inches taller and outweighed me by a couple of stone. I didn't know what I was thinking. It would never be a fair fight. I pushed him back, but he barely moved. A fist came at my face. I ducked and Jon's knuckles caught the side of my head. I hadn't been in a fight in years, not since the third year. I wasn't sure how to throw a punch well. Jon, on the other hand, had been in a few scraps in his life and was known for dishing out a beating. I was out-gunned and out-manoeuvred. Collapsing to a ball, fists fell upon my forearms as I sheltered from the raining blows. The cacophony of yells, deafening music and cheering revellers added to my confusion. Praying for a respite, the blows eased, almost stopped. I risked an upward glance and could see Jon was tiring, quickly. I punched out at what was within my eye-line, his groin. He buckled, clutching his most prized possessions.

59

I was about to make a break for it when a bouncer stepped into the lane, gripping me by the back of the t-shirt. I tried to pull away, but I wasn't strong enough.

'What the fuck is going on here?' The grim-faced, middle-aged bruiser held me in one hand and Jon in the other.

Before answers were forthcoming, Rob and Tom appeared at the door.

'It's ok, mate, they're friends,' Tom offered as an accord.

'A lover's tiff, my friend, we can take it from here,' Rob stepped in.

The bouncer looked at us like a pair of kids separated in the playground.

'No more fighting or you're both out, got it?' He walked away, shaking his head.

As if the situation couldn't get more awkward, Jennifer rocked up, confusion etched onto her exquisite features.

'What's going on? Why were you fighting?' Her question was directed at Jon.

Of course, it was. Why would she ask me anything? I had nothing to offer her.

I was emotionally hurt, psychologically hurt, and to top it all off, physically hurt. My head and my forearms throbbed. I know I would be bruised tomorrow but her attention for her cheating fuck of a boyfriend really drove a skewer into my tender heart.

'Go on! Tell her!' I yelled.

It hurt to see her wounded eyes dart between us. There was distrust in the glance toward me. Yet I was the one fighting – getting beaten up – for her honour.

'He was getting a blow job.' I had to say it.

As unprepared I was for fighting, I saw Jon's shoulders twist and my reaction was to dodge backwards. A fist swung past my chin, completely missing me, but catching Rob squarely on the bridge of the nose, blood exploding from his nostrils. I threw all my weight behind a right hand, catching Jon in the middle of his face. He was stunned but not hurt and retaliated with a left hand. It didn't reach me. Jon's blow was parried by Rob and countered with a right hand of his own. The damage I was unable to do, Rob managed in his drunken state; bloody nose and all.

This time two bouncers threw themselves into the fight, grabbing both Jon and Rob, dragging them down the lane toward the street.

Tear-filled eyes gazed at me.

'Was that true?' The distress in her voice was too obvious to miss. Jennifer had a look of hatred toward me, as though I had caused this upset.

I nodded and wanted to speak some words of comfort, but she raced away.

I tried to follow but too many bodies stepped into my path, and I lost her in the crowd.

After traipsing around Debrett's for a few minutes, I figured I was the only one of the gang still in the club and decided to leave.

The night air was cooling in contrast to the stifling atmosphere back inside the club. There were a few people milling around on Hamilton Terrace. Some would probably head back to the Starboard for a lock-in; some would go to get some food. There was no sign of Jennifer, Jon or Rob. Leaning against the wall, chatting away, were Tom and Sarah.

'Where did you disappear to?' I asked Sarah.

'I needed to get some fresh air. One too many drinks – one too many jibes,' she winked at me as she said it.

'Have you seen the others?' It was only Jennifer I was concerned about. Rob and Jon were big enough and ugly enough to look after themselves.

Tom piped up, 'Jennifer got into a taxi – alone. She was crying.'

I wasn't happy about the crying, but I was happy about the alone bit. This would all look very different in the morning, and I was hoping not to look like the bad guy. I know I wasn't, Jon was, but in the heat of the moment, with the added ingredient of alcohol, this could look so different depending on which side of the argument you stood.

'You guys going home now?' I asked.

'I'm going for some food,' Tom said. 'Anybody wanna join me?'

I shook my head. Sarah declined also. We bid him farewell and watched him head down to the burger van at the end of Hakin Bridge.

'Shall I walk you home?' Sarah asked.

'No,' I said indignantly. 'I shall walk you home, instead.'

'Maybe some of the way.'

Sarah lived on Vicary Street, the second right after The Rath. A ten-minute walk. I'd walked with her many times before and it was a very calming stroll on a mild summer night. Milford Haven's waterway was lined with oil refineries, and although they spoiled the daytime view with colossal tankers berthed at the jetties, generators thrumming away constantly, the night view was something different. There was still the noise of the generators, but the jetties and ships were adorned in lights of all colours. On a cool, calm night, the lights were beautiful, penetrating the dark of the unlit waterway.

'So, what happened?' Sarah asked as we casually strolled up Hamilton Terrace, passing the war memorial like we'd done a thousand times before, just the two of us.

'Jon was getting a blow job in the lane – and not from Jennifer.' The words were bitter on my tongue.

'Anyone we know?'

'I couldn't tell. It was dark.'

'One of his old tarts. Or one of his new tarts, probably.' Sarah had missed the whole thing and was digging for gold.

'Don't know – don't care. I just hope Jennifer is ok.' I was running ideas around my head about how I could come out the winner, maybe looking like the hero of the hour, but they all hinged on how

Jennifer would be with Jon afterwards. I hoped she wouldn't forgive him.

'I'll pop round and see her tomorrow,' Sarah said.

I just nodded, walking in silence.

We approached the Belgian monument at the start of The Rath – a sort of Cleopatra's needle but smaller. Sarah stopped and turned toward me.

'I can see myself home from here, Will.'

'Are you sure?'

'Absolutely.' She paused then laughed before she spoke. 'I'm sorry your birthday night was so shit.'

'Hey, it ain't over yet. Anything could happen,' I said, my arms splayed open in the hope for good fortune.

'You fool.' Then she kissed me. On the mouth, her lips parted slightly but the contact didn't linger for more than a second. 'Happy birthday.'

I watched her walk away. She didn't turn to see if I was still there, she just carried on her merry way.

I headed for home via the park opposite the council offices and took the long way round on to Robert Street to avoid the police station on Charles Street. I didn't want to top the night off by being arrested for underage drinking or something.

Under the orange glow of the street-lighting, most of the roads looked the same. In the distance I could hear taxis driving up Hamilton Terrace, taking people revellers to their homes to sleep off whatever drink they'd downed. I didn't need a taxi. The long walk down Robert Street wouldn't take long. Passing Dan's house, I noticed there were no lights on. I figured he hadn't gone home but had gone to Nikita's house instead. I could only imagine the stories he'd tell me tomorrow.

I smiled a sad smile and continued on my way.

Up ahead, I could hear the clipping of heels heading in my direction. I wasn't sure which way to turn, or even if I should turn. I had as much right to be on the street as anyone else.

63

But as the heels drew near, I recognised the shape of the owner of those heels. I wasn't sure how I was going to play this one.

17

1986

'You're heading home early?' Tina said looking at her watch under the orange glow.

I wasn't sure what to say. Did I say I'd been in a fight? Did I say the night had been completely shit and the only saving grace was that Jon and Jennifer might have broken up because he's a dickhead and she deserves better? I know what I shouldn't say: I shouldn't say that her eldest offspring is making the beast with two backs with one of the best-looking girls in town. That one I would keep to myself.

I kept it simple. 'Yeah, I ran out of money.'

She gave me a quizzical stare, like she knew I was lying. My mother also knew if I was lying. I wasn't sure if I was a bad liar or if older women were adept at seeing through bullshit. 'I don't think Dan would have let you go home early because of money – where is he by the way?'

Fuck, fuck, fuck! I may as well tell her the intimate details of the night and try to hide her son's conquest in the minor details. Dan always told me, to be a good liar you need to lie as close to the truth as possible, and that way, if you are found out, you can claim you didn't know all the facts to begin with. I had to say something.

'I think he's making sure one of the guys gets home.' I avoided her gaze for fear of being caught in a white lie.

'What's her name?' Tina smiled her perfect white smile. From her smile I could see she was telling me that she used to be that young once and knew the score. If your best friend wasn't with you at the end of the night, it was highly likely they had gotten lucky.

I smiled back and could see I wouldn't get anything past her. 'Nikita.'

'Nikita Brown?' I could see the admiration in her eyes as she asked the question.

I just nodded. There weren't roving gangs of girls called 'Nikita' on the streets of Milford Haven. It was the one and only.

Arguably the second-best looking girl in our year – Jennifer being the first, of course – but probably the third best looking female I knew.

The second best was standing with me in the street, making small talk.

'So,' she landed a loaded pause into her words. 'If you've not had much to drink, would you like to have a drink with me?'

I frowned in my confusion. She merely smiled and pointed toward her front door, just thirty yards or so behind me.

'Ok,' I said.

She led the way. I was a step behind and watched how she walked, tottering on her heels, the shape of her legs, the sway of her behind. It was poetry.

In the time between her pulling the keys out of her clutch bag and opening the door, I had scanned the street. I was aware that I was stepping into a house with an attractive woman and whoever saw could very well get the wrong end of the stick.

'What's your poison?' Tina said, leading the way toward her kitchen.

'What have you got?' My mind flashed back to the last time I was in this kitchen – just the two of us. She was in her skimpy dressing gown, and I was in a weaken state from too much booze. However, this situation felt very different. Maybe it was because I was a little older and wiser. No chance. It was because of a layer of alcohol I was wearing like body armour. My confidence was stratospheric, and my inhibitions were lower than whale shit. Somehow, I had found the balance.

'Lager, wine or vodka,' she said, grabbing a tumbler from her cupboard.

'What are you having?'

'Vodka and orange.'

I nodded in agreement. She grabbed a second tumbler.

With drinks in hand and the lights dimmed, we shared the sofa in the living room.

'So.' There was another of those loaded pauses she seemed to be dropping on me, as though she knew the answer before she even asked the question. 'What really happened tonight? Why were you heading for home at midnight on your sixteenth birthday?'

I told her everything. I told her about the way Jon was ignoring Jennifer; about how they were being mean to Sarah; about how I caught Jon with another girl; about the fight; how I took a beating and how Jon and Rob were kicked out of the club. I deemed it useless to try and hide anything from her. And what did it matter? I wasn't in the wrong. If she'd have asked me anything I'm sure I would have told her. She had that way about her. Dan was lucky to have a mother like her. My mother was a drunken piece of shit that would put the feelings of some guy she'd just dragged off the street ahead of mine. Tina was different. She didn't make you feel like you were talking to an elder, she made you feel like an equal.

'So, are you going to make a move on Jennifer, or are you going to suffer in silence and miss your chance, leaving it to the next guy to come along and sweep her off her feet?'

'Probably the latter.' At least I was being honest. 'I don't think I could sweep anybody off their feet.'

Tina gave me one of those pregnant pauses and held my gaze for longer than was necessary. 'Don't be so harsh on yourself. Confidence with women takes time and you've got all the time in the world. Take a few chances – learn a few lessons.'

'I wouldn't know where to start.'

'Try asking her-' I could see she was going to deliver some advice for me to try but she was interrupted by the phone ringing.

We both glanced at the clock. It was a little before one in the morning. Tina walked into the hallway to answer it. I could only hear her side of the conversation.

'Hello... hi sweetie... uh huh... yeah, that's ok... goodnight. See you in the morning.'

She walked back in with a wry smile on her face.

'What?' I asked.

67

'Dan is staying over and won't be home tonight.'

'Oh?' I made out like it was a surprise.

'Yes.' Tina's voice dropped a few decibels as though she was about to reveal a secret. 'He's staying at a friend's house tonight.'

'Whose house?'

'Yours!' She laughed.

I didn't know where to go with that. I just joined in with the laughter. Dan was caught out.

Picking up her glass, she drained it without setting it down again. 'Do you want another?'

I threw the drink back and handed her the empty glass.

I couldn't see her, but I could hear the clipping of her heels against the tiled kitchen floor. I heard the light switch click and the glow from the hallway extinguished. Walking back in, she placed one glass in front of me and then kicked off her heels and sat down on the sofa, right next to me, so close our legs were touching.

'Will you ask Jennifer out?' Tina asked.

'I don't think I'm up to that. I think she wants someone with a little more to offer.' I was being truthful. I was the only son of the town slag; my prospects were limited. Jennifer was raised by her schoolteacher mother and taught to be independent at an early age. As people, we were poles apart.

'You have plenty to offer, and not just to her…' her sentence trailed off as she leaned into me. I don't know what I was expecting but youthful fantasy was not it. Tina placed her open lips against mine, kissing me in a way I could have only dreamed of. I responded, kissing her back, my arms wrapping around her. I opened my mouth wide, forcing my tongue into her mouth. She pulled back.

Oh my God, what had I just done? My mind flicked into overthinking overdrive. I had crossed a line and Tina was repulsed. How could I face her again? How could I face Dan? What do I do next? My brain wasn't coming up with any solutions to the million and one questions my conscience was asking. I was too busy worrying to see Tina was laughing.

Why was she laughing?

'Slow down,' she said.

I went to speak but she placed a finger on my lips, sealing them.

'You won't be impressing Jennifer with that tongue action.' Tina smiled as the next words seductively fell from her lips, 'Open your mouth only as much as I do. Match what I do. If you feel my tongue in your mouth, then – and only then – may you put your tongue in mine.'

She leaned in and continued kissing me. I kissed her back, heeding her instructions. There was no pulling away now. I'd kissed girls before and there was a buzz, an excitement to it. But this was something else – she was something else. This was a woman – an older woman – with experience older than I was. I heard one of my mother's boyfriends say that women reach their sexual peak in their thirties. I'd never been sure whether he had been telling the truth or not but, based on the last few minutes, I'd say he was on the money.

Tina had one hand on the back of my head and the other on the small of my back. She pulled me closer, drawing me in, her tongue touching against mine. My heartbeat so loud I feared she could hear it pounding, drowning out the eager moans she was letting slip. Both my hands were around her back, but I made a move to cup her breast. It was firm yet supple. I'd never touched one before. To my friends, I'd touched loads. In reality, I'd never even had a glancing touch. I continued to squeeze and stroke without being too harsh. Whatever I was doing was getting a response. Tina gripped my hair and kissed me harder. My hand dropped to her thigh – her bare, silken thigh. I could feel her legs part slightly. I took this as an invitation. I slid my fingertips up the inside of her thigh until I touched the lace of her panties. Her legs opened wider. I gently pulled the thin material to one side, touching what lay underneath. The soft mess of pubic hair with a warm, moist opening felt comfortable but new – like foreign territory I had permission to explore. So, I explored.

Then she stopped me.

I looked at her expression, waiting for approval or displeasure. I saw neither. Instead, she took me by the hand and led me to the stairs.

I had always thought that the road to adulthood was a progressive journey, marked on the calendar until the date came and went. I was wrong. The road to adulthood was a road paved with moments such as this; landmark events that would make or break the journey. Whatever happened from here on in, I was leaping forward. I only hoped that my young conscience could bare the weight of the secret I was about to be a part of.

18

1986

I stepped out into the cool summer morning not sure if what had just happened was real or a dream. Turning to my right would take me home to Trafalgar Road. Instead, I turned left and took a walk into the darkness of the early hours. Somewhere, beyond the box-grid street design, I could hear a taxi either ferrying someone home or returning to the depot at the end of the shift. I looked at my watch. It was 3am.

My mind was awash with the events of the night, so much had happened, but one was racing to the front for attention. I had just lost my virginity, and not in chaotic fumbling on a park bench, or a stolen moment in the bedroom of an empty house. I had been guided through the doorway of sexual maturity by a beautiful woman with experience, and in an unrushed scenario that I couldn't have been more comfortable in. I was still riding high on the flow of serotonin mixed with boundless adrenalin. But for all the euphoria smothering my stroll into the next phase of my life, there was a harsh sadness I had to take with me.

I couldn't tell anyone.

Somewhere, in a darkened bedroom on the Westhill Estate – the rich end of town – my best friend had crossed the same threshold as I had, or at least I assumed he had. I'd know tomorrow – later today, actually – and he would tell me all the intimate details; what she looked like, what she felt like, what she did, what he did, how it felt. It wouldn't be bragging. It would be the sharing of a pivotal moment in a young man's life.

I wouldn't be able to have the same conversation. Nobody would know about my night. Nobody would hear about the intimate details of Tina's flawless body; the delicacy of her caress; the skill in which she had instructed me. I feared I would have to carry the experience to the grave, unable to share it with anyone.

At the top of Robert Street, I turned and followed the slope of North Road passed St Katherine's church, down Sandhurst Road and onto The Rath.

I dropped onto a bench above the path leading to the outdoor swimming pool. Dwelling in the dark orange glow had a comfort all its own. I gazed across the black water; lights reflected off the waves of water constantly in motion. The mixture of jetty and tanker lighting provided enough stimulation for my eyes while my soul floated on the breeze, wishing to be somewhere other than my hometown. I couldn't take back what had happened, nor did I want to, but I had to live with it, burying it deep within the fabric of my conscience, only to be revealed once an eternity had come to pass.

It wasn't an eternity, but after a while I had achieved a certain degree of peace, revelling in the minor comfort brought on by the rhythmic thrum of a tanker's generator. It told me that somewhere there was someone away from their home and family, making the best of their choices. Whereas I was still within the same ten-mile radius that I had been since I'd fallen from my mother's womb, and I'd never felt more like a stranger than I did now. It was time to wander to my mother's house. I wouldn't call it 'home.'

19

Present day

Brooks stood at the top of the stairs outside the budget hotel he and Delgado had been booked into. The hotel shared the site with a motorway services just outside Cardiff and was about as comfortable as sleeping in the boot of a car in winter. Wrapped in the long heavy coat he wore over his suit, Brooks still shivered against the February chill. His breath was casting clouds of vapour, and he hadn't yet lit his cigarette. He often joked that smoking outside in the winter might result in smokers passing out as they didn't know when they were done exhaling.

He placed a cigarette between his lips, struggling to light it against the gusting cold air. Burying himself into the corner of the lobby, he managed to catch a spark and drew heavily on his first smoke in an hour. He told himself he'd give up. He lied to himself often.

After stubbing out his smoke, he was about to head to Burger King to be completely disappointed by the image of the food he was overpaying for but, before the disappointment could begin, Delgado appeared from the hotel entrance carrying a file.

'Have we a winner?' Brooks asked.

'I've got a couple but some of the statements in this one mention a fight before the disappearance,' Delgado said.

Brooks glanced at the name on the cover. The file was old and faded.

'Where did that one come from – out of the Ark?'

'No – the eighties,' Delgado smiled. 'Like your dress sense.'

Brooks snatched the file from his younger colleague's hand. 'It's your turn to spring for food – I'll have a quarter pounder, large fries and lemonade. And get me some of those cheesy jalapeno things.'

Brooks took a seat, opening the file while Delgado headed toward the food counter.

The file was a missing person's file, as opposed to a murder file, but had quite a few leaves of dog-eared A4 bulking up the paperwork. Eyes scanned through witness statements handwritten in black ink on pre-printed forms: all the dates were from 1986. Brooks couldn't help but feel sorrow while reading the parents witness statement; the scrawled penmanship of a fellow officer, recording the last known movements of a teenage lad on the cusp of life some thirty-odd years ago. For all anyone knew, the lad could have runaway and set himself up in another town, never to return. Brooks had seen it so many times before. And he had been the arresting officer many a time when those runaways ran out of money and ended up trying to steal a way out of their situation. A conviction is a formality but a theft stamp on their record closes many doors that may have remained open if they had stayed at home. He felt sorry for runaways. Brooks was under no illusion that leaving the old life behind and casting oneself into the unknown was a desperate act. Was the information before him the last known act of a desperate boy or the last testament of a murder victim? This case was only just beginning. The first stumbling step of a perilous journey was laid out on a plastic table in a motorway fast-food joint. There was nothing glamourous about police work.

20

1986

The rattling second hand of my battery powered alarm clock had become hypnotic, but not enough to allow me to sleep. The sweeping red hand, in contrast to the silver minute and hour hands, had made its revolutions under my watchful eye for the last five hours.

I heard my mother's alarm clock radio click on. Bohemian Rhapsody by Queen was halfway through, blaring out of the crackly mono speaker, serenading her while she coughed up last night's cigarettes to herald in the new day. Over Freddy Mercury's vocals and the harsh ingrained ticking of my clock, I could hear her moving around on the squeaky mattress, reaching for the packet of John Player Specials to light up the first of the forty smokes she would puff through today. If nothing else, she was a creature of habit, and I was heavy on the word *'creature.'*

Working several jobs would come across as admirable to the casual observer. My mother worked in shops, in pubs, in restaurants, in laundromats; anywhere there was a quid to be made. She did most of her work off the books and lived for a cash-in-hand lifestyle. Some weeks she would be putting in up to sixty hours of hard graft but would still be totally broke by the time Sunday came. Her chaotic work ethic funded her smoking, drinking and general whoring around town. It was only because my grandmother had left the house in her will that we had a permanent place to live. I'm sure we would have been blacklisted by every landlord in Pembrokeshire by now if the rent fell under her responsibility.

I knew it was coming – and I was right – my door swung open and in walked my mother, puffing clouds of nicotine into my room.

'What'd you get up to last night?'

No *'morning,'* just aggression. That was my mother. Judy Taylor, a forty-two-year-old mother of one who walked about the place like a twenty-six-year-old mother of none and doing it all while looking like a sixty-two-year-old mother of a drinking problem. There was not a single maternal bone in her body. I was a burden to her, and she let me know it on a daily basis.

'Nothing,' I snorted from under the covers.

She stopped and stared at me for a moment, the curling tendrils of smoke oozed from the glowing bud at the end of her cigarette. 'Did you fall over? Were you drunk?'

My hand went to the side of my face. There was a lump, about the size of half an egg between my left cheek bone and ear. I don't know what it looked like from where she was standing but it felt large to me and hurt like a bitch. It must have been where Jon caught me when I tried to dodge his first punch.

'I fell – I think.' It was all I had to give in my confused, sleep deprived apathy.

'Fell? You're a useless shite, boy. You need to get off your arse and down the job centre first thing Monday morning. You need to get yourself a better job than picking fucking spuds. There won't be any spuds to pick in the winter, so don't expect me to be paying for your upkeep.' With that, she stormed out of the room, slamming the door behind her. The rush of air swirled the remaining cigarette smoke into a vortex. I was hoping that it might suck me up and deposit me somewhere other than here. If there was anywhere I could be, it would be Tina's bedroom again. Making sweet love with a woman of experience might have spoiled sex for me, or it could have given me a massive advantage for the future. With only the one point of reference, I would have to live under the assumption that last night was a high calibre carnal adventure and use it as a benchmark if ever I was fortunate enough to end up in a similar situation.

I hopped out of bed, wearing nothing but my boxer shorts, and slid up the sash window. The morning air poured in, extracting some of the nicotine stench. I reached for a can of Insignia body spray, squirting it into the centre of the room to exorcise the remaining smell. I needed to get out of the house and out of her way.

I dived into my wardrobe, pulled on a pair of clean jeans and a t-shirt and headed to the bathroom. The door was shut, but unfortunately, we had a glass panelled door to our bathroom. Mercifully, the glass was mottled for privacy but that didn't hide the shape of my mother sitting on the toilet, cigarette glowing from her lips. I figured I'd try and get some breakfast down me and then worry about my ablutions later. As I made the turn on the stairs, I heard the rasping sound of my mother breaking wind, followed by the splash as she emptied her bowels. She was a fucking delight.

I knew how she attracted men. She was kind of pretty – in a heavily made up, blouse-busting-tits kind of way – but on the inside, she was ugly to the core. The men may stay for a night, but after a morning with my mother, it often proved to be one morning too many.

I wolfed down a bowl of cereal then headed straight for the bathroom once I'd heard the door open. I should have given it more than a minute. The legacy of my mother's takeaway and booze diet hung in the air for an eternity. It's very difficult to brush your teeth and hold your breath at the same time.

With shoes and socks on I was good to go but not even in stealth mode could I escape a final passing comment from my mother's wretched mouth.

'When you get back home, we're going to have a long talk-'

I wasn't staying to hear how that sentence ended. I knew the answer: job – job – job.

Even though it was August there was still a chill to the morning. The sky was overcast but through the night there had been no cloud cover, allowing the heat of the previous day to escape into the ether. With no sunshine at all it was quite dull.

I wasn't sure where I was going but I knew I couldn't go to Dan's; not yet anyway. He probably wouldn't be home, and if he was, how would I ever be able to be in the same room as Tina again. I mean, I wanted to be in the same room as her again – the bedroom – but I didn't know how she was going to be around me. I could have gone to see Rob or Tom, but I decided against it. The last thing I needed was a rank amateur's view of the current political situation and talked into becoming a communist. And I definitely didn't need to be subjected to a barrage of badly copied porn. No, there was only one place for me to go.

1986

I don't know why I had thought it was a great idea to be knocking on someone's door at nine-thirty, on a Sunday morning, after a Saturday night on the sauce, but I did it anyway. I knocked once and waited, almost afraid of what might be said when somebody eventually answered. But there was no answer. I knocked again – three short raps on the old wooden door. The noise echoed into the hollow hallway beyond the door. I waited for a moment and was just about to leave when I heard sounds of movement from inside. I could have run off and ducked into the alleyway between Vicary Street and Brick Houses, but I decided that I should stay and face the music.

I heard the deadbolt drop followed by the latch clicking as it was turned. Sarah's squinting eyes appeared at the crack in the door.

'Will?' yawning as my name fell from her mouth, 'What are you doing here?'

'Escaping?'

She knew only too well the issues I had with my mother. She had a few with her own and was sympathetic to my plight, but how sympathetic she was likely to be at this early hour would remain to be seen.

The door was opened just enough for me to enter.

'Put the kettle on while I throw on some clothes.' She scurried upstairs without waiting for a reply.

I tiptoed through the lounge to the kitchen. There was a stack of unwashed dishes on the side and an even bigger one of half-washed items in the sink. I had to remove two saucepans from the scummy, greasy water to be able to place the kettle under the tarnished mixer tap.

The kettle had barely started to rumble when Sarah walked into the kitchen. She was in pink pyjamas. That was not a colour I would normally associate with Sarah: black, blue or purple maybe. But pink? Definitely not.

'What's the emergency?' she asked. I could see her craning her head to look at the lump on the side of my face.

'I had to get out of the house. I just had to get out and speak with someone.' My mind was racing, running through the various scenarios from the last twelve hours or so, trying to put them in an order so that I might be able to process them and give her some, if not all, the details. I wasn't sure what I could tell her and what I couldn't.

The Tina question raised its head.

Did I say *raised its head?* It was screaming at me like some demonic heckler, trying to provoke me into spilling every little detail so that I might be exorcised of the guilt I felt. The weight of this secret would crush me at some point, this I knew.

'What do you need me to hear, Will?' Her eyebrows were arched high as though it was a surprise for me to speak to her about anything serious. I went to her with most things. This wasn't anything new.

'I just wanted to... you know...' I was stammering over the truth. I didn't know what to tell her and I didn't know why she seemed so genuinely surprised that I would be talking to her, '...talk about last night... the fight and stuff.'

'Is that all?' She snapped. 'I hope there's more to this than just you wanting to get stuff off your chest, because that's all I ever seem to be good enough for these days – I'm everyone's ear for a problem but nobody wants to be mine.'

I could feel my face redden. I saw her notice it. I handed her a mug of coffee and tightened my lips, not knowing what to tell her. I felt embarrassed for how one-sided our relationship appeared to her. Maybe, I wasn't such a great friend. Maybe, I was one of those friends who just used others for my own needs and fucked off once I'd gotten what I could. I didn't think I was like that but perhaps I was. Is that why my mother hated me so much? If there was a lesson to be learned, I would have to figure it out later.

'Hey,' I said, eventually, 'I wanted to see if you got home ok and how you were feeling, too.'

I lied.

Sarah gave me a tight-lipped guilty smile but said nothing.

'So, how are you?' I returned her smile with a wide-eyed, beamer of my own.

She laughed. 'You're such a dickhead, Will. I'm sorry I snapped at you. I think the moon may be at that critical point in the lunar cycle.'

That was Sarah's code phrase for 'getting her period.' We were good enough friends to say it out loud, but we needed humour to broach the subject sometimes.

'Shall I grab the cork out of the spaghetti jar?' I asked – a wry smile on my lips.

She cast a confused glare.

'You know-' I didn't know if I was overstepping the mark, but I went for it anyway. '-to plug up your really big fanny.'

The punch in the arm was playful but delivered with enough force to hurt. I figured I was forgiven for my one-sided assumptions, and we went up to her bedroom to drink our coffee.

We talked for a while about the events of the previous night but made no firm conclusions about how things would work out for Jon and Jennifer. We agreed that Jon was a prick and would go full-charm mode to win Jennifer back. We also agreed that Jennifer would fall for all the bullshit and go back to being a doormat for his ego.

Sarah perched at the head of the bed, sitting cross-legged, her unfinished coffee cupped in her hands. I couldn't help noticing that she looked like she had lost some weight. I'd been her friend for the past five years and she had always been the chubby girl, not that I would ever say anything of the sort to her. But, in the here and now, without makeup on, in the cold light of day, I could see a difference. There was more definition in her jawline, less flesh around chin and her face looked narrower. Whatever was happening with her, it made her green eyes stand out, and when she smiled, I could detect some dimples in her cheeks. I'd never looked at her in such detail before.

'What is it?' She wore a confused frown.

'Nothing,' I lied again. 'I just enjoy being here.'

'Even with my music playing?'

She was playing her Toto album – the one with Rosanna and Africa – it was one of the albums I could tolerate to the point that it wasn't bad.

'Even with your music playing.'

For a moment there was a new level of understanding. I don't know what it was. My inexperience in social situations wasn't giving me the answers, but I felt I could tell her anything right at that moment. The question of the Tina situation reared its beautiful, completely inappropriate head once more, but I swiftly ushered it away.

We talked some more. And then some more. Sarah put on her Mr Mister album and then an old Fleetwood Mac album, and I don't know if it was my constant exposure to her taste, or maybe just the relaxed atmosphere in which we chatted, but I didn't hate the music this time around.

We were on our fourth coffee a piece, and because it was lunchtime, Sarah had rustled up a plate of tuna mayo sandwiches. She had said that her mother was away with the latest boyfriend and had been left to fend for herself. Sarah was fit to travel and had the skills to survive on her own for a weekend or more, even if the mountain of washing up suggested otherwise.

Sarah was about to grant me some respite and put on a Simple Minds tape when the phone rang. She ran downstairs to answer it. I couldn't hear the conversation, and I didn't try, but I was summoned to the top of the stairs.

'Yeah, what's up?' I said.

'Have you seen Rob today?' Sarah asked.

'I haven't seen anyone but you, today.' I was being glib, not realising the seriousness of the question.

'It's his Mum on the phone. He didn't come home last night.'

I shook my head. Sarah responded to the voice at the other end of the line in the negative, apologised and hung up.

82

'He probably got drunk and crashed at someone's place. He'll turn up,' Sarah said.

I didn't agree or disagree, out loud. Silently, I thought something else.

22

1986

Sarah was wrong for once. Rob didn't just turn up. Not later that day; not the next day, or the day after that. A week passed before the police arrived. Two wooden tops had sat on my grandmother's tatty bequeathed settee to take a statement from me, with my mother present, on the last known whereabouts of Robert Sherman.

I told them everything; the fight, the drinking, being thrown out. I assumed that was what everyone else would have said and so I didn't add anything. I told them what I did know, not what I didn't know.

I also didn't say anything about my after-midnight liaison with my best friend's mother. To my mind, it was best kept between just me and her. Since that night, I hadn't been near Dan's house. He had come to mine, but I was steering clear. I don't know what I was trying to achieve. Avoidance was the only course of action available to me. I thought that if I entered a room with the woman who had taken my virginity in it, a neon sign would drop from the ceiling announcing the fact that we had engaged in an inappropriate carnal coupling. I was sure it wouldn't, but I couldn't take the chance of my face reddening in guilt and doing much the same thing.

And while I couldn't say a thing about it to my oldest friend, he had carte blanche to tell me all the intricate details of his mediocre first time. Knowing Dan as well as I did, I knew that he would be embellishing the story; it's what he did. He was great at telling stories, making a journey seem like an epic quest when, in reality, it was just a long walk to the chip shop. I'm sure he would have thrown in a few dragons and unicorns for good measure if he could have gotten away with it. I won't go into the details because let's be fair, they are likely to be exaggerated, but he said that there was lots of kissing, a bit of boob action – apparently Nikita's were gravity defying – followed by complete nakedness and penetration, with a condom, on the living room floor of Nikita's parent's house. Dan felt obliged to show me the remnants of the carpet burns he had sustained to his knees as a result of frantic shagging on the shagpile.

Dan had his interview with the police, too, but he had even less to tell them as he and Nikita had departed just before I caught Jon balls deep in some random girl's face.

Outside of our close circle of friends, only a few other people were questioned about Rob's movements on that night. He was officially a missing person, and that's how it would stay.

To us, Rob would be forever young.

23

Present Day

Brooks strolled into the Heath for the second day in a row. There were results to obtain and two more bodies to be examined. He had the bulky 1980s file under his arm and a coffee in his hand. He'd sent Delgado back to a local police station to use the HOLMES computer system and start digging for more missing persons from Pembrokeshire. It seemed hard to believe that most of the information they had available to them was only on paper.

The HOLMES (Home Office Large Major Enquiry System) is the information system used by all UK police forces for the investigation of major incidents. The system was introduced in 1985 on a trial basis to check for teething problems and rolled out to all forces over a period of several years. The Pembrokeshire force, part of Dyfed Powys Police, didn't have access to the HOLMES system until the late 80s. That was why the case notes on Robert Sherman were handwritten and stored in a box file. Brooks had sent Delgado to see if Robert Sherman popped up somewhere on the system in other parts of the country. It was logical to assume that if the young man had gone missing from Milford Haven in 1986 and his body was later found in Milford Haven, he had probably never left the town and his remains had lain undisturbed since then. It was logical but Brooks assumed nothing.

Thirty-four years had passed since the disappearance and anything could have happened in that time, although the key factors would be centred at the immediate time frame preceding the last known sighting. Brooks was already planning on asking his superiors for a press conference and possible reconstruction. Brooks never wanted to be a poster boy for the police but if getting his face on the BBC boosted his profile, while putting a few noses out of joint and antagonising his ex-wife, then so be it.

Whatever the findings from the pathology report, they were going to be significant, maybe not the biggest case Brooks had worked on before but big enough to cause a media sensation. As the SIO, Brooks knew that he would fall under some tough scrutiny, not only from his superiors, but also from journalists and the public who would no doubt be following every beat of the case.

Milford Haven, as a reasonably sized town at the far end of Wales, was no stranger to murder cases. In the year before Robert Sherman's disappearance, the town was rocked by a horrific double murder. The Scoveston Park Farm case in which Richard and Helen Thomas, a brother and sister who were 58 and 54 years old, respectively, were murdered in their own home, shocking the local community to the core. In towns like Milford, where everybody knew everybody else's business, the crime was a mystery. While there was much speculation, there were no clues to motive or culprit. The apparent running away of a teenage lad slips well beneath the radar when a murderer is thought to be walking the streets. It soon became clear that there could in fact have been two murderers walking the streets. Again, just to be thorough, Brooks would have to investigate the Scoveston Park Farm case just to establish or dismiss any connection.

Three years after the Richard and Helen Thomas' murders, there was another double murder on the Pembrokeshire coastal path. Peter and Gwenda Dixon, who were holidaying in Pembrokeshire, were tied up, robbed and shot in the face with a sawn-off shotgun. How can a rural tourist location have two brutal events happen so close together, in time and locality?

It was easy to answer that question after the cases were solved. They were committed by the same man: John William Cooper. Cooper was a local man with a history of violence and criminal activity. He burgled houses, sexually assaulted women and committed murder. He was nicknamed 'The Bullseye Killer.' Not because he was a crack shot with a weapon, but because his appearance on the television quiz show 'Bullseye,' lead to him being investigated for his similarity to an artist's impression of a person of interest. It took twenty-five years from the Scoveston Park Farm event for there to be a conviction on the case. Cooper was sent to prison for the murder of the Thomases, the Dixons, and the rape and sexual assault of two teenage girls.

Procedure would insist on Cooper being spoken to about the missing boy. Brooks knew this was a whole different crime but wouldn't overlook the possibility of a connection. But at the same time, he wondered how long it would take to gain enough evidence to investigate anything with any certainty, never mind have enough for a conviction. If another major investigation took twenty-five years to gain a result, how long would this one take? They were already thirty-odd years behind the curve.

24

Present Day

I walked The Rath as I had done a thousand times before, and how I had the night of my sixteenth birthday celebration. The large flagstone pavements had been replaced with cobbles, the outdoor pool had been replaced with The Water Gardens and, most significantly, the dull scar across my guilt had been replaced with a raw gaping wound. Everything else had remained mostly unchanged.

I sat upon a bench, like the one I had sat on nearly thirty-four years ago and gazed across the Cleddau River: the haven. The same haven from where the town gained its name: Milford Haven.

It's funny how most of the residents drop the Haven part of the name, me included. Haven: a safe place. Ironically that was the opposite to how people were feeling about the town these days. What would it take for the ghosts of the past to be laid to rest and the residents to breathe a sigh of relief? A suspect? A confession? A conviction? Who knew? For now, Milford would stay Milford and it would be a long time before anyone felt safe.

I stood up, my joints creaking – the years were starting to take a toll – and strolled along the pavement. The trees of the Water Gardens blocked my view for a time, and then I saw it.

The Mine Depot.

The rumours had spread like a virus, mutating as they went, changing from the time they had oozed from the gossip's tongue and arrived on the slab to be dissected badly by the bad news brigade. That's how it goes with rumours in a small town; like a malevolent Chinese whisper, growing in stature with every telling.

I leaned on the railings next the old Minesweeper memorial, staring down at the derelict buildings in the distance. The once busy armaments depot had long since been closed and forgotten; sitting idle as the passage of time eroded the bricks and mortar. The only life existing for that place now were the weeds growing from the cracks in the tarmac.

I pulled up the collar of my jacket to keep out the brisk February gusts which sought access to my flesh. I remember that night, so long ago, and how I had walked this road in just a t-shirt and jeans. A cool August night was much warmer than a mild winter's day. I could recall how I stood upon the cusp of life, looking into the future with the uncertainty of youth.

Now I could look back on all those years with experience and deduced that we are all just floundering through life, trying to make it through the day, the week, the year, until there was a moment of respite to catch a breath. I would have been catching mine if I could actually breathe at all. Life had ground to a halt, and I couldn't help but feel the guilt resting heavy on my mature bones.

Three bodies had been pulled from that building and although unnamed, I knew who they were. I prayed that I could shed the burden once the truth came out, regardless of how much responsibility I bore. It was time.

25

Present Day

The clip-clip-clip of a firm dress shoe against the hard floor surface echoed in the confines of the corridor. The sound flowed and swirled on a mix of caffeine and dopamine, breaking through the silent barriers that protected a soul from its dreams. Brooks could hear it, but his brain could barely register it.

With a snap, his head lurched upwards, twisting away from the uncomfortable angle it had hung.

'Did I wake you?' Delgado stood in the corridor, a cup of coffee in each hand.

Brooks shook his weary head to clear the fog. 'I was just resting my eyes.'

Delgado smiled and handed his superior a latte. Brooks nodded a 'thank you' and sipped on the hot liquid.

It wasn't the first time Delgado had caught his boss napping. The blackened rings around Brooks' eyes were enough to tell anyone the man had a difficult relationship with sleep. Whatever worries he carried to keep sleep at bay he kept to himself. Police officers saw a lot of evil if they were unlucky enough. Brooks never considered himself to be lucky.

Maybe the good fortune was to be had in the folder Delgado had tucked under his arm.

The men had their differences. They were not friends, they were colleagues. Outside the force they probably wouldn't have any sort of relationship. Not one that would be pleasant at least.

'What have you got in there?' Brooks asked.

'An active line of enquiry,' Delgado said nonchalantly.

Brooks sighed, flipping open the heavy paper file that had become his comforter for the last twenty-four hours. 'Have you anything in there about these witnesses?'

Brooks believed while there could have been any number of possible suspects to Robert Sherman's murder, he firmly believed that, in such an intimate town, the murderer would have been known to the victim. He was just playing the odds, but the odds were good.

Delgado scanned the page scrawled with Brooks' handwriting and opened his file for a comparison. 'Yeah, this one,' Delgado said pointing at a name on the list.

Brooks was about to follow up with another question when the pathologist's door opened.

'Officer Brooks, Officer Delgado, would you like to come through? We are about to examine the second body.' Dr Davenport ushered them toward the door as though they didn't have a choice. In truth, they didn't.

As they moved through the office and into the short corridor leading to the autopsy room, the smell of disinfectant intensified. The chemical odour was preferable to the stench of decomposition, but in this case, there was hardly any flesh remaining.

The police officers donned gowns, masks and hats to offer some protection against cross contamination and entered the cold, sterile room with a steel table displaying the remains of some person as yet unknown. Brooks recalled the first time he had ever attended an autopsy. In that case, the victim was identified as Laura Birkett. The killer was still unknown. That was the killer who got away; the one case that always reared its head to cast doubt into Brooks' mind about his ability as a detective. One day that crime would be solved.

One day.

Not today.

In the darkness, when the demons called, Brooks would see only her face and ask for forgiveness. Brooks put all thoughts about the dead woman to one side, for now. Today was another day with another victim.

Davenport stood in front of the officers like a street magician about to pull off some incredible illusion. As a doctor of death, he was all about the theatrics of the event.

Pulling on a pair of blue nitrile gloves, Davenport opened with the punchline, 'Before we start, I would like you to notice the slight nicks to the lower ribs.'

Brooks and Delgado leaned in with trepidation, staring towards the areas the doctor pointed to, while the earthy stench of death filtered into their nostrils.

'Yes?' Brooks asked.

'Knife wounds – this was definitely a murder.' Davenport wasn't messing around. He normally liked to tease his audience, displaying subtle evidence as a kind of foreplay before edging his way toward the climax. Not today.

For the next forty minutes or so, the police officers stood in silence listening to so many medical terms and Latin words that the language morphed into something incomprehensible. Doctor-speak for the under-educated and over-tired.

While Davenport was rattling on about something they didn't understand, on a part of the body they couldn't pronounce, Brooks leaned into Delgado.

'Why did you point at that name?'

'Because they were interviewed about the first victim, and now, they're also a missing person,' Delgado replied without taking his eyes off the skin and mostly bones on the slab.

'When did they go missing?' Brooks ventured.

'1991.'

26

1986

The weeks that followed Rob's disappearance held the group in limbo. We didn't really hangout like we used to – we'd be together – but it wasn't the same. It amazed me how much the dynamic of the gang changed without our left-wing, self-righteous brother. The fallout from my birthday celebration had taken on a whole other dimension. The catalyst for the fight had been almost forgotten about. There were bigger issues to deal with and oh boy were we dealing with them.

My personal feelings were put to one side. I felt guilt, I felt loss and I felt sadness, but I never shared that with anyone in the group. Not Sarah and not Dan.

There was a distance growing between Dan and myself. We had been best friends for ten of our sixteen years but the glue that had bonded us had ruptured, forming a chasm. Most of that chasm came in the shape of Nikita. Before the hook-up, I saw Dan four or five times a week, sometimes more. Now, with teenage love in the air – and a lot of sexual barriers being torn down – I was lucky to see him once a week.

Sarah had also been distant, but I thought that could have had something to do with how the whole Rob situation was affecting me. I was angry and withdrawn. I didn't need people talking about it. She would call at my house every now and then, stopping for a cup of tea and a chat but it was strained to say the least. I was affected – she was affected – everything was affected. Our friendship was treading water in rough seas and salvation was nowhere on the horizon. It was how we all felt.

As for Jon and Jennifer and the grand romance, that was interrupted. The betrayal split them up and quite rightly so, but the disappearance brought them back together; two people with a brief history, seeking comfort in difficult times their immature brains couldn't fathom. They lasted a month and split for good.

I saw Tom from time to time, but the conversation only went two ways – Rob or porn – and I didn't really want to broach either subject. The only thing I noticed about Tom was how upset he was about Rob. I'd seen Nikita and Jennifer cry on more than one occasion when the subject came up, but Tom was the only one of the male members of the group I had seen show genuine sorrow over the loss of a friend. It made me sad to see how much he was feeling the loss.

That was how it was for what seemed like an age, but it was no more than a few months. As the nights pulled in and Christmas approached, the group seemed to recover some of its former glory. Even at our most complete, there was a gap that couldn't be filled. Was this what life would be like? Was it about loss and change and all the things in between?

I didn't like how life was shaping up for me.

I didn't like who I was becoming either.

In normal circumstances, I would have turned to Dan and spilled my guts but that was no longer an option. Our waning friendship was not only strained because of Nikita. There was another reason.

Tina.

As much as I tried to stay away from her, I couldn't keep it up for long. I was drawn to her – addicted to her. She filled a need that had been missing in my life for as long as I could remember. I needed to be wanted and that was what she did. I became significant in her life, and she in mine. In those few desperately mournful months after a night that would change us all forever, she was there for me, taking me away from the hurt that infected every part of my life. A missing friend – an unrequited love – a neglectful mother; those pieces of my wounded soul fitted together too well. Tina drew a veil over all of that and, for the precious moments we spent together, I felt relief. It was what I needed. What I lost in seeing Dan, I made up in seeing his mother. I could say that I loved her. I could, but I won't. Lust? Maybe. Connection? Definitely. But love? What is love, anyway?

And like all good things, it came to an end. Tina met someone else, and I was alone once again, but alone with newfound confidence and experience. As 1986 ended I took myself off to find work beyond

Milford Haven, beyond the county of Pembrokeshire and most definitely beyond Wales. New Year – new beginnings – new me.

27

1991

My return to Milford in 1991 was not spectacular or earth-shattering. It was just me and two suitcases, rocking up at the railway station on a Tuesday afternoon. It wasn't the first time I'd been back, but it was the first time I felt trepidation about being back in my hometown.

I had made a point of coming back for a cathartic reunion to celebrate Rob's disappearance. August 9th was the date, and we would get together on the Saturday immediately following or preceding the anniversary. We always joked that maybe one year he would make an appearance and tell us where he'd been. It hadn't happened so far.

This year would be different. Rob wouldn't turn up, we never expected that. No, this year would be the first year that we might all be together. And it wouldn't be on the anniversary either.

This year Milford was hosting the Tall Ships race. It was a big deal for the maritime community and the businesses in the surrounding area. A big event like that would bring in some serious coin for those who could organise themselves for the chaos that would ensue. I'd already experienced a Tall Ships Race and knew what to expect.

In the previous summer, I had been working as a barman in The Grand Hotel on Plymouth Hoe – the year Plymouth hosted the event. It was where I raked in a ton of cash working on and off the books. I worked a fulltime job at the hotel, covering mainly daytime shifts, and then I moonlighted in The Cider Press in the heart of the marina community, cash-in-hand; add the generous tips from sailors unfamiliar with the currency, and I pulled in a month's wages in one week just from the bar work alone. I was hoping to do the same this time around. I had a month to secure a bar job.

Looking down at the pair of battered suitcases, I figured a taxi sure beat walking to my digs and I strolled up to a pale blue Ford Sierra. The driver continued reading his copy of The Sun, flicking fag ash out of the open window as if it was an inconvenience to his downtime.

I stated my destination. He stated a price. I threw my cases in the boot and climbed into the backseat.

There wasn't much conversation and that suited me just fine. She's Got the Look by Roxette struggled out of the crackling speakers, serenading my return to the streets I had wandered so many times. Hamilton Terrace seemed somehow shorter and narrower than I remember, maybe because I had travelled to bigger and better places, experienced other towns and other people. My mind wasn't as narrow as it had been when I left five years earlier. I still couldn't decide if that was a good thing or not. Only time would tell.

Zipping past The Lord Nelson Hotel, Debrett's and The Starboard, I recalled the many hazy evenings that turned into regret-filled mornings, and staggering home to the subtle thrum of a trawler engine, bringing a bizarre comfort in the orange glow of the early hours. Many would say they were good times. I remember it differently, remembering one night more vividly than any other. Sad times.

I asked the driver if he would take a detour. He grunted and indicated to turn right at the very familiar Belgian Monument.

Although I had returned to Milford twice since leaving in 1986, I hadn't walked The Rath on either of those visits. It had changed. The old outdoor pool, where we sometimes had school swimming galas, had been removed and in its place was a garden. I asked the driver when the pool had been removed.

'Last year,' he said through his husky cigarette voice. 'Put the Water Gardens there instead – bloody waste of money, if you ask me.'

Unfortunately, I had asked him.

I didn't say another word, letting the dulcet tones on the radio substitute for conversation. Beats International and Dub be Good to Me forced itself from the speakers and I settled back into the cigarette scented seats to continue the journey.

Thankfully, the driver pulled up at the address I had given him just as Michael Bolton started to wail some sappy love song. I made a mental note not to listen to Radio 2 any time soon. I dropped some coins into the driver's hand, and he was gone in a cloud of diesel fumes before I could even take a step down the path.

Pausing for a moment, nerves suddenly seeped into the worldly-wide confidence I thought I had. What was the worst that could happen? I decided to get over myself and walked to the door. But I didn't have to knock. A figure appeared in the frosted glass of the front door window, and I knew who it was straightaway.

'Hello, stranger!' Dan stood in the doorway, his arms extended, his smile wide.

'Hello,' I said. It was a little awkward but necessary. Dan had shoulder length hair and a wispy beard. The boy was all grown up. He wore a shabby denim shirt unbutton to the waist and ragged jeans. I was careful not to stand on his bare feet as I embraced him. I caught a whiff of body odour and hoped that the house was cleaner than he was.

He wasn't living with his mother and sister anymore. Dan had moved into a semi in Coombs Drive with Tom Magee. I imagined it would be a beer can scattered porn den. I wasn't far wrong. In five years, some things hadn't changed. Something I was happy about.

28

1991

Sitting in Dan's poky living room felt comforting. Even though it was sparsely furnished and basic, it seemed familiar and homely as though I'd been here before. I hadn't, of course, but it was just how it felt. Like a weird Deja-vu but with a whiff of body odour and unwashed socks.

'So,' Dan said, walking into the room armed with two mugs of coffee. 'How have you been?'

I took the mug. It was a Liverpool FC mug. I had drunk from it many times when he lived with Tina.

'Not bad, not bad at all,' I lied. I was freefalling through life, hoping to catch a fortunate breeze to save myself from being smashed into the earth at maximum velocity. 'I've been doing a bit of bar work – here and there – and was hoping to get some work around here.'

'Awesome!' Dan lifted his mug as though toasting an epic victory with champagne.

'What about you? What going on with you?' I knew a few things about Dan's life since I vanished on a train, five years ago. And it wasn't as though this was the first time I'd seen him to talk to. On both the previous times I'd come home we had met up to raise a glass to Rob and to chew the fat.

The first time, a year after I'd left, he'd still been in a relationship with Nikita. They seemed happy enough but there wasn't the passion about them that some couples have. They kissed, they hugged, but on the surface, they looked like two friends who had gotten caught up in the pace of life, finding each other just to fill the spaces between the dawn and the dusk. When I came home again two years after, I wasn't surprised that they had broken up. I also wasn't surprised that it seemed amicable. Nikita had gone off to University in Cardiff to study Maths. Dan always joked that she had to take her shoes and socks off just to check her change, so something more complicated like statistics or calculus must melt her brain.

'I'm working out at Consort. Packing machinery and loading wagons,' he said. His eyes dropped, not at all hidden behind the steam rising from his coffee. There was disappointment in his gaze. I wouldn't know the problem now, but maybe later, once we had become reacquainted, I would learn more of what was happening behind the scenes.

'At least you're working.' This was awkward. It was strained, and not in a good way.

'Tom's working, too,' Dan offered. 'He's waiting tables at The Mariner's.'

The Mariner's Hotel was in Haverfordwest, the next big town along. I saw an opportunity to maybe bag some bar work. Although, I'd have preferred to work in Milford; no bus fare meant more money.

'When does he find the time? Is he still addicted to porn?' I asked, already knowing the answer.

'I don't let him make my food. I can never tell where his hands have been. The job is probably saving his eyesight. It's hard to masturbate frantically while handling plates, but I'm sure he's had a go, just for shits and giggles.' Whatever the reason for the sadness he still had a razor-sharp wit. It was nice to know some things don't change.

'Do you still see the rest of the guys?' It was a loaded question. I wanted to know about one of the guys, and only one.

Dan wasn't stupid but he wasn't going to play ball. He would make me drag it out of him.

'I see them when they're home,' he smiled. 'And for students, they seem to be home quite a lot.'

'Who have you seen?'

'All of them.'

I was frustrated and he was enjoying watching me squirm.

'Are any of them home at the moment?' I would keep going until I had to ask directly, but I was trying to play it cool. But whether I liked it or not, my face was reddening with frustration.

'Yeah.'

101

He was such a dick!

'Which ones?' My internal monologue splurged out with the question.

Dan laughed at how transparent I had become. I was a man – twenty years old – I had moved away from home, gotten jobs, been drunk, gotten laid, bought stuff, sold stuff, given advice with experience and been right. But just five minutes back in my hometown with my best friend and I had been reduced back to a spluttering teenager, stumbling over my words because my pride wouldn't ask a direct question.

I caved.

'Ok. Have you seen Jennifer?'

'Yes, I have. And yes, she's home at the moment.'

The flow of my breathing heightened as though a wave of cold fear stole the air from my lungs. Even after all this time, just the thought of her made my resolve crumble. If just talking about her was having this effect, how would it be to actually see her?

'How does she look?'

'Fat and ugly!'

My brain didn't compute the information and it showed on my face.

Dan started laughing again. I liked to see him laugh. He had one of those machine gun laughs – rapid and reverberating.

'You should see your face, man,' he said, trying to stifle another bout of guffawing. 'She looks good – in fact – she looks better than good.'

I nodded in mock approval of his assessment. I had to see her. I hadn't seen her since the Christmas I left. We kept missing each other by a day or so upon our trips back to Milford. We had written to each other a few times and spoken on the phone once, but I hadn't actually laid eyes on her in five years: five years was a big chunk of life when approaching twenty-one and still having no clue what my life plan was.

'We should all meet up,' I suggested.

'Sarah's already beaten you to it.'

In my haste to know the ins and outs of Jennifer's whereabouts, I had forgotten about Sarah. A pang of guilt struck and suddenly I didn't feel like I was a very good friend to her anymore.

Sarah sent me a letter once a month, without fail. She also would call once a fortnight if our schedules allowed. Sarah was studying to be a nurse in Bristol and had very little time off, with working and lectures eating into her timetable. But now she was home for six weeks and had made sure that our paths would cross. I felt a warming glow in the pit of my stomach at the thought of someone going out of their way for me.

I was about to ask what the plan was, but there was a knock at the door.

Dan got up and answered it. I heard a child's voice and the voice of a woman. From what I could make out Dan clearly knew them and invited them in.

'...and look who's here, visiting.' Dan said as he stepped back into the room.

I heard the woman say '*Who.*' That one syllable was all I needed to hear to know who it was. My mind immediately raced back over the years, arriving at a point in time that defined part of my being. I was no longer sitting in a house in Coombs Drive. I was back in the front room of the house in Robert Street. I also knew why the room had seemed so familiar. The sofa that took up most of the living room – the one I had been sitting on – was the same one that had been the venue for Tina's seduction. And now, five years later, she walked in behind Dan.

'Er... Hi, Will.' It was the most awkward greeting in the history of the world.

'Hi, Tina,' I used to call her Mrs James before we had shared a bed and bodily fluids. Calling her Tina in front of her son for the first time felt wrong and inappropriate, much like our previous relationship.

Dan seemed oblivious to the dip in the atmosphere and carried on as usual. 'And this is my little sister, Kayleigh.' He said, picking up the infant and blowing a raspberry on her cheek, making her giggle.

In any of the communications and two times I had met up with Dan in the past few years, he had not mentioned that his mother had had another child. I know she had entered into a relationship with another man about the time I had left town. I think there was even a mention of marriage and possibly of a separation, but no mention of a sister.

'How old is she?' I asked.

'Nearly four,' Dan replied. 'Yes, you're a big girl now.'

In the midst of the affectionate tussle between big brother and little sister, my mind dropped into calculating mode, trying to work out the years, the months, the days. I'd left Milford four and a half years ago. Regardless of the truth, my head was only coming up with one question.

Was Kayleigh my daughter?

29

1991

The acid adrenalin was still burning its way through my system, melting away the resolve I'd built up for coming home. My head was shot to pieces. Could I be a father and not even known about it? Whatever fears and regrets that had been chasing me down my entire life, they had now been washed aside by a crushing wave of reality. For every action, there is a consequence. The consequence of my actions with my best friend's mother, I thought, was an uncomfortable shame laced with triumph. But it was totally possible that the consequence was a child named after a song written by an alcoholic.

Tina and her daughter left very shortly after arriving and I could sense Dan's eyes on me after the visit. I wasn't sure what signs I was throwing out for him to pick up on, but I made my excuses and left to run a fictional errand.

Normally, I would have been admiring the beauty of the day, and how my hometown always looked at its best under a blue cloudless sky. Instead, my mind wasn't home, it was in a whole new version of Hell, and I had just been given the guided tour. There was only one person I could go to.

I knew that if I was to have Sarah's ear for what could be the most difficult discussion of my young life, I would have to tell her the truth.

Secrets were secrets for a reason. I was contemplating exposing one the blackest secrets I had. What was I doing?

30

1991

The door of the house on Vicary Street didn't look any different than it did the last time I knocked on it. I hadn't been a very good friend to Sarah. We wrote often. We phoned frequently. But since the time I had left town, almost five years ago, I hadn't laid eyes on the one person who had never turned their back on me. I wasn't sure how I was going to play this.

I rapped my knuckles against the flaking wood. The hollow sound, so familiar to me, resonated into the unseen hallway. I waited for a moment.

There was no sound from within.

I knocked again.

Somewhere in the depths of the house I heard movement. A moment later there was the sound of footsteps upon the staircase and then a rattling of the latch.

I didn't know what I was expecting.

Sarah's mother – the evil old witch – or maybe a new stepfather that Sarah was too ashamed to admit to knowing. My mind was already blown to bits. I wasn't prepared for what came next.

The door opened and it wasn't Sarah's mother, or an anonymous father figure, but more surprisingly, it wasn't Sarah. It was Jennifer.

I had to look twice. I almost slapped my face to see if I was dreaming.

I was about to say something when she launched forward and hugged me. I hugged her back.

Oh my God.

I can't describe how good it felt to have her arms wrapped around me. I had dreamed of this for an eternity, and it was happening, here and now, in the instant that my life had become so terribly difficult and confusing, I had been given a moment of satisfaction to soften the blow. I didn't want it to end.

But it did.

That's when I received the next surprise. And again, oh my God, did it take the wind out of my sails.

Sarah was right behind Jennifer. I hadn't seen the girl in years, and she was different.

In the few months before I left Milford, I had noticed that Sarah was looking slimmer than she had been in school. She had always been that dumpy, frumpy girl that took some abuse over her plain looks, old clothes and excess weight. But now, as a woman of nearly twenty-one years of age, she had blossomed. She wasn't just slimmer – she was slim. I wasn't good when it came to guessing a girl's size, but I can remember Sarah having a size sixteen dress that ripped because it was too tight on her. If I had to guess, I'd have said she was a size ten, twelve at the most. Slim legs, slim arms, slim neck; I had to look at her twice just to make sure it was her. The eyes still had the same sparkle but there was more wisdom behind them. Her cheekbones were high and very prominent. I'd never seen them before. I'd never seen her look so good.

'Wow!' I can't believe I said it out loud, but I did.

I could see the satisfaction in her eyes; that feeling of attraction she had been looking for when she was a teenager. If that was her intention, she had succeeded.

She reached up and wrapped her arms around my shoulders. I placed my arms around her waist. She felt so different. I remember feeling the softness of her body the last few times I held her like this. I never judged her for how she was or how she looked but her reason for being bullied was obvious. But now, now she was a whole different animal. Lean and firm.

'Wow yourself,' Sarah's mouth was so close to my ear I could feel the heat of her breath as she spoke. 'Haven't you grown up into a handsome young man.'

I released her to take another look.

'I think you've gotten me beat in the growing up stakes. Look at you. What did you do?' I didn't want the attention on me just yet. I was due my turn, but I wasn't sure I'd be able to open-up with Jennifer there.

Her perfect smile revealed her dimples which seemed so much more prominent than ever before.

'I'm a student. I can't afford to eat, and I have to walk miles to get to lectures. It's the fresher's diet – guaranteed to work. When you lump in all the drinking on an empty stomach and throwing up the next day, you've got a winning formula.'

She was more than a year past being a fresher, but I understood what she meant. I remember from all the letters she wrote and how hard the first year seemed to be. Once the adjustments were made, she seemed to settle in. At least that's what I took from her correspondence. At the time, I was struggling to make the many adjustments in my own life, and it was such a distraction, I probably wasn't thinking of my friend's plight.

Jennifer broke the deadlock – I had almost forgotten she was there – with a similar line of questioning to mine.

'You look so different yourself, Will,' Jennifer was looking me up and down. She had never done that before, at least not with a look of admiration in her eyes. 'You filled out a bit, haven't you?'

She wasn't wrong. Bar work isn't just about pulling pints and mixing the odd cocktail. It was about unloading cases of bottled beer, moving kegs around the cellar and humping bin bags full of empty bottles. A fulltime bar job was as taxing as a labouring job sometimes. Yes, there could be quiet times when the only thing under pressure was my elbows against a cold wooden bar but, for the most part, it was hard graft. The evidence was in the wiry arms and broad shoulders I had developed. If Sarah could have a Fresher's diet, I could have the Cellar Boy workout.

I was also sporting three days of stubble across my jawline. The last time these guys had spent any time with me, the only hair on my face other than my eyebrows was a few wispy hairs on my top lip, such was my physical immaturity.

It was laughable – so much for my physical immaturity. I might not have been able to grow a half decent moustache, but it seems I might have been able to father a child. That thought was right there at the forefront of my brain once more. The wows and cooing about how much we'd all changed was over and done with. And now I had another problem to deal with. For the first time ever, I would have to try and get rid of Jennifer so that I could confide in my best friend. I knew coming home was a mistake.

31

1991

So much for going to see Sarah and bearing my tortured soul to her. It seemed that she and Jennifer were bosom buddies.

Back in school – when life often seemed to be at its most complicated – they had been more like casual acquaintances than friends. Jennifer hung out with the more popular girls from the wealthier areas of the town, while Sarah made friends with anyone who would be her friend. It was only through the mutual friendship of Nikita that the girls ever hung out together at all.

That dynamic must have changed drastically in the last few years, or so it seemed. I had to sit in the chair in the corner of the room while the girls did lots of girlie stuff – stuff I wasn't used to seeing Sarah do. First there was manicuring of fingernails, then toenails, then painting of the aforementioned nails. They offered to do mine, but I graciously declined. I was struggling with potential fatherhood and didn't need to add cross-dressing to my CV.

Between the preening and giggling, there was some relevant conversation and it happened to pass that Sarah was going back to Bristol that day – in fact, in the next couple of hours. Whatever I had to say would have to wait.

I stayed until she left, helping her pack up her little car. She must have been earning some good money, even as a student, because she was driving a virtually new car: a 1989 Ford Fiesta. Sarah told me the colour was Maritime Blue and she would have preferred a black one, but the dealer didn't have one. I was impressed that she had a car and had passed her test; the colour of her ride was irrelevant. It seemed important to her though, she insisted that she never drove around Bristol, walking everywhere to stay fit but also because parking was a nightmare.

I waved her off and decided to go back to Dan's house. A lift was offered and declined. Jennifer did the same and walked with me. It felt funny, but nice.

'So, do you meet many girls on your travels?' Jennifer asked.

'You know me – I don't have much luck with girls,' I was lying. I had met a few girls here and there. Apparently, my subtle Welsh accent was deemed 'cute' by young ladies from the North of England, but I wasn't about to start telling her the sordid details of my brief liaisons during the holiday season on the south coast.

'Maybe you just haven't found the right girl yet – I'm sure you will,' she gave me a wry smile when she spoke.

I could have said the truth. I could have said that the only girl I had ever wanted to be with was her. That every other girl couldn't compare to her. I could have told her that while walking and talking so candidly. In truth, I was a step closer than I ever thought I was likely to get to her. I could have said that, and so much more.

'Maybe. Only time will tell.'

I felt such a pathetic loser that my own inner voice was berating my squandering of such a perfect opportunity. My own personal nirvana was pounding on the door, and I was hunched in a corner with my fingers in my ears. I needed to man up.

'Oh, Will, I'm sure time will tell you so much more than that. How about we go out for a drink and try and steer you at some girls.'

I was stunned by the offer. 'When? Tonight?' I blurted.

She laughed at me. 'No, silly. It's a Tuesday. Nobody goes out on the prowl on a Tuesday. Saturday night? Are you up for it?'

I nodded my answer just as we reached the corner of Coombs Drive, and the point where our conversation would end. She leaned in and hugged me again, kissing me on the cheek as she broke away. As I bid her farewell, I felt a moment of golden joy – my heart sighed in complete and utter satisfaction. It had entered a place it had longed to be, and I was dragged along for the ride. For a moment I had forgotten about the fatherhood revelation. But as I watched her step away, the reality of a past encounter rushed back to my consciousness, spoiling one of the most perfect moments I had even experienced.

32

Present Day

Brooks stepped into the carpark of the busy university hospital and sparked up the cigarette that had been nagging at his addiction for the last two hours. The last remains of some poor lost soul had been thoroughly examined, every detail logged and photographed, every word of the pathologist recorded digitally. All Brooks had to do was stand in the room, taking in what details he could, sift through the relevant and discard what wasn't. It was a mountain of a task made harder by the lack of physical evidence to steer the investigation.

The exhaled smoke wisped around his face, creating an air of comfort to dwell in. Brooks knew that while three bodies should have three times the evidence, the age of the grave, and the apparent animal activity, would significantly affect the lines of enquiry. He wasn't easily disturbed but Brooks flinched when the pathologist had described how there were gnawing marks on many of the bones of the second victim, and how one of the femurs had been split at the hip joint, the marrow removed almost in its entirety. While Brooks would always remain objective, inhabiting the middle ground on emotional attachments, he also couldn't help but feel an overwhelming sense of sympathy for the victim, and the yet unknown family.

Stubbing his cigarette butt against a cast iron bin, Brooks watched a woman, wearing a scarf around an obviously bald head, being helped from a car by an over-attentive husband. It was clear from the pale skin stretched over the bones of her face, and the spindly limbs that could barely support her meagre weight, she was possibly a cancer patient, potentially at the end of her fight. Brooks felt guilty placing his smouldering stub into the ash box. The husband of the woman gave a weak smile as he shuffled past the police officer. Brooks returned the smile, wishing he could have brought the woman's murderer – cancer – to justice before the illness could steal her last breath.

As he watched the couple disappear inside the hospital, Delgado pulled up in an unmarked Vauxhall Insignia.

'You, ok?' Delgado asked, sensing something was wrong.

'I'm fine,' Brooks lied. 'What did you get from that?'

Delgado assumed his superior was talking about the autopsy.

'What – other than the murder victim? I'm not quite sure yet. We've still got a body left and we've got little else to go on but the bones.'

Brooks said nothing for a while. He was mulling over the more disturbing items in the pathologist's report. 'What did you make to the cause of death?'

Delgado gave his gaffer a sideways glance while maintaining a view on the road ahead. 'He was stabbed – many times. That's pretty conclusive to me.'

'I get he was stabbed to death,' Brooks snapped, 'but this killing was frenzied. For every nick of the bone there must be many others that just hit soft tissue. This murder was personal.'

'They're all personal. Ask the victim's families.'

Brooks didn't reply. He knew Delgado was correct, after a fashion, but what was going through his mind, after years of experience and in-depth research into other crimes, he knew this killing was personal for the murderer. There was hate carved into the dead bones, left and discarded, to be picked at by tiny scavengers until no flesh remained.

Brooks was about to reveal his thoughts when his phone rang. Staring at the screen, the number withheld, he tapped the answer icon.

'Officer Brooks?'

'Yes.'

'Davenport here – I just wanted to let you know that something was bothering me, and I had to examine the skull in more detail.'

'Go ahead,' Brooks wondered how much more he could have examined the skull.

113

'Well – I think I said that there must have been significant animal activity in the eye sockets-.'

'I remember.' How could he not. Both he and Delgado flinched when the pathologist indicated that the eyes must have been chewed out of the sockets.

'I looked at the markings again, and while many were the teeth marks of rodents, I spotted some very linear marking on the bone at the back of the eye socket, too linear to be made by teeth. I'm sure they were made by the knife, and I will be amending the report to reflect that.'

'Ok. So, what are you telling me?'

'That the victim had a knife put into their eyes.'

Brooks bid the good doctor a farewell and hung up.

'What did he say?' Delgado asked, only hearing one side of the conversation.

'That this *was* personal.'

'How so?'

'Because the murderer cut the fucking eyes out.'

The revelation kept them in silence all the way to the hotel.

33

1991

Hometown blues was something that could only be felt if you lived in a dead-end town for too long. I didn't consider Milford to be a dead-end town, and I was merely passing through for the summer. But I was starting to feel anxiety about the place I had grown up in with every passing day.

The day after my arrival I had been acting bizarrely to say the least.

Dan could see I was dancing around a certain subject and instead of dismissing it – as I would expect a good friend to do – he tackled the question head on.

'Why are you so nervous around my mother?'

There were many possible answers I could have given. They would have been lies, but they may have been believable if delivered correctly. I decided to dance as close to the truth as I dared and hope for the best.

'It's really odd to see you have another sister.' It wasn't a lie – it was a moronic statement – but it was the truth.

'And that's why you jumped in the air when she turned up here? Are you still traumatised by the two little girls in The Shining or something?' His face wore doubt, badly.

'No… er…' When pausing over a question there was an appropriate amount of time that could be endured before the pause looked like avoidance and all credibility in the following reply would evaporate. I had stepped into that timeframe and didn't look to be escaping any time soon. 'Look… It's just a bit weird to – you know – see your mother starting over again. It must be hard for you and Charlotte.'

Dan shook his head. 'She is starting over *yet* again. She's leaving my stepdad.'

I was shocked and I stated my sympathy.

'I'm sure she's got another man on the go,' Dan continued, 'that's why she came round yesterday – to tell me she had kicked out my stepdad and not to side with him.'

For a moment, my head went to that place in my ego where all the selfish thoughts lived and I waivered over the idea that maybe it was because I was back in town, and she wanted to be with the father of her child instead of the imposter she settled for. That thought slid through my brain swiftly, not even pausing to wipe its feet.

'What about your little sister – what's going to happen about her?' I threw in a question of concern to hopefully distract the attention away from the initial question.

Dan shrugged his shoulders. 'I don't really know. She – my mum – was saying my stepdad wants Kayleigh on her birthday.'

'When is that?' If there was one question, I needed to know the answer to, it was this one. All the anxiety that had pent up inside me for the last twenty-four hours could be completely undone with a simple answer to a simple question. More so than at any time in my life, I needed to know the birthday of a child I had absolutely no connection with.

He shot me a bemused glance, shaking his head before answering. 'September fifteenth.'

The inside of my head turned into one of those computers you see in the old James Bond movies: a big room with multiple tape reels, all spinning at a million miles an hour, many breaking off their mountings, spilling an untold quantity of magnetic tape under the pressure of the most important calculation known to man. I resorted to counting on my fingers and had to triple check my answer before I could take a breath.

And it was a breath of relief.

Even with my inaccurate method of calculating a due date, I established that Kayleigh would have been conceived after mid-December. Tina and I had ceased our illicit liaisons at the end of November. It was close but there was at least a three-week gap,

116

possibly four, which felt like enough. It didn't take away the guilt I felt but at least I hadn't spawned a child I didn't know.

After I had let the revelation wash over me, I was able to settle into spending quality time with my best friend again. Somewhere, under the surface, I could sense Dan felt my relief too. That was a lesson learned the hard way.

34

1991

My first few days back in the old hometown had been bordering on boring. After thinking I had spawned a child and then discovering that I hadn't, the time had tapered down to fitting into the working routine of my housemates. I was calling them housemates because that's how it felt, and I was contributing to the household by tidying up after Dan and Tom and springing for a chippy tea on one night and a Chinese on another. If I was staying long-term, I would want to have a bit of a say in what they did too.

I was cleaning up the kitchen after breakfast – and by breakfast – I meant the mess Dan had made over every inch of the worktop with his Rice Krispies. He hadn't changed in all the years I'd known him and would eat the same breakfast, every day. Rice Krispies made with warm milk. Pouring the cereal and the milk into a bowl and chucking it into the microwave wasn't going to cut it. He needed the milk warmed separately and then added to a bowl of his preferred cereal. He was a funny lad.

After removing a plethora of crushed crisped rice from the surfaces, I boiled the kettle to make some tea for myself and Tom.

Dan had gone to work but Tom was on an evening shift at the hotel and didn't need to leave for hours.

Tom wandered into the kitchen in nothing but his underwear – a pair of saggy boxer shorts that must have seen their best days during the 80s.

'Two sugars?' I asked just to be on the safe side.

'Cheers!' Tom said, thrusting himself up onto the counter I had not long wiped down. I made a mental note to wipe the counter again after Tom had removed his hairy arse from it.

'So, what's your plan for the day?'

I had an answer, but it wasn't one I wanted to share. I needed to go and see my mother. I didn't want to go but I had to go. It was Friday, the fourth day of my return and as yet I hadn't ventured back to

Trafalgar Road. There was no doubt that mother knew of my return because I had seen a few of her old muckers knocking around the town and news travels fast in a one-horse town where everyone knows everyone else's business.

'I'm not really sure.' It was a white lie, and I was sticking to it.

'Well, if you're stuck for something to do, I've a stack of new *merchandise* on top of the wardrobe in my room. You're more than welcome to have a look, but be warned, Dan is silent when he comes home, and you wouldn't want him walking in on you.' A double thumbs up punctuated the end of that sentence.

I had no intention of being caught in a frenzy of angry masturbation by my mates. Dan had already told me that he couldn't count the number of times he had caught Tom 'peeling one out' to some Swedish erotica in the living room on a return from work. Dan thought it had to be deliberate for him to walk in on Tom so often.

'Thanks, but I think I'll skip it,' I tried not to sound too ungrateful.

I'm sure he was going to descend into a detailed review of his latest blue movie fetish but thankfully the doorbell chimed.

Unabashed about his attire, Tom hopped off the counter and answered the door.

I heard a voice. My heart sank.

There are many times in a person's life when something so small can be blown up into something overwhelming. It may only last for a second or it can last for days, weeks or even months, but the feeling is sparked by something as small as a picture or a memory, or in this case, a voice.

Tom scooted back into the kitchen followed by the owner of the voice.

'Fuck me! You've filled out a bit.' The comment was accompanied by a hearty slap on the back. It hurt like Hell, but I prayed that I didn't show my flinching.

119

Jon stood in the centre of the kitchen like he was the prodigal son returning to the scene of his greatest achievement. He might have said that I'd filled out, but he too was carrying a few too many pounds since the last time I saw him. And not in a good way.

The strong jawline that all the girls seemed to like had softened and there was a subtle double chin threatening to be exposed. His whole body seemed bigger, rounder, less defined. I would have to say that he had 'porked up' considerably but I wouldn't utter it out loud.

'Hello, Jon, it's good to see you.' I wasn't good at lying to someone's face and I don't think I was pulling it off now.

'Yeah, good to see you too.'

He wasn't too good at hiding a lie either.

'What can I do you for?' Tom thankfully interrupted the potential stand-off.

Jon switched straight into his usual *'I'm in charge'* demeanour.

'I need to borrow something "high quality" from you,' he made the air-quotes, 'and your video camera.'

'Not a problem. I've got some new gear and a choice of cameras.' Tom dashed out of the room and up the stairs.

I was hoping Jon was going to follow but instead he stayed in the kitchen. Just the two of us.

An awkward silence would be too cliché. I wanted to avoid it.

'So,' I was hoping to show that I was the bigger person, 'what are you doing with yourself?'

'I'm a student, in London – studying to be an architect.'

'Nice!' It was all I had.

'It's ok. I'm temping with a firm in Hounslow. I'm earning and learning at the same time.'

I nodded interestingly. 'Good money?'

'Better than average.' His smug smile showed more of the pouch of fat growing under his chin.

I imagined that his wages were enough to buy him all the pasta and ciabatta he could stomach.

Luckily, Tom barged back in, a holdall in one hand and a fistful of VHS tapes in the other. A selection was made. Instructions were given. Jon was out of the house within five minutes.

'He's still a fucking dickhead!' I said, after he had left.

'He might be, but he's got something on the go,' Tom said, winking his eye and touching the side of his nose.

'What do you mean?' I asked.

Tom hopped off the counter again. I had to avert my eyes because I'm sure one of his nuts fell out of the leg of his saggy pants.

'He's got a new woman on the go,' Tom said, licking his lips like the festering pervert that he was.

'Really!?'

'Really! But he won't say too much. He did say that they were going to watch a movie together and maybe make one of their own.'

I couldn't look at Tom's drooling face anymore. And I definitely couldn't take Jon's smug grin out of my head. Today was going to be a tough day. And just to make it tougher, I figured I'd go and see my mother. I was a glutton for punishment.

1991

I trudged to Trafalgar Road to see if my mother was home. Unfortunately, she was. Friday was apparently her day off from the several jobs she was barely holding down.

'Do you want a cup of tea?' she yelled from the kitchen through a dense cloud of cigarette smoke.

I responded with a yes but inwardly I wanted to say, *'No thank you, I don't want to drink from one of your piss-stained mugs.'*

I was sitting on the plastic sofa, counting the fag burns in the cheap cotton throw she'd chucked on to cover a multitude of sins. The room seemed a whole lot smaller than I remember but, that said, I only have one photograph of myself in the back living room, and it was on a Christmas day many years ago. I'm playing with a multi-coloured toy camera and standing in front of a small, wooden box television, clearly unaware of the poverty I was being dragged up in.

Mother walked in, fresh cigarette in one hand, a dirty mug in the other. The mug was placed in front of me. I wasn't going to be drinking from it.

'So,' she glared at me with a face that wanted to ask a million and one questions, 'how long have you been back in town?'

One down – a million to go.

'A couple of days,' it was a white lie. I hoped *four days* didn't fall out of my mouth at any point.

'You were seen at the station on Tuesday. Couldn't come and see your mum any sooner, could you?'

I wasn't expecting her stealth patrol to be roaming the lower end of Milford. I could have apologised but I wasn't sorry. I could have come up with a story, but I didn't think she was owed a poor excuse, or any excuse, for that matter. I had managed to get by for the last few years without her help so my days of explaining myself were over. I merely shrugged and picked up the mug.

'How long are you back for?' She took a long draw from a superking cigarette.

'The summer – maybe longer – depends on what work I can get.' I replaced the mug after thinking better of taking a sip.

'What kind of work are you looking for?' She exhaled her lungs into the room.

I figured that it would be question after question unless I gave her more than just enough information to cover her query. I decided to give her a chunk to chew on and hope the interrogation would run out of steam. I told her which towns I'd been working in and the kind of places I'd worked for. I went into some detail and told a few stories about the drunks I'd had to deal with during the bar work. She remained pensive throughout my description of the last couple of years and I could see the cogs turning with the questions mounting up behind her yellow stained teeth, but she didn't ask another thing of me.

We sat in silence for an uncomfortable moment, sizing each other up. I hadn't spent much time in her presence in the last few years but what I could see didn't fill me with nostalgic glee. I reckon she had aged ten years in the last five, losing weight off her face and legs, yet gaining it on her belly and hips. I was no Columbo, but I could have deduced that she was living off chips, booze and fags, and the overall effect was going to be sending her to the cemetery before her time. I should have felt some sorrow about the deterioration of my own mother, but it was difficult to detect the frayed ends of a maternal bond that had been severed so many years ago. Having a new 'Dad' for every Christmas and birthday would do that. For every different Dad she was a different Mum, and not one that prioritised her only son – not for a day, not for a minute. We were strangers with the same surname and that was the limit of our bond.

I wanted to make my excuses and leave. I wanted to step away from my unhappy childhood home, never to return. I wanted so many things. I wanted a mother who might actually give a shit about me. I wanted to have nothing but joyful memories from within the four walls that had housed me for so long. But I learned a very long time ago – you don't get what you want, you get what you need. In my heart of hearts, I knew this distance – this disconnection – was to be for my betterment, and her eventual downfall.

I left the house.

Instead of turning right, heading up the street back toward Coombs Drive, I walked down to The Haven Fish Café. It was lunchtime and the aroma of fresh chips was too good. Especially in contrast to the smoke-filled air I'd been breathing in. I stepped inside and perused the menu on the wall behind the counter. I placed my order with a young woman fighting with her sweat-compromised make-up and waited patiently for the chips to cook.

I looked back up the road toward my mother's house, wondering if I had been too harsh, if I should have been the better person. In her eyes, I would never be the better person. To try would have been a waste of my time.

I took my tray of chips and gravy and strolled out onto Dartmouth Street. Taking the turn just past Griff's sweet shop, I walked up Robert Street. I don't know why I took that route, but it was often the way I would go to Dan's when he lived at home. The Robert Street carpark was half full as usual. As kids, Dan and I would often drop into the Italian shop and armed with a packet of pickled onion Monster Munch and a can of coke, would sit on the wall overlooking the carpark pretending we owned the best car we could see.

Good times. Old times.

I finished my chips as I was passing the sorting office. I thought, one time, I might like to have been a postman, but I always had an issue with waking up before 8am. Maybe it wasn't for me.

I could have changed direction at any time, taking a much shorter route back to the house but, for some reason, I had to walk past Dan's old house: the house where Tina still lived. There were a million different reasons why I wanted to walk past the scene of my past crimes but, for the life of me, I couldn't think of one. If I saw Tina, it would have been a bonus.

124

I wasn't far away, and I wasn't really paying attention to my surroundings. My eyes were dead ahead and staring at the doorstep that I had crossed one night when I shouldn't have. I could have knocked upon the door and said hello. I could have but I didn't. I didn't get the chance.

I saw a figure walk out onto that doorstep. I stopped dead in my tracks. I couldn't take another step. That familiar nausea overwhelmed me, threatening to spill the freshly consumed chips onto the pavement.

I found my feet and ducked into the flats. Peering around the corner, my initial sight was confirmed. The person stepping out of Dan's house, bidding an over-friendly farewell to Tina was none other than Jon, armed with the video camera bag. His expression wasn't one of disappointment. It was the familiar satisfied smugness.

I emptied my guts onto the grass next to the path. That man tainted everything I ever cared about. I hated him as much as I hated my mother. And that was a lot of hate.

36

1991

I curled up on the camp bed mattress thrown into the corner of Dan's bedroom, trying to get my head around what I had witnessed. My brain was struggling so hard with the situation that I had no idea whether I should tell Dan or not. There were other things to consider. I didn't know if Jon knew what he wasn't supposed to know, like the liaisons between Tina and myself. It was possible he might know something about it if he too was sleeping with her. But maybe that was my paranoia working overtime.

There was a fine line – so fine I could barely see it – but I still had to tread carefully in case I said anything that would reveal something from my bag of dark secrets. At this stage of my life, I had very few resources to fall back on in an emergency. Dan was one of my main fall backs. I didn't like to rely on anyone, and I hadn't needed to for most of my life, but times were changing, life was changing. I had limited options and my friends were the stopgap for now. I wasn't using them, I was accepting their help, for which I was eternally grateful. I hoped to return the favour someday, but I couldn't do that if a smug, loud-mouth prick spilled the beans that I'd shagged my best friend's mother.

I flipped onto my back, wondering when sleep would come. It was still early but I'd spent most of the afternoon and all of the evening under a duvet on the wafer-thin mattress trying to sleep my way out of my shit life.

Trying to empty my mind of the last few hours was proving pointless. I observed the orange shapes cast by the filtering of the streetlights and my eyes scanned for shapes and symbols that might add meaning to the anxiety eating away at my fragile mind. I saw nothing.

I shifted my position again and pressed another sore point of contact against the limited comfort beneath me. I could hear action vibrating through the hollow floorboards. Dan was watching a movie and volume was not something he seemed concerned with. I, on the other hand, was concerned by everything. I would have to wait until tomorrow and see what Saturday night would bring.

I was hoping for a heart-to-heart with Jennifer. I was hoping that maybe her subtle hints and not-so subtle glances were aimed only for me. It was wishful thinking but at least it was thinking that brought some comfort. More comfort than the floor at least.

Somehow, at some time, I eventually drifted off to sleep. It wasn't a good sleep, but at least it was some sleep, and for that, I was grateful.

37

1991

I had gotten up at the crack of dawn, made a cup of tea and curled up on the living room sofa with a book. Dan was big into his horror authors and so I pulled a James Herbert from the shelf and started reading. It was the first time in years that I'd read anything other than the newspaper or a magazine. It felt good to lose my restless mind in the pages of a nightmare and escape the nightmare of my own life.

I figured that I must have started the book at about 6.30am. I finished it by 10. I put it to rest on the coffee table next to the mug I had filled three times as I heard Tom come down over the stairs. He had a shift at the hotel that afternoon and needed to catch the bus.

'You're up early,' Tom hollered through the door on his way to the kitchen.

I didn't reply. I wasn't in the mood for idle chit-chat that would no doubt turn into a random porn related conversation. My hope was he would run for the bus and be gone before he stirred thoughts of Tina and Jon that I'd been trying to rid from my brain the previous night.

I was lucky. He grabbed some toast, shot back upstairs, got dressed and left.

My morning was planned out. I had found a recording of the movie The Untouchables and had planned to watch it when I got a moments peace. That moment was now. I was merely counting down the hours until tonight. Drinks with the gang but, more specifically, with Jennifer. I had decided to tell her how I felt. And I felt brave enough to handle the rejection.

I had managed to get to the part of the film where Kevin Costner and Sean Connery were picking Andy Garcia to be a part of their crew when Dan stumbled in.

'What time is it?'

'Nearly midday,' I said.

He grunted and staggered into the kitchen. I heard the click of the kettle and the rustling of the bread bag. A few minutes later he returned with some tea and toast.

We watched the rest of the film together and chatted like old times. It felt so comforting to be like our old selves. We talked about the times we had our names taken by the dock police for jumping off fuel tanks onto bags of fertiliser; when we would play on rope-swing in the woods; or when we would creep over the rocks toward Hakin Point and spy on older girls sunbathing in bikinis. Our history was solid, so was our friendship, I couldn't think of any reason why I would want to jeopardise that. The secrets I held were staying with me, for now. But big secrets were hard to keep in a small town like Milford.

38

1991

The tick-tock of the clock on the mantelpiece seemed to be slowing time down. I was sure that I'd seen the minute hands on other clocks spin twice as fast. But it wasn't important anymore. The time had arrived, and we were ready.

Dan was wearing baggy jeans, Reebok trainers and an oversized t-shirt. He'd also thrown on enough aftershave to repel predators up to five miles away. I wasn't sure what the fragrance was, but he smelled like the queue for the bar of a 1970s working men's club.

I, on the other hand, had a very subtle fragrance bought for me for Christmas by Sarah: Cerruti 1881. I wasn't sure it was going to have the desired effect if I was standing down wind of Dan, but I was sure that his particular stench would numb the senses of anyone who stood too close to him. I had to hope my casual look of Levi's 501s, a grandad shirt and a pair of brown brogues would do the trick.

We headed out at 7pm. Tom didn't finish his shift until 8pm and then had to catch the bus home. We expected to see him at around ten-ish, wherever the hell we were. Everybody else was turning up at The Starboard in their own time.

It was looking to be a lovely evening. The sky was a flawless azure with the sun hanging over the mouth of the haven, casting long shadows as we strolled to the pub. It was on days like this that I really enjoyed my hometown. Although the streets were overfamiliar, the favourable weather made it seem like a different place – a better place – like on holiday, with a perfect climate. It's almost as though the sunshine was part of a package deal. I was used to bracing winds and fine, penetrating rain, keeping the town in a permanent state of autumn. But the evening felt like a fine summer day, and I would treat it as such.

The trek into town wasn't all sunshine and perfection, though. The most picturesque route took us past Rob's house. It had been a while since anyone had had a conversation with me about Rob, but

Dan had said Rob's parents had moved to Steynton, the better end of the town. The old house on North Road probably housed too many memories, too many good times that couldn't be enjoyed anymore. The loss would be felt at the bar tonight. No political talk. No lefty discussions.

Making our way along Hamilton Terrace, the three storey Georgian townhouses seemed so much grander under the sun's rays; the whites were whiter, the colours more vivid.

Dan's conversation was also becoming more vivid, going in directions that I considered dangerous territory for a guy like Dan. He was a sucker for a pretty face, regardless of the personality.

'I'm hoping the new barmaid is on in The Starboard tonight – she's magnificent!' Dan enthused.

'Have you tried to *crack-on* yet?' That was the current phrase for attempting to pull.

'Not yet, although Jon's already had a go.'

'How well did he do?' I knew the answer before it was said.

'He shagged her,' Dan pointed to the other side of the road, 'over that bench, about a month ago.'

I needed a drink.

I didn't say another word, wanting the conversation as far away from the subject of Jon as possible. The lad didn't even need to be in my presence and he still annoyed the shit out of me.

But Dan continued, 'He's like a walking gland. If it's got a pulse, he wants to fuck it.'

'I pray for impotence to strike him down.' It was as much as I dared say.

'He might end up that way if he keeps visiting Tom's pornographic emporium. He might pull his cock off from wanking too much,' Dan laughed.

I laughed with him but in reality, I wanted to find a Genie in a lamp to grant my three wishes – the first wish would be to have that scenario come true.

131

I asked the question I hoped would be answered with a firm 'No.'

'Is he coming out tonight?'

'Yeah,' Dan nodded weakly, as though he knew it was not the answer I wanted to hear.

Great!

Tonight, was freefalling into an abyss of disasters. And we hadn't even hit the pub yet.

39

1991

Dan had just returned with our third pint of the night when the girls arrived: and by 'the girls' I meant Jennifer, Nikita, *and* Sarah. I was under the impression that Sarah had gone back to Bristol for the weekend, but apparently her plans had changed. I was disappointed, I was surprised. I liked being out with Sarah, she was my wingman, in all kinds of situations. But with her being back, I wouldn't get much of a look-in with Jennifer.

Once everyone – and by everyone I meant Dan, myself and the girls – had a drink in hand, we took up residence in one of the window benches of the Starboard. It was the best seat in the house if you liked to watch the world go by. I was settled into one of the nooks in the seating, allowing me to look up Hamilton Terrace, watching the cars and people toing and froing on a pleasant sunny evening. They were going places. We were going nowhere.

For the most part, we were just chatting shit like we always did. Nothing had changed. The only difference in the content of the conversation was the addition of more life experience and less childish outbursts.

As the talk drifted on, I gazed up the road, watching the streetlights come on. The evening had succumbed to the night. Conversation had become background noise to my mental meanderings. With the alcohol swirling through the grey matter, my mind took me back to that first night with Tina again. It was a similar night to tonight. Hopefully it would have a similar ending but without the prior argument and fighting.

My daydream ended abruptly when I caught sight of Tom sauntering down Hamilton Terrace. It wasn't Tom who had killed my nostalgic vibe. It was who was with him.

Jon.

The pair of them burst in, clearly already in a drinking mood. Tom looked as though he had been throwing down the booze since the minute his shift had finished. Jon looked less drunk but more smug than usual.

'Alright, losers?' Jon opened the tone of his dialogue for the evening.

There were a few grunts and gestures of greeting, but the gang could feel the atmosphere drop. Even Nikita, who was supposed to be a good friend of Jon's, was a little hesitant to engage with him. My hope was he would get swept away under the tidal wave of his own hormones and hook up with some willing participant who wasn't sat at our table.

The pair returned from the bar and joined the crowd. Tom fell into the corner seat next to Sarah, spilling some of his lager onto her long black skirt. There was a fuss made about the spillage, but Sarah didn't seem too put out and didn't mind when Tom dropped to his knees to suck the beer from the wet material.

'Look out! Someone's getting lucky tonight – or unlucky – I can't really tell,' Jon said, looking down his nose at Sarah's nonchalance.

'Unlucky, if they get you,' Sarah fired back.

'Calm down, chubbs, that's the most action you'll get this weekend,' Jon laughed at his insult.

I was seething. The burning hatred I had for that lad was coursing through me. I held my tongue because what I wanted to say wouldn't be taken as a joke and I didn't want things to kick off.

Thankfully, there's always Dan. Drink or no drink, his wit was always rapier quick.

'Chubbs?' Dan said, 'Have you seen your chin? Oh sorry, my mistake – *chins*.'

'Fuck off!' Jon already knew he was beat.

'I know you've been away, working hard as architect, but from where I'm sitting – and that's in your considerable shadow – you look like you've been failing to overcome your cake addiction.'

The group, except Jon, started to giggle.

134

'Oh, here we go, Dan putting in the effort to be funny.' It was a lame retort from Jon.

'Well, you seem to be putting in the effort to get type two diabetes. What sports have you been playing up in London, Sumo?'

That was enough for Jon. He grabbed his drink, storming off to the poolroom.

'Bravo,' I said, giving Dan a well-earned round of applause.

'It was nothing, unlike his gut.'

'I think you may have upset him,' I said.

'No. He's just gone to walk off some of that cake baby he's carrying.'

Beer shot out of my nose.

*

After a few more drinks, we moved on to Debrett's. It wasn't called that anymore. It was called something else, but nobody knew what the new name was, and because there had never been any signage, we still called it Debrett's.

It was just the six of us for now. Jon had stayed away for the rest of the evening and when it was time to leave nobody went to get him. Jennifer, Nikita and Sarah waltzed into the nightclub arm-in-arm. Dan and I had to do the same for Tom who was certainly beyond ordering anymore drinks, or even engaging in simple forms of communication for that matter.

We dropped him in a corner booth where he curled up and promptly fell asleep.

Instead of drinking, the girls hit the dance floor. I headed to the bar; Dan followed. We bought some vodka and went to sit next to Tom but found a couple devouring each other in the space next to him. There were some stools next to a table, so we took one each and tried to talk. It was very difficult to maintain a conversation with MC Hammer – You Can't Touch This, belting out at over a hundred decibels. We gave up our stools and moved to the very front of the club, there was an empty area just at the top of the stairs, near the entrance, where we could sit on the floor and chat.

'Are you going to ask Jennifer out?' Dan asked, shouting the question at me.

'I'm going to have a chat with her and see where it goes. I'm not pinning any hopes on it.' That's what I was telling him, but the reality was different. I had missed too many opportunities before and, in my head, it was now or never.

We chatted some more and then the girls turned up, their faces covered in a sheen of sweat and condensation. The area near the door was nice and cool and they had come to have a breather. Jennifer had taken the bit of floor right next to me. This was my chance.

'Did you have a good dance?' I asked. Mr Small-talk, I wasn't.

'Yeah, not bad. You should come and have a dance,' she beamed. Even with a fine sheen of moisture ruining her makeup, she still looked stunning. Years of being away hadn't changed anything about the way I felt. If anything, it had reinforced what I already knew. She was the girl for me. That was what my head was telling me, and even with a fair quantity of cheap booze topping up my courage, I needed to act on it.

'Maybe. Maybe you'll save the last dance for me.' It was a cheesy line, but it was the best I had.

She smiled her wide perfect smile, looking straight at me with those bottomless blue eyes and paused for a moment, holding my gaze. And then she said...

And then she said nothing.

She didn't get a chance.

One of our casual acquaintances barged into the area and informed us that Tom was currently vomiting in his corner booth. The moment ruined, we felt obliged to go and check on him.

So close, yet so far.

That was our night over and done with. We left the girls to dance the night away and walked our housemate home, stopping every now and then to allow more vomit action. All thoughts of Jennifer were lost to the sound of retching and splatter.

I was sure it must have been some kind of galactic conspiracy against me and my happiness.

40

1991

While I wasn't so fortunate with the ladies, I had better luck finding employment. My first few weeks back in Milford had proved to be fruitful. I had landed two jobs; working dayshifts at The Nelson Hotel, and a few evening shifts in a brand-new pub on the docks called Martha's Vineyard. I had wondered who Martha was, or where her vineyard was to be found, but it turns out, it was an island off the coast of America. The film Jaws was made there.

It seemed odd to be back on the docks after so long. The last time I remember being there, Dan and I were being chased by the dock police for riding our bikes through the fish market. A stroll through the now new and improved 'marina' showed how much things had changed. Martha's Vineyard was smack bang in the middle of where the fish market used to be. All the sheds that had lined the rear of the docks had been bulldozed. What remained was a scarred and flattened rubble waste ground. A lot of the other buildings around the edge of the docks had gone too. I remembered, as a kid watching the huge blocks of ice slide down the chute of the ice making factory, but that had gone too. The face of Milford was changing, and I suspected that many of the residents would be reluctant of change.

One such resident was my mother.

I had popped in to visit her, on more than one occasion, and it always seemed like a massive mistake. I called in on the morning of her day off, a little after eleven and it was a shocker.

I wasn't sure if she had spent the whole morning drinking, or if she was still drunk from the night before but, on that morning, she could barely string a sentence together. I had made her enough black coffee to wake the dead, but somehow it had no effect on her inebriated state. She just slumped in her chair, sparking up cigarettes, smoking them down to the filter before lighting another immediately. If there was no work for her, she would sink into the bottom of a bottle and stay there. On every occasion I called in, she smelled of drink and fags, whether she was working or not. This was someone who wasn't changing. This was someone reinforcing themselves, doubling their efforts to remain the same.

While my only parent was immovable, I was adapting to my circumstances well. I now had my own room in the house I shared with Dan and Tom. I had a bed, a bed side table and a wardrobe. I didn't need much more. Living with two of my best friends was proving to have a calming effect on me. For years, I had anxiety as I moved through life, aimlessly; a ship with a broken rudder and no sails to catch the wind. I was still young, but I had a sense of urgency about everything I was trying to do, although not everything was happening quickly. There was no foot up my sorry arse when it came to chasing Jennifer.

But, racing myself into the grave aside, everything else was trundling along pretty much as well as could be expected. Occasionally, Jon would turn up, unannounced, and spoil the atmosphere – ok, only my atmosphere – but once he had been fobbed off with a tape of some European debauchery, he would be gone.

Tonight, was going to be a good night, though. It was Saturday. Nobody was working tomorrow. And Jon was away all weekend. It seemed that conditions were near perfect for Operation: Win Jennifer.

I had to give it a name.

Opening my second can of the night, there was a knock at the door. Swigging away, I opened the door to the girls. It was the ideal ratio for the night: three girls, three boys. In my head I was working out the pairings.

Dan had been with Nikita before, and they were both single. They were already comfortable with each other so there could be a chance of a brief rekindling for one night only.

On the last night out, Tom – long before he had thrown up – had looked to be getting cosy with Sarah. Whether Sarah was getting cosy with him was another matter but if they hooked up it would solve two problems. One, I wouldn't be preoccupied with Sarah, and two,

Jennifer wouldn't be preoccupied with Sarah. I just had to hope that I could steer Tom into being preoccupied with Sarah. I vowed to keep them drunk and in close proximity to each other.

That left only one pairing. Me and Jennifer. No Jon to spoil the party.

Drinks were poured; snacks were consumed; laughter ensued. After several drinks had raised the mood, we left the house and headed into town.

Phase one of the plan was working out. Dan and Nikita automatically fell into a twosome, strolling ahead of the group. As I had been rallying around Tom and Sarah in conversation at the house, they had become accustomed to engaging more than they were used to and seemed to want to continue doing more of the same. Result.

That left me, with the idol of my affections, bringing up the rear. We chatted, we laughed, and I think we even flirted a bit; if this was my plan, it was working. Our pace slowed, dropping us away from the others. And this wasn't my doing. It was all her. Even with a quantity of alcohol in me, I could still feel the rush of adrenalin stealing power from my legs, dancing in my stomach, and making my heart race. This was a good feeling.

I looked at her. She looked back, her head down, her eyes wide. She was coy. Oh my God, it was happening. My hopes and dreams were going to be answered. All those years of teenage heartbreak were going to be mended, here and now. I could feel it.

Then it happened. It had started. The courtship was on. She laced her fingers into mine and held my hand as we walked. Instantly, it was just us. There were no other friends – no other people – just us and the stars and the moon. We were the only two people in the world.

And then she spoke.

'I have a secret,' she said, giggling as she spoke.

'So do I,' I said back.

'What's yours?'

'You go first,' I said, smiling a Cheshire cat smile, hoping and praying she would say the words I wanted her to say.

140

'Are you sure? Yours could be far my important than mine.'

'Of course, I'm sure.'

'Can I whisper it in your ear?' she asked.

I didn't know why declaring her undying love for me needed to be whispered but clearly it was something she needed to do.

'Go ahead.'

She leaned in placing her mouth so close to my ear that it I thought she had kissed it. I could feel the warmth of her breath wrapped around the words ushered from her lips.

I heard the words.

They were not the ones I wanted to hear.

'What?' It was all I had. I was confused. Had I read the signals wrong? What she had just said – the information given to me – made no sense. No sense at all. The moment was ruined. So was my life.

41

1991

'What do you mean by *Sarah wants you?*' I was running close to hysterical, which was not the sure-fire way to win over the love of my life a minute after she had dropped a bombshell.

'Exactly as it sounds – she wants you. She wants to be more than friends.' Jennifer said the words, but her eyes were looking ahead trying to see if Sarah had heard my outburst.

'Did she put you up to this?' I wasn't sure what kind of emotion I was displaying – either anger or confusion – but I was sure as shit wasn't playing it cool.

'Er… no. Not exactly.'

All logic had drifted out of my tiny mind. I had a clear goal for the night – an objective I was destined to conquer. For as long as I could remember, I had wanted the woman standing before me and I had planned to tell her everything. How I had loved her since I saw her gappy smile beaming at me on the North Road school field when we were just seven years old; how I had loved her even more when our class – for a laugh – decided to sit boy-girl and she chose me to be the boy she sat next to; how I loved her more still when she chose me to dance with her at the school disco in 1982. Everything this woman did – from times when she wasn't even a woman – made me feel special in so many ways. Just being with her, here and now, having this confusing, awkward conversation was still special. And still, it made her *The One,* in my eyes.

But I was in a hole, and I didn't have the boots to climb out.

I stood on the pavement, the raucous noise from The Kimberly pub, just a few yards away, blocking out any rational thoughts from being conjured up.

'Will?' Jennifer reached out and took my hand, 'Are you ok?'

She always knew what to do to leave me completely disarmed. I don't think it was deliberate, I just think it was the effect she had on me. The warmth of her subtle grip brought me back down to earth. Not with a bump, but with the compassionate nuances only she could pull off. I was going to have to go for broke.

'I'm ok. It's just a bit of a shock. I wasn't prepared for that.' I was playing for time as I had my own bombshell to drop.

'A good shock or a bad shock?'

'I couldn't tell you.' It was a bad shock – definitely a bad shock.

Those wonderful blue eyes gazed at me, trying to figure my mood.

I was giving very little away, I hoped.

'Sooo,' it was a long drawn out 'so' that girls often used to start a loaded question, 'do you want to do anything about it?'

I pondered all possible answers and decided to give her the one she wasn't expecting.

'No. She's my friend and that's how I view her. She's the sister I never had – it would be weird.' Now was my chance, 'Besides, I have my heart set on someone else.'

Jennifer smirked. Her eyes fell to the pavement for a moment and then back at me.

'Who?' she asked.

I couldn't help but think she already knew the answer. I couldn't help but think that she had been waiting for me to ask for as long as I had loved her. She was one of those girls who knew this kind of stuff. And if she knew, I was toast.

'You.'

I was sure the dinosaurs could have evolved all over again and become extinct in the eternity it took for her to reply. There was no longer noise drifting from The Kimberly. The cars that zipped past on North Road did so in silence. The only sound I could hear was the thunderous beating of my rapid heart and the deafening silence between Jennifer and me.

The reply was not exactly as I had expected. It was worse. Much worse.

'I know, Will,' she said, melancholy flooding into her expression. 'I've always known.'

Game over.

42

1991

'If you've always known, why have you not said anything before?' This was as bad as finding out that Father Christmas didn't exist. I always had a belief that she knew nothing, that I was her very good friend and could be told everything. The chasm between what I thought I knew and the truth, couldn't be bridged with a few planks of wood. I needed Brunel and all the civil engineering shit he knew.

'Because I didn't want things to be awkward between us,' she soothed, holding my hand as she did so. 'I really do care about you, Will. You're so special to me, you've such a good heart and I would never want to hurt you.'

'But...?' I was pre-empting.

'But nothing. I'm your friend, I'm Sarah's friend, and she's liked you for a very long time – since school.'

And now I was hearing about it. I was about to pin my hopes on the girl I wanted. I thought long and hard – all two seconds of it – about my next course of action.

'If Sarah wasn't interested in me, would you be?' I could sense a painful, yet necessary answer coming my way.

She took a moment to answer. Maybe she was considering her options, or just trying to pick the words that wouldn't hurt or encourage me because either would be detrimental to our relationship. I was totally at her mercy.

'What do you want to hear?' she said eventually.

'I want the truth: plain and simple.'

'I can honestly say that out of all the men I've ever known, I know you would never hurt me. I can't say that the possibility of *you and me* hasn't entered my mind, because it has, but it's not something I ever wanted to pursue because of Sarah. That girl has had enough to deal with in her time. I didn't want to add to it.'

I knew what she was saying regarding Sarah. The bullying about her weight and her plain looks were just the tip of the iceberg.

Sarah suffered at the hands of her mother and various stepfathers over the years – suffered in ways that she would never tell. It amazed me how resilient she was.

But now I was getting side-tracked. The overwhelming desire I had to tell Jennifer everything had been brushed aside to make way for a massive dose of sympathy for our mutual friend. Regardless of what was said, I needed to have the truth.

'I can't deal with Sarah's feelings for me now. I need to know where you are. If Sarah was not in the picture, would you be interested? Please, give me an honest answer.'

'Maybe!' Her expression was one of confusion. I imagined it was how my face looked a few minutes ago.

My heart pounded out of my chest, sticking in my throat, preventing the words from falling out. I wanted to scream, *what did 'maybe' mean?* I wanted to but couldn't.

'Will,' the confusion on her face had spread to her tone, 'say something.'

Where would I start? Where would it end? I couldn't be helped for my outburst in this situation. I didn't want my infatuation Tourette's to get the better of me and have words spill out into the here and now with no chance to retrieve them.

I had to say something.

'I love you.'

That was the wrong thing to say.

Those three little words had only ever passed my lips when drunkenly singing to the Ramones at a bedsit party when I lived in Plymouth. I knew my infatuation Tourette's would let me down once alcohol and desperation were thrown into the emotional cauldron.

'You don't love me, Will, you think you do but you don't. And being in love with me has never worked out. I get hurt and they get hurt, which means, you'll get hurt.'

'I don't think a day has passed in the last six or seven years where I haven't thought about there being an *us*. I believe that I am the

146

guy for you, and I know you're the girl for me. I've thought about it for so long that I don't think I can undo it.'

'Why are you saying all this now? You've had years to say it.'

Of course, she was right. I'd been afraid of rejection. I should have been used to it with living in a constant state of rejection from my own mother. But that was my mother. I expected it from her. I never wanted to feel it from Jennifer, but here I was, staring down the barrel of rejection with no place for cover.

'I didn't have the guts,' I said, 'plus, you were always involved with someone. Right here and now, you are single. So am I. Let's make a go of it.'

Her expression softened. She stepped toward me and placed a hand on either side of my face, holding it as though to focus my attention on her.

'You're so sweet and lovely and such a good friend, but there are other things to-'

She didn't get to finish the sentence. I reached forward, placing my hands on her face as she had on mine, and I kissed her.

For the briefest of moments, she held her ground, letting her lips respond. It was joy. In that second, I felt the burning rush of belonging and I didn't want it to end.

But it did end.

Jennifer twisted her face away from mine, pushing herself free.

'What are you doing?' she asked, her face flushed. I wasn't sure if it was anger or embarrassment.

'I thought I was kissing you…' my dialogue ran out of steam when I saw her lip quiver. What had I done?

'I'm sorry,' I said it because I meant it, but it sounded hollow as it echoed from the empty shell of my wasted heart.

'It's ok,' she said, wiping away a tear, 'I can't blame you for how you feel. I just didn't expect that to happen.'

147

There was something else she wasn't telling me, but I was too afraid to ask what was going on inside her head.

'Still, I'm sorry, I shouldn't have done that.'

'Oh, Will, what a mess. We shouldn't be kissing. People are going to get hurt.'

'Who?' I was prepared for hurt. My childhood had been forged in the crucible of hurt. With a mother like mine, I learned about hurt before I learned how to walk.

'You – me – Sarah,' there was anger in her tone.

'I won't hurt you – I would never hurt you. And as for me; I'm a big boy now and I can take the hurt.' I was fired up but not yet shouting back.

'What about Sarah?' Jennifer bellowed.

'I don't care about Sarah; I care about us.'

I shouldn't have said that.

'*Thanks*, Will! *Thanks* a bunch!' Sarah's voice drifted over my shoulder.

That was my safety net cut free. The weight of guilt from the million-and-one things she had done for me landed as though dropped from a B52. I said nothing more. I didn't trust my own tongue. I went home. Alone.

43

1991

What a fucking twat! That's what I thought of myself. How the Hell did I do this time and time again? In the dictionary under the entry, *Fuck Up*, there wasn't a definition, just a picture of me with a sad face. Not only had I screwed up any chance with Jennifer, but I had also alienated one of my dearest friends.

What a mess.

That's what Jennifer had said, and she wasn't wrong.

With my night over before it had begun, I hit the fridge for the last few beers. Three cans of Carling had been chilling on the beer shelf and now all three were lined up on the coffee table, waiting for my attention.

I dug around the video cabinet for something to watch, deciding to go for an old faithful film to crowbar some comfort back into my life. Highlander was the movie that the gang used to watch together when the weather was bad and there was bugger all on TV to watch. I strapped myself in – can in hand – and let the Queen soundtrack wash over me as the story of Connor McLeod unfolded in grainy pirate quality.

I finished the third can just as the credits were rolling. Suitably tipsy but not completely smashed, I opened a bottle of vodka, mixing it with some orange squash to make a screwdriver. It was the drink I had shared with Tina, five years ago.

I had attempted to watch Terminator as well but switched it off after half an hour. The growing intoxication, coupled with an annoying ripple of the movie on the screen every minute or so was vexing my already frayed emotions. I decided sleep would be my only respite tonight. The drink had made it possible.

As easy as it was to fall asleep, my slumber was shallow, and I was attuned to every noise. Several taxis had been shuttling into the street; revved engines and slammed doors, jarred me from my weird dreams back into a foggy reality.

The front door slammed.

I grabbed my watch and blinked at the time. It was just after 2am.

There were voices. There were footsteps. I pulled my ragged pillow over my head to block out the noise. It wasn't enough to block out what came next.

I was used to hearing sexual activity penetrating the wall that divided bedrooms, but usually it was accompanied by a lame soundtrack or some nondescript rock music if the brand of pirated pornography was from the 1970s. Tonight, the sounds of sex were accompanied by the banging of the headboard against the plasterboard and woodchip divide. Unless I was very much mistaken, Tom was putting in his best efforts with a real girl instead of finishing off into a tissue, only to drop it onto his bedroom floor. The more I tried to ignore the noise, the more I heard. It seemed like the desensitising of daily porn and three-wanks-a-day, plus the drink from the night, was having a positive effect on his performance. The moans of the first encounter lasted for a solid fifteen minutes. There was a brief pause in the *lovemaking* before it continued for another hour or so. I left my bedroom after ten minutes into round three.

I could have curled up on the sofa, but Tom's room was directly above the living room, and I would have been subjected to just as much noise but without the comfort of a bed. Instead, I opted for the kitchen with a book.

The clock on the oven was just creeping up on 4am, and I was sipping my third cup of tea, when the door opened. Tom staggered in, naked, his semi erect penis dangling for all to see.

'Have you got any Johnnies?' Tom said, no apologises for the disturbance or the noise.

'Not on me,' I said, 'I'm not likely to encounter available women in the kitchen at this hour.'

Un-phased, Tom continued, 'Do you know of any in the house?'

'Try the bathroom cabinet. I think Dan had a pack in there.'

150

Without a *thank you*, he disappeared back upstairs. I heard the slide of the mirrored door and the joyous *'Yes!'* as he no doubt found the condoms. I stayed put for a while longer, waiting for the sounds of sex to subside. By 5am I was back in my bed and the frantic headboard action had finished.

I dozed off a few times but kept waking myself up. Sleep didn't seem like a possibility, and by 8am I was back in the kitchen trying to stave off a hangover with tea and toast. It wasn't working.

I was throwing down a couple of paracetamols with some water when the door to the kitchen opened.

I froze, trying to register what was happening.

Standing in the doorway, barely dressed in a t-shirt and panties was Tom's conquest for the night. I think it was the most awkward I had ever felt in my entire life. Not because they must have known I heard everything that had happened, but because I think it was deliberate that I heard everything.

She took two mugs out of the cabinet and filled them with water, barely acknowledging my existence, before scurrying back upstairs. Within five minutes the sex started all over again.

Tom's partner in lust was Sarah. I guess she hated me now.

44

1991

It had been two weeks since I opened my big mouth and upset one of the most important people in my life.

Sarah had spent all of the day after my outburst in Tom's room engaging in some form of depravity with Milford Haven's premier pervert, broadcasting unstifled moans of ecstasy, so much so that one of the neighbours from over the road knocked the door and ask for the noise to be kept to a minimum. I took that as my cue to leave the house. I spent the afternoon walking past all the closed shops on Charles Street, many times, as I performed laps to fill the time. By the time I got back, Sarah had gone, and Tom was sleeping off a mixture of hangover and sexual exuberance. She didn't put in an appearance again.

I filled the time working, eating or sleeping, trying not to think of the hurt I had caused. Working was where my focus was, and I was squeezing in a day shift at Martha's Vineyard because the bar manager wanted me to train up a new barmaid starting that day. Talk about in at the deep end. The Tall Ships Race had kicked off, and what a shock to the system it was.

Every inch of the docks was filled with sailing vessels of one kind or another. There wasn't a clear view of the sky because of the multitude of masts and rigging blocking the line of sight. I imagined this was how Milford Haven looked in its heyday when it was known for whaling and fishing.

There were vessels of every shape and size from every nation moored around the dock perimeter until there was no space left.

All those ships had eager crews who seemed more eager for the drink and chat in a strange location than they were for the race that brought them to the town. The crews flooded the closest watering hole and were lined up to wait their turn at the bar – some wanted drink, some wanted to talk to the novice barmaid. I wanted to talk to her too, but the swirling throng of empty glasses and thirsty sailors put an end to that.

It's not that I didn't know her, because I did. The new barmaid was Dan's little sister, Charlotte. But she wasn't so little anymore. Eighteen years old and with the best of the genetics her gorgeous mother had to offer. She was turning heads from every corner of the bar. Turning mine more than was appropriate, and I was only three feet away.

After four hours of frantic, relentless bar work, we were able to knock off for the day, relieved by the evening staff who hit the ground running to a throng three deep at the bar.

Feeling sticky from the beer and sweaty from the work, I almost didn't want to ask if she wanted to go for a drink. But I shouldn't have worried.

'I know we've just finished serving a million pints, and you're probably sick to death of looking at glasses of booze, but I was wondering if you'd like to go for a drink?' Charlotte asked.

'After *that* shift what I need *is* a drink.' I couldn't believe my luck. She was doing the work for me.

Since I had had only minimal contact with Jennifer, and when I did see her, she was very standoffish, I figured that the possibility of me and her was completely off the table and that I should try and move on.

Moving on to Dan's sister was not the plan but it was the opportunity that had presented itself. I know, when I had my liaison with Tina, it was so wrong and there was no chart on which to measure how wrong it was. Dan's mother – no, no, no.

Dan's sister, however, was an entirely different matter.

It was considered flattering if your mates fancied your sister. I didn't know, I was an only child, but back in school we regularly discussed the hot girls we would encounter on a day-to-day basis and Charlotte often came up in conversation as a hottie of the future.

And here we were, both adults, both single, and the age difference was neither here nor there. She was eighteen and I was a matter of weeks away from my twenty-first birthday. It would have been rude not to explore the possibilities.

We rocked into The Nelson, shamelessly still wearing our black Martha's Vineyard polo shirts. With a pint of Carling for me and a pint of Strongbow for her, we resigned ourselves to the only empty picnic bench in the beer garden. From our elevated, suntrap position we could see the massive Russian sailing ship, Dar Mlodziezy, anchored out in the middle of the haven. The hull shone a brilliant white under sunlight, yet it seemed an unhappy sight without any sails on its three towering masts. A sailing ship was meant to have sails. We would just have to wait until the start of the race in a few days' time to see it in all its glory. Then it would sail away, never to return, or something just as romantic.

'A penny for them,' Charlotte said, cutting through my daydream with expert precision.

'I'm just thinking about all those ships – all those crews – the places they go to and experiences they have. It must be a great life to get away from home and visit new places,' I was wishing that I could go with them. Maybe I could stowaway on a ship, only to be discovered a thousand miles from home. But, looking across the table and taking in the beauty of my companion, I figured that being here wasn't so bad.

Charlotte had the same looks as her mother; the same chestnut hair; the same bronze eyes; and the same womanly figure. She was her mother's daughter, of that there was no doubt. She even had the same freckles across her nose. It made me wonder if she was the same as her mother in other ways: the ways that I shouldn't know about but did, only too well.

'But you've been away. You lived away for a few years – wasn't it like you expected?' she quizzed.

'Nothing's ever as you expect it to be. Living away, working away, it has its good points, but it also has its bad.' I didn't want to bring down the atmosphere, so I didn't go into detail. Yes, it was great to get away and work in other places, have a change of scenery and

154

mix with new people. But after a while the scenery starts to become familiar – the people too – the novelty wears off and there's a sudden realisation that one thing never changes. You.

You think that changing location will change your life, but the reality is never that simple. The one thing that stays the same is yourself and that's the one thing you've been trying to change. Personality and upbringing cannot be altered by living under a different postcode. Real change, as I discovered, starts from within and not by changing your surroundings.

'Did you miss Milford?'

'I missed my friends, and I missed the sunsets,' as I said it, I raised my glass to the glowing orb above us and took a swig in its honour.

'Surely all sunsets are the same. It's the same sun and it sets in the same place,' she debated, playfully.

'The foreground is different. A sunset in the city is black and daunting – tall buildings block the best of the view. Sunsets on the coast are magical, especially if the view west is nothing but sea on the horizon. You can literally watch the sun disappear behind the earth. It's beautiful.'

'Wow!' she said, lifting her glass for a drink, 'You seem to have grown up since leaving town.'

'I've seen some things; I've done some stuff, and I read quite a lot. It's all good for the brain. You've done a bit of growing up yourself.'

She smiled the same coy smile that her mother had. 'All of my brother's friends have noticed that.'

'I bet,' I was curious by what she meant but didn't want to pry because maybe it was something I didn't want to know.

'Tom and Jon are bad lads by themselves and even worse when they get together,' she said.

I didn't need telling. I knew. And I shuddered to think what those two had tried it on with the young lady sitting opposite me. Is

155

that why Jon had gone after Tina? He couldn't have the daughter, so he went after the next best thing. It was his style, after all.

'Did you get asked out on a date?' I ventured.

She laughed into her drink, spraying some onto the table. 'I got asked but not for a date – not a date in my experience, anyway.'

'What *do* you call a date?'

'This!' she said, holding my gaze, looking for a reaction.

I smiled and became a little animated in my embarrassment. 'Is this a date?'

'I'd like to think so.'

And that's all that was said for a long moment. Maybe this was supposed to happen. It was too early to tell, and not enough alcohol had been consumed. I extended the pause by buying another round. The possibilities were endless.

1991

Five drinks in and the conversation was yet to slow down. I think the drink was having an effect as I could tell I was starting to slur the odd word here and there. Charlotte seemed to be holding her own, either that or I hadn't noticed any drunken behaviour because my lager filter had blocked out the signs.

The sun was now out of sight, hidden behind the hotel, but still casting its orange glow upon the wisps of cloud forming on the clear, purple sky. The temperature in the beer garden had dropped too, making the work polo shirts completely inadequate for the job of alfresco drinking. We decided to retire to the warmth of the bar and maybe have just one more drink.

It was Charlotte's turn to get in the round. I took refuge in the corner booth which looked out onto Hamilton Terrace. Even with the view of the haven slightly obscured, the Russian sailing ship was still the obvious sight to see. I was lost to another drunken daydream on the deck of that magnificent ship when interruption came from a pint glass being placed with a thud in front of me. Maybe Charlotte wasn't holding up as well as I'd first thought.

The bar of the Nelson was very full. We had been lucky to bag a seat when we did. While there were a few familiar faces, the bulk of the patrons were strangers – not just to me – but to the town. Some young men with French accents were debating loudly at which tracks to put on the jukebox. I don't know who won the argument but Sinead O'Connor's Nothing Compares 2 U came droning out of the speakers, taking the atmosphere down a notch.

'What do you want to do next?' she asked me, her eyes had expectation in them. It was a look I very rarely experienced. I never put value into my own worth and never saw myself as anything more than average in the big wide world. Why this beautiful young lady was looking at me was beyond my comprehension.

'We could get some food, if you like?' Food might make it seem like a real date. I was hoping for a positive response.

'What do you like to eat?' she had a habit of answering a question with a question.

'I'm easy,' I said.

'That's what I'm banking on...' She giggled into her glass as she took a swig.

'Excuse me!?'

'It doesn't matter. Do you like Chinese food?'

'Who doesn't?' I said, skipping over her previous comment.

'Ok,' she said, putting down her glass with purpose, 'that's settled it. We will finish this drink and then go to The Mandarin.'

I nodded and took hold of my glass. The Mandarin Chinese restaurant was only about a hundred yards away but with my stomach rattling under the lack of food, a hundred yards was feeling pretty far away. Empty stomach or not, I was racing down the lager. After Sinead had finished whining about the hardships of life, Elton John's Sacrifice oozed into the bar. I don't who those French guys were, but they knew how to kill the vibe. I gestured my empty glass to Charlotte, and we left to get some food.

*

After stuffing ourselves to the point of death with Chinese food, we staggered out on to Hamilton Terrace. The food had been washed down with several vodkas, and the vodka had been soaked up with an endless supply of prawn crackers.

There was an opportunity to drop into the Starboard, but we passed it by. Dizzy heads and overloaded stomachs were not to be helped by more drinking.

'Do you want to come to mine for a coffee?' Charlotte asked as we climbed the steep hill of Barlow Street.

'I don't think it would be a good idea.' My heart was telling me to go for it, but my woozy head was telling me not to because Tina might be there, and it would be beyond awkward.

'Why not?' Her face was filled with confusion.

'We're drunk and it might lead somewhere – a bit too fast – and your mother might not approve of me,' I said, trying to play the gentleman.

'Yes, we are drunk, and it will lead wherever it leads. As for my mother, why does it matter what she thinks? She's not going to know.'

'Don't you live with her?'

'No. I moved out months ago,' her face beamed with pride, 'I share a flat with my friend and she's away for the weekend.'

Opportunities seemed to be opening up all over the place. Loving thoughts of Jennifer and concern for Sarah were thrown to the curb for now. It was time for me to start living in the moment.

46

1991

Charlotte's shared flat was just a few doors up from her mother's house on Robert Street. While I wasn't likely to bump into Tina in the bathroom or the kitchen on the morning after the night before, it was possible that a mother's curiosity could prompt an early morning visit and I decided it was best that I wasn't there if that happened.

I'd left Charlotte sleeping, getting myself dressed in stealth mode, before scribbling a note and stepping out of the front door just after 8am. I made sure I wasn't seen from Tina's house, legging it to the corner, ducking down the alley towards Warwick Road but immediately regretting that decision. The countless drinks and heavy Chinese food from the night before still hung in my guts and running on a hangover was never a smart move. I leaned against a garage door, taking shallow breaths to try and regain some composure.

Trying to distract myself from the nausea, I reflected over the past hours, from the time we knocked off at Martha's, wondering how it had happened. I'd never just end up in bed with a beautiful girl, or any girl, it just wasn't me. Yes, I'd done it before, but it was a rarity. I didn't have an endless list of one-night stands. I didn't need all the fingers on both hands to count the number of conquests I'd had in the last five years. Even Tom, the raging fucking pervert, was on double figures, and that didn't come from his boasting, that came from Dan keeping count.

That's how it was in the 90s. It wasn't like the fear of death from AIDS in the 80s, when we were forced to watch adverts, voiced by John Hurt, scaring the shit out of you, informing the ignorant that if they had so much as an improper thought towards someone, they found sexually attractive, they would explode and die, instantly. In the 90s, we all carried condoms, including the girls, declaring ourselves the informed generation of the next sexual revolution. How ridiculous.

With the fear of vomiting easing, I carried on back to the house. I didn't know what I was going to say when asked where I'd been. I could lie but Charlotte could tell her brother that she was getting *done* by his best friend and the cat would be out of the bag. To be honest, I didn't know how Dan would take the news. Last night, I'd been driven by my instinct to mate with a female, bop her on the head and drag her back to my cave, and all fuelled by an excess of alcohol. In fact, it was Charlotte who had dragged me back to her cave and there was no need for anyone to get bopped on the head. But that's not how it was going to look in the cold light of day.

I figured I'd creep back into the house, hoping both Dan and Tom were still fast asleep and fall into bed where I could claim to have been there all night. It was a long shot.

My walk of shame took me along North Road, where I had to be vigilant to avoid dog shit and vomit. Every now and then my mind would wander back to the wee hours of the night, when Charlotte and I were naked in bed together. She was stunning in every way.

Tina was beautiful but her legacy had been perfected in the second of her offspring. Charlotte was flawless: the curve of her hip; the swell of her breast; the tone of her skin. Perfection. I doubted I would ever be with a more perfect woman: except maybe for Jennifer.

I was still carrying that torch like an anvil.

Struggling.

I also started to struggle with my hangover. The nausea had returned. My mouth was watering even though I was severely dehydrated, and a fine sweat was rising on my back. I ducked into the petrol station to buy a can of diet Coke – my preferred recovery drink – and a packet of Polo mints. There was a taste in my mouth, and I needed it gone.

I popped a mint in my mouth and prayed in might stave off the vomit I could feel rising from my core. The traffic was louder and more aggressive to my fragile senses. A bus rushed past me, its wind nearly knocking me off my feet and left me breathing in a thick cloud of diesel fumes.

Staggering uncomfortably, I gripped on to the railing of the old North Road Boys School. I stared into the now deserted

161

playground where I had once been a soldier, a cop, a robber, a superhero, a victim – for real and at play – or anything a game had required me to be. I didn't enjoy my childhood, and I didn't enjoy my time in that school. I was beaten, bullied and caned. But I'd go back to it in an instant, to a time when I didn't know what heartbreak and hangovers were, if I could rid myself of the sickness washing over me.

I pressed on, trying not to think about it.

I managed to cross the road by Al's Gym, next to the vets, narrowly avoiding a transit van that seemed destined to hit me. With less than a hundred yards to go, I could hear my bed calling me. It was a day off for me, so if I could, I would sleep all day, I just had to keep putting one foot in front of the other.

The path to the front door had never looked so good, but that soon changed when the door opened, and Dan stepped out in his work clothes.

'Where've you been?' He had a wry smile on his chops, knowing I would've only stayed out for one reason. 'Was she worth it?'

A shrug of the shoulders was all I could muster, and I passed him by without a word. The interrogation would come later. I could feel it. For now, I had to get myself right. I promptly went to the bathroom, threw my guts up and retired to my bedroom. I stayed there for the rest of the day, swearing I would never drink again, like I had done a million times before.

47

1991

After wasting a day to the drink, I decided that I would make the best of my newfound connection and see if this Charlotte thing had legs. When a girl is forward with me, I assume she is like that with other guys too and that makes me feel less special. I would have to investigate, or so I thought.

I had a shift at the Nelson in the afternoon and a shift in Martha's in the evening. The good thing about part-time bar work was the ability to fit in other work if needed.

It was about halfway through my shift at the Nelson when Charlotte came in. I'm not good at hiding my feelings, my face giving away what I was thinking with the smile that emerged as soon as she walked in.

'You seem pleased to see me,' she said, taking a seat at the end of the bar.

'*I am* very pleased to see you.' It was an understatement. 'So, what brings you here?'

'You, of course.' Her eyes had the same flirtatious sparkle as they did two nights ago.

'Is this because I'm an amazing barman?'

My banter was lame…

'No, it's because you're amazing in bed.'

…but apparently my love making skills were satisfactory.

'Well, I can't hear that enough…' My brain was still stumbling over what I'd just heard, and all the words of reply suddenly ground to a halt.

She perched on her seat, staring at me while I served an older gent who spoke with a Yorkshire accent. The Tall Ships race was pulling in people from all over the country and when they weren't looking at ships, they were drinking and eating.

With no more customers to serve, I sidled down to the end of the bar to dig into the reasons why Charlotte had popped in, other than my prowess between the sheets, of course.

'I'm going out with my friends at the weekend,' she said. 'Would you like to meet up and see where this goes?'

She was either keen or I was foolish, whichever way it was, I had my doubts. I had to weigh-up the pros and cons of dating my best friend's sister. I didn't think it was Dan that was going to be the problem. It was likely to be Tina. Jumping ahead a million years, if me and Charlotte worked out, we could be married, have a family and have family get-togethers. How would it be if my sexual liaisons with my mother-in-law ever came out? My thoughts of the future were sabotaging my life in the present, based on things from my past. Talk about fucked up.

'Um, yeah?' I didn't mean it to sound like a question, but it did, so I had to own it.

'You don't have to sound too enthusiastic about it,' she was abrupt but didn't appear angry.

'It's not that,' I lied, 'I don't know if I've been put on the rota for Saturday night.' I knew very well what my hours were for the week, I was just buying time to consider the question and any other options.

'I checked already. You're off.' Her smile returned.

Pressured into a corner, I said the first thing that came into my head. 'In that case, yeah.'

'Cool!' With that she got up, leaned across the bar and kissed me on the lips. Not a snog, but not a peck. The kind of kiss a girlfriend gives her boyfriend.

'I'll see you then,' I said, my eyes following her as she went.

'Yes, you will.' She waved a goodbye and ducked out the side door.

I wanted a moment to consider my options. I wanted to be able to sit down, put my feet up and think about a strategy for telling the key people about my new relationship.

But that wasn't going to happen.

No sooner had she left, Charlotte quickly returned, but no further than the door to crane her neck around. 'Oh, and I forgot to say. Dan knows about us.'

Shit.

At least I didn't have to tell him now.

'Oh,' she continued, 'and so does my mum. Bye.' She waved once more and was gone.

I was royally fucked.

48

1991

After six hours of serving beer and spirits I wasn't sure I was up for a night out. Aside from Charlotte insisting that we meet up during the night at some point, I had Dan and Tom hounding me to go out as we hadn't been drinking together in the last few weeks. They had, I hadn't. The last time I'd tried going out with them, I'd alienated one of my best friends and had to witness the indignity of her shaming herself with the likes of Tom. It wasn't that I didn't like Tom, I did, but he had such little respect for females in general that I didn't want a close friend of mine being used and abused to fulfil his sexual needs.

On my return home, I walked into the house only to find my housemates playing a drinking game version of Connect Four. I wasn't sure what the rules were but there was an egg timer and a lot of empty Budweiser cans littering the living room.

I grabbed a can to drink while getting ready and decided that I definitely needed a shower. After six hours of gruelling work behind a busy bar, getting splashed with various beers and having the cigarette smoke of the patrons exhaled onto me while sweating my tits off, I desperately needed to wash the stench off.

But that was easier said than done with the bathroom facilities in our rented house.

The shower was so under-powered that I could probably stand on my head and produce more water if I pissed on myself. The water would trickle out, rapidly change temperature, stop, resume with cold water, heat up to an unbearably hot temperature and then repeat the cycle. I had my shower routine down to about two minutes as that is as much time as I could bear it for.

I washed, dressed and was back downstairs within twenty minutes.

The boys had given up on the alcohol infused game of Connect Four and were laughing about something and nothing while downing more cans. I walked in and grabbed one of the few remaining cans.

'So, what's the deal with you and my sister?' Fuelled by the booze, Dan had little restraint. He seemed buoyant, most likely from the excessive drink, and not pissed off at all.

'I don't know yet. Ask me in a week's time,' I said, trying to evade an inquisition.

'Come on, Will,' Tom piped up, his words slurring already, and we hadn't even left the house yet. 'He wants to know if you've pumped his sister yet.'

'No, I don't,' Dan fired back.

Tom nodded slowly, whispering loudly, 'Yes, he does.'

'Of course, I did,' I said. 'I banged her like a shed door in a gale force wind. She's a dirty girl. She took it in the mouth, took it in the pussy, took it in the ass, took it in one of her earholes and I even tried for a nostril – she was loving it! I even brought your mother along for moral support. She had to have a go on my cock too. And she's *even* dirtier! I was chopping and changing them so often I didn't know which one I was fucking. I'm really quite tired now. Can I go for a lie down?'

There was a moment of utter silence. The calm before the storm? No emotion on their faces.

Then Dan exploded.

Into laughter.

Tom followed, and I wasn't far behind. The three of us belly laughed as a collective. It was humour that bonded us. And through humour, I had managed to dodge the awkward question.

With tears in his eyes and colour in his cheeks, Dan stood up to fetch some more beers but not without slapping me on the shoulder. 'That's the funniest thing you've ever said. You can fuck my sister; you have my permission. Hell – fuck my mother too, while you're at it. What are friends for?'

I continued to giggle, but not about what I'd said, but about what Dan had just said. If only he knew the truth. One day, I figured he

167

would, and his reaction wouldn't be filled with hilarity, and we'd remember that moment for as long as we both lived. That was a certainty. Betrayal had a habit of being memorable.

49

1991

The night out started at the docks for a change. Foolishly, we thought that starting at Martha's would be the best idea to embrace the spirit of the Tall Ships Race, mingling with the many visitors, both from the crews and those wishing to spectate, but it wasn't to be. There was standing room only at the bar in Martha's, with a fight to know where the queue for the bar started and ended.

It was clear for all to see that, while the event brought much needed trade to our small town, the development of the docks/marina was maybe a year behind being prepared for such an event. A marquee next to Martha's was the mediocre solution. There was a bar at one end and a scattering of white plastic patio tables and chairs throughout. Every seat was occupied.

Still having to elbow our way to the trestle bar, we ordered two drinks a piece to avoid a further scrum when the plastic glasses we were drinking from ran dry.

I gazed around, what was essentially a beer tent, to see if I could spot any familiar faces, namely Charlotte, possibly Jennifer. While I did see a few people who we went to school with, and a group of older locals hunched around a couple of tables, everyone else was a stranger to me. They could have been residents but there was nobody else I knew by sight.

We engaged in some light banter, but it was obvious than Tom wouldn't last the night if he kept throwing down the booze like he was. I was determined not to miss out on any opportunities because of his poor relationship with alcohol and the vomiting that often followed.

You didn't need to be medically trained to see Tom was a statistic waiting to happen. I remember talking to Sarah about it when I visited her on my first day back. She had said that cirrhosis of the liver was a growing concern in younger people, and she'd done a module about it in her nursing degree. Tom was a prime candidate. I never used to pay attention to how much any member of the group was drinking on a night out but living with the boys had been an eye-opener. Dan might have had a can or two if we were watching a movie or had a takeaway, but Tom would buy a case of twenty-four every week and finish it by Friday, sometimes sooner. I could see premature aging, if not a premature death, if he carried on the way he was going. I watched him struggle to place both pint glasses on the rough floor then try to extract a cigarette from the packet he'd bought on the way down into town. He said he was a social smoker, but it seemed that every night had become a social event.

'S-so…' Tom struggled with his words as much as he was struggling with his smokes, 'w-where are we going after this?'

I exchanged a few glances with Dan as we watched Tom fail to strike a flame from the lighter he had bought just thirty minutes earlier.

'We'll head back into town. Nelson or Starboard, I'm easy.' I had to take control of the schedule. Dan never cared and Tom didn't look like he could control a cigarette, never mind making decisions about our drinking habits too.

'Shounds like a plan,' he slurred, promptly knocking over one of his beers as he bent down to retrieve them. 'Fuck it!'

I thought to myself he might be thankful for that accident later on, but it was most likely us who would be thankful.

We swiftly drank up and moved on, walking the long way round to give Tom a chance to get some air.

I'd never seen so many boats crammed into the docks. There seemed to be more than before. The colourful flags adorning the rigging of the many fine sailing vessels fluttered under a light breeze; the noise was a comforting sound. The clacking of rope against mast gave life to the old docks on its transformation from working dock to working marina. I walked the paths of this place so many times before, back when the smells of the dock were of fish and diesel. That had all changed now. The new look came with new odours; beer and street

170

food for all to indulge in. It was a privilege to be a part of the festivities.

We took a steep walk up Hamilton Terrace from the entrance of the dock, hoping the exertion might force the booze out of Tom's system. It didn't. It made him thirsty.

We skipped a visit to The Haven Hotel or The Con Club. One was too low brow and the other too high. We stayed with what we knew and took the direct route straight to the Nelson.

It was heaving at the bar. The other locals had come to be somewhere familiar. Great minds think alike. But in this case, great minds had a hell of a wait at the bar. Dan volunteered to get the round in while I took Tom outside to maintain the fresh air to his brain. Even for all the crowds, we managed to find an empty picnic bench to sit at. Tom immediately sparked up and attempted to blow smoke rings to impress a table full of girls just a few feet away. I was sober enough to know that he wasn't winning them over.

I decided I needed to open the can of worms that had been nagging at me over the last week or and so I asked the fatal question.

'So, what's the deal with you and Sarah?'

There was a delay in his recognition of what I had said. His eyes blinked slowly, and his mouth moved even slower. 'Nothing. It was just some good... good old-fashioned sex,'

'So, it's not going to happen again?' I don't know where or why I had started this, but I could see it was going to descend into a pornfest from the perv-meister general.

'I dunno.' He punctuated his reply with a long pull on his cigarette. 'If she wants to do it again, I'll do it again.'

'You're not going to go out with her then?'

'Fuck no! I'm a free... free agent – playing the field – fucking what I want.'

I hated Tom when he was like this. We all knew he had very little respect for women. And even less for the ones he ended up having sex with.

'Does she know this?'

171

'I dunno. I know she likes you. You should fuck her. She's not bad for a plain girl. Good boobs.'

I didn't reply. I waited for Dan to come and change the conversation. I should have thrown that can of worms to the back of my closet of regret, allowing it to rot away to nothing.

After Hell had frozen over, Dan appeared carrying three pints of lager. I eagerly thanked him and engaged him in conversation that didn't involve sex, Tom, or Sarah. After our love of music, movies came next, and we were still waiting for the highly anticipated Terminator 2: Judgement Day to arrive at the Torch Theatre. That was the problem with living in the ass-end of nowhere; we were always the last to get anything new.

The movie chat rolled on for quite a while, entertaining us through the next two rounds. By now, Dan was starting to slur his words and Tom was barely able to speak. I was still holding it together, competent enough to advise Tom to have a pint of water or something soft to aid his survival of the night. He reluctantly agreed and his first drink at the Starboard was a pint of orange squash. I made sure he had the same for his second and third, too.

Time was getting on. Midnight was approaching, and so far, we'd not seen anybody else from the gang. I understood why. Jennifer probably felt awkward around me, Sarah wasn't speaking to me, and Nikita and Jon were more *their* friends than *my* friends. If there was a permanent split in the group, it would have been my fault. I knew I'd have to suck it up and fix the rift.

As we shuffled down to Debrett's, it seemed the baton for drunkenness had been handed over. Tom was talking again, still slurred but the squash had done the job and curbed his descent into booze-fuelled oblivion. But I couldn't say the same for Dan. He was stumbling like a baby who'd only just taken their first steps. On one occasion, I had to grab his arm and pull him upright to stop him stepping off the kerb and falling into the road. How I got him past the door staff of the nightclub, I'll never know.

I told Dan to sit himself down because I was going to do for him as I'd done for Tom. I was going to bring him some soft drinks to dilute the booze, hopefully staving off complete and utter obliteration. It took a while for the idea to filter its way past the alcohol fog, but when it did, I left the lads drunkenly mumbling to themselves and went to the bar.

There was a queue, three, sometimes four deep the full length of the bar. I even had a couple of girls push in front of me, using their best lines and flashes of cleavage to distract my attention. In truth, I was in no hurry to get the drinks. The booze was starting to penetrate the cast iron constitution I had developed, and I would have to simmer down if I was to finish the night upright.

As I got my elbows to the bar there was a tap on my shoulder. I don't know who I was expecting but my hopes were that it would be Charlotte. I turned and witnessed my place at the bar taken by another girl who pounced in my spot like a tramp on a bag of chips.

I don't know if the booze had delayed my reaction, or maybe because registering the face of the shoulder tapper was nothing out of the ordinary, but as soon as my brain caught up, I knew I needed to eat some humble pie.

It wasn't Charlotte, or Jennifer, or even one of the boys.

It was Sarah. She didn't look pleased.

50

1991

Move Any Mountain by The Shamen was blasting out at top volume, vibrating the walls, making any conversation impossible. I tried anyway. I had to move the mountain between us. I leaned down to Sarah, put my lips next to her ear and said, loudly, 'I'm so sorry.'

She placed her lips against my ear to respond.

I waited for some words to come from her, but nothing did. I turned to look at her to see if she was talking but I couldn't hear over the din within the confines of the small venue. Her lips weren't moving for talking. They were quivering as she cried. I lifted my hand to touch her face, to comfort her in the only way I knew how but she slapped it away.

Then she slapped me across the cheek, tears running from her eyes as though it was her who had been struck. I'd never seen her like this. I was stunned, not knowing what to do for the best. I pulled her to one side, away from the bar and the prying eyes of everyone queuing for a drink.

'I don't know what to tell you,' I yelled, 'I didn't mean what I said. Of course, I care about you-'

She lunged forward, kissing me on the lips. I should have pulled away, but I couldn't reject her, not while she was in this state. Her arms encircled my neck, drawing me down, her kiss becoming more passionate; her tongue slipping into my mouth. I could taste the salt of her tears mixing with the vodka on her tongue.

Then she released me. 'I fucking love you, Will. I always have and I always will. Not being with you hurts me, every single day.'

'I had no idea.' I would state the fucking obvious.

'No, of course you don't.' Her face screwed up, the emotion causing her physical pain. 'You're too caught up in your pointless feelings for Jennifer. Nobody ever notices me-'

'That's not true.' I was annoyed by her outburst. Not because it wasn't true because I didn't feel the same way about her, but because it wasn't my fault. As much as I valued her friendship, and all the things she did for me, I wasn't going to be blackmailed into saying things I didn't mean and feeling things I couldn't feel.

'Who notices me? Can you tell me, because I sure can't?' She was like an open wound, the hurt pouring from her.

'What about Tom?'

'Are you that stupid?' She shook her head in frustration, 'I don't want him. I want you. I just wanted to be wanted by someone – anyone – him. Do you know how hard it is for me to see you and not be able to tell you how I feel? It's impossible.'

They say, *If you speak of the devil, the devil appears.* I shouldn't have mentioned his name, and we shouldn't have made such a public scene.

'Hey, darling, why are you so upset?' Tom wasn't known for his tact and now was not the time to be opening the charm on a distraught Sarah.

'FUCK OFF!" she screamed, storming away into the throng.

'What did you do to her?' Tom said, perplexed, 'I thought I was on a promise tonight, but you've fucked it up.'

'I really don't need this. Go and sit down.' I was raging inside, barely holding it together.

'Don't tell me what to do... WILL.' The screaming of my name wasn't enough to punctuate his sentence, he pressed his forehead against mine, pushing me backwards.

I pushed him away and walked off after Sarah. I had to see if I could fix the mess I'd caused.

I didn't get far.

Stepping out of the illuminated area of the bar, into the darkened area surrounding the dancefloor, movement proved to be difficult, the mass of people packed into the club stopped any progress. I was sure there was a limit to how many patrons could be in the club

175

at any one time, but tonight, it looked as though the limit had been binned.

As I was halted by a wall of revellers, I felt a firm hand clap me on the shoulder. I turned to see who it was, but I was met with a fist. The blow struck me on the left cheek. Going from the light to the dark, plus the alcohol, and the surprise of the punch, disorientated didn't sum it up. I would have dropped to the ground but for the dense crowd giving me something to fall against. I threw out a punch of my own but hit nothing. I wasn't aiming because I couldn't see where the strike had come from… until I got smacked again. This time there was not so much force. And I could see why. It was a very drunken Dan.

Still reeling from the first blow, the second one felt like nothing. I knew Dan wasn't a scrapper; this was his drunken persona coming to the fore. We'd had fights before, but he knew I was tough for my size: A few of my mother's boyfriends thought they could teach me a lesson or two, but all they taught me was how to defend myself against drunken old men. Dan was a drunken young man and had been lucky with the first punch.

'What are you fucking doing?' I bellowed over the music.

'Fucking cheat!' Dan could hardly stand. I was surprised he didn't fall over after swinging at me.

'What?'

'I… saw… ya...' Dan's eyes couldn't focus. I wasn't sure what he saw but it would have been blurred.

I gripped him by the wrists of his raised fists and lead him back into the light, back to the seats, but our seats had been taken by some Russian sailors, so I guided Dan to the wall, trying to keep him upright. With the risk of attack diminished, I asked the question, 'What do you think I've done?'

'I saw ya! You kissed… Sarah… on the lips.'

'I didn't kiss Sarah. She kissed me.' It was the truth.

It took a while for the information to filter through to the booze addled brain cells. I wasn't sure what Dan was battling with the most – the penny to drop or the gravity pushing him down. A half smile broke on his lips.

'Y-you… still like my… sister?'

'Yes. I want Charlotte, not Sarah.'

He nodded; his eyes closed as though he were about to fall into a coma. Then he hugged me and shook a fist with a raised thumb at me. I took this to mean we were ok.

'Look, I must go and find Sarah to see if she's ok. Stay here and…' I tried my best Schwarzenegger accent, 'I'll be back!'

He raised a smile while sliding down the wall. I left him there to sleep some of the booze off, mentally noting to return to see if he was alright.

I had to barge my way through the mass of drunken club goers, checking faces as I passed in case Sarah was there, alone, upset and standing in the crowd. I didn't want her to feel ignored, forgotten about.

But she wasn't being forgotten about, in fact, quite the opposite.

I walked into the seating area behind the DJ pulpit to find Sarah engaged in a clumsy tryst with Tom. She was reclined into him, head on his shoulder, with her arms loose and open, her left hand fumbling over the crotch of his jeans. He had his left arm hooked around her head with his hand inside her bra, squeezing at her ample breasts; his right hand between her legs, the action of his right arm suggested to me that he was two knuckles deep and trying to go further.

I felt sick hearing their sexual encounter from the next bedroom, but to see them going at it, in a deafening room full of drunken voyeurs, it felt so desperate. So disappointing. As much as I needed to speak to her, I didn't think this was the time to have a heart-to-heart. She was in a totally different headspace than the heartbroken Sarah of just a few minutes ago. She had crawled into that pit of self-loathing where she found the most comfort and she had company.

51

1991

I not only left Sarah and Tom to their illicit encounter, but I also left the club, too.

I knew that I should have been meeting Charlotte, but she was nowhere to be found. I had seen a few of her mates milling around the bar area of Debrett's but they were without her. As much as I wanted to hook up with her, I wasn't feeling it anymore. Not that night.

I took the long stroll home, walking the full length of Hamilton Terrace, turning left at St Katherine's church and walking the full length of Great North Road. The route home always looked different under the muted orange glow of the street lighting with a quantity of alcohol on board. Generally, I found a drunken stroll with my tail between my legs was often the start of some philosophical meanderings. The meaning of life would present itself to me, in perfect clarity, and I would formulate some life-altering decisions based on all the facts available to me, only to have the new strategy evaporate into thin air the very second after I'd woken up the next day. It was as if the morning erased all traces of my good intentions. I was determined that it wasn't going to happen this time around.

The house felt desperately lonely as I stepped into the living room. The evidence of our start to the night was still spread across the coffee table and the floor. A dozen cans of Budweiser, with various quantities of beer still remaining in them, were scattered everywhere. You could see where I'd been, where Tom had been and... Oh shit! In my state, I'd forgotten to check on Dan. It was a twenty-minute walk back to the club, where I'd have to pay to get in again, and there was no guarantee that Dan would still be there.

He was a big boy. He'd have to fend for himself.

I really wasn't earning any merit badges from my friends today.

I filled a pint glass with water and drank eagerly. I didn't want to polish off the night with a grade A hangover, so I took the necessary measures. Once I'd finished the glass, I refilled it and headed for bed. I didn't read or put on the TV, but I did drop a tape into my Walkman and placed the headphones on. I thought the Enigma album would take away all my fears and send me, peacefully, into the nurturing arms of sleep's comforting embrace.

It never failed.

*

Whatever solace I had descended into, I was now in the limbo between dream sleep and the conscious cusp of awakening. I was aware of sound, of breathing, of movement, but where it came from was unknown. Was it in the waking reality, or subtle overflow of my dreams, I wasn't sure.

There was touching – sensation – arousal.

Whether a dream or not, I couldn't help but be swept along, my body was useless to resist. Whatever my mind was creating for me, it was ecstasy. The strobe lights of the nightclub still flickered in my imagination, while the intense ringing that accompanied a night of loud music was fixed in reality. I would ride out these feelings until sleep took me once more.

A crash from downstairs confirmed my presence in the waking world. The pleasure ceased immediately. I heard Dan's slurred voice state 'Oops!' and I figured he must be ok. I glanced at the glowing red diodes of my radio alarm clock, telling me it was almost four in the morning – too late for me to be getting up now. I tried to turn over and settle back into the same erotic dream, but I couldn't. I was pinned into the bed. There was a weight upon my lower limbs that I was unable to see in the blackness of my room.

Then it started again.

The pleasure.

My sense of confusion didn't quite outweigh my sense of gratification. I knew what was happening. I wasn't a Don Juan by any stretch of the imagination, but I had had my dick in enough mouths to know how a blowjob felt.

I ripped back the duvet and flicked on the bedside lamp.

Sarah's eyes held my gaze, my erect cock still in her mouth. She didn't stop. She continued slowly, her eyes never leaving mine. As much as I knew it was wrong, I didn't want her to stop. It spurred her on, increasing the speed of her action as she chased my climax down, her eyes still refusing to look elsewhere. I was caught in the trap – her trap. I should have broken free, told her to stop, told her it was wrong. But I couldn't. She watched my face intently. I wouldn't know what she was looking for until it was too late – until I had gone too far. My eyes closed and my mouth opened. A pleasurable moan fell from my lips.

That was her cue.

She took my penis from her mouth and climbed on top of me, sinking down onto my shaft. The grinding of her hips intensified the sensation and I had nowhere else to go. I thrust my hips to meet hers, climaxing into her. For the first time since the light had been switched on her eyes closed. A tremble ran over her body, flushing her face and chest as she descended into her own climax, the breath rinsed from her lungs.

Stunned and breathless, we remained adjoined for a just a moment, the reality of the act washing over us. I was about to speak when her stern post-coital expression morphed into a smile. And not a happy smile, a sinister grin of a plan well executed.

She lifted her naked body off mine and walked out of the room, shutting the door behind her.

And then all Hell broke loose.

52

1991

'What the fuck is this?' Tom raged at the pair of us. He was standing on the landing wearing nothing but his pants.

Sarah ignored him, walked into his bedroom and proceeded to get dressed.

'I don't fucking know,' I yelled back, 'I was asleep, and I woke up and she was sucking my cock.'

'You must have tried *so* hard to fight her off.' His sarcastic sneer didn't sit well on his drunken face.

'Fuck you, Tom. What do you care? You've only pounced on her cos she's drunk and vulnerable.'

'And what were you doing, giving her a comfortable place to sit?'

My rage was already off the charts, but he must have been watching to know what was going on and that sent my spike through the roof.

'Were you fucking watching?' I jabbed a finger in his face.

He pressed his forehead against mine, trying to use his superior height to push me back into the bedroom. 'So, what if I was? You didn't seem to care what was going on a minute ago.'

I shoved him away. 'Get out of my face!'

'Then stay away from my bird.' It was his turn to jab a finger in my face.

I slapped away his hand. 'Your bird? Did you say? "Your bird." To you, she's one step up from your wank sock. If tissues had tits, you wouldn't look at her twice.'

'STOP!' Sarah, now dressed, screamed at top volume, 'Stop talking about me as if I'm not here. You've had your way with me tonight, both of you, so you should be happy about it and move on-'

'Hey,' I butted in, 'that's not fair. I didn't-'

'Fair. You want to talk about fair do you, Will?' If she had been drunk before, she was now stone-cold sober and controlling the argument. 'I've been in love with you for ever. That's not fair. I've had to watch you drooling over Jennifer since junior school, and that's not fair. It doesn't matter which men I try to replace you with, they aren't you, and that's not fair. And when I look for some affection off Tom, you go ape shit, and guess what?'

'That's not fair…' Why did I always see things from only my perspective?

'Bingo!' She may have been small of stature, but her rage towered over us in the cramped dim landing.

With anguished tears running down her face, she fled into the night.

I threw on some clothes and raced out of the door. I needed to see if she was ok. It wasn't right that I was constantly thinking of myself. Others had to come first, sometimes. I think my selfish streak came from my upbringing, or up-dragging, as I liked to call it. Being an only child with a self-absorbed mother made me think that if I didn't put myself first then no one else would. I was wrong, of course.

I cast a glance toward the kitchen just as I was about to leave. I could see a disorientated Dan trying to pick up some pots and pans that had fallen out of a cupboard. He was moving, so he was alive. On that front, my conscience was clear. I left the house, hoping to clear even more.

Because I had been asleep for a few hours, I had no concept of what the time was. I knew what my watch said but my head was thinking something different entirely. Instead of the pitch black of the early hours, the sky was a dull grey/blue and I knew that would mean the sunrise wasn't too far away. I wasn't inclined to run because I wanted to hold on to my stomach contents. Instead, I paced as fast as could toward Vicary Street, hoping to see her figure in the muted light of the morning. I saw nothing.

I had assumed that she would have headed for home and that's the way I went. There was more than one way to her house from ours, but I had taken the most direct route. In the predawn silence I slowed my pace to listen for footsteps. I heard nothing definite. No footsteps. No cars. No revellers.

I approached the house but there were no signs of life. I could have knocked but that might have brought me under the wrath of Sarah's mother, and nobody wanted that. Instead, I walked onto The Rath, sitting on the nearest bench and stared out at the lights on the refinery jetties and contemplated my life. As always, The Rath is never quiet. The thrum of a tanker's engine ruined the still morning air, stealing whatever peace I had tried to find. I stayed there, alone, thinking about everything and nothing. The time passed but no comfort came.

The sky started to darken, as it always did just before dawn, and I could see two figures approaching from where the old outdoor pool used to be. They were walking sedately in the cool of the morn. It was Sarah and Tom.

I stood to greet them – maybe to apologise, maybe to explain, or maybe just to ask why. My mouth opened but I was cut off before any words came out.

'We don't want to hear it, Will,' Tom said with a raised hand.

'Hear what?' So much for the calm approach.

'Go home, Will. When you've sobered up, you'll see the error of your ways and can apologise.' Tom seemed to be in the driving seat.

'Me, sober up? Have you seen yourself?' I could feel the warmth of rage drawing up from my toes.

'Do as he says, Will,' Sarah chipped in.

The anger animated my limbs before anything raged from my lips.

'What have you got to say about all of this, after all, you are the instigator?' I insisted.

'He's delusional. Let's go.' Tom gripped her by the arm to lead her away.

Instead of letting them go – the sensible thing to do – I grabbed his arm and faced up to him. 'What do you mean by delusional?'

An open palm pushed my face away and that's how the fight started. There was gripping, pushing, shoving, and then there was a punch. The searing pain exploded from my cheekbone. I was stunned, but not enough that I couldn't return a blow. It was more grabbing and wrestling than anything: the type of fight you had in the schoolyard, not the ones you see on TV. I could hear Sarah shouting for the brawl to stop but it was lost words. Both Tom and I went over the bench, rolling down the steep embankment that ran from the pavement down to the path leading to Ward's Yard. I saw a tumbling procession of

184

lights and then grass and then more lights as my body was at the mercy of gravity. I could hear Tom's grunts as well as my own, but I didn't know where he was in relation to me. The burning friction of grass gripping at the bare skin of my arms stung but not as much as the raw pain when my nose hit hard against the ground. The spinning infinity of my circumstance was brought to sudden stop when my skull met Tarmac.

*

I was awoken by a hundred pinpricks against the skin on my back. I tried to move but couldn't, my arms were pinned behind me. In the confusion of my situation, I had no bearing on where I was. I could see the orange sky of the sunrise merged with the dark blue of the night and that was as much of a view as I had.

When I eventually reclaimed my grasp on reality, I realised I was trapped in a bush and the pinpricks were the brambles on which I was lying. Dragging myself from my snare, I couldn't understand how I'd gotten to where I was. I wasn't at the bottom of the embankment. I was practically on the train tracks on the other side of the hedgerow. I figured I must have staggered down here and collapsed.

I got to my feet and looked down at myself. I was covered in dirt, grass stains and, most significantly, blood. My hands, my arms, my clothes, and I imagined my face too, were covered in blood. I had to get home. Unseen.

What the fuck had happened?

54

1991

I'm not one for running away from a problem, but I am someone who occasionally needs space to gather my thoughts and address the issue once I've regrouped. The cover of my watch was broken but it still told the time: 7.30am and I hoped that my mother would still be the same creature of habit she always had been.

I walked the full length of the hedgerow path to get off The Rath, heading up Slip Hill to get onto Hamilton Terrace. The steep incline made my tired thighs burn with every step. If they hadn't been hurting before, Slip Hill was making sure they were now, and I could feel it to the bone.

Hamilton Terrace looked very different than it normally did. I'd done this walk hundreds of times before and there would always be a handful of cars parked against the pavement on the north-side of the street, the south-side being completely free of cars because of the double-yellow lines. With the Tall Ships Race being in town, every single space on the north-side was filled and there were also a few cars parked up on the pavement on the south. I couldn't help thinking someone was making money out of this, and it wasn't me.

The extra cars were cover enough against the odd car passing by as I scurried along. I dived up Barlow Street, climbing the steps that lead to Charles Street, ducking across the road to the narrow lane that came out next to Haven Heights carpark.

I think I had done a pretty good job of being unseen until I was about to cross Priory Road. Two cars, filled with ship's crews, sailed past. Young faces stared out at me, pointing at the sight I must have been. I sprinted down the alley next to the Italian shop and along the open lane at the back of Dartmouth Gardens. Within a minute, I was walking breathlessly up the lane between Dartmouth Gardens and Trafalgar Road.

The latch of mother's backyard door opened effortlessly. I hoped it would be the same with the backdoor. I had a key anyway, but she would often leave it unlocked in case she lost her keys, which was regularly.

I crept into house, listening out for signs of life. There was nothing. Not even my mother's tobacco clogged snoring could be heard. I guessed the house was empty. If she was sleeping, she'd be snoring. If she was awake, she'd be hacking. I quietly checked all the rooms. The house was empty.

I stood in front of the mirror and couldn't quite believe what I was seeing.

I knew my face felt dirty and rough. I figured it was from the earth from the tumble down the embankment. But it wasn't. It was mostly blood.

I had a gash on the right side of my head, leaving a thick trail of blood across my cheek and down to my jaw. To me, it would suggest that I had lain on my face for some time while I was bleeding. But when I had woken up, I had been on my back with no way to turn over and a good distance from the path. I must have dragged myself there.

Apart from the gash on my head, I had blood clogged in my nose, and cuts and bruises across my face, hands and forearms. There was a sharp pain in my ribs when I breathed, and my knees and back felt sore to the touch. I was lost to find a place where I didn't have an injury.

I quickly ran a bath; it would be cold because the immersion heater hadn't been on but at least I could get myself clean. While the bath was filling, I went to my old room. I knew there were a few old clothes still left in the wardrobe. I just had to hope they would still fit me.

*

One cold bath later, I was dressed in a pair of Wrangler jeans and a blue Levi's sweatshirt. I had found my old Adidas school bag and filled it with trousers, some passable t-shirts and every item of

187

underwear I could find. I had enough for a week or so. I had also found a pair of Nike trainers that were a size too small, but they would have to do. The white canvas deck shoes I had been wearing the night before were stained with blood and grass and were too far gone.

I had to leave town. Not for good, but until the whole saga had blown over.

If I was travelling, I would need money. I had about three quid in change and my bank card was broken.

But as I always say, mother was a creature of habit. She had an over-sized whiskey bottle filled with change in her bedroom. I couldn't take too much from that or she'd notice. I took all the pound coins and left the rest. In the kitchen she had an old sweet tin where she would keep her bill money. I took half of it. She wouldn't know. She would frequently grab a few notes before heading out the door, promising to replace it but never doing so. I banked on her thinking that she would have been the reason for the shortage.

With no more than a hundred quid in my pocket, I headed upstairs to grab the sports bag and make sure the bathroom had no trace of me.

Then the front door opened.

Shit.

It was mother. And she wasn't alone.

55

1991

For all my injuries and bruising, I was still agile enough to drop to the floor and roll under the bed, dragging my old school bag as I went. I heard the voices but not the words. Both were familiar to me, but I didn't understand why one of them was here.

I heard the voices getting louder and footsteps on the stairs. They were coming up.

My fragile system was handling too much alcohol to have my heart rate rise like it was. I was sure they had to be able to hear the pounding from under bed.

But they never entered the room.

'We're worried about Will. Nobody's seen him since last night,' Sarah's voice was low and restrained.

'Well, he isn't here. He never comes here. Why would he? He couldn't give a shit for his own mother, so what makes you think he gives a shit about you or any of his other friends.'

With my mother wielding such a character assassination, I didn't feel so bad about stealing her money.

'I'm sure that's not-,' Sarah didn't get to finish her defence of me.

'Well, it is! He's a selfish little shit – always was, always will be. If you want my advice, you be better off just forgetting about him: I know I am.' The rasp of her lighter and gush of cigarette smoke was typical. She always lit up when she was done talking.

'Please, if you see him or hear from him, tell him to get in touch.' I could imagine the pained expression on Sarah's face. It was always Sarah who looked out for me. Why had I been so foolish to ignore her? Now wasn't the time for such questions. I wasn't sure I had the answers, or ever would have. I still needed the space to regroup.

'If I see him – which I won't – I'll tell him. Now, I need to get on. See yourself out.'

Oh, my mother, always the hostess.

I heard the door slam. That was one of my problems out of the way for now. All I needed was for my mother to slip into a drunken coma somewhere other than the staircase and I could be on my way. I was expecting it. While my mother could often maintain a cohesive conversation with an unhealthy supply of vodka on board, the one thing she couldn't disguise was the smell of drink. Granted, the chain smoking often diluted her alcoholic odour, but first thing in morning was when she smelled the worst.

Fixed in my place of refuge, I listened to her pottering about the house for a few minutes: watering the plants, opening the windows and throwing clothes into the washing machine. This was her routine – her 'I'm spending all day asleep' routine. It wasn't long before she shuffled into the front bedroom. I heard clothes being removed and the duvet being drawn back. After much tossing and turning, and a few hacking coughs, a silence fell over her room. When the silence was punctured by the reverberation of her snoring, I slid from under the bed and sneaked downstairs.

I was about to disappear the same way I had arrived – through the back door – when I noticed a handbag on the kitchen table. Inside was my mother's purse. There was eighty quid inside. Not wishing to prove her wrong, I selfishly took a twenty-pound note. That was the price of a railway ticket covered.

Thanks, mum, you've funded my escape.

56

1991

Mother's money didn't go as far as I would have liked. I returned to Milford after just eight days of slumming it at a B&B in Swansea. The highlight of my brief respite was eating at Pizza Hut and going to the cinema by myself: I watched Point Break. Time away to myself helped me reflect on the past few weeks and made my vision clearer regarding the people I had around me, putting life into perspective.

After wandering in the wilderness for a few years, going back to my hometown felt like an inevitable step backwards. It wasn't something I had planned on doing on a permanent basis. It was supposed to be a return to see my friends, look at how far I'd gone in life, earn a bit of travelling money and head back out into the world, refreshed and motivated.

That's not what was happening.

I had found a triad of possibilities that somehow derailed my ongoing aspirations.

First there was Jennifer – the focus of all my childhood crushed and fantasies – who had revealed that she had some modest interest in me but was put off because of the feelings Sarah had. A frustrating situation if ever there was one.

Then there was Charlotte. She was gorgeous, she was funny, and she had the hots for me. What was there not to like about this corner of the triad? But that was the problem. I couldn't like it. It didn't feel right. She was my best friend's sister and if it all went tits up, I could stand to lose one of my closest allies. In relationships, there is always an element of risk. Charlotte was not worth the risk.

And then there was Sarah: the person who I turned to the most in any given situation. Going back as far as junior school, even when we were in separate schools, although right next door to each other, she was there for me. I loved Sarah – like a brother loves a sister. She was the beacon leading me out of the dark, through the worst periods of my meagre existence, steering me toward better things. Yet, a week and a half ago, she put my penis inside herself. That was a boundary that should have never been crossed.

When I stepped down off the train there was no welcoming committee. I wasn't expecting one, so there was no disappointment. No one knew that I had gone, and no one would know where to look for me. That was how I liked it. But there were downsides.

Rummaging around in my pockets, I didn't have enough change to hire a taxi to the house and that left me with an uncomfortable walk home. Not because I didn't like the walk, but because it would give me more time to think while I passed by all the reminders of why I decided to leave in the first place.

When I got to the house it was empty. In my head, I thought they would be waiting in for me. Who was I kidding? The only thing waiting for me was a few envelopes. I opened everything in my pile and found out that I had been sacked from both The Nelson and Martha's Vineyard for going AWOL. I only had myself to blame.

To drown my sorrows, I made a cup of tea and put on some toast. Then I took a bath and changed my old teenage clothes for something more current. I began to feel more normal again. A walk to the job centre would be prudent, under the circumstances.

I took the scenic route along The Rath, the haven looked so different – naked – without the multitude of masts and colourful rigging of the tall ships. Milford had returned to its dull, normal, town-on-the-edge-of-nowhere status.

I paused at the bench where the fight had started, looking down at the hedgerow where I had woken up and dragged myself from. The scratches and cuts had all but healed, but the wounds to my pride they were still just as raw. I figured it would take a while longer for them to heal and an eternity for the scars to fade.

I walked on, trying to create an argument in my head for how I should best broach the subject of that night with Sarah and Tom: more so with Sarah than with Tom. It was impossible. I would just have to wing it when the time came. I wasn't good at winging it.

192

The haven looked invitingly blue under the warmth of the July sun. I had always thought of how it would be to swim across the haven to the other side and then swim back. It wasn't something I could do. I'd never learned to swim. Maybe in the future, when life was less complicated, I may find the time to learn. I had so many other things to learn and the curve was steep.

My pondering on the future was ended abruptly with the harsh screech of rubber against tarmac.

The blue Fiesta bumped the kerb as it swerved to stop. The door opened and the driver was on the pavement, in a flash, standing in front of me, staring in disbelief.

'Where the fuck have you been?' The question was followed by a lot of tears. I had never seen Sarah so distressed.

57

1991

I wasn't sure how to answer the question, or if I should answer it at all. I thought that maybe I should just give her a hug and hope for the best.

I caved in. 'I just needed some space to clear my head,' I said, smiling, hoping the answer would be understood.

'Why didn't you call? I thought you were dead.' I could sense some relief in her words but there was still too much anguish to release herself fully from the burden of her tears.

I hugged her, tight. I felt her respond, arms squeezing my midsection, making the shudder of her distress more exaggerated. We held each other in silence.

'Why would you think I was dead?' I said, feeling her relax a little.

'Because of the fall, because you banged your head: you must have been knocked out.'

'You could have just called for an ambulance.' I thought it was the most obvious thing to do.

'Tom wouldn't let me. He thought he would have gone to prison for manslaughter or something.'

'So, what did you do?' I was itching to hear this answer.

'He tried to drag you off the path and down to Ward's Beach. I said he was crazy.' Sarah's face was a puffy, red mess of tears and bloodshot eyes. She looked more like the girl I used to hang with when we were ten years old, and not like the woman – trainee nurse – she was supposed to be.

'So, you left me?'

There was a pause as she tried to collect her thoughts and compose herself. 'He dragged me back to my house, told me to do nothing and that he was going to get away and would call the police once he was far enough away.'

'And you accepted that?'

'No,' her eyes welled with tears again as she shook her head. 'He wouldn't leave the house in case I phoned the police. I kept protesting but he wouldn't listen. I got him to leave in the morning – telling him to catch the early train if he wanted to get away. As soon as he left, I ran back to find you.'

'And?' Inside, I was reeling that I had been left for dead by one of my so-called best friends, but on the outside, I hoped I retained my calmness.

'And you weren't there. I looked on the beach, on Ward's Yard, I ran up the track towards the docks; everywhere. I even went to your mother's. You were gone.'

I knew that I wasn't there. I knew that just after dawn I was scrabbling along the path, battered and bloodstained, looking for a way out of my shit life. I ran away, only as far as Swansea. I wonder how far Tom got.

58

1991

After the tears and regrets and anger and even more tears, Sarah dropped me back at the house. Sure enough, Tom wasn't there. His sports bag was also gone, along with a selection of his clothes, although the trainers he always wore were still in the porch. A bag packed in a rush after killing someone is never going to be packed efficiently. I knew I wasn't thinking right when I woke up in a hedge, covered in blood. I can imagine Tom's head was just as fucked as mine.

I spent the rest of the afternoon watching videos, eating crisps, and generally killing time until I had some company. At five-thirty sharp, Dan wandered through the door. He was as pleased to see me as Sarah was.

'Where the fuck have you been?' he snapped, his work rucksack still slung over one shoulder as though he hadn't planned on staying.

'Just putting a bit of distance between myself and whole Sarah/Tom situation,' I said.

The rucksack was thrown onto the sofa. Dan meant business. 'Couldn't you have called or something? I've had Sarah here every single day. Jennifer popped in a few times too. Oh, and my sister: what's happened there? I thought you two were making a go of things.'

I hadn't given Charlotte much thought, if I was being honest. She was the least of my worries. 'Sorry, man, I wasn't thinking-.'

'I even went to see your mother, you know, to see if you were hiding out there.'

'How did that go?' I asked, preparing for the worst answer imaginable.

'You're dead to that woman. I wouldn't give her the time of day, if I were you.'

'I've been dead to her since before I set foot in junior school. You're not telling me anything I don't already know.' I was saying it out loud, but Dan already knew it. Anytime someone else was looking after me, like a neighbour or the education system, my mother was happy. I was an inconvenience to her. Always was, always will be. I often wondered what would happen when she died. Who would show up to her funeral? I knew there'd be a pile of landlords in this town whose takings were going to take a nosedive because she wasn't drinking herself into oblivion in their pubs.

'Have you eaten?' Dan asked.

'Only the shit from the cupboard.' He knew what I meant.

'I can't be arsed to cook. Do you want a chippy?'

I didn't need asking twice. We were out the door and heading towards Marble Hall chippy faster than you could say, "Jumbo battered sausage."

*

Sitting in the unlit living room of the house we called home; two greasy plates on the coffee table sharing space with some empty beer cans and two pairs of feet, we reclined with our stomachs full, watching a video. It was The Breakfast Club, a John Hughes classic, and one of Dan's favourite films because he had a thing for Molly Ringwald. The VHS tape had seen better days; the constant rewinding and replaying had caused some interference on playback in the form of lines running along the top of the screen. Even some of Tom's pirated porn played with less distortion than this film did.

I was just ripping the ring-pull of my third can of the night when there was a knock at the door. Whoever it was, it sounded loud and official, shaking the door in its frame.

'Who's that at this time of night?' Dan asked, nearly spitting out his beer at the same time.

'God knows!' I got up to answer it.

'If it's those Jehovah's again, tell them to "Fuck off" and they can keep their Watchtower this time.'

I chuckled to myself; more so about how un-politically correct Dan was on a daily basis than how funny his quip was.

The laughter on my tongue and the smile on my lips swiftly disappeared when I opened the door. It was the police.

Present Day

Brooks slumped over the endless files before him. The chair in the hotel room wasn't comfortable at all but it was all he had other than the bed. To accompany his aching back, his eyes were burning under the strain of the endless reading: the poorly photocopied reports; the handwritten statements – the old ways were definitely not the best ways when it came to police reporting. In today's rapid response, social media generation, appeals for information could be raised instantly, shared far and wide, reaching beyond the locality of the crime and the gathered information loaded onto databases nationwide. Back in the 80s and 90s it was all about boots on the ground, knocking on doors and handwritten reports. Computing for policing was in its infancy back then.

As much as his eyes were hurting, they were still catching the sight of the cigarette packet protruding from the pocket of his discarded jacket. Willpower was not something Brooks practiced when it came to his personal vices. He pulled open the drawer of the fake walnut bureau and lifted out a half bottle of vodka.

He stared at it for a moment, giving himself time to consider the implications if he was to take a drink. He wasn't an alcoholic, but he was sure his liver would have something to say about that if it could talk. With the top unscrewed, he took a short swig on the liquid, allowing himself just enough to say he'd had a drink, but not so much to say he had a problem. But a drink would always be followed by the craving for a smoke.

Grabbing his jacket and key card, he headed out the door and down to the reception.

The night air was crisp and clear. The moon glow made silhouettes out of everything in the middle distance, and picture-perfect postcard images of everything else and beyond. It was the kind of night that reminded him of his days as a beat cop, walking the mean streets of Bristol. The same kind of the night he had seen his first dead body.

Back in the early 90s, when Brooks was still wet behind the ears, he would never forget the night he was introduced to human mortality. At the tender age of twenty-one, and only six months on the job, Brooks still had his parents, although both were divorced and had remarried. This gave him four sets of grandparents and they were all still in the land of the living. Death, to him, was something that happened to other people and their relations. That all changed on a cloudless night in March 1993.

A mid-week nightshift was often a very boring experience. If there wasn't a burglary or domestic dispute to deal with, the empty night hours were the time to catch up on paperwork, of which there was a lot. Brooks had been buddied up with PC Doug MacBride, a hard man from Glasgow with fifteen years of service and had seen it all.

The call came in just after 2am. The station, which looked more like a house in a back lane than a police station, was just up the road from Clifton Down railway station on Whiteladies Road, and about a mile from the suspension bridge. The caller had stated they had seen someone jump from the bridge. MacBride took the police issue Vauxhall Cavalier down onto the A4, the road that ran under Brunel's brainchild, and brought along the rookie Brooks for the experience.

The portion of the A4, known as Hotwell Road, appeared almost ethereal under the full moon; elevated three storey houses on the one side, the unseen Avon River on the other, with the iconic Clifton Suspension Bridge spanning the gorge, bathed in a blue glow. If the circumstances hadn't been so tragic it would have been a beautiful sight.

'Och, I tell ya, more happens on a full moon than on any other night of the month – check the records – more on a cloudless night when the crazies can see it, mark my words,' MacBride's Scottish drawl often needed translation, but tonight, in the calm before the anticipated storm of a suicide investigation, it was almost in perfect clarity.

While Brooks and MacBride were at the bottom of the gorge, attempting to find a body, another unit were on the bridge aiming torch beams into the darkness. There was a crackle over the radio and the distorted message stated the body was on top of the tunnel that protected the road from things being dropped from above: litter, stones, bodies.

Locating the body was only half of the job. They still needed to determine if the person was dead or alive.

There wasn't a quick way up onto the tunnel without the aid of a ladder. MacBride had already called for an ambulance, but to contact the fire brigade wasn't something they would automatically do in a suicide situation. Brooks wanted to be a man of action. He wanted to be the cop that went above and beyond the call of duty. Without comment or advice, Brooks started to scale a tree on the footpath next to the external wall of the tunnel. He was strong and youthful and on top of the grass covered tunnel roof in a matter of seconds.

'What are ya doin, ya wee shite?' MacBride bellowed his disapproval from the footpath.

'Looking for the jumper. Throw me your torch!' Brooks was defiant.

'I'll throw ya in the river if ya donnay get back doon here.' Whatever clarity MacBride had developed had swiftly disappeared along with his patience for the young officer.

'Throw me in when I get back down, but for now, throw me the torch.'

The black plastic flashlight reflected the moon glow as it spun in the air. Brooks caught it easily, flicking it on with his thumb. Damp grass and soil felt like a slippery sponge under the soles of his work issue shoes. There was also a gradient to climb, made much more difficult under the blue light of the moon. The torch beam swept across the grass followed by Brooks' eyes, but he wasn't watching where he was putting his feet. It only took a moment or two of skidding on the slick surface for him to find the body.

The broken figure of a young man in jeans and a heavy knitted jumper lay before him. The deceased was much the same age as Brooks was. He didn't need to check the pulse to know if the victim was dead; the unnatural angle of the neck and the size of the blood splatter confirmed that fact. Brooks still placed two fingers on the wrist. Nothing. The body was warm, but life had expired. It was a sad ending to witness. Brooks could detect the odour of cigarettes and alcohol and wondered if this was an intoxicated stunt rather than a suicide. No one would ever know. A forensic pathologist would speak for the victim of murder, but no one would speak for a victim of suicide. The case would be open and shut, much like the casket on this poor wretch.

Brooks walked away from the body to tell his colleague the sombre news, but halfway back to the edge he stopped to vomit. It was his first dead body. It wouldn't be his last, but it would be the one he would remember most vividly.

60

1991

There was something about speaking to police that always made me feel guilty. I'd had harsh words from many a police officer when I was a kid and it filled me with the fear of God. I guess it was a sensation I would always feel, whether I was innocent or guilty, I would fear *They* had something on me.

Upon closing the door to the two officers, I went straight to the fridge and grabbed a can. Half the liquid was gone in two gulps, but it didn't have the desired effect.

'What the fuck's wrong with you?' Dan asked. He also grabbed a can but was in no urgency to glug it down as I did.

'Did that *not* freak you out?' My question was asked between the last swigs of my beer.

'A bit. But not so much that I wanna rush for a beer and throw one down my neck.'

True enough. Before he had even finished what he was saying I had already pulled out another can.

'They think Tom has been murdered: that's enough to make anyone drink.'

'You're fucking paranoid.' Dan looked at me as though I was stupid. 'That's not what they said. That's not what they said at all. He's missing. They are looking for him, and you were one of the last people to see him. What's the big deal?'

What was the big deal? This wasn't the first time I'd been questioned about a missing person, that's what. Five years ago, I'd had an almost identical conversation with two other police officers in relation to Rob's disappearance. Both times I'd been drunk. Both times I'd been in a fight. And both times they had gone missing. Two disappearances – one common denominator. Me.

My mother was forever saying that I was the bad penny that would always turn up. I didn't disagree. I was my own bad luck talisman, often feeling that I should be swinging from a chain around a criminal's neck, doing hard time because luck wasn't something he could steal. My mind started to spin back through my memories, to that old mantra swirling through my head. Take responsibility. I was unaware of it at the time, as many young people are, that we can have a second chance on any given day, all we had to do is decide was take it.

With a raw epiphany tugging at the fraying strings that held me up, I was unable to answer him. Right at that moment I wished I was Dan. If my jealous pride would ever admit it, I always wanted to be Dan; the rapier sharp wit, a mother who gave a fuck, siblings, hope. He had so much that I didn't. Was it normal for me to want him to fall on his face just once? Maybe that was my problem. I wanted everyone else to suffer the same problems that I seem to conjure from thin air without effort. That would make the world fair to me. I was too young, too stupid and too stubborn to realise that for my world to change, I would need to change. This situation was confirming that. I wanted to run, never to return, never to walk these streets again. They say the streets of London are paved with gold. In my hometown, the streets were paved with the blood of my friends and disappointment. I needed to escape.

61

Present Day

Brooks sauntered back towards his room in that godawful budget hotel. The grim magnolia corridor with its contrasting blue patterned carpet was sucking the soul from him with every step. He didn't expect luxury on a Police expense account, but he also didn't expect to feel like he needed a shower every time he left his room. And the shower: that was another tale of woe. The tepid water dripped from the tarnished showerhead with the same pressure as an octogenarian with a swollen prostate and a bladder infection. And there was little difference when it was on or when it was off.

The well-worn key slid into the lock easily as it had no doubt done for the hundreds of other guests who had shared this room across the years. Brooks wondered how many lives had been made or destroyed by the activity that took place behind the shabby fire door when the lights went out. He mused to himself on his first night in residence on how much DNA evidence would be discovered, and subsequently discarded, if such a room became a crime scene. The more he thought about such things, the more appealing the backseat of the unmarked police car became as a bed for the night. All thoughts of a good night's sleep in a Vauxhall Insignia were interrupted by a knock at the door.

Yet another DNA trace added to the countless others.

'How are you getting on?' Delgado's question substituted for a greeting.

'Badly.' Brooks beckoned his colleague in, shutting out the sounds of over-loud televisions and frantic fornication with a slam of the portal to hospitality disappointment.

Brooks would have offered to make a coffee if he hadn't already used what was available. He really did need to think ahead on these matters. Police work was powered on caffeine, nicotine and alcohol. At least his was.

'The victims had to have known each other,' Delgado said.

'That's hardly a stretch.' Brooks frowned. 'They lived in the same town at the arse-end of nowhere. They were roughly the same age, probably went to the same school, and shagged the same girls. I'm sure that they had more in common than just having their corpses dumped in the same hole in the ground, albeit years apart.'

'All three had to have been friends. They moved in exactly the same circles with exactly the same people.'

'It was the 80s. They didn't have social media. They had socialising – in the real world.'

'I know,' Delgado's tone matched the level of sarcasm of his superior. 'I was a teenager back the 80s too. They probably played footie in the road and only went home when the streetlights came on too, like I did.'

Brooks paced as he talked. 'We need more than the obvious. The obvious will be explored to death by the speculation of whoever we interview. We need to think of not only the details, but the details of the details. Three decades have robbed us of those details.

'Until a week ago, they were missing persons. Now they are murder victims. We have to sift through the failing memories of some middle-aged people about events that happened more than half a lifetime ago. Do we even know if any of the friends are still alive?'

Delgado knew the methodology of Brooks. There would be a lot of pacing, stamping, shouting and repeating of the case details until the fog of old evidence cleared, revealing the subtle nuances which might point toward rhyme or reason. Old School thinking and twenty-first century technology was how this case would be solved. They just had to feed the correct ingredients into the cauldron of the investigation and see what magic they were able to brew.

Delgado had some names scribbled down on his pad. He knew where they should start.

62

Present Day

The repetitive beats by some unusually named artist, rattled from the speakers to merge with the irritating swipe of the blades across the windscreen. It was just background noise to drown out the ripples of rain against the roof and the swooshing of the tyres cutting through the sodden motorway. Brooks hated driving in the rain, but he hated being a passenger more and that's why he chose to deal with the early morning traffic while Delgado sipped coffee and read the file.

'You got anything good to tell me yet?' Brooks said, his eyes dancing between the cars ahead and the open words sat in the lap of his colleague.

'You keep your eyes on the road – I'll keep my eyes on the file.' Delgado hated being a passenger too. The officers returned to silence, leaving the radio and road noise to fill the void in their conversation.

The miles dissolved as did the clouds pounding onto the road ahead. By the time the motorway had given way to dual carriageway, the rain had stopped. By the time the dual carriageway became 'A' roads, the sun had made an appearance and the sky was more blue than grey.

'So?' Brooks had driven for an eternity before his patience gave way.

'So, if you concentrate on the road we might get to this guy's house before breakfast,' Delgado said, without taking his eyes from the dog-eared sheets of A4 bundled in his lap.

'How can you read and be a passenger at the same time? It makes me sick.'

'You learn to when you're always the passenger.'

Brooks felt the barb of the reply, but it didn't scratch the surface of his conscience. Brooks was the superior. He'd earned his place.

After a few more miles without conversation, Brooks played his ace card to get his colleague talking. 'Breakfast? My treat.'

Delgado's eyes were off the file for the first time in about an hour. 'Sounds good! It's your turn anyway.'

The suggestion had only been made because Brooks could feel the pangs of hunger creeping in and there was a McDonalds at the end of the bypass. Haverfordwest was their manor, so to speak, and the local Drive-Thru, their eatery of choice.

Overall, their patch was reasonably quiet in the way of murder but deafeningly loud when it came to drug related crimes. With 180+ miles of coastline to police, there were plenty of gaps for drug gangs to filter their wares through. In the last few years alone, a large boat landed at Fishguard harbour carrying millions of pounds worth of cocaine. It made the national news and created headaches for the Dyfed Powys Police force. On a much more personal level, Brooks and Delgado had to investigate a murder on one of the local beaches that turned out to be an organised crime related killing. Murder is seldom without reason. There must be a necessity for it. Profit, revenge, hatred: you could pick a reason, but it wouldn't remove the tragedy of the act, only expand it.

They sat in the restaurant, amongst the students about to head into the nearby college and the workmen starting their day by filling their bellies.

'What have you managed to find on this guy?' Brooks asked.

Delgado was wolfing down one of the two breakfast muffins he had ordered.

'William Taylor, 49 years old. He's got the usual social media: Facebook, Instagram and Twitter. He's not especially active on either of them. He used to run a bar in Milford Haven but, at this moment in time, there are no records of what he does.'

'Married?'

'Not sure,' Delgado answered just as he was about to bite into his second muffin.

'Kids?'

208

Delgado shrugged. His mouth too full to answer.

'How do you know all these accounts belong to him?'

'He's got the same profile picture on all of them – I imagine it's an old photo from maybe more than a decade ago – there's a picture of him in the file. He's not changed much.'

'Lucky bastard.' Brooks took a swig from his coffee.

Delgado laughed, spraying some of his food. 'Who knows what he looks like now? He could be bald, fat and grey by now.'

'Could he be dead?'

'Facebook account shows activity in the last week or so. I imagine the discovery of the bodies have stirred up the past.'

Brooks smiled. That's exactly what he was hoping for. A suspect with a guilty conscience, maybe?

63

Present Day

In the solitude of an empty house, my mind stretched back over the years, barely able to touch some of the memories I needed to access. While so much was branded onto my recollection of those early years, the subtle nuances of the days, weeks and months leading up to and after the events were hazy. I had to resign myself to the fact that I wouldn't be able to recall everything I was witness to, and I wouldn't be able to talk about the things I had blanked from my experience by the euphoria of teenage drinking.

I switched off the television. The news was nothing but a depressing series of mainly foreign news, interspersed with some home-grown gripes about poor political judgement and commercial scandal. The most worrying news item was about a virus outbreak in China, convincing myself that it was nothing but speculation, I tried to go about my day.

And how was I going to fill my day?

I'd lost my job when the bar I was managing went under. "Yet another casualty of post-Brexit Britain," at least that was what my former employer had said. It didn't matter to him, he had other bars in other locations to make his money. I was thrown onto the scrapheap once more and had been looking for work since the New Year. Twenty-five applications filled in; three interviews; no positions offered. Thankfully, I didn't have a mortgage to pay.

The only thing I received from my mother's death was the unhappy home I'd grown up in. There was no will written out. If there had been, the bricks and mortar I currently festered in would have been left to a cat's home, or maybe sold off to provide a decent chunk of money to put behind the various bars of all the pubs she frequented. As the only member of her family – although I was all but dead to her – I had inherited the house on Trafalgar Road. I'd always thought that her liver would give out from the daily cocktail of vodka, gin and whiskey she worked through, but no, she was found dead at the bottom of the stairs after a fall. Her body had lain undisturbed for the best part of two weeks. Nobody had reported her missing. The neighbours were alerted by a noxious odour and a swarm of flies which plagued the street. When I got the call – I'm ashamed to say it – I felt relief, not sadness. Luckily, I didn't have to identify the body.

I always wondered if I'd have recognised her. I only had one positive recollection of her in my head and that was at a christening for one of her old school friend's children. I think I must have been about six years old. All the older ladies seemed to be making a fuss of me and my mother was forced into doing the same. Looking back, it was all for show but in the mind of a child who knew no different, she was vibrant and smiling and showering me with the affection I so craved.

But when the party was over, so was the act.

For an afternoon I felt loved. But that single afternoon wasn't enough to mute the pain of the disappointment I had thrown at me for the next couple of decades. Whatever had happened to my only parent between the time of that christening and the moment of her death? She bore no resemblance to the woman at that event.

It was still early, so I decided on some breakfast to break-up the morning. I'd been wide awake since 5am and, with the clock advancing on 9am, I figured I should make some effort to form the day into a collection of coherent actions. Waiting for the kettle to boil in that claustrophobic kitchen, I gazed out onto the small yard where I played as a kid. I'd often been handed a toy of some description, provided by my mother's boyfriend of the hour, and left to fend for myself while she entertained him upstairs. I can't count the number of times I found the backdoor locked and I had to pee in the drain, or shelter from the rain in the spider-infested shed. I'm sure, if I went to see a psychiatrist, they would be able to dismantle my fragile sensitivities and write an epic thesis on how my life was forged in the smithy of my mother's alcohol and sex addiction.

Before the kettle clicked off and pulled me back from the abyss of my childhood, there was a knock on the door. From the echo

211

it cast through the hallway, it sounded like the knock of someone who knew their visit wasn't always welcome.

Much like how I had felt in my mother's life.

64

Present Day

It was the police at the door. They introduced themselves and I let them in. I knew this was coming. It was always a *when* not an *if* kind of situation. The inevitability of everything coming together after all this time was now bearing down on me. I left them sitting in the front room while I went to make some tea, but what I was brewing was a steaming case of anxiety I didn't think was possible to hide.

I brought in a tray with three mugs and a plate of biscuits. I don't know why I put the biscuits on the tray. It was barely 9am. Who eats biscuits for breakfast? Police officers, apparently.

They sat together on the old sofa with their back to the window. I took a seat on one of my grandmother's wingback chairs. My mother had never been one to furnish her house and the old armchairs were a reminder of happier times when my grandmother still had some influence.

The larger of the two men spoke first, Brooks, I believe he said his name was. He was a typical cop, his mere presence screaming authority. In my head, I could imagine that five minutes in an interview room with this man would make even the most hardened criminal spill their guts to crimes they hadn't committed.

'So, Mr Taylor, I don't doubt that you've heard about the discovery at the Mining Depot?'

Of course, I had. 'Yes.'

'I imagine there has been some speculation as to the findings, but I can confirm that three bodies were discovered on the site-'

'Three bodies.' I interrupted him. I don't know why.

'Yes, that's right, three bodies… If I may continue,'

He was in charge. I was nothing but a person of interest. I might not have been a suspect but that was how he made me feel: guilty as charged.

'Sorry, please go on.'

'Now, we've identified two of the bodies and we'll be hoping for the identity of the third later this afternoon.' Brooks shifted in his seat like he was handing over a baton in a relay.

The other officer, Delgado, took over. He looked like a Spanish waiter that you'd befriend on holiday. A stocky man with dark Latin looks, his short black hair flecked with grey. He may have had the looks and the name of someone from the Mediterranean region, but his accent was that of a Valley boy, rolling his *Rs* and elongating his vowels. 'It is our understanding that you knew the two people we have identified, and we'd like to ask you some questions in regard to your relationship with them.'

'Who are they?' I knew who they were, but I needed him to say the names I hadn't said in years.

'Robert Sherman and Thomas Magee. Can you verify your...'

I could see that he was still talking but I couldn't hear any the words falling from his lips. I'd been cast into a vacuum by the mere mention of their names. I couldn't breathe, I couldn't speak, I couldn't hear. It was as though the mad professor behind the curtain in the engine room of my brain had slammed his fist down on the emergency stop button, killing all communication between my senses and my conscious mind. Desperately, I was trying to override the kill-switch while struggling to take a breath. The walls started to draw in like the trash compactors in Star Wars, except I wasn't Luke Skywalker, and I couldn't call for help. I wasn't getting out of here on the Millennium Falcon. The room started to spin, details blurred, my temperature spiked.

'Mr Taylor?'

Breathe.

Inhale. Exhale.

'MR TAYLOR?'

Brooks had his hand on my shoulder.

'Mr Taylor, are you alright?'

The room dropped back into minor focus. I could hear the words but struggling to know what the police officer was saying over the pounding of my deafening heart. There was a sweat on my back like a sheet of ice. I was both hot and cold, without reason.

'Mr Taylor, is there anything we can do for you?' Brooks said. 'Do we need to call anyone?'

I shook my head. Not only to answer him, but to shake the confusion from my mind.

'No, no, no,' I managed, 'It…it's a shock. That's what it is. I'll be fine in a minute.' I fired down the sweet tea I'd made earlier hoping the old wife's tale was true.

'Are you sure, Mr Taylor? We can do this another time if now is inconvenient,' Brooks said the words, but I could see it wasn't what he wanted to do. I might have been dazed by the news, but I still had some brain function. I wasn't sure which bits, but I hoped it was the bits that would see me out of the abyss of shit I'd fallen into.

'Let's do this.' I was determined to see it through.

'Like I said,' Delgado resumed, as though nothing had happened. 'Can you verify your relationship with the deceased?'

The deceased. That's not a word you want thrown your way at low ebb. I gathered my thoughts, bundled what I could from the splintered remnants of my memories and poured them at the police officers with their note pads and recording devices.

I talked about what I could recall when we were all in The Meads Infants School; playing war in the playground; splashing in the water table; queueing up for the nit nurse. Every grazed knee. Every bumped head. Next, I laid out the endless recounting of banal anecdotes from North Road Boys School. All boys together, only sharing time with the girls in the summertime when playtimes spilled out onto the sports field. But, with prompting, I had to go into some detail about how we forged our friendships in the last chunk of education before we were thrown out into the big wide world.

Rob Sherman wasn't thrown very far.

He was thrown away.

Discarded like some useless item.

215

'What do you remember of that night, the last night before he disappeared?' Brooks had taken back the reins.

'It's all kinda hazy.' That was a lie. It was crystal clear in my mind. The thirty-four-year timespan, even with the volume of alcohol consumed at the time, hadn't erased a thing from my recollection of *that* night. 'There was a big fight – words were exchanged – insults traded. I got punched in the face and took myself off home.'

That wasn't where the story ended. I knew it. And I'm sure they knew it too.

I didn't want to talk about the drink with Tina: how I'd lost my virginity to my best friend's mother. I didn't want to talk about what came next; about the early morning walk on The Rath, what I had seen and done.

I could have taken their investigation in so many different directions; true or false. But I knew to say too much would send their eyes in my direction. Suspect number one.

'What about the night that Thomas Magee left town?' Delgado flicked through the file in his lap.

'We thought he had left town – packed a bag and disappeared,' I said.

'I've got a Police report dated from July 1991 in which you stated that you had been involved in a fight with Thomas and you suggested that he had left town because he assumed that you had been accidentally killed in the fight. Is that right?'

'Pretty much.'

They wanted me to give them all the same details I had given to the police officers nearly thirty years ago. Not just of the night in question but to the build-up and how I'd ended up living in the same house. They asked the same questions in ten different ways. I imagined it was to catch me out and to see how much my account would differ from the old police report. At the end of the interview both Brooks and Delgado were poker faced. They didn't give anything away. There'd been a lot of questions but, unlike my exams, they weren't grading my paper and giving me a score.

216

As the officers stepped into the hall, Brooks spotted a picture frame on the hall table. It was small but it had been put there to fill the space with something of meaning. He picked it up.

'Your wedding day?' he asked me.

'Yes,' I answered, flatly, not trying to give him anything.

'Should I assume you are still married?'

'My wife is at work at the moment.'

'What's her name?'

I told him. There seemed to be a moment of recognition in his expression.

'So, she was present at some of these nights too?' Eyebrows risen as if it was a detail I should have mentioned.

'Yes, we were all part of the same crowd.'

'Children?'

'A daughter – she's nineteen – twenty, later this year,' I gave the addition information before they asked.

'We're going to need to speak to your wife, as well. Good day, Mr Taylor.'

And with that, they left.

The world of shit I'd built for myself had just gotten a whole lot deeper.

65

Present Day

Brooks and Delgado climbed back into the Insignia and pulled away. Each could feel the other's frustration at the interview that had just taken place. There was silence in the car until they left the town limits, both needing a moment or two to gather their thoughts and postulate a theory. The mundane chat of the radio DJ and the squeak of the windscreen wipers did nothing to ease the thought process. Much like the weather of the day, theories were changing rapidly.

'What did you make of that?' Delgado spoke first. He knew what his superior was going to say.

'He's hiding everything,' Brooks replied. 'But giving so much away.'

'Agreed.'

'He filled the space with so much background, there was little room for any detail involving the nights in question. He wants to appear compliant without adding anything to his involvement.'

Years of experience in witness interviews had honed the officers' skills. It was never just about what was relevant but also what was irrelevant. To bulk up the mass of an interview so that the major points were buried was often the ploy of a less than innocent person. The fact that there were a lot of lines to read between told them pretty much what they needed to know. He was putting down layers of information to distance himself from the crimes.

'He wasn't curious either,' Delgado said.

He was right. They had just told a man that two of his friends – childhood, lifelong friends – were dead, and at no point did he ask about how they died. You didn't need to have years of experience to understand that if three bodies are found in the exact same location but placed there at different times, they wouldn't have happened to be there by accident. A police officer would know this but so would any would-be armchair detective.

But there were no questions about how they died.

There was not even a question about the third body. Brooks had deliberately not asked the question to see if there would be any curiosity about who the unknown victim might be. There was none.

The pair didn't exchange much in the way of speculation as they took the winding course of country roads heading back to the motorway and eventually, Cardiff. They knew how each other thought, anticipating the other's mindset. With the evidence they had, albeit meagre, adding the interview that had just taken place, they had both made their first conclusion. They had their first solid suspect.

66

Present Day

I stared out of the window, willing the car to pull away. It took a few minutes, but I was thankful when I saw the officers leave the street. I needed to get out. I needed to air the swirling mess of thoughts rammed into my head. I had to exorcise the demons once more, like I had a million times before, but this time I feared it might be the last opportunity I would ever have.

I wasn't a police officer. I didn't know how they worked or what techniques they used. But I could tell they didn't believe a word I said. Guilt wasn't a badge of honour, but I must have been wearing it like a headdress while they were here. I'm surprised they didn't cuff me then and there. Maybe that was the plan. Maybe they wanted to leave me with my freedom; freedom to make more mistakes; freedom to make their job easier.

There was only one place I needed to be.

I stepped out of the house, looking both ways, checking to see if the police were hiding around the corner to follow my movements. I don't know what it was about that street, Trafalgar Road, my childhood stomping ground. The road seemed so much smaller, constricted, insignificant, than it did when I was a child. I know I was smaller, and the world would have appeared much bigger, but that wasn't it. I only had one photo of my mother and me when I was an infant. I was sitting in a pram, I guess I was about eighteen months, on the corner of Dewsland Street and Trafalgar Road. It was a beautiful sunny day; my mother was handing me a bottle to drink from. The background to image was the empty street. It was completely clear of vehicles. Today, in 2020, you can barely park a car in the street. In the 70s, it was no problem at all. Maybe the empty street was why I remember it being so big, so wide.

Convinced that nobody was waiting to pounce, I stepped back into the house to grab my jacket.

I had never learned to drive. It was something that had never interested me. If I needed to be anywhere there was always a bus or a train, sometimes a taxi and, when all else failed, I had my legs. And I would need them now.

Taking no chances, I headed out the back of the house and down the lane between Trafalgar and Dartmouth Gardens. Again, it was one of those places where I played as a kid, and it seemed much smaller than I remember. When I was nine or ten years old, I could recall one of the girls from the street customising a black Morris Minor van in the lane. I didn't know what she was designing at the time, but it turned to be the prism off the cover of Pink Floyd's Dark Side of the Moon on one side of the van, and the man kicking the star that made up the logo for The Old Grey Whistle Test on the other. I used to sit on the wall of the yard, watching it happen. A moment of calm in a childhood of chaos.

I ducked out of the lane heading into Nantucket Avenue. The old streets, named by the families of the Quaker whaling community over two hundred years ago, were often a talking point to outsiders. I walked the lane between Starbuck Road and Dewsland Street too, if I could get from A to B without being seen on the streets then all the better. I took every lane, every alleyway and every shortcut I knew.

Eventually, I arrived at my destination on the other side of town.

I knocked the door.

I could see movement from behind the frosted glass panel and breathed easier. A car on the drive had never proved to be a reliable indicator of someone being home.

She opened the door and without a word, let me in.

'The police came today,' I said. The words stuck in my throat, gagging me.

She stared back at me, waiting for more. I didn't know what else I could say to her.

'They've identified Rob and Tom.'

'And…?' Her eyes asking what her lips dare not.

221

It was the question on my lips too, but I had been too scared to speak it aloud in front of the police: the identity of the third body. I knew. She knew. We all knew.

Her arms clamped around me like I had just saved her from edge of the precipice. I held her tightly because I didn't want to fall any further. I was already in too deep, and she had been keeping me safe these last few years.

When our embrace relaxed, our eyes met, then our mouths. Our tongues. In a frenzy of passion and desperate fear, we staggered into the lounge. Our lovemaking was angry – furious – but only so because of the levels of guilt we carried with us, wishing to be free. The infrequent moments of union we had shared were mere respite from the burden we bore.

Yes, I was married. Yes, I was having an affair. But no, I did not feel bad. Of all the things I've been a party to in my life this was the one thing I could bear the guilt of.

67

Present Day

Brooks yanked the wheel, pulling the unmarked police car into the first available space. He could see the car wasn't in the space square but that was of little concern. An accident on the M4 had slowed the traffic to a crawl, adding forty minutes to their return to Cardiff and the post-mortem. The appointment – they had to attend – was about to start in three minutes.

The officers jogged into the building, finding a path through the warren of corridors, avoiding random patients and medical staff who just happened to be in their way. They took the stairs rather than waiting for the lift and eventually landed at the floor where the pathologists roamed.

'Officers Brooks, Delgado – can I get you anything? A coffee, a sandwich, a watch that works?' Davenport said through the mask and visor he wore.

Brooks waved an apology as he breathlessly pulled on a mask and gown, struggling to fit the gown over his suit jacket: Delgado, having even more of an issue because of the girth of his frame.

Davenport stood with his nitrile gloved hands clasped in front of him, his stance sarcastic.

They entered the post-mortem room. The familiar shape of a body under a white sheet, laid out on a steel table with a gutter, was never a scene to get comfortable with. Brooks had stood in rooms like this many times before and, to his satisfaction, it was never a place he felt at home in. The crimes that humans committed against other humans never ceased to dumbfound him. He knew cops who had been exposed to too many crimes scenes; too many dead bodies in various states of dismemberment; and he had seen how numb they had become to it. He never wanted to become that desensitised to the crimes he investigated.

With the sheet pulled back, the earthy smell of old buildings was released into the air. It didn't matter how much disinfectant had been used in the room before prep; the smell of the dead would always work its way through to the senses.

The body lying before them was in a marginally better condition than the other two. The clothes were recognisable – a check shirt and jeans – no shoes or socks because the feet had separated from the skeleton, probably the work of animal activity. Brooks always thought, when he saw a victim still dressed, that they had no idea that these would be the last clothes they would ever wear with breath in their lungs. He imagined it would be the same for us all one day: a last outfit to meet our maker. He'd mentioned it to Delgado at another post-mortem a few years previously, just in passing. Delgado had remarked at the time that he hoped his last outfit was his birthday suit, and that he met his end by being shot dead on his 100th birthday by the jealous husband of the 25-year-old lingerie model girlfriend he was caught in bed with. Brooks never understood his colleague's dark humour, or at least, never found it funny.

Methodically, the body was stripped of the rags it had lain in for the last two decades. They had approximated the time of death to late 1999 early 2000. In the back pocket of the jeans, there had been a handwritten receipt from a local butcher. The date of the receipt was the 23rd of December 1999 for a Christmas turkey. The unspoken question was whether the victim ever got to eat the turkey, or did they meet their end before the stuffing balls had been rolled and the giblets removed.

With the clothing bagged and the partially skeletonised body naked, Davenport carefully began the task of looking for injuries. He changed out his visor for a pair of over-sized bifocals and scanned along every limb, every joint, every digit. Brooks and Delgado had to wait patiently, their presence a legal requirement, watching the expert pathologist search every inch of the deceased.

'The throat has been cut,' he said, pointing to a small bone attached to some desiccated sinew in the neck.

224

'Are you sure?' Brooks asked, happy to be able to move for the first time in a while.

'Pretty sure,' Davenport said, staring at the police officers over his glasses. 'I'm going to check the bone with a microscope, but I'd say the blade was serrated – like a steak knife.'

'How can you tell?' Delgado posed the question.

'There is a uniform groove in the hyoid bone which corresponds with a mark of similar depth and width on the lower edge of the jawbone.' Davenport drew his finger along the edge of the jaw without touching it. 'Although it's not obvious, the groove has some striation which is usually indicative of a serrated blade like that of a steak knife.'

'Not of a saw blade: like a hacksaw, for instance?' Delgado asked.

'No. A hacksaw had its serration staggered, leaving a much wider plane of cutting action. A steak knife or serrated kitchen knife would have the serration on one side – maybe both, but the injury made is narrower and leaves identifying marks.'

Both officers nodded in satisfaction and added to their hand-written notes. Davenport returned to the body, looking for anything significant.

With the post-mortem over, Brooks and Delgado walked through into the prep room, the strong hospital disinfectant aroma overwhelming them but a welcome odour over the smell of old corpse. They stripped off the gowns, masks, and hats, throwing them into the appropriate bin.

Davenport popped his head into the room, his gloved hand gripping the door. 'I might have an ID by tomorrow. I've sent off dental x-rays and DNA and we might come up lucky on this one.'

Brooks nodded but didn't mouth a response. He knew exactly what the pathologist was getting at. This was the later crime – the one committed within the last twenty years – there was every chance that computerised evidence of who this person was existed, narrowing

225

down the search, or even pinpointing exactly who it was. It was about time they caught a lucky break.

68

Present Day

My heart satisfied, I snaked my way home, back through the lanes and shortcuts. It was just a matter of getting the timing right as to when I would leave my wife. Getting the timing right was the story of my life. I always seemed to be in the right place at the wrong time or the wrong place at the right time. There was never a point, to my mind, that serendipity had shined on me. You'd have thought after nearly fifty years of scratching around on God's green Earth I might have caught a break at some point.

I slid the key in the door and carefully pushed it open.

'Anyone home?'

Silence.

That's not to say my daughter wasn't home. She often had earbuds glued into her lugholes because, in her words, *'The silence is oh so dreary.'*

She wasn't quite twenty, but she spoke like a ninety-year-old widow who remembers the *'Good Ole Days'* as the time when Hitler was bombing the shit out of the country and a singsong in the Anderson shelter was the only way to keep your spirits up.

I had a quick check upstairs and found I was on my own. The solitude of this old house, the bad memories hanging to the walls like the old woodchip used to, was not a calming environment for my inner demons. I had made a life I no longer wanted. Constructed a reality from the broken pieces of my fragmented childhood and shattered early adulthood, and whatever good had graced my futile existence, I just needed to be done with it. With a half century of experience, I was still fucking things up.

I loved my daughter, Jessie, I truly did. I can fondly recall all those moments when I took her to playgroup. How she would run up to me shouting 'Daddy, Daddy,' hugging me tightly and descending into a barrage of broken sentences about what she had done that morning. I was there for her first day at school; the tears, the sobbing, the streaming nose. I was there for it all. From grazed knees, to riding a bike, from the undying infant love to the endless teenage moods; I lived and breathed every moment. Now it was time to let her go. Because I knew if I left her mother, I was going to lose her too.

I'm not sure how I did as a parent. I guess I did ok. I'm sure I made all the same mistakes as other parents did: overprotective when I should have allowed more freedom; gave too much freedom when restraint should have been the answer. There was no handbook to being a parent, and if there was, the trouble-shooting guide would be too extensive to get to grips with. I was going to take having a nineteen-year-old with a clear vision of what she wanted to do in life as a big win.

When I think how I was back at her age, I didn't have a clue what I was going to do. I was falling through life, scrabbling around for a quid here and there, thinking I had a career in bar work because I had seen Tom Cruise in Cocktail more than twice. And although I had been working in and out of bars ever since, it wasn't how I envisaged my life was going to be.

If I had my time over, would I do it differently? Absolutely.

Would I have married the woman I was anchored to? Absolutely not.

But that raises the question of if I would have been happier without my daughter in my life, and I knew the answer was a firm 'No.'

In the dim light of the back room, I wallowed in the self-pity I had created for myself. The woman I loved – truly loved – I never fought hard enough for until it was too late. Was now too late? Who knew? The woman I'd married I thought was everything I'd been looking for. How could I have got it so wrong? Because that's what I always did, got it wrong, timed it wrong or took the wrong path.

Three bodies were lying somewhere, under a sheet, I imagined, stored in a fridge or a morgue, and there because I made the wrong choices: three friends gone because I made the wrong choices. And the third, as yet unnamed body, was the one that impacted my life the most. I think I would trade anything just to take back the moment that started that chain of events.

69

1999

The interim years between 1991 and 1999 were productive for me. I managed to acquire a few qualifications in bar management. I went from being a barman to a bar manager, and at one point, a hospitality manager in a hotel – a bit like being a bar manager but with a ton of additional responsibilities nobody else wanted to do. I worked in wine bars, pubs, hotels, nightclubs; I even did a stint on a ferry but couldn't handle trying to do a job while throwing up. The career I had fallen into had taken me from the arse-end of Wales to Bristol, Birmingham, Liverpool, Brighton, Belfast, Glasgow, and everywhere in between. There was a point when I worked in Ibiza for four weeks, but the piss-poor pay and competition made it more hassle than it was worth. The simple ability to pour a pint and maintain a bit of banter with the customer had managed to keep me fed and watered for the best part of a decade. There was one thing I had learned: experience would take you a long way.

My current employment was somewhat different to all other bar management positions I'd had. Christmas was coming, the geese were getting fat, and I had landed a job working in one of the local caravan parks, overseeing the three bars on the site. The summer was frantic, often unreasonably busy, but the winter was when everything shut down. We still had to stay open because a significant chunk of the statics – they weren't really caravans; they were static homes – were privately owned. The owners rented out their statics, either by themselves or through the park, making a few quid from their investment throughout the year, and picked a few key weeks for their own use. Some of the owners were in permanent residence but, for legal reasons, had to be off site for at least six weeks of the year. Most would spend the Christmas break in foreign climes or with family, but a good chunk of the less permanent residents would spend their Christmas in a prefabricated dwelling with only the basics of home comfort. And it was because of these owners I had to spend the Christmas period working. I didn't mind, it came with the job, and this year I'd landed lucky.

It was my third Christmas on this site, just outside Tenby. In the first two years, I had spent Christmas and New Year living on the site, opening the bars over the two-week holiday period, including Christmas Day and New Year's Eve. This year I had managed to bag both off, even though New Year's Eve was also Millennium Eve.

While other people would be worrying about aeroplanes falling out of the sky and the banking system crashing due to the Millennium Bug, I would be balls-deep in beer and Pringles and merriment with my friends. Dan had arranged a big party at his house and all the gang were invited. It would be great to see them all, even Jon.

I'd bumped into Jon a few times in recent months. He was much less of an asshole than I remembered. He was one of the few who had already hit the magic age of thirty and the years were already showing on him. Walking everywhere, lifting cases of alcohol and moving barrels had kept me in reasonably good shape. I still had all my hair and not a single grey. Jon wasn't so fortunate.

Yes, he was thirty – the rest of us were all still twenty-nine – but he looked ten years older. Summers in the sun had carved the crow's feet onto his face; his hair had started to recede in his mid-twenties and the hair that remained had turned grey: all of it. His job as a freelance architect would pin him to a desk, drawing and designing, but with a constant flow of coffee and baked goods supplied by his assistant. What had been a toned and athletic physique back in the 80s was now an ever-expanding soft body. Another reason why I think he was less of an asshole: diminished self-esteem.

With the party a little over a week away, I had already made my contribution. Having a wholesale card was a job perk that often came in handy when the entertainment fell at a friend's expense. Dan had thrown a few quid at me and had given me a list of stuff to buy. I tossed some of my own money into the pot and made it a party worth having. I had to recruit Sarah to be the transport.

She was back for good, or so it seemed. Her mother had died at Easter and Sarah, being an only child, inherited the house. Everyone thought she would sell it and buy something in Bristol where she had been working as a nurse for the last few years. Nobody thought that she would move back to Milford and take up residence in the house that held so many painful memories for her.

Sarah's childhood was almost as tragic as mine, but, whereas my mother was never present, her mother was always home. She couldn't escape the barrage of abuse her mother doled out. It was only on the rare occasions when her mother went on shopping trips to Carmarthen or Swansea, or on holiday, that we went to her house. I'd known Sarah twenty-five years, and although I often called at her house, I had only been inside about three dozen times, only twice when her mother was home. On those occasions she had seemed pleasant enough, but Sarah insisted it was just an act.

Sarah's mother was found dead in bed after accidently overdosing on both her insulin and sleeping tablets. Sarah had to drive all the way down from Bristol, finding the body after a family friend had called her to say they couldn't reach her mother. Apparently, Mrs Gardener – Sarah's mother, I never knew her first name – had become confused over the months leading up to her death. We had seen a lot of Sarah over that time. She was constantly driving between Milford and Bristol because of the increasingly erratic behaviour her mother was displaying. According to her only child, Mrs Gardener would forget about medication; sometimes not taking it at all, sometimes taking it twice. On the night she had died, she had taken two lots of sleeping pills and three shots of insulin. She was sixty-eight years old.

We supported Sarah through that time, but she seemed to handle it well, saying it was a weight off her shoulders. I could believe that. At the time I thought it was bravado, but in her position, I would probably feel the same way about my mother dying. It would be one less thing for me to worry about. God knows I needed that. But sometimes you have to be careful what you wish for.

70

1999

A colleague dropped me off outside what was now Sarah's house and bid me a Merry Christmas. When you were the boss, like I was, and didn't have a driver's license, it paid to hire staff from the same town and rota them accordingly. I was fixed for lifts most of the time, but if I wasn't, there was accommodation on the park for a limited number of staff. For me, it was usually the sofa in my office. It was well-worn but comfortable.

Sarah had invited me for Christmas dinner, and I had gratefully accepted. She also insisted on me spending Christmas Eve with her and waking up at her house on Christmas morning. So, under her insistence, I did as I was told.

It was a little after seven and she was planning to get a takeaway for us. I'd redirected some of the booze planned for Dan's millennium bash so that we would be able to celebrate together. A case of Budweiser and a case of Bacardi Breezers – orange flavour – were already split into the fridge, chilling ahead of a night of shit TV and Chinese food.

The door opened and Sarah invited me in. In the last few years, she had transformed herself. The Sarah of old was a short, dumpy girl, no makeup, bland hair and a little overweight. When she was in Bristol, studying, she kind of reinvented herself. The hair had already been addressed by regular colour changes from the minute she left school, but the other changes took a while to take. A diet and exercise regime dropped her weight, giving her some confidence to add a little pizazz to her wardrobe choices. As the years passed, the changes grew.

The Sarah who opened the door to me was wearing a black low-cut loose top, white hotpants and black heels. It was December. Her legs were sculpted; tiny ankles flared to shapely athletic calves, defined knees pinched at the bottom of strong, toned thighs. The top rose, showing the makings of a six-pack, yet dropped off the shoulder to display prominent collar bones and a killer cleavage. If I had to guess at her dress size, I'd say she was an eight or less. Her hard work had paid off. Coupled with a new knowledge for make-up learned from her relationship with Jennifer, her green eyes and pretty smile were highlighted by significantly defined cheekbones and dimples. She was a brand-new woman.

'Wow!' I said, 'You look amazing.'

'Why thank you, kind Sir,' she giggled. 'I was just trying on outfits for the Party. I'll take it that this is a winner.'

I just held up a thumb and gave her a cheesy grin.

She guided me upstairs to where I would be sleeping. It was her bedroom.

'Where are you going to sleep?' I asked, frowning that a spare room hadn't been available.

'I'll take the sofa,' she shrugged.

'I'll sleep on the sofa. You sleep in the bed.'

'You're the guest, I'm the host. You'll sleep where I tell you, got it!' The stern look could barely hide the smile behind it.

'Yes, hostess.' I dumped my bag and discarded my jacket.

She then whipped off her top and stood before me in just a lacy black bra and the hotpants/heels ensemble. Regardless of the weight loss, she still had boobs. It was hard not to notice.

'What are you doing?' I wasn't sure where my eyes were looking but I tried to focus on her beautifully made-up face.

'I'm getting changed. I'm not going to The Happy Garden dressed like a dog's dinner.' Her hand was behind her back, fumbling for her bra clasp.

'Whoa. Whoa. Whoa. At least let me leave the room.'

'You've seen me naked before,' she laughed, the bra clasp pinged open, but the garment held onto her lean shoulders.

'Y-yes, I have,' I stumbled over my words, reaching for something funny to say. 'But that was a long time ago and I will not be held responsible for an automatic reaction of certain parts of my anatomy.'

She brought up her forearm to shield her breasts as she unhooked the bra from her shoulders. 'Being a nurse, I've seen too many automatic reactions from many a man's anatomy. It doesn't really bother me anymore, but if it bothers you, you'd better go.'

I shut the door behind me. It didn't block out the laughter from the other side.

*

The Vicar of Dibley was on the TV, but we were barely watching it. Two dirty plates rested on the coffee table: one with my ribs, picked clean, and the remnants of some rice and curry sauce, and Sarah's with half a beef chow mein congealing slowly. There were also eight Budweiser and five Bacardi Breezer bottles randomly strewn between plates and coasters and the remote control.

'Thank you for that,' Sarah said, her normal toned, flattened tummy bulged under her sweatshirt.

'No problem. Thank you for the invite.'

I was truly grateful to be there. I had nowhere else to go for Christmas. My mother had never invited me, nor did I expect her to, as her idea of Christmas dinner was a cheese toasty while she drank her way through an entire bottle of vodka before the Queen's speech.

It was the sensible choice for Sarah and me to spend the day together. Dan would be at his mother's house with his sisters. Jennifer was with her parents, Nikita with hers. Jon was spending the day at his brother's house, probably fending off his nieces. When there were no siblings or parents – or ones that gave a fuck – the only thing to do was to spend it with the next best thing to family.

There had been the offer of a movie on DVD – Sarah was at one with the new technology – but I declined. I'd had a hard day stocking up all the bars and tidying the storerooms so that the minions I had left in charge wouldn't have much to do other than serve drinks. This was my Christmas gift to them. Plus, the weight of the food and

236

several beers were dragging down the last of my resolve. It was time to hit the hay and approach Christmas day with vigour and a sense of optimism.

Who was I kidding?

I was expecting to be half-cut by noon and asleep by the evening. That was my idea of Christmas.

I went to bed, falling asleep relatively quickly.

I wasn't sure of the time, but I was awakened by the creaking of the door. Light pouring in until the landing light was flicked off. I felt the bed lurch under the weight of somebody climbing in. Motionless, I pretended to be asleep. An arm slipped around my waist, and I could feel naked flesh press against my bare back. I could have reacted, but I didn't, I lay still and waited. Before I could ponder the options, sleep cast a spell on me again and I succumbed to the elements of the day. The sleep was restful because it was comfortable. I was comfortable because Sarah made me feel that way.

71

1999

I had woken up the same way I had every Christmas morning in my life. Single. Relationships came and went, as did Christmas, I just never found myself in a position of being with anyone on the big day. Today would be no different.

Sarah must have snuck out early.

I reached for my watch. It was a little after eight. I felt well rested and comfortable; the same comfort I had felt when Sarah slipped in beside me. Nothing happened. She just slept next to me. Maybe she was lonely, or scared, or cold. Who knows?

I threw on my jeans and wandered to the toilet. I'd finished what I was doing and was washing my hands when I heard the kettle click off downstairs. My foot creaked against the very top step when I heard a yell from the kitchen.

'William Bartholomew Taylor!' Sarah said, in her sternest sister on the ward voice. My middle name wasn't Bartholomew. That was our little joke because I didn't have one. My mother was too lazy to think of two names to give me 'Do not set foot downstairs. I am preparing Christmas and would appreciate it if you would just fuck off back to bed for a few minutes. Thank you!'

I did as I was told, lost my jeans and slipped back under the covers.

A few minutes later I heard her scaling the stairs. I could hear rattling.

The door was carefully kicked open. I sat bolt upright in mock attention to her efforts, waiting patiently for Christmas to start.

'Merry Christmas, William.' Sarah, wearing nothing but an oversized sleep t-shirt, came in carrying a tray with breakfast. It was a large tray, holding a plate of warmed croissants, butter, jam, grapes, strawberries, slices of ham and cheese, two champagne flutes filled with Buck's Fizz, two empty side plates, and a mug of steaming tea. Milk and two, just the way I like it.

'Wow!' Nobody had ever brought me breakfast in bed before.

'I thought I'd spoil you – us – actually.' She smiled broadly at her correction. 'Merry Christmas, Will.'

She leaned in, kissing me on the lips. Not a passionate kiss but her lips lingered against mine longer than a friend's kiss should. Then we tucked into the feast, the tray between us.

We ate, we chatted, we laughed; it felt so natural – so comfortable. There was that word again. Comfortable. I'd never experienced the warming sensation of belonging so strongly before. For a perfect moment, all the pieces of my life seemed to fit. Like the stars had aligned for the first time in many millennia. Is this what happiness felt like? It was all new to me.

With the breakfast devoured, we continued to chat. Smalltalk really, anecdotes from our places of work. She had more stories than I did. I imagined lots more happened in hospitals than would happen in a bar. There was only so many times you could start stories with *'One time, there was this drunk guy...'*

She didn't seem to mind my mindless rambling. She didn't seem to mind anything I ever did. Even all the times I hadn't been the best of friends to her, ignoring her feelings for me, selfishly being absorbed in my own little world and blanking her out. She forgave it all.

'Right, Mister, downstairs in five minutes. I think Santa may have been,' her grin was at its cheesy best. 'It looks like you must have made it onto the *Good List*.'

I just laughed at her silliness. She laughed with me and then stretched her arms, lifting the thin sleep top she wore, exposing herself briefly. She was wearing no underwear at all. I noticed. She noticed I noticed. And did nothing.

She hopped off the bed and grabbed the tray, kicking the door open with a bare foot.

'Downstairs – five minutes. Got it?'

I nodded and pulled on some clothes.

239

Luckily, I had some foresight and had bought her some presents too. I'd pulled out all the stops and even wrapped them. And when I say, 'wrapped them,' I mean I had one of the bar staff who knew what they were doing wrap the presents for me. I'd dibbed out on the gift wrap and the only stuff I could find had the pattern a small child would have on their presents. No matter, I'd bought it all, and they had been wrapped.

Although, I felt like a twat when I walked in and saw the living room.

There was a pile of presents on the armchair, all wrapped identically, and all wrapped immaculately. Blue and gold masculine gift wrap tied with gold ribbon that had been twisted to perfection.

'Oh, you shouldn't have gone to-.' I didn't get to finish.

'It was no bother. And trust me it looks more than it actually is.'

As ever, Sarah was bending the truth. While there were a few silly items – a twelve pack of Coke Cola, a Toblerone, a bag of jelly babies, three cans of Lynx deodorant – all individually wrapped, but she had also bought me a pair of beige chinos, like the ones I always wore for work, a Ralph Lauren blue canvas shirt, and a box set of Yves Saint Laurent Opium aftershave. The frivolous items had cost a few quid, but the big three would have cost the best part of a week's wages. The luxury bath pamper set, box of Milk Tray and Snoopy sleep t-shirt I had bought seemed a very poor offering. But if she was disappointed, she didn't show it.

And that's what our relationship had become – me, overthinking the situation, and her, well, she just seemed to be happy in my company. Somewhere in the depths of my live-for-the-moment attitude, there was a penny teetering at the edge, waiting to plunge at any moment.

72

1999

Somewhere between the time that Sarah had snuck out of bed, and I had woken up, she had been a busy girl and prepared all the vegetables for our Christmas feast. Carrots and peas for boiling and potatoes and parsnips for roasting were already in saucepans on the hob. She had pigs-in-blankets and stuffing balls ready rolled in the fridge and a turkey crown cooking slowly in the oven. We'd both agreed that we didn't do sprouts.

With everything well in hand, we both got showered and dressed – separately – and ready to leave the house.

Dan was doing very well for himself as a factory under manager. He had also struck it lucky on the lottery, not millions, but he had picked himself five numbers and the bonus ball earning a little over fifty grand. He bought a car and put down a deposit on a house on The Rath, only a couple of hundred yards from Sarah's house on Vicary Street. We had arranged to show up and exchange presents before he slinked off to his mother's house for Christmas dinner.

'Merry Christmas, everyone!' It was clear that Dan had more than just Buck's Fizz with his breakfast. He hugged us both, dragging us towards his lounge. Beige carpet, white walls, brown leather matching sofas, and a huge television on an oak stand in one corner. Since earning and winning money, he certainly liked the finer things in life. The rear end of the lounge, which had been a separate room at some point, had an eight-seater dining table, a dresser unit, with a hi-fi on top, and a real Christmas tree, bent at the top because it was too tall for the room. The massive bay window looked over the vista of the haven – the Watergardens to the right, Wards pier to the left and the three stacks of the refinery directly opposite. When you lived in Milford, you couldn't overlook the presence of the petrochemical industry, so it was better to observe the beauty of the natural harbour in spite of the jetties and tankers.

Our visit was short and sweet. Twenty minutes tops. We had a drink – Dan had two – we exchanged presents and then we left. There was a moment of hilarity when Dan and I opened our presents simultaneously, discovering that we had both bought a Lynx Africa gift set for the other. They were merely token gifts. I'm sure if we were serious about our gift choices, Dan would have bought something more expensive. I wasn't ungrateful, far from it, but the guy was my best friend, and he had a brand-new Audi on the drive. I reckon he could have stretched to a bottle of vodka or something less trivial.

With the afternoon ours, Sarah and I ate too much, and drank even more. The Christmas feast went down well, as did the bottle of white wine she had bought to accompany the meal. We drank a second bottle while watching Robin Williams cause chaos in Jumanji; the afternoon film on BBC1. As the day dimmed into night, the Pringles, nuts and pretzels came out with a plethora of Budweiser and Bacardi Breezers. By 10pm, we were both a little worse for wear; unsteady on our legs and bottoming out on our inhibitions.

It was time for bed.

And that posed another unspoken question.

Who was sleeping where?

The question had already been answered after I staggered out of the bathroom.

Sarah was under the covers, wearing her new Snoopy nightie. I didn't say a word. I climbed into bed and flicked off the bedside light. The blackness encouraged silence and the only sound was that of our breathing. A long moment passed.

I felt Sarah sit up and reach up over her head. She had taken off the nightie. I dropped onto my back. I knew what was going to happen next. As anticipated, a leg straddled me, and Sarah's small frame was on top of me before I could resist. But I didn't want to resist. For the first time in forever this seemed right. Her lips met mine in the darkness, her tongue slipping into my mouth. I reciprocated, kissing her back. Our arms wrapped around each other in the darkness,

242

feeling our way through unchartered territory in our relationship. We relaxed into it. Wanting it. Needing it. Without conscience or debate, we made love until the alcohol fuelled passion left nothing but sleep as respite to our perfect day. We couldn't take it back. Nor did we want to. The deed was done.

73

1999

The morning after my first night with *any* woman always filled me with a sense of shame. Shame because I knew it would go nowhere. Shame because I felt that somehow, I had taken advantage of whoever it was. Or shame because I wanted to be out of there as fast as possible with the chance of return taken out of the equation.

This morning, lying beneath the covers with Sarah's warm, naked body wrapped around me, I felt no such shame. What was more disturbing to me was that it felt comfortable. Yes, I had been in some short-term relationships where things were comfortable for a month or two, but the spark fizzled out pretty quickly, and before I knew it, I was heading for the door.

I glanced at my watch. My lift was coming to get me in just short of an hour. One of the terms of my having Christmas Day and New Year's Eve off was to work full days from Boxing Day until the 30th. I thought it was a fair deal and had arranged to stay at the park during that period. Now my head was all over the place. Maybe I should travel back and see Sarah every night. I knew she wouldn't mind; in fact, she'd probably encourage it. As conflicted as I was, I came to the decision to stick to the plan and not to return until I finished my shift on the evening of the 30th.

Feeling confident in my decision, I slinked out of bed and took a shower.

I don't know how long I was under the water, but on my return to the bedroom to get dressed, Sarah had gone, but there was a steaming mug of tea and a plate of toast waiting for me.

I smiled to myself and got dressed.

When I entered the kitchen carrying the empty plate and mug, Sarah was perched at the kitchen table, a mug of coffee and a plate with one piece of toast in front of her. There was a single bite out of the toast.

'Morning,' I said, cheerily but with some trepidation.

'Morning,' she replied. The greeting was returned with a smile but there was sadness to it.

'What's up?' It was loaded question. I could see there was a multitude of emotions pent up behind her false smile and I was inviting the possibility that I was about to hear some things I didn't want to. But I had to ask. If there was one thing life had taught me, it was to seize the opportunities quickly and move passed the mistakes even quicker. If this had been a huge mistake, she was about to tell me.

'About last night…' her voice tailed off. The defences were coming down and I could feel the tsunami of regret lapping over the top.

'What about it?' I needed to hear what she had to say but I was also conscious of the time and wanted her to get it off her chest – for her sake, as well as mine.

'It was special to me.' She bit her bottom lip to stop the wrong words tumbling out. 'But it was only special to me because you are special to me. You've known for the longest time how I feel about you, and I don't want this to be the wedge that finally pushes you out of my life because you aren't prepared to give me what I want from you. Do you understand?'

I understood. She had given me a free pass knowing how I was when it came to relationships. She understood that I had felt disposable for most of my life and treated people in much the same way. Now, after years of infatuation, she had managed to cross the threshold of our relationship but didn't want it to change the dynamic. She didn't want the act to mean I'd drop out of her life completely, nor did she ask me to commit to her the way she had always wanted.

I smiled at her, leaned in and kissed her on the forehead.

'Last night was special for me too,' I could say it with all honesty. 'And I won't be going anywhere. You've always had my back, even when I didn't deserve it, and I hope you know that I'm here for you too. Last night was incredible and it felt right-.'

'But?' she anticipated.

'It's a soft *"but,"* but a *"but"* all the same. Let's not rush – let's not put any pressure on ourselves. You and I will always be something to each other, so let's not make a regret of running before we can walk.'

She smiled a tight-lipped smile and rose from the chair. We hugged and we kissed. Not a kiss like lovers, a kiss like lifelong friends who needed each other when times were tough.

There were probably a million things we could have said or done but the moment was broken up by the tooting of a horn from outside. We wouldn't see each other until the day before the party and it seemed like an eternity to wait. Maybe I was changing for the better.

74

1999

Four days dallied by in tedious beer-stained confusion. Twelve-hour days that only warranted about four hours of bar work lacked the pace I was used to. I spent most of my time mopping, polishing and cleaning anything and everything, whether it needed it or not. I had to keep my mind occupied because otherwise I would descend into self-destructive mode and think about nothing else but Christmas night and the consummation of a relationship that had never needed consummating. Not at my end, at least.

I had decided not to go back to Sarah's late on the night of the 30th. I phoned her and made up an excuse. Instead, I stayed at the park an extra night, kipping on the sofa in my office, and hitched a ride back to Milford on the morning of New Year's Eve with the dray lorry. I had a good relationship with all the drivers, and we had agreed that I'd open early so they could drop off some of the kegs ordered in for the park's Millennium party if they dropped me to Milford on their way to deliver to the Nelson. It was mutually beneficial as I didn't have to spend an awkward night with Sarah and the dray lads would get home early to go to whatever parties they had planned.

Dropped off at the far end of The Rath, I sauntered toward Sarah's house. Too many times I had walked this picturesque place and had nothing but sorrow or hardship for company. Too many times had I come here, hoping that all the answers I needed would appear, or that my troubles would be caught on the breeze, taken from me and lost into the ether. Too many times.

This was not such a time.

I felt calm and controlled. There was no trepidation with each footfall. No second guessing whether I had made a huge mistake. There had been a choice to make. No, not a choice to make; an attitude to adopt. I was going to live each day as it came and not worry about what had past or what was to come. They say that a new year brings new attitudes. This would be mine. I'd always lived for the moment but never with an eye out for a positive outcome.

I strolled by the Water Gardens and the Minesweeper monument, the view of the haven filtering through the trees. I also gave a casual glance toward Dan's house, where the party to end all parties was to be held. The drive was empty, but I knew Dan was at work. No chance for a quick cuppa and some idle chat. That would be reserved for tonight when it would be beer and nibbles, and a dozen other people to interrupt the flow.

I walked on.

Eventually, I arrived at Sarah's house on Vicary Street. Her car was gone. I'd completely lost track of days and it had slipped my mind that it was a Friday. Sarah would be working having taken a role at Withybush Hospital, working one of the clinics, Monday to Friday, 9 to 5.

There was a note taped to the door.

"You know what to do. See you later, S x."

I did know what to do.

I nipped down the alley into the large parking area between Brick Houses and the backyard of Sarah's house. The gate was latched but not locked. Underneath a flowerpot on the back step was a key to the back door. I let myself in.

The house had a comforting aroma about it. Sarah was always burning incense sticks or scented candles to create a positive atmosphere. And if she wasn't burning something, she was cooking something that smelled divine. I was getting the cinnamon scent of a Christmas candle she had been lighting over the festive period.

On the table was a handwritten note: Sarah's carefully crafted letters sitting in the middle of the lined paper.

"Lunch is in the fridge. I'll sort myself out
when I get home. S x."

248

I pulled open the fridge door to find a plate of tuna sandwiches, an unopened bag of ready salted crisps, a yoghurt and a bottle of Budweiser. A smiled at her thoughtful gesture but was bemused at her madness of putting crisps in the fridge. Who puts crisps in the fridge?

But then a flash of panic raced across my conscience. This felt very "girlfriend" behaviour.

Committed.

Taken.

Involved.

But then I remembered. This was Sarah. This is what she did.

75

1999

After my initial panic and the thought of being "wifed up" had passed, I had spent the afternoon watching a movie. Sarah had an extensive collection of DVDs, from all genres, so I had a choice. I settled for Saving Private Ryan. I couldn't have timed it any better. Sarah walked through the door just as Tom Hanks was reclined against a wall, wounded, firing his pistol at an approaching tank. It was the last few minutes of the film.

'Made yourself at home, I see,' she said, her lips tight in mock sarcasm.

'If I'd have done that, I'd have been sat in my pants, watching porn,' I jested.

Sarah giggled. I laughed too. But under the veil of our laughter would always be sadness for Tom. It seemed an awful legacy to leave but none of our group could mention pornography, even in jest, and not think of Tom Magee: Porn King of Milford Haven.

'Did you want a cup of tea?' Sarah was busying herself in the kitchen, still in her blue scrubs.

I flashed the open bottle of Budweiser at her, and she nodded her understanding.

As the credits of the epic war movie started to scroll, Sarah dropped onto the sofa next to me. A mug of coffee and a plate of peanut butter on toast placed on the table.

'You know there's food at the party, right?' I asked.

'Yeah, but I'm starving – two drinks and I'll be in a coma.'

'Like always.'

A sharp elbow to ribs was her way of response. We giggled while a brief wrestling match broke out. I could feel the warmth of our friendship like a blanket that bound us together. It felt good.

Very good.

Too good.

We chatted as she nibbled on her toast then both decided it was time to get ready. I had bagged the first shower as Sarah still had to decide what to wear to the biggest party of the Millennium. Her low-cut top/hot pants combo had been discarded.

I had washed my hair, conditioned it too, soaped myself from head to foot, making sure I did my pits and my bits. When I was convinced that I had cleaned every nook and cranny I could reach, I stepped back under the flow of water, letting it wash away the lathered-up shower gel. Facing the wall, with my eyes closed, I felt a calmness wash over me with the warming water. Then I felt a hand against my back. Then another. I was about to turn when a voice told me otherwise.

'Stay still. I'll wash your back,' Sarah said. I could feel her nakedness behind me.

She soaped by back, massaged my skin, scrubbed it with a textured shower pad; spinning me around once she was done so the water could rinse away the lather. In an endless moment, I stared at her perfect naked body, water dripping off her shoulders, down her breasts and lost to the soapy mess at our toes. I could have said anything. I could have done anything. My body reacted in the way that it should, but I decided not to act on it.

Slowly, Will. Slowly.

'Swap places and I'll do your back,' I said, with a grateful smile.

I returned the favour, rubbing a fruit scented gel into a pink lather on her sculpted back, from the nape of her slender neck, down the groove of her spine, to the swell of her pert buttocks.

Without a word, she turned to me. Her eyes filled with expectation.

'You can do my front, if you want.' Those pretty green eyes fluttered through the mist of warm water enveloping her face.

I could sense what she wanted, or at least I thought I did. In this situation, with anyone else, I'd have not hesitated. Lust would have conquered reason and we would have made love under the water.

251

But she wasn't anyone else. She was special and deserved my respect. Respect was hard for me to show in a reasonable fashion to someone I was as close to as I was her.

I did it in my own clumsy way.

'Nah, you're all right.' I leaned forward and kissed her wet forehead. 'You can wash yourself, you lazy cow.'

I felt a damp sponge hit me on the back of the head just as I was about to escape the bathroom.

*

An hour later, after some more preening and plucking, and a couple of drinks, we were making our way to Dan's house. I was wearing the chinos and shirt that had been my Christmas presents. Sarah was in a figure hugging little black dress; a pair of four-inch heels lengthened her legs, defining the toned shape of her calves and muscles above her knees. Her burgundy bobbed hair, shining from a layer of hairspray, framing her exquisitely made-up face. She looked stunning.

Although it was a short walk to the party, we dragged it out, strolling along the haven side of the road. The familiar rumble of a tanker's engine gave the night some life while the lighting on the jetties gave us something to view. The Cleddau River was black and invisible apart from the odd, fleeting reflection.

She broke the silence first.

'So, where are we?'

'We're on The Rath.' I couldn't resist being glib.

A backhand to the arm. 'No, Doofus. Where are *we*? I have to ask.'

Of course, she did, it was the question I needed an answer to as well, but I felt wholly unqualified to answer. I had to be honest with her. She deserved that much.

'I don't know – that's the truth. My life has never had much structure – normality. I've tumbled through life without a care in the world. It's not been the best strategy: not for me or my friends. You,

252

for example, seem to have life all figured out. I couldn't figure out what to wear tonight.' I was being honest, but I had to ask a question myself. 'How do you see it?'

She laughed, interlocking her fingers in mine as we continued to walk, walking straight past Dan's house as though the journey was too short to resolve out issue.

'I won't labour the point of how much you mean to me, again. That much you already know. But what I will say is this – I will take whatever you have to offer because it's all I've ever wanted. Having you in my life is important and I want you there regardless of how that is. As our circle gets smaller, the meaning we have for each other grows larger. We didn't think this way when we were young and stupid – we thought we'd live forever. It took all these years to show us how wrong we were. No more Rob, no more Tom. Who'll be next? We're not immortal and that has been shown to us. If nothing else, we need to learn from it and appreciate what we have.'

I understood what she was getting at, but I wasn't convinced she was being altogether truthful. She was dancing a vague waltz around what I needed to hear and what I believed she wanted to say.

'So,' it was my turn to use that loaded start to a sentence. 'Are we just good friends without expectation?'

She stopped and turned to me, pausing for a moment before nodding. 'Yeah, just good friends.'

'Cool,' I replied.

'And speaking of cool, it's fucking freezing. Can we go to the party now?'

I didn't answer her. I just grabbed her hand and playfully dragged her tottering on her heels back towards Dan's house. It was time for our party to begin.

76

1999

I hate being the first to arrive at a party but that's what Sarah and I were: the first to arrive. It didn't make much difference. We spent the time in the kitchen as Dan was still preparing food. We laughed as he burned his fingers on a tray of sausage rolls and laughed even harder when his beer frothed over, spilling down his Dolce & Gabbana jeans. For all our age and experience, it still only took something simple to reduce our mentality back to playground rules. Other than the banter and the laughs, Dan talked about taking some time off work to go travelling. We had previously discussed spending some time in Australia and New Zealand and going together. I was never sure if it was something I wanted to do but Dan was keen to spread his wings. He had hinted about moving to Australia, permanently, and this was to be his initial recce. He was keen for the idea because Jon's brother, who was home for Christmas and the Millennium, had moved to New Zealand some years ago, and Jon was going out there in a few months' time. Dan said that he had discussed the idea at work and could take a sabbatical. He urged me to do the same during the quiet, pre-season months. I agreed to satisfy Dan's want and changed the subject.

Over the next hour and a half, the guests started to arrive.

The first to arrive, about an hour after us, was Jon. He was dressed in a grey suit and was wearing a tie with his button-down burgundy shirt. I didn't want to cast too much judgement on him, but I'd have said that he'd been under attack from a battalion of carbohydrates since the last time I'd seen him. There were no sharp edges to his appearance, and I couldn't stop staring at how his hairline started halfway up his scalp. With a treble chin nestling in the gap where his tie should have held his shirt closed, he looked as if he'd given up. Maybe this was karma.

'How's the architect business going?' I asked, making the smallest of small talk.

'Yeah, yeah, not bad.' His head was bobbing as he answered, revealing far too much movement in the loose flesh around his neck. 'I've got a few projects on the go – a few more for the new year. Yeah, yeah, things are pretty good at the moment. How are things with you?'

He asked to be polite, not because he wanted to know. If there was one thing I knew about Jon it was he didn't give a shit about anyone else. He only ever wanted to know what others were up to so that he could compare his life with theirs and see who was winning.

'Good, pretty stable, just the way I like it. There're a few opportunities in the pipeline too,' I lied. It would bug the shit out of Jon if he thought someone was getting a promotion because of their work ethic. Jon was self-employed; he couldn't get promoted. 'I've got to weight up the pros and cons, but in the meantime, I'll keep doing what I'm doing. It keeps me slim, if nothing else.'

One nil, to me.

We shared a fake laugh and a lot of head nodding. I pretended I needed the toilet and he pretended to be interested in whatever Sarah had to say.

By the time I had returned from not having a pee, Tina and Charlotte had turned up. Talk about double awkward.

It was the mother/daughter combo that I had started (and finished) the 'Wild Oats' period of my life with. Both were still as gorgeous as ever.

Tina was heading for divorce and apparently had a younger man on the go – she always liked the younger men – and looked stunning in a figure-hugging blue dress with matching heels. She was 47 but looked ten years younger. She may have had an extra line or two on her face since the last time I saw her, but it didn't matter, she could still turn heads.

Charlotte was also still a stunning girl and had the same pedigree of youthfulness as her mother. She was married and had two kids: one of them less than a year old. She had come dressed in skin-tight black trousers – which didn't hide the tiny amount of baby weight she still carried – and a low-cut red blouse – which couldn't hide what

255

she had been feeding the child with. She looked mumsy and mature, but comfortable with it, and still could command a room with her bronze eyes and winning smile. Her husband was also in tow. A nice guy called Dave, who was from up north. He wanted to talk fast cars and Manchester United, but I'd have rather removed my own spleen than talk about his Subaru and season ticket. We exchanged a few words throughout the night but nothing of any substance.

There were a few other guests; work colleagues and neighbours of Dan's. Some I vaguely knew; some I'd never seen before in my life. The diversity of the guests added to ambiance of the party. One guest, in particular, changed the party for Dan. A pretty admin girl at his office called, Estelle. She was toned and tanned and showing it off in her pink cocktail dress; her long, straight, jet-black hair scooped back into a single ponytail, revealing a long, slender neck. She was early twenties and flirted endlessly with Dan, but at no point did we see the two of them kiss. If they weren't already making the beast with two backs, it wasn't far away. They had chemistry.

The last to arrive was Nikita, and her guest. Her guest was the love of her life – a woman of Italian extraction.

Nikita had dropped off the radar about seven years ago. She had gotten her maths degree and tried to be an accountant but was soon bored of office life. As it turned out, she took herself off to France, working in a vineyard for a few years. She had an aptitude for languages and could speak French fluently in next to no time. Adding to her maths degree, she took a qualification to teach English as a foreign language and trekked off to West Africa teaching the kids English on The Ivory Coast. That's where she met her life partner, Florence, or 'Flo,' as she liked to be called. Flo had typical Latin looks; olive skin, dark hair, dark eyes and added sophistication to everything she said or did. She was a handsome woman with an androgynous look; the combat trousers and army boots didn't help to soften her appearance, but she wore a white vest top to show that she was all woman.

256

Nikita's look was equally striking. Her hair had been shaved at the sides, but the top was long, dyed red and hung over to one side. She was wearing a tie-dyed t-shirt, denim dungarees and a pair of well-worn black canvas Converse boots. She was still beautiful but out of reach. There were plenty of stories flowing from her and her partner. They had also taken the precaution of bringing their own food as they were both vegans.

All in all, Dan's Millennium party was looking to be a success; plenty of food, plenty of drink, and about thirty guests, all rubbing along together nicely.

It was almost too good to be true.

And that's because it was.

77

1999

As Millennium parties go, I'm sure this one wasn't a bad effort. Everything flowed, the drink, the food, the conversation. There was mingling and laughter, debate and understanding; all the elements of the party weaved together to form a warm atmosphere for everyone to enjoy. I was being swept along without much thought for anything but the moment. I hadn't even thought about my mother.

On Christmas day, I'd rung her house to wish her a merry Christmas and was confronted with a slurred reciprocation of the sentiment. I'd called at midday. I had to assume that either she was still drunk from the night before, or she had been downing vodka for breakfast. Either way, she had spent Christmas the way she always did, drunk as a skunk. I gave her no more thought. I'm sure she would have returned the favour too.

A few of us were heavily engaged in a conversation about wine. Dan's kitchen was almost as big as his lounge diner and had a six-seater table in the middle of the room. Nobody was sitting, we were all leaning against the oak units and marble topped counters. Dan had a cast iron wine rack filled with a variety of wines from a variety of countries. Regardless of how unimportant the item was, it had prompted a conversation between me, Dan, Nikita, Flo and Jon.

'So why do the bottles have to lie on the side?' Jon was asking. He claimed to be an expert on many things, and he was trying to say he knew a bit about wine but that had quickly become an error on his part.

'The cork had to be kept moist – if it dries out, the cork shrinks; if the cork shrinks, the air gets in and the wine spoils,' Nikita said, drawing on her experience at the vineyard.

'So why do these ones have dents in the bottom?' Jon had a bottle of supermarket wine in his hand. He had brought two bottles to the party. He had put his finger into the indentation by way of a demonstration.

'It's called *a punt*,' I said.

'A cunt!?' Jon mocked an outraged face and then descended into laughter at his own joke to which we collectively feigned smiles.

'No, no, that's you, Jon,' Dan was as sharp as ever.

It was at that point we started to laugh for real.

Jon was oblivious to the slight and continued with his exploration of all things wine related, the excess drink in his system clearly fuelling his quest.

'But what's it for?' Jon asked, again poking the dent.

'It's so the sediment in red wine can collect and doesn't get poured into the glass.' I had been on a wine course as part of my bar manager training.

'Oo, look at Jilly Cooper.' Another fall-flat joke.

'Do you write erotic fiction, Will?' Dan asked, again drawing laughter from the rest of the kitchen crowd.

'Not the last time I looked.' Dan and I high fived.

'No, no, no,' Jon tried to cut into the humour, 'that blonde woman with the posh voice, on that wine programme.'

'Yeah, that's Jilly Goolden, *not* Jilly Cooper.' Dan gave Jon a slap on the shoulder. 'Don't give up your day job, Jon. The world of comedy just isn't ready for you.'

I'm sure there would have been more poor-quality jokes had it not been for the doorbell ringing.

I heard the door opening; I heard voices pitched in surprise; I heard the door shut; and then I heard stiletto heels clipping against the mosaic tiled hallway.

There was a murmur amongst the guests: looks exchanged in bemused anticipation. Who could this be?

There could only be one answer.

There were introductions for the strangers, and hugs for those more familiar with the late arrival. I was the last of a long line.

'Oh my God, Will, how long has it been?' Jennifer hugged me tightly. It also seemed to be a longer hug than everyone else received.

'Too long,' I said, my mind had just been broadsided by a flotilla of battleships. Blown way was an understatement.

'You look so well – so handsome. Life must be treating you to some of the good stuff,' she beamed, her eyes not leaving mine for a second.

'I could say the same to you. You look... I don't know... incredible,' I stammered over the appropriate compliment. There were no words I could pull from my arsenal that would do her justice. Her flowing blonde hair hung perfectly, yet so naturally, cascading over her bare shoulders. The red party dress she wore left nothing to the imagination; off the shoulder, low-cut in the front, and high cut at the hem, showing three quarters of her slender, long thighs. She was already tall but three-inch heels brought us face-to-face, and that was how we stood now, face-to-face, so close I could feel the warmth of her breath on my lips.

'Thank you, Will, you've always been so sweet towards me. I've never thanked you for all those times you made me smile when I really didn't feel like smiling.' She leaned in and kissed me on the cheek.

All the feelings that I had forgotten about, all those heart-breaking moments in time that had been carved across my heart, they all came rushing back to me. But not to hurt me or to remind me of how lame I was to think that a girl – woman – like her could ever look at me, but instead it lifted me; focused me into thinking that maybe now was the time. Twenty-odd years of patience could potentially pay-off and I could be heading into the new millennium with a fresh perspective and renewed hope that I was worthy of all I had ever dreamed of. Was it too much to ask? I didn't think so.

I was about to rush into a million and one questions about her life and what she had been up to since I'd seen her last, but that was interrupted, briefly.

'Hi, Jen...nif...fer. How. Are. You?' Sarah staggered in. Dan had bought a case of Red Bull and two additional bottles of vodka. Sarah had apparently slammed down a few too many in a very short space of time. She could barely stand.

'Wow!' Jennifer said. It wasn't a sincere exclamation. It was, *'Oh my God, you are so drunk'* kind of *'wow!'*

'Wow?' Sarah probed. Her face screwed up in inebriated confusion.

'Yeah, Sarah – wow! I can't believe how great you look. You're beautiful. You always were, but now... Yeah, I think *wow* is the appropriate word.' Jennifer made a great save under pressure.

'Well... you look beaut... beau-ti-ful, too!' Sarah eyes were everywhere but the direction she was barely facing.

Dan had noticed the state of our mutual friend and sidled up to Sarah to put an arm around her waist to hold her up.

'Hold on there, girl, I think there's too much blood in your alcohol system,' Dan quipped.

'You... you're... always... fun-ny,' Sarah couldn't even keep her eyes open to speak.

Dan eased her into a chair at his kitchen table. She slumped forward, her head falling onto her arms.

'Did she just fall asleep?' Dan asked.

'It's your company, comrade – always stimulating,' I said, gazing down at our drunken friend and wondering how to deal with her.

Dan looked at his Tag Heuer watch. 'It's not even eleven. Shall we put her in my spare room?'

I nodded in agreement. I picked her up like I would pick up a baby. She was small enough and light enough – lighter than a beer keg – to be carried by one person. Dan led the way and we put her into a single bed in his office-cum-spare bedroom. A bucket was deposited at the side of the bed for the inevitable bout of vomiting.

Back downstairs, Jennifer and I carried on where we left off and had no more interruptions until the stroke of midnight. It was a perfect hour in perfect company. I didn't want it to end. And I think she felt the same way.

78

1999/2000

At five to midnight, I crept into the room where Sarah was sprawled out. She was still on her side, exactly the way we had left her, just in case she vomited in her sleep. I called her name quietly but there was no response. Deciding that sleep was probably for the best for her, I left the room, closing the door behind me.

Downstairs, Dan had poured flutes of champagne for everyone. The front door was open, and the TV was on. I grabbed a glass and leaned against the kitchen counter.

Jennifer sidled up alongside me glass in hand, a wry smile on her face.

'Are you ready for the new millennium?' she asked.

'As ready as I'll ever be. What about you?'

'This year will be a year of change, that's for sure.'

During our conversation, she had revealed her last few years and what she had been getting up to. She had worked as a personal assist for a businesswoman in London, living the highlife and all that it entailed. Jetting off to Florida, Dubai, Australia, wherever she needed to go, and most of her time was spent taking phone calls or making phone calls. The job could result in twenty-hour working days but there was often time to take in the surroundings. During her employment, Jennifer had earned a big bonus from her boss – a five figure bonus – and while it was a drop in the bucket by London standards, it had allowed her to buy two repossessed houses in Pembrokeshire. Over the next couple of years, she had managed to buy another two houses and rented them out for profit. While the money she earned from four rental properties was nowhere near the figure she earned as a P.A. she was able to build up a nest egg of money and buy houses at auction. She'd quit being a P.A. and turned to fulltime property development. With a property portfolio of four rental houses providing a stable residual income, she was able to buy, refurbish and sell on properties, furthering her income opportunities while growing a business. Jennifer was her own woman: her own boss. And it made her even more attractive. Not because she had money, but because she had a determined, confident spirit that was difficult to resist.

'What changes are you making?' I asked, casually hoping I could find a way in.

'I'm thinking of selling my rentals and developing a piece of land, putting ten to twelve houses on it and selling them on.' She was nodding as I watched the words fall from her perfect lips. It was mesmerising to hear her plans. But for all her apparent success, she had just moved back into a humble home in the middle of Milford. Yet another house purchased at auction.

'Sounds like a plan. Got any others?' I jested.

'Well.' She dropped her head slightly, gazing coyly at me. 'I'm standing next to you because I want to kiss you first at the stroke of midnight. Does that sound like a plan you'd want to be a part of?'

Speechless, I just nodded and downed the champagne I should have been saving for the clock chime. In life, there are many moments that seem too good to be true. If she kissed me, and kissed me like I always wanted her to, then it might be true. But one kiss was never what I wanted. I had dreamed my whole lifetime up until this point to have her as mine for the rest of my days. I was overthinking that, somehow, I'd misread the situation, or dreamed the whole thing up from a cocktail of alcohol and nostalgia, but there was another element of this scenario that hadn't been overlooked. Sarah.

The countdown had begun. I'd grabbed a spare flute of champagne and started to shout the backward count with my fellow revellers.

'Five!'
Would she really kiss me?
'Four!'
Was it going to be a friend's kiss?
'Three!'
Maybe a passionate kiss, who knew?
'Two!'

Was I overthinking the overthinking?

'One!'

Too late now.

'Happy New Millennium!' we yelled in unison.

There were hugs and kisses: words of gratitude and salutation. I didn't hear or see what the others did. I was too engaged with Jennifer. She had wrapped her long slender arms around my shoulders and pulled me close, placing her lips against mine, kissing me hard. I responded with the same. Lost in a moment I never wanted to end. I heard a single round of applause: one pair of hands clapping just a few feet away. Then another joined in, then another. Then a wolf whistle.

The kiss was interrupted. Jennifer and I opened our eyes, maintaining contact for a second before we turned to see a few of the guests applauding our moment of passion – Dan and Jon amongst them. Luckily, we could laugh about it. It was nice to have something to laugh about in that moment, because, like most things in my life, the happy moments didn't last long.

79

2000

The moments after midnight tumbled on, more drink, more chat, more food. Jennifer and I were in the kitchen nibbling on cheesy Doritos and ham sandwiches while sharing a bottle of wine and, more importantly, sharing time. We had exchanged a few kisses, had some tactile moments and generally seemed comfortable around each other. The level of involvement we shared left us in the dark as to who was still at the party and who had left.

Jon, of course, was still drinking and talking shit. He was sitting with Dave, Charlotte's husband, and boring the poor fella to tears with talk of architecture and his planned trip to the Southern Hemisphere. Charlotte and Tina were engaged in an in-depth conversation with Nikita and Flo, leaving Dan and Estelle looking a little too comfortable together on the sofa. The rest of the guests must have made their excuses and left already.

I nipped upstairs to check on Sarah; she hadn't moved a muscle and was snoring soundly. I figured she'd be good until the morning and left her to sleep it off.

Back in the kitchen I could see Jennifer had a frown on.

'What's up?' I asked.

She hooked a thumb at the doorway to the lounge where everybody else was. 'I think Jon has had too much to drink.'

'You think? I could have told you that about two hours ago,' I laughed, trying to make light of her concerns but I sometimes forget they had been in a relationship.

'He's telling old war stories: drunken fights and one-night stands. He's currently talking about the one you and he had when he cheated on me.' I could hear the disappointment in her tone.

'...anyway... me and Rob and Will... were fight... ting... there's blood...' Jon was rocking back and forth on the edge of the chair, as though sitting was a difficulty.

'Yeah, that was a long time ago – water under the bridge,' I said, interrupting the tale as I walked into the room.

'Like your jealousy,' Jon was able to string those words together. It was almost as if he'd practiced them a million times in the mirror.

'Relax, Jon, everything was like a million years ago. Nobody cares,' I kept my tone in check, but it still seemed loud as the room fell into silence.

'There's… lots of stuff people would… still care about if the truth came out,' he left quite a long pause between words, but no one was biting to take his bait. 'Eh, Tina? Lots of stuff…'

Tina said nothing, her face, grim, any joy from the party had instantly evaporated. I held my breath like I had done for the last thirteen years or so. I didn't know where he was going with his insinuation, but I knew Jon wasn't the kind of guy to give a fuck when he was sober. And he was a million miles away from that.

Whatever atmosphere there had been was now sucked out of the room. Jon's head was bobbing and weaving loosely on the stem of his neck, as though he was dodging punches. There were probably a few he deserved but nobody was moving to deliver them.

'What do you mean by that?' Dan's attention was on his very drunk school friend and no longer on the pretty girl sitting beside him.

'Oh… don't you know?' Jon started an over enthusiastic fake laugh. 'Ask your mum. Or maybe… ask him.'

Jon wagging finger was pointing straight at me.

'Mum? Will? What the fuck…?' Dan couldn't finish his question.

Whatever euphoria I had been feeling was now evaporating on the heat of my anger. Not just for Jon, but for myself too. I had gotten myself into the situation and had been burdened with the shame ever since. What Tina had felt, I never knew, but from the expression etched into her pretty face, I could see it wasn't far away from what I had felt.

267

Tina spoke first. 'Darling, he's drunk and doesn't know what he's saying. Thank you for a lovely evening but it's late and time to go.'

In unison, Tina, Charlotte and Dave, stood up.

'I know… what I'm saying… don't I, Will?'

'He *really* doesn't, darling,' Tina said, leaning to kiss her son on the cheek. 'Pay him no attention.'

The goodbyes were rapid and executed with precision, almost as quickly as the party's flavour had been tainted. The night was over.

80

2000

'Are you going to tell me what the fuck this is about, or what?' Dan had sobered up, significantly.

'There's nothing to tell,' I said, emphatically.

What I had to tell was the stuff of Freudian nightmares.

What was I going to say? Was I going to blurt out, *'Sorry, Dan, your mum popped my cherry, and we were doing it for a few months afterwards. No harm done?'*

'That's not the way Jon tells it.'

'The guy's drunk and looking for attention – who the fuck knows what's going on in his head.' I knew I didn't. It wasn't a case of what he knew; it was a case of *how* much he knew. There could have been a lot of guesswork involved, or he could have known all the sordid details. My mind was racing around all the houses, and no one was answering. The only solid thought I had was from the time when I had seen Jon coming out of Tina's armed with a video camera. I remember him saying that he was going to film himself shagging someone but, like so many other things that fell from Jon's gob, I thought it was bullshit. But he knew something.

Jon and the rest of the guests had left already. It was just me, Dan, Jennifer and the sleeping Sarah. And that was still two too many.

'I saw how my mum reacted. I saw how quickly she wanted to leave. I'll speak to her tomorrow, but you're here, now.' Dan wasn't letting it go. Who could blame him?

'Maybe we should speak tomorrow too – it's late – we've been drinking-' I didn't get to finish.

Dan slammed me into the protrusion that divided the room, his hands gripping my shirt. I could feel the spittle from his exposed teeth hit my cheek.

'You will tell me. NOW!'

Jennifer stepped in but I forced Dan away from me before she could get hurt in the melee. We grappled, we shoved. Dan threw a punch, but it only scraped the top of my head. He was off-balance by his over-extension, so I caught him easily on the chin with a straight right hand. He went down. Hard.

Stunned, but not unconscious, Dan looked up at me as if to ask why. I had no answer for him. We'd been friends all our lives and this was only the second time we had properly come to blows. And for what? Drunken ramblings of a guy from our past. What a fuck up.

'Speak to your mum. Speak to Jon. And when you've done that, then you can speak to me,' I pointed my instructions at him, pinning the words to him so he wouldn't forget.

With that I left, slamming the door behind me, raging into the cold morning air.

I'd barely travelled thirty yards or so when I heard the distinctive sound of clipping heels against paving slabs.

'Will, wait for me,' Jennifer insisted, tottering up behind me.

I shook my head in bewilderment at the night's events and she understood not to ask questions. Holding my hand, she walked alongside me, in silence, as I ran through the details in my head. This would need sorting out. But not now.

We ambled toward the end of The Rath, the muted sounds of parties continuing elsewhere in the town brought little comfort. This was supposed to be a new start – a new millennium. Initially, it had started so well. But, as with all things I'm involved with, it rapidly turns to shit and disorder.

'Are you going to walk me home?' Jennifer said. It was the first thing she'd said since catching up with me.

I smiled at her attempt to distract me. It was nice to have someone other than Sarah thinking of me for a change. I know that I'd given up thinking of myself. Days, weeks, months pass, and I was taking it all a minute at a time. But a minute like this – one where I seemed to be the focus – I wished I could savour for an eternity.

'Of course, I will. Where do you live?'

She laughed at my ignorance. We'd talk about all manner of things in the last few hours, but her address wasn't one of them. I had told her of the pokey bedsit I was renting on Hamilton Terrace, and how I didn't spend too much time sleeping there, more content to sleep on a shabby sofa in my office or in a vacant static caravan.

Jennifer was renovating a house at the end of Charles Street, opposite the police station. It wasn't too much of a detour.

She opened the front door to a stark contrast to Dan's well maintained detached house. The hallway was bare plaster and floorboards; the air was gritty and had the odour of fresh paint. A single lightbulb, harsh without a shade, cast shadows in all directions, illuminating the work in progress.

I was led into the kitchen. It was also halfway through a refitting. All the base cabinets and counters were in place; a microwave, toaster and kettle crammed into one corner. The wall units were still flat packed in boxes leaning against a shabby looking under-counter fridge.

'Do you want a coffee?' She asked, lifting two mugs from out of a cabinet.

'No.'

I didn't wait for further conversation.

I turned her to face me and kissed her hard. She responded, arms wrapping around me, tongue probing my mouth. Frantic; ardent; exquisite. I was lost to her. She was all I had ever wanted – needed – and in one of those moments I existed for, she was here driving the agenda. Flesh was exposed, gripped roughly, angrily. Teeth gnashed at bare skin; lips sucked; tongues tasted. Naked and unashamed, we lost ourselves to desire. The staggering, swaying love making started right there, in the kitchen, moving onto the sofa bed in the living room. Hours passed. Passion burned.

When the collapse came, the dawn light had started to show itself through the thin material adorning the windows, heralding the morning after the night before. The New Year started here, and I wasn't releasing my grip too easy.

2000

We dozed until noon, made love again, and parted ways. Jennifer saw me to the door, kissed me in the way I had always imagined she would, and left me to my hangover. As much as I had always wanted to be with her, make love to her, call her my girlfriend, there was one thing spoiling everything about this crazy turn of events.

Sarah.

I didn't want the scope of my life narrowed by the sensitivities of one of my best friends. But at the same time, I didn't want to alienate a friend, narrowing my social circle and cutting off the better portion of the support network I'd had for as long as I can remember.

I stood at the corner of Charles Street and North Road, debating with myself on which route to take back to Sarah's house. I could have nipped onto The Rath, but I didn't want to run into Dan. I wasn't ready for him yet. I would have to talk to Tina and Jon to see who knew what and why and find out how much I could or couldn't say. With any luck Jon knew fuck all and we could just move on with it being one of his egocentric bullshit stories. He was known to have a few. But Tina was likely to be caught in the direct firing line of whatever rumours had been spreading. I understand that she was complicit in the act, after all, she was the adult at the time, while I was barely anything, and just floating on the cusp of adulthood; my age of consent clasped in one hand and a beautiful willing woman in the other. It wasn't as if I was going to turn her down.

I headed down Pill Lane, taking the coward's way out.

I passed a few revellers still looking as though they were deep in the party mood and looking for another venue. My watch said it was mid-afternoon. Clearly, the millennium was running on.

I unlocked the backdoor and walked into warm moist air and the scent of strawberries. It was obvious that the shower had been on.

Heading toward the bedroom to grab my things, I stuck my head into the bathroom, but it was empty: the condensation thick, the air humid.

Pushing open the bedroom door, I was confronted by a naked Sarah.

'Oh my God, I'm so sorry,' I turned to walk out.

'Don't be daft,' she said, her voice raw. 'A week ago, I was bouncing on your cock. You've seen me naked before and you'll probably see me naked again.'

I didn't leave the room, but I did avert my eyes to give her some privacy.

'How are you feeling?' In my head – and judging by the sound of her voice – I figured she was going to be feeling rough.

'Like a dog's chew toy. How did I get so drunk?' She was sitting on the bed, a dressing gown barely covering her modesty.

'You were caning it back. What time did you get home?'

'I rocked up about half an hour ago. I thought I'd better make myself scarce. Dan was not best pleased.'

There could have been any number of reasons why Dan was angry – I could guess at the main reason – but I thought I'd allow her to tell me what's what.

'I vomited on his floor and in his bed. Then I was expecting it to be rag week in a few days, but I came on in the bed too – hence the shower,' she said, open armed as if to prove her cleanliness. 'Someone had also spilled red wine on his beige carpet. But I think the main reason he was pissed off was because of you.'

I paused to let her continue but nothing was forthcoming.

'Did he say why?' I figured she would know.

'Did you sleep with Tina?'

I had avoided that question for so long. I had felt it coming for years, chasing me down, every so often getting close enough that I could feel its breath on my neck, but I always managed to evade it. But here I was, not exactly cornered, but in a position I didn't want to be in with a person who I thought might understand. There was too much alcohol, too little sleep, and too many life-changing events running riot

273

through my brain for me to think my way out of this. Fight or flight? Parry or evade?

'What did he say?'

'He said you might, or might not have, shagged his mother. He didn't say much more than that.' Her eyes were all over me. I wasn't sure if it was in judgement or if the booze was finding fault she had never seen in me before.

'I need to speak to Tina and Jon before I speak to him. I imagine he's going to do the same too,' I said.

'So, did you do it, did you shag his mum?' She said it as if she was asking me if I ate the last biscuit in the pack; a little judgement, a little pissed off, but nothing serious.

An age past without a word being uttered; I couldn't think how to answer and make it sound less than it was.

'So, you did?' Sarah said, eventually.

'Why do you say that?'

'It takes a nanosecond to say "No" when you haven't done something. You haven't said No – you haven't said anything, and that tells me you did it. You don't have to be a mind reader or a psychologist to know that.' The disappointment in her voice was tangible.

Half a lifetime away but somehow it had caught up with me – caught up with Tina. It was foolish to think that I had the shit end of this deal. I was the teenage virgin popping his cherry with the first female to say ok, and she was the mother of the friend of that teenager and would now have to answer for why she thought it was such a spiffing plan to deflower a skinny sixteen-year-old. It was such a fuck up.

'I'm not going to talk about this now. I need to get my head straight. I've got to-'

'Oh. My. God! It's all about you, isn't it?' She let her hurt out with a yell. 'If you thought about other people for a change then maybe this shit wouldn't happen. You make mistakes and other people get

274

hurt as a consequence. For once in your fucking life, think about the other person.'

She wasn't wrong but I wasn't going to give her a free pass.

'You know the shit I've had to put up with. You know that if I didn't think of myself nobody else would. I know I've fucked up but now is not the time or the place to talk about it, ok?'

'Well maybe it's not but you're gonna have to deal with it, and soon. And you are *not* the only person to think about you. I've been looking after you for as long as I can remember, and I get very little in return. You're a selfish fucking bastard, Will Taylor, and you don't deserve me, sometimes.'

The truth of her feelings was threatening to overwhelm the argument. The hurt in her tone stung me like little barbs of hate; all the wrongs I had done unto her were being returned, sharpened, and thrown with more force.

'I'm not going to-'

'You're not going to *what,* deal with this? Talk about it because it makes *you* uncomfortable?' She wasn't backing down. 'Well let's all do what Will wants, shall we?'

'I'm out of here.' I resisted defending myself. Instead, I grabbed my holdall and headed for the door.

'Oh, where are you going – are you running back to Jennifer?' Venomous fury flowed into the room.

I paused. I wanted to say so much – too much – but I held my tongue. Nothing valuable is ever said in the heat of an argument. I guess she knew about last night: about Jennifer. It saved me the job of explaining, although, I wondered how she knew.

She told me anyway.

'Yes, I know. Dan said you two were cosy last night, and here you are, standing in my bedroom – the bedroom you fucked me in, less than a week ago – and you're stinking of your sex with her. I can smell that bitch on your skin.' She was on the brink of tears, but she held them back, unlike the words she threw out. 'Get the fuck out! Get the fuck out of my house and never come back.'

275

I left, her hatred ringing in my ears. What a complete fuck up of a life – my life. Why did I expect anything different?

82

2000

My eyes flickered open: my brain tried to register where I was. Of course, I knew in a moment. I dragged myself upright, sitting on the battered sofa in my office instead of lying on it, which seemed to be my preferred use of that piece of furniture. I had spent the first week of the new millennium living in the office with the occasion shift behind a bar, somewhere on the park.

The first day of the new millennium had started well, was shit in the middle, and then got predictably worse.

Instead of a day of recovery and reflection, I was called up and dragged into work. One of my bar supervisors – the one covering for me – had downed too much vino at a party and ended up in hospital having their stomach pumped. As bar staff professionals, we are supposed to advise customers to drink responsibly and refuse service to those who seem incapable of making decisions about their own welfare. Unfortunately, us bar staff professionals, me included, are not too clear on the rules that govern us. Often, we break the guidelines we are supposed to adhere to. So, as fragile as I was, I had to go into work, and I'd been there ever since.

I had tried to call Jennifer but the mobile phone I had just purchased didn't have signal in the park. I was able to walk out to the main road and pick up one bar of signal but that wasn't enough to make a call. I sent a text instead. My first text to Jennifer was my first text to anyone. Mobile phones were the current revolution, but I had resisted until a few months ago because of all the confusion over the notorious Millennium Bug.

The text I received back wasn't what I had hoped for or expected.

My phone – a chunky little Nokia – only had a dozen numbers stored into its memory. Dan's, Sarah's, and Jennifer's – which had only been input at the party – and the rest were work colleagues and my boss. I know Jennifer didn't have a landline available to her; she had told me the constant moving house was a nightmare in terms of communication. Also, because calling a mobile from a landline incurred massive charges, I was reluctant to break the company policy on phone usage. It was texts or nothing if signal was going to be an issue.

I'd sent a brief message in the best text speak I knew.

> *ME: 'Hi Jennifer how R U? It was gr8 meeting up with U and I can't wait 2 C U again. Give me a call when U can. Will X.'*

It was the buzz of the phone that stirred me from a booze induced slumber. A week after the party – three days after I had sent my text – I was still hoping for a positive reply. I wasn't about to have my wish granted. Why would I expect anything different?

> *JENNIFER: 'Hi Will. It was great seeing you too. Unfortunately, I spoke to Sarah, and she told me about you two. I didn't know you were more than just friends. I think we made a hasty mistake and got caught up in spirit of the New Year. I'm sorry. I hope we can still be friends. Bye. Jennifer x.'*

I dreaded to think what Sarah had told her. How much venom – how much exaggeration – would be wrapped around the story Sarah told Jennifer.

I had been obsessed with one woman for as long as I could remember. Also, one woman had been obsessed with me for as long as she could remember. These two women were friends. It seemed their loyalty to each other was greater than my lifelong desires. My life was like the plotline of a piss poor soap opera. I wished I could just flick a

278

switch and switch it off, but I couldn't. Alcohol and work were my only distractions. I put my faith in them to see how far it would get me. Not far it would seem. Not far at all.

83

2000

Days tumbled into weeks, and the weeks tumbled by rapidly. Before I had time to breathe, it was the first event on the calendar that we would make a special effort for. St Valentine's Day.

So far, the new millennium had been a blast, and not in a good way.

For a start, Jennifer had stuck to her guns on our just being friends and declined any conversation to the contrary. It felt like I had just climbed Everest and some shitty Sherpa had dragged me back down to base camp before I set my boot upon the summit. I'd been shown the prize but hadn't been allowed to take it home. Most of my texts went without reply. Regardless of how it appeared, rejection was rejection.

Also, I couldn't speak to Dan anymore. His employers and his mother said he had gone travelling. Tina hadn't spoken to him since the party, but a text had been sent to say he was going to Australia to put some distance between him and the situation and that he would be in touch. The *Dan and Will* travel plan had been put into action minus the 'Will' part. My rejection had guilt for company, and they were not the most agreeable bedfellows.

And the worst – and I never thought this would be the worst – was the break in contact with Sarah. She had blanked me. I called, I texted, and I even knocked on her door. She didn't want to see me. I was all at sea without the people I had grown up with. Seeking solace with the people I worked with was ok, but it wasn't the same. I couldn't rely on Nikita as she had gone back to Africa and all her communication seemed to be in the form of Airmail. There were no instant answers to be found via Airmail. And I definitely didn't want any contact with Jon. It was his big mouth that started this rift, so I figured anything that spilled from his gob was likely to be bullshit or bravado, or both.

I sat on the sofa in my office, blowing up pink balloons for the Valentine's Special we had planned for the owners. There was nothing overly romantic about pink balloons, chocolate hearts and a glass of Buck's Fizz, while an endless playlist of love songs blasted out of the speakers in a tardy bar. If I was being honest, it was just a night out with glitter and false expectation.

My morning was all prep work. I had a box of chocolate hearts, half a box of party poppers, two cases of cheap Buck's Fizz and a million balloons with love heart messages embossed on them. It was cheap and tacky romance at a cheap and tacky venue for cheap and tacky people. Between the squealing of the helium canister, I was catching the tunes playing on Radio One. They say that music can lift your spirits. It can. It can also send you down the spiralling rabbit hole of oblivion if the tune playing exaggerates the bad mood brewing. A current dance tune was lifting my general apathy with its simple beat and lyrics, but it was swiftly followed by She's the One from Robbie Williams, the sadness of the tune dragged my tolerance down and I was back where I started. And as if to add insult to injury, the next track was the Euro-crap hit by Eiffel 65: Blue. I felt that stamping on the radio, smashing the irritatingly shit noise from its circuits, would not have been an overreaction.

I switched the frequency to Radio Two and was greeted by the comforting sound of Glen Campbell and The Wichita Lineman. It wasn't my usual taste, but it was a song my grandmother used to play, reminding me of a time when life was simple.

Once again, all was right with the world.

Such was my life; it didn't last very long.

The phone in my office started to ring. I never received calls in the morning unless it was a problem or the drayman. I wasn't expecting either.

'Hello?' Outside lines were a rarity to my office landline.

I was asked a question.

'Yes, I am William Taylor,' I answered the question.

281

I listened to the police officer at the other end of the line. My day at work ended abruptly. The news was a shock but not really a surprise. My mother was dead.

84

2000

She wouldn't have felt a thing, they said. It would have been over very quickly, they said. It was just an accident, they said. They said a lot of things: none of it of any consequence. My mother was dead. Fallen down her own staircase – drunk – bashing her head in on the door frame at the foot of the stairs. She was 56 years old. She looked 76 years old.

According to the coroner's office and the police report, my mother had lain at the foot of her stairs for about two weeks. There wasn't much left to identify so I had been spared that task. The neighbours were alerted, not only because of the increased numbers of blow flies inhabiting Trafalgar Road in February, but because of the swarm of blow flies attached to the glass panel in the front door. The neighbour who raised the alarm, had no sense of tact or decorum and quite happily told me he could hear the buzzing through the walls.

With nothing but my dark sense of humour for company, I joked to myself that at least the flies had had a meal, and most probably a drink too, which is more than I ever got while she was alive. That was changing now she was dead.

As her only living relative, the only child of an only child, I stood to inherit the house my grandmother had left her when she died twenty-something years ago. As much as I wasn't looking forward to the prospect of owning a property that had only bad memories for me, the idea of being a homeowner before my thirtieth birthday without ever having a mortgage, seemed like something I could accept.

Once the dust had settled and everything had been sorted out, I would be living rent free in a two-bedroom house, instead of paying 200 quid a month for a box with a toilet. No doubt, I would probably spend most of my nights curled up on my office sofa, slowly crippling my back and eroding my self-worth. And that was on a good day.

The last week had been a bit of a blur. From the time of the phone call to the morning of the funeral, I thought I'd made the jump to light speed. Those seven days had flashed by so quickly I could barely recall what had happened. I knew the bullet points but that was it. Luckily, I had a bit of money saved up and could afford half of the funeral costs. After a quick scoot around my mother's house, I found a few hundred quid stashed under her bed, in her old coffee jar and in a handbag buried at the bottom of her wardrobe. Using what I had, what I had found, and some money loaned from the bank, I was able to arrange a cremation. I didn't want a grave to visit. There was no point in me standing next to a headstone, occasionally placing flowers and trying to remember the good times.

There were no good times.

There were no good memories.

On my days in limbo, I spent hours going through cupboards and drawers and old boxes, looking for anything that might prove me wrong about my mother's complete disregard for her only offspring. What I did find surprised me.

At the top of the landing was a cupboard filled with junk she had been saving up or was too lazy to get rid of. I found an old record player fitted with a round pin plug. It looked like a small suitcase when shut, covered in a shabby pale blue material, two clasps on one side and a full-length hinge on the other side. Inside the box, with the turntable, were bundles of letters, each tied with a ribbon – like something out of a Jane Austen novel. The letters received were from an old boyfriend, a Danish fisherman. Beautifully handwritten messages of love and longing from a man who had met a woman he truly cared for. Such heartfelt words, carefully crafted, from a man whose first language was not the one the words were written in.

There was something else I noticed. The record player had been near the top of the stack of junk. There was dust and cobwebs throughout the cupboard, but that record player was dust free. That said to me it was removed and looked through on a regular basis; maybe recently.

284

One of the bundles had a familiar smell about it.

Vodka.

The letters in that bundle were dirty; the pages so thin they felt like tissue. I didn't need forensics to tell me these letters were read and reread, repeatedly. The words inside were an indication of why my mother was so fucked in the head; why life was cheap to her. They were rejection letters. There was love woven into the words, but words of regret and sadness all the same. The regret was about a child – a child born out of wedlock – a boy child, born in 1970.

I was that child. These letters were from my father. The man I had heard about but never seen.

Digging through the cupboard, I found a shoebox buried under a mountain of old shit. Inside were a hundred letters – never addressed, never sent. They were all written by my mother saying the same thing in as many ways as possible. Saying that she wanted to be loved and wanted him to come back and see the child he had sired. In several there were photos.

I'd never seen any of the images before. Some were of me. Some were of me and my mother. She looked happy – smiling – young – pretty – all the things I could no longer remember her being. All the memories were blotted out by her contempt for me.

I raked through box after box looking for something else; looking for a hope that somewhere there might be a reason tied up with string, some kind of indication of why this woman who could write such words of love, as well as inspiring love from another, would lose that feeling for the flesh and blood whom she had given birth to.

It wasn't to be found.

What I did find was a photograph.

The image was of a tall, rugged looking man, wearing jeans, a beige thick-knitted sweater and fisherman's boots. He had mid-brown hair – like mine – large round eyes – like mine – and a cheery smile. The backdrop to the picture was Milford docks, the fish market clearly visible. I suspected that mother may have taken the picture. There was a name written on the back in blue biro: *Carl Bruun.*

Amongst the boxes of old ornaments and junk, I found an empty picture frame; a double one that would close with a clasp but could be opened to show two photos. I placed the picture of the man I believed to be my father and a picture of my mother holding me into the frame, resting it on the mantelpiece in the front room: images of a happy family never to be.

From then on, I stared at that picture every single time I came into the house and pondered on the 'What ifs.' I stared at the frame for the longest time just before I left to go to the funeral. Newings, the local undertaker, pulled up in the narrow road: hearse at the front, family car at the rear. I was alone in the family car. That's all that was left of her family. Just me.

The slow drive to the crematorium seemed to never end. All I could do was sit and contemplate the possibilities of how I would move forward. I also thought about the prospect of being the only one at the service, but that was soon short-lived. As the short convoy pulled up, I could see a few people milling around; dressed in black and smoking cigarettes. A dozen men and a couple of women, around the same age as my mother, parted to allow the vehicles to pull into the covered entrance. I recognised some of the male faces as men who would be found sharing a bed with my mother when the drink had gotten the better of them. One of the men, Graham, I remembered him as he was in a rush to get away, way back when I was but a teenager. I could recall him placing a wedding band back on the third finger of his left hand as he scrambled out the door.

He still had the ring on that finger. I could see it as he clutched the hand of his wife, comforting her as she cried. I wondered how many tears she would have shed if she had only known the truth. Maybe she already did. Who knew?

The real surprise for me was standing back, away from the rest of the mourners. Sarah and Jennifer were dressed in almost identical long black coats; both sombre faced and yet beautiful.

As much as the day was not something to be enjoyed, it lifted my mood to see them there. The service was short – a few words, two hymns, and the Lord's Prayer – fifteen minutes of recognition for a woman who had been barely sober long enough to recognise her own self.

With the service over, I stood at the end of the flower gallery, waiting for people to pay their respects. The men shook my hand. The women kissed my cheek. Sarah and Jennifer hugged me, kissed my cheek and said nothing.

I was informed of a small wake being held at my mother's local and that I was welcome to attend. I'm sure she would have approved, but there should have been a wake in all the other pubs she frequented; The Victoria, The Kimberley, The Three Crowns. In fact, every pub in town could have raised a glass in remembrance to her.

I politely declined and went back to my bedsit where I sent texts to both Sarah and Jennifer, thanking them for attending. I didn't receive a reply from either.

I had found myself alone in the world. I had brought it all upon myself. Some lessons were hard to take. I would take mine in a shot glass, neat.

2000

In the two weeks following the funeral I had spent my days working at the holiday park and my evenings clearing crap out of my mother's house. I was still waiting on all the legal mumbo jumbo to be sorted out, not believing that the house was going to be mine until I had to sign for the deeds. I'd scraped together some more cash and threw it at a solicitor to do all the leg work. I figured it to be an investment. Once I stopped paying rent – the biggest chunk of my monthly outlay – I would be far better off; a few hundred quid to a crook in a suit seemed like small potatoes in the grand scheme.

After a particularly nondescript day at the pumps, my colleague, and lift, Jason, dropped me at the bottom end of Trafalgar Road. It was pushing 7pm, I was hungry and the smell of chips wafting up from the Haven Fish Café was often overpowering. I grabbed a large bag of chips and gravy before wandering up to *my* house to continue packing up fifty-odd years' worth of shit and clutter.

I had a lager from the fridge and sprawled out on the sofa, the aroma of the chippy tea overcoming the scent of decomposition that still lingered. I popped on the TV to find an episode of A Question of Sport had just started. I didn't go much on sport but the banter between John Parrot and Ali McCoist was quite entertaining. Once I'd finished my food, I sank another can of lager, then another. And then another. The sport quiz had run on to a crime programme with Sue Lawley and, because I didn't watch EastEnders, I flicked over to watch University Challenge. No boxes were being packed tonight. For the first time ever, I seemed to be relaxed within the four walls that had held so much pain and dread for me. I was beginning to realise that the trauma wasn't in the bricks and mortar, it was in the memories I had forced upon me by my alcoholic mother.

As I reclined against the moth-eaten cushions I remembered from my childhood, my gaze drifted from the TV to the picture frame on the mantelpiece. The shifting light of the screen, the only source of light in the room, illuminating the tattered photos I had placed behind glass. The 'what ifs' bounced around the room with the reflected light, caught in the shabby woodchip wallpaper like echoes from the past: a past that never was. The contrast of light and shadow became almost a comfort and, before I knew it, I'd fallen asleep.

The dawn's dim arrival was enough to shake me from the slumber I had been lost to. I squinted at my watch in the half light, pressing the button to illuminate the screen. It was 6:43am. I had about an hour and a half to get back to my bedsit, wash, change and be ready to be picked up to start another day.

I was putting on my shoes when I heard the post drop onto the floor, the postman clattering the rusty front gate on his way up the street. More junk mail, I figured. Everyday something new landed onto the not-so-welcome mat.

I shuffled out, my back in spasm after a crippling night on the fifty-year-old sofa in my mother's old front room. It wasn't half as comfortable as the one in my office. Maybe there was something to be said for cheap modern furniture.

Amongst a few bills, a bank statement and circular from the Reader's Digest – all addressed to my mother – was an envelope addressed to me. The handwriting was familiar.

There was something inside other than a letter.

I tipped out the contents onto the semi-circular metal and glass table in the hallway. The item was wrapped in a note written on lined paper, the perforated edge facing me. Unfurling the note, the item fell with a soft clunk to the glass topped table. I read the note first.

> *Hi,*
> *It's yours! I'm keeping it.*
> *How much you want to be involved is up*
> *to you.*
> *Call me.*

I read the name signed at the bottom of the note. Again, I reread the note and looked at the item, then went back to the note before finally picking up the plastic tube from the table.

It was a pregnancy test: two blue lines showed in the little window, confirming conception. It seemed that fate – and sexual stupidity – had chosen the next move of my life. I wasn't sure if I was ready, but in this situation, who was?

86

2000

The few months that followed on from the doorstep revelation had become a blur. Things were moving fast, faster than I would have liked, in fact, faster than was normal in anyone's eyes, for sure. On the 29th of February I found out I was going to be a father. By the middle of June, I was married: a small registry office affair with a small gathering of friends and family.

There was one friend who wasn't there – the friend I would have asked to be my best man in a heartbeat – Dan.

Dan had been declared missing in April. Almost four months of no contact would do that. Tina had started the ball rolling when she still hadn't had any contact from her son by February. The process was a bit more complicated than a quick call to the police when the missing person had been planning to go travelling for some time. After a lot of nagging and pleading, Tina managed to get the police to open an investigation into her son's whereabouts.

I was interviewed for an hour in the comfort of my own home. But there was nothing comfortable about it. It had been noted by the investigating office – a DCI Watts – that I had been interviewed about the disappearances of my other missing friends too. The fact was they were my friends, it seemed logical that I would be interviewed about them. I also added that with so many of them disappearing, I was waiting for my turn to come and that I'd probably be found dumped in a hole somewhere. Watts didn't like that comment and I regretted it the second it fell out of my mouth. His tone took on a more severe turn, and his line of questioning changed as though there was a crime scene he'd just walked from, and I was sitting there covered in blood. After a significant grilling, they left, and I never heard from them again. I did, however, discover that Dan's passport had never been used and there was never a booking in his name to fly to Australia, or anywhere, for that matter.

He might have been missing but he never got far.

Maybe like Rob. Maybe like Tom.

Whatever happened between me and Dan, and whatever betrayal I had dropped on him, I still missed his presence. I missed his rapier sharp sense of humour and how he could turn any situation into a dark humour moment, no matter how sad or sick it was.

I'd lost my best friend, my best man, and the first person I would have asked to be a godfather to my unborn child.

Being a parent scared the shit out of me. I had sleepless nights thinking about how badly I would perform. My only parental example was a complete fuck-up, leading me to believe that was a complete fuck-up too. The way I acted when around other people who cared about me, I was inclined to agree wholeheartedly with that prognosis. I was going to be shit as a father and shit as a husband. For the last few years, I had dreamed about finding a sense of normality in life, finding a purpose, a path. I had believed that family life would be the making of me.

How wrong could I get it? I had everything I ever wanted under one roof; a beautiful wife; a child on the way; and it didn't feel like enough. Or maybe *enough* wasn't the right word.

Maybe I wasn't enough. Who knows? I know I didn't. My life was the self-destructive mess it had always been. And that's how it continued.

Present Day

'Daniel James. Twenty-nine-years-old. Last seen on New Year's Day, 2000,' Delgado announced, dropping the file onto the plastic topped table of the Burger King that had become their eatery of no choice.

'We've got our victims. Now all we need is our killer.' Brooks sipped on his scalding coffee.

'We may already have him.' Delgado started flicking through the handwritten notes, looking for a smoking gun.

Brooks chuckled. Brooks didn't do levity often, but this was a gallows humour moment. He knew where his colleague was going before Delgado could thumb his way into the centre of the dog-eared file. In small town killings, the killer was often known to the victim. And not always as people passing each other daily; sometimes the killer was an integral part of the victim's life, often a friend or relative. There was no real mystery to murder. There was a necessity on the killer's part and the victim's death was the result of that necessity. To the real friends and family, it was an enigma. To psychologists and criminologists, it was routine. The difficult part was figuring out the necessity and following the evidence to its natural conclusion. Murder was seldom without reason and the reason would only be important to the killer.

Delgado stopped at the page he had been looking for.

Brooks spoke without looking down at the page. 'So, did Mr William Taylor get into a fight with Mr James on the day in question, like he did with the other two before they disappeared?'

The wry smile on Delgado's lips was confirmation enough. They had their number one suspect, and they already knew he wasn't telling them the truth.

Present Day

It was nearly that date again: St Valentine's Day. For as long as I could remember I would always be prepping for an event that celebrated the love people shared, whether it was new or old; from first sparks to the enduring end.

And here I was being a hypocrite to all the sentiment I used to tape to walls, sprinkle on tables, and profess to visiting patrons back when I had a job.

I had visited a card shop and a supermarket. The supermarket to buy a simple card and gift to give to my wife, as expected, and the card shop to buy something a little more special, plus the nice wrap, ribbon and gift bag that would adorn the gift I had purchased for my lover.

I'd been living two lives for so long; I didn't know where one life ended, and the other began. My dual existence had become so fluid that I couldn't see the joins anymore. As soon as I stepped outside my front door, I was a different man. I was, Will, the reason for another's joy; sharing a love that faced many challenges, but we were in it together to the bitter end.

Behind the door I was, Will, Dad, husband, or whatever title fitted the role I was masquerading in. The black hole of my marriage had sucked me in, and its gravity kept me where I hated to be. I was one row from leaving forever. But that row never came. There was no anger or complacency directed at me. It was as though every action was steered toward keeping me captive. No escape seemed possible from the singularity of my marriage.

But now there were other things to worry about, things much bigger than my life, and how fucked up it was. My constant grabbing for tiny slices of joy, thrown down from my master's table, would have to stop, for now. There was a storm coming. The blackening clouds of a police investigation were threatening to engulf my pathetic little world, and there was nothing I could do.

Back at my empty house I prepared the two sets of gifts, safe in the knowledge that my wife and daughter would not be home any time soon. They were off at a spa day: my daughter's gift to her mother. Her connections in the beauty business were wide and varied, proving to be quite fortuitous at times. The good fortune fell on me also. I was able to gift wrap an expensive necklace without being disturbed.

My mind was already a constant disturbance. As luck – or the lack of it – would dictate, St Valentine's Day was also the anniversary of the discovery of my mother's death. Those twenty years had passed by without so much as a backward glance. Had the spiteful old bitch been more of a mother, I might have mourned for her. Maybe this was why I was so incapable of accepting love from someone like my wife. I felt the closeness, but not the need. I wanted love, but I couldn't find a way to express it. It was as though there was a gene missing from my biology and I had inherited it from a woman who loved drink more than she could ever love her son.

Another chance was what I needed. Whether I would have it or not would be decided over the course of the next few weeks, months, or however long it took to investigate the crimes in my hometown. I knew I would be subject to more police grilling. My conscience felt the guilt my tongue wouldn't speak.

I think the investigating officers knew this too. That's why they came to me first.

89

Present Day

I'd never been in a police station before, but it was exactly how I imagined it would be: high-counter custody desk, pale blue walls and lots of doors to various unseen rooms. Officer Delgado was leading the way to one such room.

I took a perch on a chrome framed chair, Delgado sitting directly opposite. I placed the coffee I had been given in front of me, contemplating what I was going to be asked. Before any questions were asked, the officer told me, quite informally, exactly what was going to happen. The interview was going to be recorded on audio because they didn't have a significant witness suite available and couldn't video record my questioning. There was CCTV but it couldn't record the audio and was told to respond to the questions as though the camera wasn't there at all.

Informal or not, it didn't make the process any easier to swallow.

We sat making small talk about my trip to Haverfordwest. He asked about the traffic; I said I took the bus. Other than a brief discussion about the terrible weather we'd been having and the news about the Chinese virus, we didn't say much else.

Apart from the mock chestnut desk and the pale blue walls, my eyes fell to my watch more often than was reasonable. I'd been sitting across from the Hispanic Valley boy for almost ten minutes before his colleague entered the room. I wasn't sure if it was police procedure or an interview technique to make me nervous. I was sitting in a police interview room; I was already nervous.

DCI Brooks entered the room, closing the door behind him. 'Sorry to keep you Mr Taylor, I'm sure you can appreciate things are a little crazy at the moment.'

The man seemed distracted, like he didn't want to be there. I wasn't sure if this was more underhand interview witchcraft or just his general demeanour.

'Do you mean in regard to this case, or in the wider world?' I don't know why I was responding but my brain was going into full-on anxiety chatter mood. If I didn't watch my own mouth, I was likely to confess to anything just to get out of the room.

'Both.' Brooks replied, the hard stare that followed indicated that the small talk was over.

He switched on the recording device and stated his name, his colleague did the same and then gestured to me to do the same. Brooks then stated the date and the reason for the interview.

'As you are aware, Will – may I call you *Will*?'

I nodded.

'As you are aware, Will, three bodies were recovered from one of the buildings on the old M.O.D. site near Blackbridge, in Milford Haven, over a week ago. We've had the identities of all three confirmed and the next of kin have been informed. We've already established that all three were known to you but, as part of our ongoing investigation, we would like to explore your relationship with the deceased so that we may be able to build up a picture of their last known movements. Does that make sense?'

I nodded again.

'For the benefit of the recording, Mr Taylor is nodding,' Delgado added, his stiff smile indicating it would be better if I spoke my answers instead of him filling in the dead air.

'Yes, it makes sense,' I replied, just to let them know that I was getting with the programme.

'Good.' The tone of his voice wasn't selling 'good' as part of his patter. 'At the time of our last – informal – meeting we informed you that we had identified two of the persons as Robert Sherman and Thomas Magee. We can now confirm the third person as one Daniel James. Can you confirm that you were familiar with Mr James?'

I nodded.

'For the benefit of-' Delgado started, but I finished.

'Yes!' I blurted out, remembering my place. 'Yes, I am familiar with Daniel James.'

There was a long moment before another word was uttered.

'You don't seem that surprised that Mr James is the third body. Why is that?' Delgado asked.

It was obvious to me, and I guessed it would be obvious to anyone else, including the police why I wouldn't seem surprised. My mind was awash with the potential scenarios the investigating team were theorising, but still I was able to think clearly enough to answer and not place myself at the top of their suspect list, yet.

'Dan – Mr James – has been missing for twenty years. If three of my friends go missing and you tell me two of the bodies are my friends, I'm naturally going to assume who the third one is. If there was an unnamed body found in the area, there would be a lot of people jumping to that conclusion too, don't you think?'

'Indeed,' Brooks said. 'Do you have any thoughts on how three of your friends happened to have met their end?'

I pondered my response for a moment – long enough to give a reasonable answer but not too long that the officers would think I was constructing one out of thin air.

'I have absolutely no idea of what happened, or who would do such a thing.' While the first part of the statement was true, the second part, not so much. 'These were my friends. I can tell you how they lived but not how they died.'

'Well, let's take them one by one and see where it takes us. Is that ok with you?'

I responded positively and opened myself to three hours of questioning. Every possible nook and cranny of my life was ripped apart and exposed to police scrutiny, and yet I still had to dance around my darkest secrets, not wishing to shine a light on anything that could be a potential motive. By the end of it, I was convinced I'd be convicted, regardless of what could be proven or not.

90

Present Day

'Am I under suspicion?' I yelled the question at the officers, spittle landing on the desk between us. I had been asked and re-asked the same questions repeatedly. The same questions they had asked me in my own home. I knew they were doing their job, but I felt like they were pinning all their hopes on me. To their minds, I was in the frame.

'We need to establish the events leading up to the murders and we need to be thorough. And I won't lie to you – your direct relationship, and the disagreements you had on the nights in question do not absolve you from any involvement. You were very much involved – by your own admission – in the events of said nights. How would it look to you if you were sitting this side of the desk?' Brooks' volume was restrained, but I could tell he could blow at any minute.

'Are you going to arrest me? Are you going to charge me? Should I be heading for the border right now? Hire a lawyer? You tell me – what is going on here?' I dropped my pitch down to match the investigating officer's.

'For now? No. We still need to talk to the other people in your friendship group, including your wife. Is there anyone else you can suggest?'

'What, and put them through this, I don't think so.'

'Mr Taylor, there had been three incidents to which you have been directly involved in. You are a significant witness in this case, and we would not be doing our jobs correctly if we did not investigate you thoroughly. We're a little behind the times here – thirty-plus years in one instance – and we need to be on the same page as the killer. Do you understand?'

I nodded and then I saw Delgado take a sharp intake of breath as if he was about to speak. Beating him to the punch, I said, 'Yes.'

Brooks looked at his watch and terminated the interview.

'You are free to go.'

The superior officer led me to the exit, opening the door for me, the bright sunshine a glaring contrast to the dim interior.

'We'll be in contact, soon,' Brooks said.

I nodded. There was no recording out here.

But before he closed the door, he said something odd.

'I'm sure you wish to know who stabbed your friends, don't you?'

'Yes,' I said.

'Unfortunately, this is part of the process. Good day, Mr Taylor.'

He closed the door before I could respond. I walked to the bus stop; my brain fried from the interrogation. I could tell I was their number one suspect. Why wouldn't I be?

91

Present Day

Brooks strolled into the small canteen area where Delgado had already boiled the kettle and prepared two mugs. There would be a quiet debrief over a coffee before moving on to their next witness.

'What did you make of that?' Delgado knew most of what was to come but he also knew his boss would want to verbalise it for his own benefit.

Brooks slammed his file onto the desk and slumped into a chair. 'He's hiding so much.'

'Agreed.' Delgado placed a mug of steaming coffee in front of his colleague, taking the seat opposite. 'Do you think he's guilty?'

'He's guilty of something. Whether it's murder – one, or all of them – remains to be seen. Where's your head at?'

'He's overly evasive which suggests he has something to hide. Is it relevant to the case? Who knows? But his story is consistent which suggests he believes what he's telling us. We're going to have to rattle a few more cages before we go back to that one.'

Brooks agreed with his younger colleague. The witness was skirting so many facts it had to be deliberate. And while the story was consistent, Brooks also knew this to be true of well-rehearsed cover stories. If anyone had been telling the same lie for thirty years, the line between the fact and the fiction would inevitably become blurred to the point where the lie became the new truth. Cross examination, even in the early stages of an investigation, would often reveal inconsistences that could be exploited later as more evidence and witness statements are gathered. Will Taylor's story, although evasive, was rock solid.

It didn't mean it was the truth, but it was a truth that he himself believed and there would need to be a defining piece of evidence to crack his story. Brooks believed for every question the witness had answered there were at least two new questions generated.

They needed to allow the witness to sweat before he changed the status officially to suspect.

'There was one thing that's bothering me,' Brooks said. 'As I let him go, I asked him if he wanted to know who stabbed his friends. There was no reaction from him, just a nod.'

'Liars tend not to speak if they don't have to. They justify the silent gesture as not *telling* a lie,' Delgado replied.

'That's true.' Brooks sipped on the bitter drink.

'So, what are you getting at?'

'I just told him that his friends – comrades in arms – drinking buddies – had been stabbed. But one of them hadn't.' A serene expression spread across Brooks' face. 'And he didn't even blink.'

92

Present Day

I stepped off the bus in Charles Street, right outside the Factory Shop. Years ago, it had been Woolworths and the central hub for all the shopping in Milford Haven. Back in the early-90s, Charles Street was the one-stop shopping destination for most. These days the world was a lot smaller with many a purchase delivered to the door with the aid of whatever online platform was the preference. I wasn't a dinosaur. I had an Amazon account, as did most, but there was something about walking into a shop and selecting an item off the shelf that felt significantly more satisfying to me than just looking at a picture, reading a blurb and clicking the Buy Now option.

I crossed the road, walked into the shop which had had too many different names to remember them all – Spar, Eurospar, CKs – it was the closest convenience store to my house and so it was my first port of call nine times out of ten. I bought a pasty, a four-pack of Stella and a local newspaper. The headline read *'TRIPLE MURDER AT M.O.D. SITE.'*

I figured I'd better read how the local media saw it before I read my own name as a suspect in print.

Climbing the hill towards my house, I heard my phone ping. I'd received a text from my wife. She had been contacted by the police also and was going to give a statement on her way back from the spa day. Our daughter was heading up to Cardiff to spend a few days with friends while taking in a trade fair. I would have the house to myself.

I had a few options at my disposal.

I could go and catch a few precious moments with my lover, but that would be foolish, for many reasons. Or I could sit in the bleak dreariness of my empty house, munch on my pasty and gloss over my general anxiety with a few cans of beer. I opted for the latter. God only knows what my wife would say about her involvement. And God only knows what she would say about mine.

I knew how much I didn't tell the police. But I couldn't predict how much she would contradict my story. It was a waiting game.

93

Present Day

The only good thing about being out of work was if a call for a paying favour came in, I was always available. The call to my mobile came in as I'd just pulled the ring-pull on my second can of Stella. The opportunity for work met two needs; one it was money, of which I had very little. Two, it saved me from pitching myself into the abyss of alcohol I was so desperate for.

I had a quick shower and threw on some appropriate attire for bar work. It was a six-hour shift in The Nelson, and if I played the game, it could lead to more work.

I set off down the hill and texted the wife on the way. It was almost two hours since she'd texted me about going to the police station and so far, there was no more word from her.

The Nelson was a very different venue from the version I had worked in all those years ago. There used to be a wall in the centre of the room, but it had been taken down to make the whole place open plan, and the plush carpets had mostly been removed to expose the bare boards near the bar.

The early part of the evening was kind of dull. A few residents were having meals and drinks; a couple of locals, who I knew, slipped in for a pint before going home. There were also a few locals who I didn't know but I knew their faces from other bars and the standard nods of recognition were adhered to.

I had a break at 8pm and stood in the beer garden to take in the evening air. My phone was still showing no response from my wife. I wondered what story she was laying out for the police.

Like some marriages of length, ours had run its course, at least on my side of the arrangement. There was no love. No emotional connection. What was once was no more, and while the police hadn't asked me anything about my marriage, I could safely assume the opposite was true of the woman I'd shared my vows with. She knew me better than most and was probably singing like a bird, the detectives hanging on her every word.

I returned to the bar at the same time Jon Samms walked in through the door. I hadn't seen him in more than a decade, which was unusual as we both still lived in Milford. Dan had always joked that Jon was pushing maximum density and it would only take a mild doughnut addiction to tip him over the type-two diabetes precipice. As if to prove that theory, here was Jon, bulked up to the max and wrapped in an ill-fitting suit which did nothing to hide his excesses. At a guess, I'd have said he was close to twenty-five stone. He was also bald with some white stubble behind his ears, showing the colour his hair would have been if he didn't clipper it.

'Hello, stranger,' he said. 'I've not seen you that side of the bar in here since… since the Tall Ships race.'

'A long time ago, Jon. What can I get you?'

He placed his order, and I pulled the pint.

'So, how have you been?' The smugness that had consumed his personality when he was a teenager was back in residence.

'Just fine. Yourself?' I made small talk. I wasn't going to be drawn into the usual conversation where he would talk about his car or his house or his latest foreign holiday.

'Not bad. Just got back from Spain.'

I could see he was tanned but I wasn't sure if he'd visited a tanning salon or something like that. Vanity was his thing if it didn't compromise his love of food and drink.

'Nice.'

I hoped the one-word answer would kill the conversation dead and he would fuck off to put his hard-earned cash into one of the fruit machines. No such luck.

'Have you heard about the boys?' he asked.

'The boys?'

'Rob, Tom and Dan – you know, the boys.'

'Yes, I know. Have you spoken to the police yet?'

306

'Not yet, but they did call me. They're popping in to see me at my studio tomorrow.

Studio? Fuck off, you pompous prick. That's what I wanted to say. But I didn't.

There was an awkward silence for the longest of moments. He sipped his beer; I wiped the counter. I prayed for some customers but there was none to distract me from the hellish interaction I was eager to avoid.

'So, have you spoken to them?' Jon asked, smashing his way through the silence.

'Yeah. Today.' I should have lied and said no.

'They're probably interested in you because of all the history.'

'We all have history with them. You were there too, remember?'

'Yeah, but – you fought with them on the nights they disappeared and... Er...'

'And what?' I snapped. If I'd been hiding how uncomfortable it was talking to him before there was no doubt of my feelings now.

'No. Nothing. You know?' He stammered.

'No. I don't know. What are you trying to say?' Out of the corner of my eye I could see heads turning. The residents were like meerkats looking for danger.

'I shouldn't have said anything,' he timidly admitted.

'Enjoy your beer, Jon.' I walked to other end of the bar where a man had thankfully appeared.

By the time I'd poured the gent a pint of bitter and a glass of wine for his wife, Jon had gone. His half empty pint-pot sitting on the bar, looking dejected, as did he before he left.

I glanced down at my phone to see there was a text. It was from my wife. I swiped the screen to see the one-word message – no kiss – telling me everything and nothing.

'Sorry.'

It was the story of my life.

Present Day

I never got to finish my shift at the Nelson. Brooks and Delgado walked in with two uniformed officers and arrested me on the spot. I spent most of that first hour in the back of a marked police car or standing at the booking-in desk with the custody officer.

As rapid as the arrest was, the urgency for the interview that followed was lacking. I was put into a cell for an hour or so – at least that's how long it seemed – while waiting for an interview suite to become available. Apparently, there was a lot going on and, even though I was deemed Pembrokeshire's number one criminal, I still had to wait my turn. I was handed a tepid tea in a polystyrene cup, deprived of my belt and shoes, and left to contemplate my fate within the pastel blue walls of a ten-by-six box. My only comfort was a wipe-clean mattress on the raised concrete platform which constituted as a bed.

Eventually, I was shuffled into the same windowless room where I had my witness interview the day before. The format was different this time. Both Brooks and Delgado stated their own names after a long introduction, announcing that I had been cautioned and other stuff that drifted over the top of my head. The interview didn't commence until I had stated my full name, address and date of birth for the record.

Brooks dived straight in. His whole demeanour had altered from the man I had met twice before. He gave the official line on my rights to state no comment, and my right to legal representation, before dropping the first question. 'Can you describe, in as much detail as you can recall, the events during the night of the 9th of August 1986, following through until the morning of the 10th of August, 1986? Do you understand the relevance of those dates?'

'I do.' My throat was drier than the Mojave Salt Flats. I downed the water provided in one hit. I could have drunk a bath-full and still feel parched.

'Could you please state your recollection of that period?'

I started from the moment I left my house, calling at Dan's, going to Rob's, and wandering down to The Starboard for a pre-nightclub drink. To use his phrase, *'in as much detail as you can recall,'* I talked about the guys who were at the house and what they were wearing; those who arrived at the nightclub and in what order; and Rob playing UB40 on his stacked stereo system before we left: the whole shebang. Like with most recollections of events more than thirty years ago, I didn't tell everything in the order it happened, I told it in the order the memories came to me. On that particular night, some events were more significantly engrained into my memory than others, and the most vivid ones being the ones I didn't wish to disclose.

I got as far as the fight in Debrett's and then the interview took a sharp turn away from my recollections and toward the agenda of the investigation. The officers had let me ramble on for long enough. It was their time to steer where they wanted the interview to go.

'After you left the club, where did you go?' Brooks' stare scythed me in two.

'I went home. There was no point in staying out on the street,' I said, emphatically.

'Home? No detours? Straight home without passing Go or collecting two hundred pounds – are you sure about that?' Brooks didn't blink.

'I think so. It was a long time ago – a lot has happened since then-'

'Not for Robert Sherman it hasn't,' Delgado cut in, making his presence felt.

'I'm well aware of that.' I wasn't going to be bullied. 'I was in a fight, and I went home. What else do you want to know? Do you want to know if I walked home on my hands? Sang ABBA tracks at the top of my voice? What else do you want?'

'We want the truth, and that's not what you're giving us.' The intensity of Brooks' stare matched his accusing tone. 'Stop wasting time and playing games – tell us what happened on that morning. We have a different story for your whereabouts in the hours after leaving The Debrett's Nightclub. So, if you please; the truth.'

I fell into silence. Who had said what? Had my wife given a different version of events from that night? Why would she do that? I was racking my brains to find not only a reason for her possible discrepancy, but for what details I could be missing out on. It was so long ago. Could I have blocked entire swathes of my memory? But I didn't think so.

Then something rolled over in my mind.

'Oh, hang on. I did walk Sarah part of the way home – only as far as The Rath, and then I went home. Is that what you're getting at?' Was that the missing detail? It seemed insignificant to me.

'Partly,' Brooks said. 'What about the part where you ended up spending over an hour at Daniel James' house when he wasn't there? Could you elaborate on the events that took place behind closed doors that night, and any other such instances that happened between you and Tina James, Daniel's mother?'

I'd never spent a minute behind the wheel of a car but the feeling that raced around the circuitry of my brain must have been akin to driving at a hundred miles an hour and having a blowout. I was no longer in control. I was in a fight to grind the forward motion down to a manageable pace so that I could digest each piece of new information without choking.

'Where did you get that from?'

'We're the ones asking the questions,' Brooks snapped. 'Would you mind answering them?'

'No.' I spat my answer back at him. 'Tell me who is saying this?'

'Are you saying it's not true, Mr Taylor?' Delgado jumped in just to remind me I was outnumbered. 'Are you saying that, at the age of sixteen, you weren't engaged in a sexual relationship with your friend's mother?'

'That's not what-'

'So, is it true, Mr Taylor, you were a romancer of older women when you were barely out of school?' Delgado continued with his glib accusations. 'The teenage Don Juan of Milford Haven, no doubt?'

'Ok. Ok. It's fucking true! Me and Tina had a brief relationship. I was over the age of consent. There was nothing illegal going on. How is it relevant to what happened to Rob?' It was the first time I had spoken it aloud in a long time. It had become a truth instead of a secret, and it was all recorded digitally to be used against me in a court of law, if they so wished.

'It might not be relevant to Mr Sherman's death,' Brooks said. 'But it could be a reason for the death of Mr James. And yes, you are right, while there was nothing illegal going on, but the same can't be said for how immoral the whole thing was. You had an inappropriate relationship, and the discovery of that relationship could be a motive to one or more of the deaths involved in this case. Surely you can understand that?'

Brooks' stance had relaxed as though he was trying to lower my guard.

'I understand. Can you tell me who told you about this? Was it Tina?' I needed to know.

'It was your wife.' Brooks was almost serene.

'My wife?'

'Yes,' Brooks continued, 'your wife, Sarah. She told us everything.'

312

95

Present Day

I had been released pending further enquiries.

I didn't know if it was part of the routine or maybe it was an exception made on my behalf, but the police took me home, dropping me off at my door. I suppose it was the done thing as they had arrested me direct from the first night's work I'd had in weeks. I could have asked for a lift, but I only really had two people I could ask. One was the woman I loved with all my heart, and I hoped that we could make a go of things. There was, of course, a tiny detail in the way – I was a major suspect in a murder investigation. The only other person I could have asked was Sarah, my wife. But she had stacked me right to the top of the suspect pile and was no longer on my Christmas card list. Not just for this Christmas, for every Christmas. I knew I was throwing out a glib attitude, but it was the only defence I had with what was happening around me. I was wearing my sense of humour like a suit of armour, hoping for some protection from my accusers. I shouldn't have bothered. They were coming at me with tanks, firing depleted uranium shells, at point-blank range. I didn't have a hope of defending myself against their twenty-first century weaponry with my medieval puns.

I climbed from the police Volvo trying not to look guilty. The police constable bid me a jovial farewell just as if I was a punter being dropped off by a cabby.

The truth was very different.

I had spent much of the last 48 hours either lying on a thin plastic mattress, failing to sleep, or sitting in an interview room, failing to answer the same questions over and over again.

I had a few questions of my own, but they would be saved for Sarah.

For as long as I could remember, she had always had my back. However, in the last few years I could feel her reluctance to commit to anything which would benefit our relationship. Maybe it was my fault. Maybe I was still the same selfish bastard I'd always been in her eyes. Twenty years of marriage failure had been realised by the discovery of our dead friends. We had been freefalling through the last half decade as though there was no point in pulling the ripcord; the parachutes that should have saved us were nothing but rags, much like the tatters our marriage hung in.

I opened the front door, feeling the oppression in the air, as though Sarah had poisoned our home against me.

I called out.

I don't know what I was expecting, but the house was empty. Not only empty of my family, but empty of any of the warmth I should have come to expect from a home. But, if I was being honest with myself, those fires had long since burned out. I was coming home to kick up the ashes and start over. I was tempted to just leave now and head to my lover's house on the other side of town, but something was waiting for me.

A letter.

I picked it up.

I recognised Sarah distinctive handwriting, feeling the weight on the pages within without breaking the seal. God only know what vitriol was awaiting me. I grabbed a bottle of vodka from the cabinet in the back room and swigged straight from the bottle. If I was going to read between the lines of her explanation, I needed something to take the edge off. I could have drunk the whole bottle, but it wouldn't have made the handwritten contents any easier to swallow. I was fighting a war, and I was going to lose, with the addition of a possible murder conviction thrown in for good measure. I was on my own.

96

Present Day

In the gloom of the back room, a 40-watt bulb barely assisting the meagre daylight creeping through the netting, I sprawled in a drunken, crumpled heap. The letter folded neatly back into the envelope after I had read and reread it. It didn't say a lot, it just gave me the bare bones of what was going on.

> *Will,*
>
> *I'm so sorry that it has come to this. I know that things haven't been right with us for some time now and I always thought we could get through anything, but I don't think even we, as strong as we are, could get through a murder enquiry. Not if we're being honest with each other and being honest with the police in terms of the investigation. I think we all feel guilty about what has happened, and I've always felt that you seemed to show more guilt than anyone else. I've never known why.*
>
> *I've taken it upon myself to move out. The tenants at Vicary Street gave notice a while back and have already moved out. I'm going to move back in for now and Jessie is coming with me. I believe our marriage is over – I believe it has been over for a while and you've been too distant to reach. I hope that we will always be friends, but I think this is the end of the road.*
>
> *Love*

S.

P.S. I've taken a few things with me, and I hope we can come to some arrangement about collecting the rest of my stuff.

As much as I knew she was right, and as much as I felt the weight of responsibility lifted from me, it still stung to be on the wrong side of rejection after all we had been through. And to think that Jessie, my beloved daughter had gone too, made it all the more painful to deal with.

The vodka wasn't helping either.

My stomach was empty, offering no defence from the ravages of the alcohol. I needed to get some food quickly. There was no chance of me making sense of the situation if I was both drunk and hungry. I opted for a quick shower and a change of clothes first. I'd been in the same gear for two days straight and I didn't want to remain feeling as shitty on the outside as I did on the inside.

As I lumbered upstairs, my joints creaked as much as the stairs did. For the first time in my life, I had a sense of my own mortality. Talking about the death of my friends would do that I suppose. The ghosts of the last thirty-four years had come back to haunt me and I'm sure I deserved it; I don't think I'd been a very good friend. I was alive, they were dead. I felt the guilt like a dead weight.

I could see where Sarah had emptied her drawers. The wardrobe door was still ajar, showing the few items left behind; old clothes that no longer fitted her.

I stripped, showered and dressed in fresh clothes. I still had a vodka fog, but the water had cut a swathe through most of it, giving me a moment of clarity – clarity enough to head to the kebab shop. I figured if I ate my own bodyweight in doner meat and chips I might die of a massive heart attack and completely miss the police investigation altogether.

Not even I was that lucky.

I headed out to discover an even worse fate. At least my life was consistently shite.

97

Present Day

I stumbled out of the kebab shop onto the old market square next to Astoria. The Astoria, as it had been called, used to be a cinema back in my grandmother's day. She used to tell tales of couples going on their first dates, watching black & white movies starring the greats of the silver screen, paying half a crown or three-and-six or whatever price she used to say it was. I might have been old, but my memory lived entirely in the decimalised world. For as long as I could remember, the Astoria was a bingo hall. On summer evenings, roaming the streets, Dan and I would often wander past, hearing the various calls that only made sense to the patrons. The stench of cigarette smoke would billow out to the road, warning us off. We never set foot inside the place.

Now it was a nightclub. With 'the' dropped, Astoria was reborn, with the current generation going there on 'dates.' Did the youngsters of today go on dates at all? Gone were the days of silly glances over popcorn. There was no holding of hands on the walk home, and if you were lucky, maybe a kiss on the cheek from the pretty girl in shiny shoes and an Alice band. The current youths were more likely to share spit behind the wheelie bins and getting lucky might be something as trivial as two fingers up to the second knuckle if she was that sort, before wandering off to consummate the relationship and simultaneously conceiving the next generation of broken children.

I smiled at my own cynicism. Would I have been any different had I been a teenager in this new social media, instant gratification world? Probably not. I'd have been one of the broken children, conceived over a park bench, rebelling against the world through alcopops and recreational drugs.

I wandered home with my food.

The best thing about living in a small town is that you know everyone.

The worst thing about living in a small town is that everyone knows you.

And I had their eyes looking at me now.

Call me paranoid but I could see the furtive glances and exchanged whispers from everyone I passed on the short walk back to my house. I ducked down the alley that joined the Robert Street carpark to Trafalgar Road via Dartmouth Gardens. I passed a dog walker from Dewsland Street. I knew the face but not the name. She recoiled, tugging the dog away from my attention, a mask of disgust worn without remorse.

The old Milford rumour mill was churning out a verdict on a trial where no charges had been made. As far as my memory would allow, I was innocent. In the eyes of my fellow townspeople, I needed hanging. Three murders committed, three decades passed and a killer still to be unmasked. If I was the first sniff of a suspect, by hook or by crook, they were already building my gallows. Maybe they'd like it to be a public hanging, in the old market square, next to Astoria; drunken patrons could come and take selfies with my hanging corpse before having a kebab and a fumble on the way home. I'd be famous for a week, forgotten about in an instant, and only recalled when Facebook showed the images as an 'On this Day' memory.

The world's memory was a social media feed, deactivated or reposted when beneficial. My memory was somewhat different. I blocked out as much shit as I could and learned to deal with that which I could not. If I could deactivate my memory, I would. Until such things were a reality, there would always be vodka.

I barged open my front door, not wishing to touch the surface with my greasy hands. Plastic forks were good and all that but doner meat should be consumed with drunken fingers. I crashed onto the sofa in the front room, tapping the standby button on the remote with the little finger on my left hand – the only finger without grease – switching on the box so that I might switch off my mind, for a while at least.

319

I was halfway through my takeaway – and an old episode of Friends – when my phone pinged. I rubbed a greasy finger on my jeans before tapping the screen.

It was a message from my lover.

My life had made more sense since I committed to her.

But the message didn't make sense. Not one bit.

> *'What have you done? Did you kill them?*
> *Did you kill them all?'*

There was no kiss.

The last bastion of hope in my life was singing from their hymn sheet. Was there any point anymore?

98

Present Day

The alcohol in my system didn't soften the blow. The back of her hand swiped across my face.

'Did you kill my son? Did you kill the others?' Tina screamed the questions from inches away.

I let her anger subside before I tried to speak. I knew how she worked. She would explode, get angry, scream and shout, and then she would feel remorse for her rage and ask for forgiveness even when it wasn't necessary.

'I didn't do it – any of it,' I could feel my words slur as they slipped over my drunken tongue. 'You have to believe me.'

'They were asking about *Us* – you and me – back when you were a teenager. Asking me if I had seduced you, whether I thought it was morally right to have sex with my dead son's best friend.' Her words lost the sharp edges, bringing forth the tears she had held for so long. 'They made me feel dirty. They made *Us* feel dirty. Do you know how that feels?'

I shook my head.

'Did they ask you about it? I bet they had a different tactic for you, didn't they?' her voice lifted in anger once more. 'I bet they made you think you were King Stud, romancing some poor old lady who couldn't get a man her own age.'

'No, they asked if it happened, and I said it did. That was it. No details, no nothing.'

We stood in silence for a long moment.

She walked into the living room to grab a tissue. I followed her to move an uncomfortable conversation into a more comfortable setting.

She no longer had the house on Robert Street. After Dan's disappearance was confirmed, they had to sell his house and the money was split between Tina, Charlotte and Kayleigh. Tina sold her house too. So full of constant reminders, she needed to escape what felt painful, taking what was precious in her heart and her photo albums. She now had a bungalow on Westhill Drive, just a few doors down from where Jennifer's parents still lived.

Charlotte and her husband funded a permanent move to Australia, while Kayleigh went off to university in Bristol and remained living there after she graduated. Tina had been living alone, mostly, with only the occasional dabbling of a relationship in the last twenty years.

'Did they ask if anything was going on now?' I couldn't help thinking it sounded like a self-absorbed question as soon as I'd said it.

'Of course, they did. And I told them the truth. We can't run away from this forever, Will. What was it you said, "It's *Us* against the world." Well guess what, the world is against *Us*.'

I went to embrace her, but she pushed me away. The hurt of her loss consumed her. I could only watch as she tried to make sense of it all. I was the enemy now. Whether this was a permanent state or a temporary one would only be known over time. It felt like the world was against me, but I couldn't be selfish as I stood witness to her pain. Whether I liked it or not, this wasn't about me, it was about three people taken in their prime. My feelings didn't matter.

'Shall I make us a drink?'

'Haven't you had enough already?' Her venom was still hot. 'I could smell the vodka before I opened the door to you. You won't be able to drink your way out of this, do you get that?'

Every time she scolded me, whether for something big or something small, I would be made to feel like the little kid I used to be, scraping along with her son, waiting for adulthood to catch us both. Regardless of the occasional reprimand, I still looked at her with love, amazed by the beauty of this incredible woman. She had recently celebrated her 67th birthday but, as always, she looked at least a decade younger than her actual age – more if I was being honest. Forty-nine didn't look bad on me but we looked of a similar age.

And at the age we were now, it really didn't matter. Love doesn't have a number.

'A tea? A coffee? Anything?' I said, taking her accusation on the chin.

'I'll have a coffee. Make one for yourself – a strong black one – you need it.' There was a flicker at the corner of her mouth, a hint of a smile maybe.

I returned with the drinks and took a seat on the sofa next to her. Much like I had thirty-four years ago on that fateful night that started this emotional roller coaster. This time we sat in silence. Not daring to speak for where it might lead.

I felt I had to end the deadlock.

'Sarah has left me.'

I could sense the statement being absorbed and dissected.

'How do you feel about it?'

'Relieved.' To say it out loud was to acknowledge the end of the sham of a marriage. Maybe life could start now. Heaven knows I've waited long enough.

Present Day

A whole week had passed since I arrived home to an empty house and, so far, I'd had no other contact from Sarah. I didn't want to text or call her. I wanted to give her the space she needed. It didn't really matter anymore. The marriage was over, of that there was no doubt.

With a steaming mug of tea before me and a screaming, vodka induced headache hanging over me, I flicked on the TV to watch some news. I needn't have bothered. The news was only about one thing these days – Coronavirus, or to give it its more official name, Covid-19. A city in China was completely locked down, there were stories of infection in parts of Italy and several cruise liners were also quarantining passengers because of suspected infections. It was Spanish Flu scary.

I switched channels to some guy getting frisked in an Australian airport, watched it for a minute, and decided my time would be better spent making breakfast before going for a walk. I wanted to walk over to see Tina, but she was out with a friend for the day; shopping in Carmarthen then a spot of lunch, or something like that. She was retired. She could do as she pleased. Also, we had cooled our affair for the time being. We weren't sure how much surveillance I would be under, and even though the police knew about our affair, we thought it best to cool it off for a while.

I was just dropping some bread into the toaster when there was a knock at the door.

It was the postman. He had a few letters and a package which wouldn't fit through the letter box. It was addressed to Sarah. Somewhere in the corner of my frazzled brain I could remember her saying something about a delay on something she'd ordered. This must have been it.

With some Marmite on toast and another mug of tea in my belly, I headed off out to clear the cobwebs. I decided to drop off the package and some other bits of mail for Sarah and Jessie while I was out.

The crisp, cloudless morning was doing exactly what I had hoped, lifting the cloud of a hangover, merging my soul with the blue sky. For the first time in a while, I had a sense of positivity.

It was a typical Milford day. The general hustle and bustle of joggers and dog walkers paraded along Hamilton Terrace, while cars and vans shuttled up and down, and all under the shadow of St Katherine's Church. The Rath was the same; joggers, dog walkers and me. The Rath held very different memories now. It was no longer the place where I could reclaim a sense of calm in the madness of my world. It was now the place that displayed the madness to me like an ancient show reel. Walking alongside the Water Gardens I could barely remember how it looked when it was an outdoor swimming pool. The whitewashed wall encroaching on where the diving platform used to be was still there, and the reception area was now a Chinese Restaurant, but the rest was gone and it was difficult to envisage how a swimming pool, with the stepped spectator area, actually fitted into the space.

Much like that spot on The Rath, my whole world was different too.

Stepping past the Minesweeper Memorial, I could see Wards Yard with its crumbling pier, the Mining Depot just beyond. Even at the distance I was from the site, I could still see the white and blue police tape, cordoning off some of the structures, fluttering loosely on the breeze. Another story added to the derelict buildings' history.

I paused, reflecting on what had been discovered, how they had come to be there and the many motives possible by way of an explanation. The sense of guilt I had hidden for so long reared its ugly head and the positivity I was feeling was carried off on a very different breeze: A wind of change I had no control over.

I continued on.

I could see Sarah's little pastel green Fiat 500 parked in the carpark behind the house but could see no sign of Jessie's Corsa. If I knew Jessie, she would be doing someone's nails while gossiping away about all and sundry. No doubt the talk of the week would be the virus. Last week it would have been my questioning; the week before, the discovery of the three bodies.

I knocked on the door. There was no answer. I knocked again and still nothing.

I had the package and some letters, and I wasn't going to take them home with me. The letters would fit through the door, but the package wouldn't.

Pondering my options, I remembered I still had a key for the house and swiftly rummaged in my pocket. Sure enough, it was still on the bunch I had on me. I knew it was a tad inappropriate, but I slipped the key into the door and opened it. I could have just dropped everything on the hall table and sent a text. But I didn't. I had a quick scope into the living room to see if there was a notepad and pen so I could leave a note, but all thoughts of that drifted away when I saw a man's jacket thrown across a chair. My mind raced with who, what and why but all thoughts were interrupted by the sound I heard coming from directly above me. The rush of adrenaline melted through me, and I knew I had to see.

100

Present Day

It felt like the room was on fire. It wasn't. I was. All the heat was being generated from within my gut; the acid spilling over to scorch my ego. I had no right to be jealous of what I could hear going on but there will always be a piece of my heart dedicated to Sarah. I knew it was her and not Jessie. I could tell by the moans of pleasure. Sarah was always vocal during sex; whether it was a quickie against the kitchen counter or a marathon between the sheets, she always made the noises a man wanted to hear. I could hear them now. And they weren't for me.

I crept upstairs. I wasn't trying to be quiet, but I also wasn't trying to announce my arrival, either. I'll let it be a surprise for my wife and her lover, whoever that was.

The floorboard creaked under my weight, stopping me dead in my tracks. I was expecting the frantic sex to cease and be discovered, but no, they were too involved with the action to hear my noisy approach. The rapid panting of their breaths in unison was loud enough to drown out anything I was doing.

Her pleasurable moans, the same moans I had heard a million times before, the first time being through the wall when Sarah had seduced Tom to spite me.

I could also hear him – the man thrusting into her. I could hear the motion of his body, the gasp of his breathing, the grunting of his effort. Someone was having the fuck of their life.

I feared my pounding heart would break my ribs and throb its way out of my body by itself. A fine sweat covered my whole body as my temperature peaked from the rush of adrenalin. My jealously was tangible. But who was I to be jealous? I had been having an affair for years. It wasn't my place to feel this way. So how come I did?

I felt like I had stood outside the door for an eternity and yet they were still going at it. I had to inwardly praise the man's stamina while questioning my own at the same time.

Fuck it!

I pushed the door open and stepped inside.

I wished I hadn't. Oh my God, I so wished I hadn't.

101

Present Day

There are very few images branded onto the surface of my memory. My brain picks and chooses what deems merit for being remembered and adjusts accordingly. I can think back and most of what is available to recall is grey around the edges with the odd detail of clarity. Like many people, I need photographs and video tape to be assured of what the brain is telling me.

But this was not something I was going to forget in a hurry, or indeed wanted to remember, ever. The scene was not so much illicit as it was pathetic.

'What the fuck are you doing here?' Sarah screeched, gripping for the duvet to hide her shame.

Jon – yes, Jon – climbed off her. His bulky appearance without the disguise of a suit was not something I envied. His large belly was lined with stretchmarks as though he had given birth to triplets at some point. The summertime poster boy image of his youth was dead and buried. I could have laughed – if the whole gig had been amusing – as he tried to pull on his trousers to hide his modesty.

'I came to drop off the *mail*, but it seems the *male* has just dropped off you,' I said, not in a position to judge what I had witnessed but also not one to avoid the obvious puns of the situation.

'Well, you don't want me, so why shouldn't I look for attention elsewhere?' Sarah was pulling on a t-shirt, momentarily getting caught in the sleeve as she tried to push her head through.

'Nice work, Taylor, couldn't you have waited until I'd finished,' Jon snapped, still stumbling into his trousers.

'I think you're already done.' I glanced down at his now flaccid penis and raised my eyebrows.

'Fuck you!'

'No, no, you carry on fucking my wife! That's what it looked like to me – just! I was reminded of that David Attenborough clip of the two tortoises fucking in The Galapagos. If Tom had had that on videotape, I'm sure it would have been classed as, *cruel and unusual.*' My subconscious brain had taken over, thank God. My heart was elsewhere, crying slowly to itself.

'Fuck off!' Jon spat, eventually managing to pull up his trousers and cover whatever dignity he had. Which wasn't much.

'See, you can dress yourself. And I thought it was the job of your butler to dress you.' I needed my mouth to stop running on autopilot, but it was difficult to rein it in.

Jon grabbed the rest of his clothes, barging past me on the way out before leaving the house. From the corner of my eye, I could see him pulling on his shirt on the road in front of the house. He seemed to be struggling with that too.

'So why are you here?' Sarah said. She was out of bed now, pulling the bed together to hide the evidence of wrongdoing.

'Like I said, just dropping off the mail.'

'So, you thought you'd let yourself in and walk into my bedroom. There's a fucking letterbox on the door – you could have posted it.' She wiped herself with a wet wipe, shamelessly, in front of me before pulling on a fresh pair of knickers.

'Well, how was I supposed to know you'd be fucking one of our school friends?'

I witnessed her flinch against the barb.

'Fuck you, Will. No, better still, why don't you go and fuck Tina – you've been doing that for long enough, haven't you.'

There was no comeback for that one. I was in no position to judge her, yet here I was, chucking insult and accusation like I was without sin. Even I wanted to yell at myself for the hypocrisy of it all.

'How long have you known?' I asked, meekly.

'I've known since 1986.'

If my brain had been one of those room-sized supercomputers from the 70s, I'm sure the reels of magnetic tape would have started to fly off the spools. Had she really known from the first time?

I didn't need to ask, though, she told me. 'On the night Rob died,' she said *died*, not *disappeared*. The detail was slowly sinking in

330

for everyone who knew him. 'I followed you home. You offered to walk me home and I refused. But, after a minute or two, I thought that maybe you wanted the company – to talk about what had happened. So, I turned around and tried to find you, but when I did, you were talking to Tina outside her house. I watched you go in, Will. I was going to knock the door to see if you were ok – to see if you wanted to talk to me – but you didn't.'

'I didn't know you were there.' It was the truth.

'And that's the story of our relationship – you never knew I was there.' She left a pregnant pause for my own mind to fill in the endless possibilities.

'That's not true. We're married. We have a child. How can I not know you were there?'

'Jessie was an accident, as much as we both love her, that's what she was – a happy accident to kick off our unhappy marriage.' Sarah was playing the victim to the best of her ability. I'd seen it before.

'I'm going.' I turned and headed for the door.

Sarah skipped around the bed to catch up with me, grabbing me by the arm. 'Where do you think you're going? Are you going to see *her*? Running off to see your whore?'

'I can't go and see her, can I?' My anger rose, 'I'm the number one suspect for killing her son, thanks to you and whatever you've said. Is that what you're doing? Getting me put away so nobody can have me? I'd take a stretch in solitary confinement if it meant I didn't have to deal with you anymore.'

She lashed out, her fists pummelling against my arms and chest. I allowed her a moment of rage, to vent the hatred I could feel gushing from her. The pain of her fists was nothing compared to the pain of her words. I had too much going on, numbing out whatever she threw at me.

I reached out, gripping her wrists, thwarting the onslaught. She struggled but soon succumbed to my resistance, although, I felt it was more a retreat than a defeat.

331

'Kiss me, Will, one last time – before you go.' She held my gaze firmer than I'd held her wrists. I could feel myself turning my head, leaning in, lowering my face to meet hers. I snapped out of it. She always did this, using her guiles to manipulate me, no matter how small the victory, she had to try it.

'Stop it, Sarah. We are done.'

I released her and walked away.

The venom overflowed and she let it all out. 'Go on then, get out. Fuck off to your old hag of a lover. I'll never be at the top of your list, you bastard! There's a queue, and I've always been at the back of it. Fuck you!'

I was twenty yards from the house before I could no longer hear the tirade of abuse. I should never have come. Hindsight was a wonderful thing.

102

Present Day

If my life didn't already suck enough, it was about to get much worse. Not as bad as some but pretty shit in the grand spectrum of my life.

Turn on the TV, flick on to any channel and the world was in meltdown: Coronavirus meltdown.

Now the story is kind of sketchy at best but apparently, if you believe the Daily Mail and other such sources of media that peddle half-truths and vague reporting, somebody in China made some soup from a dead bat and people are dying from the flu, or something resembling the flu. Every news media agency is pumping out stories about Spanish Flu, Bird Flu, SARS, Ebola, and somewhere in the text the word *Pandemic* would appear. There was a lot of talk about closing the schools down, which they did. Then there was a lot of talk about cancelling sporting events and gigs, which they did. Slowly but surely, every aspect of everyday life was stripped away. There was no such thing as normal anymore. Normal was what we used to do. What we did now was social distancing and isolation.

The Government guidelines said that we could go shopping for essentials, take daily exercise, and go to work but only if it was essential and that we should work from home, if it was possible. I was an unemployed barman. I could pour my own beer and that was as much as I could do. I couldn't even go looking for work because all pubs and restaurants had been closed indefinitely. In a dwindling job market, there had been an influx of available workers to fill the gaps left by others who were required to isolate themselves due to infection, shielding, or self-isolation.

Very early on in the crisis, I was able to stock up my cupboards to keep myself fed and watered. I was bewildered by the amount of panic buying that had gone on; shelves stripped of pasta, toilet paper, and hand-wash. I'd got lucky and managed to get some pasta, sauces, tinned goods, and potatoes. I also had a stack of cheap pizzas in the little chest freezer that lived in the cupboard under the stairs. With a case of lager and several multipacks of crisps, I was ready for the apocalypse.

I took the daily exercise recommended, mid-morning every morning, walking the streets of Milford as my step-tracker clocked up my mileage: 10,000 steps a day, minimum.

The weather was beautiful, like an early summer, blue skies, devoid of clouds and passenger planes; the sun beaming down with an uninterrupted view of a world in isolation. But even with so many people off work and allowed to take exercise in the gorgeous weather, the streets were surprisingly empty. Every day was like a Sunday in the 80s.

Even the road traffic was limited. Cars and vans were few and far between with only essential travel allowed. It was a strange new world. And I felt totally alone. No Sarah, no Jessie, no Tina, no anybody. Yet, I felt a calmness that I'd not felt in years. A peace from the routine I had established.

I would wake at the same time every day, around 9-ish, have breakfast, have a shower, get dressed and go for my walk. I'd then have a spot of lunch, read a book for about an hour and then watch a movie. Once the film had finished, I'd prepared some food, open a can of beer and put on another movie or work my way through a box set before dozing off on the sofa or eventually going to bed. The isolation magnified many issues for some, but for me, I was able to regroup and find myself.

I'd managed two weeks with limited interaction from other people until there was a knock on the door.

Brooks and Delgado were standing back out on the pavement when I opened the door. There were both wearing face masks. In the craziness of the pandemic, I kind of hoped that the insignificant case of the murder investigation would have avoided my door. How wrong was I? But then how foolish was I to think it would ever leave me alone? I was suspect number one thanks to my estranged wife.

334

103

Present Day

'So, what do you want to talk to me about, now?' I leaned against the back wall of the house while the police officers stood at the far end of the yard. Social distancing guidelines suggested two metres; the officers were further away than the guidelines, gripping mugs of coffee under a clear blue sky.

'We understand that you and your wife have separated – is that a permanent arrangement or temporary?' Brooks asked.

'Who knows? I would imagine it will be a permanent arrangement seeing as she's fucking somebody else.'

'Forgive me for asking but aren't you involved with Ms James?'

Tina had reverted to her maiden name after her divorce. It seemed odd for her to be referred to as Ms James after all the years I'd know her.

'Not during this lockdown, I'm not,' I said, before taking a big slug of tea.

'So, getting back to the subject of your wife.' Brooks disregarded my obviously belligerent attitude to continue his line of questioning. 'Who is she currently involved with?'

I told them as much as I could about Sarah and Jon's relationship status. I even told them about walking in on the pair of them making the beast with two backs on her mother's old bed. They seemed to appreciate the details but not the sarcasm I offered in abundance.

'To your knowledge, how long have they been involved?' Brooks came across as laidback, almost serene, compared to my other dealings with him and his colleague.

'Your guess is as good as mine – weeks, months, years? I don't know and, if I'm being completely honest, I don't care.'

'We appreciate your honesty, Mr Taylor,' Delgado spoke for the first time since walking through the door. 'Would it surprise you to learn that it's more likely to be years – decades, even?'

As much as I no longer gave a shit, my stomach plummeted only to be drop kicked back into place, knocking the wind out of my already fragile sails. 'What the fuck do you mean by *decades?*'

'Maybe that's something you need to discuss with your wife.'

The officers, in unison, placed their empty mugs on the flower border wall and made their way through the yard door to the lane beyond.

'No. Wait.' I called after the officers, but I could see they were in no mood to comment further.

Brooks paused as he pulled the door behind him. 'Good day to you, Mr Taylor. Stay safe.'

The rickety door clattered shut, the tarnished metal catch reverberating. But not as much as the revelation of betrayal reverberated through the only good memories I could raise about my marriage. Everything was a lie.

104

Present Day

My rage burned like acid, eating through my cast iron selfish core. I felt it rise from within, threatening to spill from my pores and scorch the air as I trekked through the streets of my hometown. I didn't know what awaited me this time, but nothing would surprise me anymore. If I walked in and there was a queue of our school friends, taking numbers while listening to a live mariachi band, I don't think it would raise an eyebrow from me.

As I stepped off the pavement at the end of The Rath, I could already see I was in for disappointment. Sarah's car wasn't there.

But Jon's car was.

Fuck it, I thought.

I marched up to the door, banging with the side of my fist to hopefully scare the Bejeezus out of whoever was inside.

But there was no answer.

I banged again, thinking he might have been on a call, on the bog or – most likely – on top of some other woman while Sarah was working.

No answer.

I still had my key and, by the looks of it, the lock hadn't been changed.

I stepped inside with some trepidation. I was trespassing, technically, and I wouldn't be able to explain my presence other than to say I'd come for a heated debate about the lack of fidelity in our marriage. Which would have been rich coming from me.

I called out a timid 'Hello.'

The house was empty. I really should have left, then and there, but curiosity had its hooks in me, and I was drawn to having a good poke around. There was nothing of interest in the lounge or the kitchen. The rooms were spotless, and the dishes were clean. I couldn't even inwardly condemn the standard of cleanliness; remembering the three beer cans I'd left on the coffee table from the previous night. Again, who was I to judge?

In for a penny, in for a pound, I was up the stairs as fast as my creaky knees would allow. But it was the same story upstairs – immaculate.

I pondered in the bedroom for a moment. It wasn't as perfect as I'd first thought. On the old mahogany dressing table, sitting on a coaster, was a mug. The mug was empty. I was going to note how shoddy it was to have one thing out of place and commit it to memory with the endless bitter anecdotes I was storing away, but instead I rested the back of my hand against the glossy china. It was still warm.

If somebody had been in the house they must have only just left and I missed them by a minute or two – maybe only seconds – but by luck, rather than judgement, I had entered unseen and now I had to do the same on the way out.

I was about to leave when something caught my eye. A tattered shoebox was tucked under the bed with just a corner fouling the valance. I recognised the box as one that had been bundled into the back of a wardrobe in my house. It was most definitely one of Sarah's. The contents had always been a mystery and I wasn't one to pry. But now, with everything that had gone on, I wanted to take a look.

I pulled it out, feeling there was a weight to it; there was something other than a pair of shoes inside. I slid back the perishing elastic band, it snapped, pinging off into the room somewhere. Inside was a stack of notebooks – diaries to be exact – all carefully scribed in Sarah's hand. Reading someone's diary was a no-no, but I was compelled to open a page to see what was written within. Lifting the first diary out of the box, I flipped through a few leaves. It started on the 1st of January, as I would have expected, and was an account of the hangover we both had and how we were avoiding Jessie's needs. I could remember that day. We went to a party with some of Sarah's work colleagues and got completely trashed, staggering home at some God-awful hour, pissing off our babysitter something terrible. I'd never kept a diary and never thought such things would be noteworthy, that is until Facebook came along with its Memories facility, reminding everyone what they had been doing on whatever day so many years previously. It was only then that I could see the validity of keeping a diary. I flicked through a few pages of mundane nothingness until a name jumped off the page at me. It was Jon's name. She had been for coffee with him. There was nothing unusual about that – two friends going for coffee – apart from the fact it was during the early years of our marriage and Jon hadn't been a factor in our life for years. Well, he hadn't featured in mine, but in Sarah's, that was a different thing. I flicked a few more pages and saw his name again. It was *that* day again: St Valentine's Day.

> *February 14th, 2010: Jon came round today. I miss him. It felt good have his company while Will was at work. I hate Will working the weekends but if it means that Jon can come over and we can... ha ha... have some fun, then so be it. Unfortunately, Will came home early from work, sick, and Jon had to shoot out through the back door. It was a close one, but I don't think Will noticed a thing. He never notices anything. Ha ha.*

The acid constantly rumbling in my guts combusted, rising until it burned the back of my throat. I could have spewed my breakfast, then and there, but I managed to hold it down. I remember that day. I was working a day shift in The Manchester Club back then, but I went home early feeling like shit. It spoiled our date plans for the night. Sarah didn't seem too worried about it when I arrived home because she said she was feeling ill too and had a temperature. I can recall her making me feel her brow and how rapid her pulse was the minute I walked through the door. But she wasn't ill, she'd been caught on the hop, and like the sucker I was, I had fallen for her story.

My whole life was a lie, and I had the documented evidence of it all, neatly stacked in a large shoebox before me.

I had to leave, but I was taking the box with me. God knows what other revelations I would discover.

I put the lid back on and got to my feet. I had a cursory look around for the elastic band, but I couldn't see it. It didn't matter, I had the diaries and that was all that was important.

Then I heard a voice; a familiar voice, in conversation.

It was Jon's voice.

He wasn't inside the house. He was out front, chatting to a neighbour, and exercising the two-metre social distancing rule.

I could see a newspaper in his hand. He must have popped out to buy it after finishing his mug of coffee – a minute before I knocked the door.

How in the hell was I going to get past him and escape with the evidence of his and her betrayal?

105

Present Day

I skidded across the grass, falling over, the contents of the shoebox spilling down the grass bank. Less haste, more speed, I thought to myself as gravity took over from my legs in moving me forward. I barely escaped from Sarah's house before Jon came in from talking to the neighbour. I'd made the decision to get out via the back door, escaping through the lane and out into the big chunk of tarmac where Brick Houses and the rear end of Vicary Street met.

It was the right decision to get out, but it wasn't such a wise choice to sprint as fast as my old legs could carry me down the uneven and precariously steep grass bank that fell away from the end of The Rath.

The tremors in my hands kept a tempo with the pulsating of my exploding heart. I could barely grip the diaries to shove them back into the fragile, aged shoebox. With my eyes scoping the grass for anything I'd left behind, I threw an occasion glance over my shoulder, feeling sure that Jon would be bearing down on me any second now. He never arrived.

Scooping up the spoils of my trespass, I headed along the low path until I could mount the steps below The Water Gardens. I paced up the path, taking the sharp turn up past the paddling pool and came back to The Rath at the junction of Sandhurst Road. On the outside, I tried to give the impression that I should have been there, carrying an old shoebox and sweating profusely. But on the inside, my ego was itching to rip open that box and devour the words of betrayal and deception.

I traversed the lonely streets of Milford to get home – to get safe. But was there such a thing as safe anymore? My life hadn't amounted to much. Fifty years had flashed by, and I was still scratching around, trying to make a living from an industry that had been shut down for the foreseeable. There was nothing that resembled *safe* in my life.

Finally, I slammed the door behind me, shutting out the world. For now, I felt kind of safe. As safe as anyone could with the police breathing down their neck and an ex-wife determined to fit me up.

I dropped the box onto the coffee table and walked into the kitchen. I stared at the kettle for a long moment, pondering on the possibilities. Instead, I grabbed a tumbler and a bottle of vodka. It was the drink of choice for watching the world unfurl.

Fuck it, I thought. If my mediocre life was going to descend into a Hell on Earth, I may as well have some good tunes to herald in the end of life as I knew it. I dropped Pink Floyd into the CD player and had the haunting sound of Shine on You Crazy Diamond as I downed my first free-poured vodka of the day. It wasn't even 11am.

*

The empty Smirnoff bottle clattered onto the floor. I had completely missed the table. I could have blamed tiredness, or hunger, but it was still light outside and I'd devoured two tubes of Pringles over the course of the last hour or so.

And, of course, I was drunk.

I'd started off with some Dutch courage as a method to my madness. I worked backwards through the dairies, starting at the latest available – 2019 – I figured I'd reverse my way back through to the point where it all went wrong. How wrong could I be?

Every instance of Jon's inclusion had to be read and reread. I clocked over a hundred times his name was mentioned in the first diary, and there were so many other times when he wasn't, but while unnamed, he still had to be the subject of some of the treachery I was trawling through. Shopping trips that weren't shopping trips; medical courses that required hotel stays were fiction; even a walk to get a takeaway that was subject to an illicit diversion along the way: a quickie in the lane between Trafalgar Road and Dartmouth Gardens.

342

She even had the forethought to bring wet wipes for the clean-up job so I wouldn't know.

Page after deceitful page – a lifetime of lies, completely documented for my consumption.

Slumping back into the sofa, I threw down the last dregs of vodka. I hoped there might be another bottle somewhere. My eyes were stinging from reading five of the diaries, completely, and there was still twenty-plus to go. But now, the light was failing, and I needed more alcohol.

I was about to start the quest for truth with a quest for more booze, but I could hear something unusual. I know what I *thought* it sounded like, so I went to investigate. It was coming from the street.

I opened the door to rapturous applause and cheering. I was so drunk I wondered what I had done to deserve a standing ovation.

They weren't clapping for me.

I glanced up a few doors to where a neighbour I had gone to school with was clapping and whooping.

Seeing the confusion on my face, she let me into the secret. 'We're clapping for the NHS and essential workers.'

I nodded and started clapping my hands together. This must have been part of the 'new normal' our lives were evolving into. My life was evolving too, rapidly, and for very different reasons. Whatever sub-branch of human evolution I fell under, I felt sure I was heading for extinction. A meteorite was going to blast me the same way as the dinosaurs. But the meteorite wasn't falling from the sky. That meteorite was sitting in a shoebox on my coffee table while I was pounding my hands together for the unseen heroes of the hour. Nobody was coming to save me, and I knew it.

106

Present Day

I was awoken by the dawn chorus chirruping merrily, heralding the start of a new day. The dim glow of the early daylight warning me that life was another day shorter, and I was another day closer to death. It wasn't such a scary prospect, under the circumstances.

I swung my legs around so that I could put my feet on the floor. My body felt broken after another night on the sofa, I was doing it a bit too often. It would have been a welcome change if I had awoken rested and refreshed, but that was a pipedream. The excess of vodka still rattled around my fuzzy head, tweaking my nausea setting to over-sensitive.

I stayed where I was for the time being. I didn't want any sudden movements triggering a sudden evacuation of my guts, not with a sink full of dishes and the only toilet a flight of stairs away. After a moment of deep breathing, I deemed it safe to move.

It took me a while to stand fully upright. It seems my rapid escape, and subsequent tumble, had left me with a few unseen reminders of the stupidity of my actions. When I first returned to the safety of my house, I thought I'd got off with a few grass stains on my clothes, a bruised knee and a friction burn to the elbow. But in the cold light of a new day, I had stiffness in every joint and my spine felt like it had been replaced with broken glass; each shard finding a new soft spot to prick as I tentatively tried to move through the house.

The grey dawn had invaded the kitchen. I flicked on the florescent light to chase away the grey and illuminate the shambles I'd left for myself. Every surface had various items of dirty crockery or takeaway cartons strewn across it. I wasn't a house-proud individual at the best of times, but this lockdown situation had exaggerated my bad habits to the max. I would have to tidy up. But not yet.

I took the only clean glass I had, an old Guinness glass, probably stolen from a pub on a night out, and filled it with cold water. Stepping out into the yard, I sipped slowly while relishing the cool air.

I could see the haze of the dawn lifting, revealing another blue-sky day to come. It seemed cruelly ironic that we were experiencing some of the best weather in years, yet unable to do anything other than sit in the garden or go for short walks. I knew that half the county lived on the beaches but, for the time being, they were closed, and people were making do with indoor entertainment. In some cases that involving a lot of drinking.

After breathing a lot of cold air and drinking half the glass, I felt better prepared for the day, going back inside to make a start on something. Anything.

The front living room was a mess, littered with the crumbs of a million Pringles, a few fragments of biscuits were stamped into the carpet, and a variety of chocolate bar wrappers were dotted everywhere. There was an empty Smirnoff bottle and a half empty Red Square vodka bottle on the table, plus a dozen beer cans, mostly Carling Black Label with a few Kronenbourg cans for when I felt like spoiling myself. If anyone was to walk into this room, today, they'd insist I had drink and snack problem. They wouldn't be wrong.

Sitting in the middle of the table was the shoebox. It held the documented destruction of my life.

I had trawled through five complete diaries before being interrupted by the applause in the street, but the fresh air had hit me hard, and I had been introduced to all the alcohol I had consumed at once. After that, I had struggled through another half a diary and fallen asleep. The next thing I knew was the fucking birds tweeting themselves awake and me with them.

I looked down at the box, and the discarded sixth diary, covered in crumbs, and knew alcohol couldn't feature in my day today. I had to get to work and pick the bones from three decades of Sarah's thoughts. I figured time was against me. It would only be a matter of time before she would discover I'd taken her scrappy memoirs and was working my way through them, word by painful word.

*

I thought somebody must have thrown bleach in my eyes, they stung so much. I had leafed through a good chunk of the battered, dog-eared diaries. Ten years of life had now been revealed to me in intimate detail, and this time I was sober enough to understand the words flying off the pages at me.

My life wasn't as clear-cut as had been presented to me. The affair that my wife and our so-called friend had been having had started, in earnest, back in 2009, although I imagine there had been plenty of intimate liaisons in the years before.

Most of that year had been filled with mundane entries about the weather and work, with the occasional gem about Jessie doing something in school, like winning a race on school sports day and achieving her 25-metre swim badge; those little milestones, so easily forgotten over time, captured in blue ink on lined paper. The only newsworthy entry I could remember was about Michael Jackson's death. Like everyone else, I was caught up in the tirade of sick and offensive jokes that were doing the rounds at the time; none of which I could remember today.

Page after page, day after day, there was little variation in the entries other than the Jessie gems and the annoyance I brought. But there was one, longer than usual entry that showed the spark of infidelity, and while it was painful to read, it also alleviated some of my guilt about Tina.

> *August 1st, 2009: Will's birthday is nearly here, and I still don't know what to buy him. Maybe I'll pop to the pound shop and buy him some cheap shit. It's all he's worth these days. When I was out and about today, trying to find something to buy, I bumped into Jon. I hadn't seen him in years, and he had changed quite a bit. He's a bit heavier than the last time I saw*

346

him, and his hair is thinner and greyer,
but that made him even more accessible
and friendly. All the girls used to fancy
him in school, me included, and he knew
it. I think he still knows it but, with a few
years on him, I think he'd settle for less.
Maybe I could tempt him with my boobs,
bum and oral skills. It's worked before – it
could work again. Anyway, we've
arranged to meet for coffee. I'll let you
know how it works out, dear diary.

This was the first note of betrayal and over the following pages, I read the first-hand account of their blossoming romance. It felt like reading a fiction of some strange character's life. These were not people I had known for years, or even met. This was the life of a couple outside of my realm of understanding. The mountain of my guilt was being rapidly eroded as the pages revealed so much more than coffee and exchanged kisses.

By the time I was ready to pick up 2008, my guilt was mere dust in the wind.

Mine and Tina's affair had started about five years ago, after a chance meeting on a night out. According to the diary entries. Sarah and Jon had a six-year head-start. I could read the apathy of feeling Sarah had for me, how her love was dwindling without much chance of recovery. Reading it from the pages only confirmed what I had been feeling this past decade. I was surplus to requirements, like in other areas of my life.

Except with Tina.

The inappropriate launch of our relationship was ancient history. We were two middle-aged people who had rediscovered each other after many years in our own personal wildernesses. Starting out as a drunken first flurry of sexual abandon, eventually to peter out a few months later, only to be rekindled in the same manner almost thirty years later. A drink, a chat, a kiss; all the ingredients required to conjure up a spell that would be difficult to break.

But at that moment it was broken. Lies and accusation had been the venom and I was searching through these pages, looking for an antidote. It was proving hard to find.

I'd taken off the reading glasses that were growing to be a more permanent fixture these days. My watch was telling me it was bedtime, but my mind was telling me to press on. Coffee, a few hours before midnight, wasn't advisable for a good night's sleep but, here I was, ten minutes past the witching hour and preparing two espressos. My entire life had turned into an endless night of revelation. Caffeine was my companion.

107

Present Day

For the second morning in a row, I had woken up as a crumpled heap on the sofa, still wearing the clothes I had pulled on 48 hours earlier. At least this time I didn't have a hangover. At least this time it didn't hurt to see the new day bleeding its colour under the curtains, awakening me to the stupidity of my cravings. I sat up and could feel the ache in my ageing joints. No more tumbling down the grass for me.

I shuffled into the kitchen and filled the kettle. The new day was looking like every other day we'd had this week; hazy to start but blue skies and cloudless until the sunset. Yesterday, I had only stepped out to sample some fresh air while trying to hold my guts down. Today would be different. Today would be better. I padded barefoot into the yard and tried to absorb the sun's energy, hoping that my damaged limbs might heal by way of photosynthesis. The crisp air and heat felt good on my skin, but I was a long way from a miracle cure, and under the current travel restrictions, I wouldn't be heading to Lourdes to be healed any time soon.

The audible click of the boiling kettle summoned me back into the house.

I went maverick and made myself two mugs of tea. After a guilty blitz on the housework the day before, I had the mugs to spare, and I wanted to save myself the minute and a half I would waste returning for a second brew. I had work to do. Diaries to read.

The whole reading of the diaries saga was starting to lose its appeal. I thought that I may garner some snippet of information of how it had all gone wrong. But I was mistaken. Reading the diaries in reverse order but always starting at New Years Day had proved difficult and jarring. Yes, I could see some events as they unfolded, but after every 365 entries – sometimes 366 – the whole world, written in the same blue ink, would shift out of alignment and I'd have to get my bearings again.

I'd managed to work my way back to 2002 before the Sandman had caught up with me. Seventeen years down, only another seventeen to go, maybe.

The record during the mid-2000s had been pretty sketchy. Every date had been handwritten in but there would often be no entry below. If there was, it would be a sentence at best, describing something insignificant that somehow marked the day as memorable. I couldn't make head nor tail of the sporadic input. From the start of 2004 until the end of 2008 – five full years, plus two leap years, 1827 days – there couldn't have been more than two hundred entries in total. Birthdays, anniversaries, day's out, holidays – it was the bare bones of those wilderness years when our marriage was coasting down a road to nowhere.

I could see why it wasn't exciting for her to experience. It wasn't exactly a barrel of laughs for me to read.

I took a swig of tea, picked up 2002's catalogue of disaster and continued the shameless invasion of privacy I felt I had earned.

There was more to this one. An entry under every date summarised to fit into two or three sentences. Baby Jessie was heading toward her second birthday and most of the words were baby related. I was mentioned in the odd note about birthdays and work and nights out, but that was it. I had expected a child to take precedence over me but not to the degree shown. I was dropped so far down the pecking order that I had to scratch around for an iota of significance.

I made short work of 2002 and 2001. I would have ploughed straight into 2000 – the year of our marriage and the birth of our child – but the crowing from my guts was distracting. I threw together an omelette, made another mug of tea, and sat out on the low wall of the yard to eat. Eating brunch al fresco always made me feel like I was on holiday. If this had been a holiday, I'd have been asking for a refund.

Trying to continue the whole *New Me* thing, I washed my plate, dried it and put it away before taking a shower. I already had the feeling that the day was going to throw some curveballs my way, and yesterday's clothes weren't going to cut it.

Freshened up and renewed, I resumed my journey back through time. I didn't feel like I was HG Wells, riding out my time machine back through the memory of a woman I clearly didn't know. I was more like Marty McFly once his image had evaporated from the photo in his pocket. Maybe the future would have been better, but I wasn't sure whether I would have been Morlock or Eloi, or maybe Doc Brown with crazy hair. Whatever, it wasn't an option for me. I picked up 2000 and opened it to the first entry.

Slam!

The realisation hit me like a home run batter who'd been served an easy ball. The first of January 2000 was the last day anyone had seen Dan. And here it was, all laid out for me, the height of my so-called wife's betrayal just a few short months before our wedding. Ok, we didn't know we were going to get married at that point. We didn't even know that Jessie was a possibility. Our relationship was casual at best, and I had no reason to judge anything Sarah did.

But I had to.

Everything I had read over the course of two days – the lies, the liaisons, the manipulation – had made me question everything my wife had ever done. There was no escaping what was being laid out for me. She was the architect of her place in the world, and I was the poor sap, falling on her ever word ever since I'd seen those two blue lines on the pregnancy test.

It appeared that another two blue lines, written in ink, were about to define the course of the twenty years that followed.

The second line of the first diary entry was painful to read. The third line sucked the very life from my marrow.

> *January 1st, 2000: Happy New Millennium!!! First day of the New Year – new millennium – and I've already had my first shag of the year, courtesy of Dan James. He blew his fertile seed into me*

twice without asking. Fucked me like there
was no tomorrow.

Fuck. My. Life. It raised a million questions, and the answers wouldn't wait.

108

Present Day

Lockdown or not, I was out through the door. I had a question to ask.

The streets were eerily quiet. Shops were shut, people were at home. That was the advice, and many were taking it. Social media was filled with pictures and videos of people doing crazy things at home; anything to lift the mood and alleviate the boredom. Others were taking it like an extended holiday as there was weather to match. People were posting pictures of glasses of wine and cans of lager being consumed before noon, daily. When all this disruption and lockdown was over, there would be a ton of people emerging from their homes with a drink problem. I knew I could be one of them if I didn't curb my yearning to crack a ring-pull.

Pacing swiftly, sober and anxious, I headed across town with a purpose.

No. A quest.

There were things I didn't know about myself, and I wasn't going to find the answers down the back of the sofa or even in the twisted journals I had been probing through into the dark hours.

I marched up to the door and banged on it.

There was the sound of movement and then I saw a figure moving behind the frosted glass porch door.

'You're not supposed to be here.' No greeting. Tina's features were like stone.

'I need to speak to you,' I said.

'We're supposed to be socially distancing. Households are not to mix. You can't be here,' she said, her face softening.

'I need to know something,' I pleaded, 'there's... something has happened – I need some answers before I can go armed with the evidence. You're the only person who can help me. Please, I beg you, five minutes.'

Tina's eyes darted back and forth with my movements. I was the proverbial Cat on a Hot Tin Roof – pacing to and fro as though my feet were being scorched.

Her face melted; the stern veil morphed into the beautiful, loving features I was more accustomed to seeing.

'Go around the back and we'll talk through the kitchen door,' she said, shutting the door behind her.

I scooted down the side of the house.

Tina took a seat on the bench just outside the back door. It was where we had shared a drink and a chat many a time over the last few years. It was the spot where we could relax and be ourselves.

Tina looked far from relaxed. She had a tumbler with what I assumed was gin. She also wasn't wearing any makeup; not that she needed it.

'Did you want a drink?'

The possibility had run a full circuit of my brain before I was obliged to decline. I was having enough difficulty thinking while sober, adding booze to the mix was not an option.

'So, what's so important that you had to break all the distancing rules?' Tina took a big swig of her drink.

'I need to ask you something that might be difficult for you to answer honestly-' I didn't get to finish.

'I haven't got the patience for your tales of woe,' she snapped. 'I've got one daughter on the other side of the world and another a few hundred miles away, both who I can't go and see. And, to top it all off, I've got the police probing around in my private life because they think my fooling around with you might have gotten my son killed. So, if you've got a personal problem and I am the only source of sympathy you've got left, I have to tell you that you're shit out of luck.'

Her words were like a slap across my face. *Shit out of luck* summed up my life. Shit or bust, I had to just come out and say it.

'Did you try to get pregnant by me?'

'What?!' Tina said, nearly spitting out the sip she'd just taken. 'Are you for real?'

'Seriously, I need to know.'

'We are a long way down the path now. I can't have any more kids. I'm retired, for God's sake.'

'Not now.' I rolled my eyes, not knowing if she was serious or just yanking my chain because the opportunity had presented itself and sarcasm was her second language. 'Back in the eighties – you know – the first time we...'

She took a breath. I could see the cogs turning. An explanation was being constructed.

'Well?' I prompted.

'I missed being a mum to small children. That's the curse of having kids so young.' Her expression was distant, thoughtful, as though remembering the nappies and the sleepless nights had killed the flow of reason. 'I was still young and had two kids who would have been flying the nest, sooner or later. I wanted to have that feeling of brand-new unconditional love while I still could, while I was still young enough. Now, as a grandparent, I hand that responsibility over to Charlotte and Kayleigh. I can still feel that love, but it's different. I only wish I could have seen Dan's children.'

A sharp intake of breath, a solitary tear; the feeling of raw loss teetered into the present.

'I need to understand something,' I said, the realisation of my inadequate fertility growing with each breath. 'You weren't using a method of birth control when we had sex all those years ago.'

She shook her head, a mask of regret affixed. I couldn't tell if it was regret that she had been so desperate, or regret because her plan didn't work.

'But Kayleigh definitely isn't mine?' I thought I knew but asked all the same.

'No.' Tina smiled, weakly. 'She's got her father's eyes – her father's smile – she isn't yours, Will. But through my own selfish

355

maternal instincts, she might have been. I don't know why it didn't happen.'

Ouch.

My brain imploded. That penny hadn't just dropped, it had thrown itself from the edge, plummeted into the abyss, exploding on impact, causing a fireball to which all my reason and truth had been sucked into; a powerful singularity from which there was no escape.

I staggered, reaching out for the wall for balance. Tina leaped up to catch me. Social distancing ignored; she could see my collapse imminent. There was grass and wall and sky and concrete – all merging into a kaleidoscope of confusion.

I blacked out. Just for a moment.

'Will? Speak to me,' Tina's concerned voice pulled me out of the void. I was sprawled on the grass, looking up at the perfect canopy of blue above. The ripples of light-headedness could still be observed but I pushed myself into a sitting position. Tina's hand was on the back of my neck, rubbing the tight stem of muscle.

'Are you ok? Do you know where you are?' she asked.

I knew where I was. More importantly, I knew who I was; or should that be, *Who I wasn't.*

I couldn't father children. Or at least that's how it seemed. Jessie might not be my daughter. But she could have been Dan's, and she could be Tina's granddaughter. The more I thought about it, the more it made sense. Jessie always had this air of familiarity about her; something I recognised in her. I always believed I was seeing her mother's traits, or my own, reborn in her. But I wasn't. I was seeing Dan.

If Sarah had been hiding that for twenty years, what else could she be hiding?

109

Present Day

I wandered back to my house on unsteady legs. It felt as though I had downed the optics shelf of a well-stocked bar. I hadn't, for a change. I did have a shot of Glenmorangie, kindly provided by Tina after she had helped me to the bench to regain my composure. After she'd gotten over the shock of learning about her potential granddaughter, and I feigned getting over the shock of discovering that I was in fact childless, we said our goodbyes and I left.

My first instinct was to race over to Sarah's house, kick the shit out of the front door and pin the deceitful bitch to the wall by the throat. That's what I wanted to do, what I felt I was due. Forearmed is forewarned, and I needed to know more. Everything I needed was back in a shoebox in my isolation bunker. I would be holed-up with frozen pizza, beer, and the memoirs of a compulsive liar. I was a glutton for punishment.

I put my key in the lock. It wouldn't turn.

I tried again. Nothing.

The lock on the door was old, sometimes temperamental, but it always opened.

But then I remembered. The old lock had a drop catch which could prevent the key from opening the door from the outside. Not many houses still had them, but mine did. Somebody was inside.

I pressed my ear to the door. I could hear the vague stomping of feet, possibly upstairs. I had two choices. Either I slam the shit out of the door to make my presence felt, or I could nip around into the lane and get in through the back door.

I opted for the latter.

My heart was already rattling off the hook in my chest, I wasn't sure if my fragile emotional state could bear a confrontation with an intruder. Still, I pressed on.

I arrived at the yard door and paused. I felt so small, so vulnerable, just as I did when I played in the lane as a kid. Trembling fear infected my fingers, the door handle rattled in my grasp. I turned it and the door swung open, slipping from my grip, clattering against the wall. I cursed. There was no way an intruder wouldn't have heard that.

With leaden limbs, weighed down by the overwhelming adrenaline, I rushed to the back door, fumbling through the keys to find the right one. My hands shook so much I couldn't get the key into the lock. I tried and I tried. Eventually, it slid in, and I gained access.

But I was too late.

I rushed through the house but as I entered the entrance hall, I could see the front door was ajar. I stepped outside and looked up the street.

Nothing.

I ran up the road to the junction of Dewsland Street.

Nothing.

I'd missed a trick. I just had to check the house to see if anything had been taken. I knew what they were after without checking. They were sly, but so was I.

110

Present Day

I went through every room in the house, checking to see if anything had been taken. There could have been but, with my standard of housekeeping, I'm not sure any would-be burglar would know how to find any of the good stuff. And I wasn't sure I'd have been able to identify to the insurance agent or the police if anything had been pinched. Although, to me, it was obvious there had been a presence in most of the rooms – a wardrobe door was open, some drawers had been pulled out, a kitchen cupboard had been raked through. These were not things I would have left, as untidy as I was.

I walked into the kitchen and filled the kettle. A strong sweet tea was called for. I was toying with the idea of calling the police about the break-in but there would be little evidence for them to go on. There was no broken glass or forced entry. The intruder had a key and that narrowed the list of possible suspects in my own personal episode of Columbo: Sarah, Jessie or, more than likely, Jon. On reflection, I figured I'd have to let it go. After all, the intruder was looking for something I had stolen from Vicary Street.

Next to the kettle was a box of lager. Twenty-four tins of Carling in a white cardboard sheath, upended, covered in plastic apart for the one end where I had ripped my way in. I lifted off the top layer of cans and placed them on the counter. Under the façade of tins – giving the impression of a full box – was the shoebox filled with diaries. My own paranoia had kicked in moments after reading the first words of deceit. I had spent the last two days with an eye over my shoulder, and that was while I was still in the house. When I left to see Tina, I made sure my ill-gotten gains were not immediately obvious.

I made my tea and sat at the kitchen table for a change. I had already made sure that all the front windows were locked and that the drop catch was down. I didn't want anyone sneaking back in. And, from the kitchen, I could see the yard door and had my rear guard covered.

I pulled out the diary for the year 2000 and continued through it.

I could remember much of what had been documented. A simple line prompted a vivid memory. Good memories. Bad memories. Life defining memories. A funeral, a wedding, a birth. 2000 was a year packed with events.

I swallowed down my tea as I swallowed down the text.

For the most part, there was nothing out of place. But somewhere, buried in my mind, something was flagging up a discrepancy. It was bothering me, but I didn't know what it was. I read on to a finish and reached for the next diary.

And the next.

And the next.

And the next.

As soon as the daylight had dimmed, the kitchen light had been flicked on. I'd made a bacon sandwich and sat down to continue. Throughout my reverse journey through the 90s I was learning nothing new. Sarah and I weren't even an item, weren't even a thing. Her life was almost completely based in Bristol, with the occasion excursion back to Milford. Most entries were work, nights out, days out, and trekking down the M4 to visit the old hometown. There was nothing special – or sinister – to report. Most of it didn't have any relevance. There were names and places I'd only heard about in passing. Nothing familiar.

I'd rolled myself through several years of blue ink nothingness before I read something that put a halt on my backward motion.

June 1st, 1996: I hated Laura Birkett with a passion. She won't be missed.

That was the entire entry for that day. I didn't know who Laura Birkett was, but I had a friend, called Google, who might. I

360

tapped in the name and awaited the results. Several articles popped up, but only one fitted the timeline.

> *Laura Birkett, 25, from Cheltenham, was found dead by a dog walker in woodland near Clifton Observatory, Bristol. Laura was a student nurse at the Southmead Hospital, Bristol, and had been missing for three weeks.*

The article was one that had been added to an online archive, but the original date was June 19th, 1996.

I dug into the case, searching every online resource I could find that had details of the Laura Birkett case. Most articles were basically the same as the last, just worded differently. All stating it was a murder investigation and was, as yet, unsolved. The victim had been stabbed.

I shuddered over the possibility but quickly dismissed it. Sarah was a devious cow, but she wasn't a killer. Maybe she was just commenting on the fact the nurse – who happened to work at the same hospital as Sarah – was missing. I made peace with that idea and returned to the diary.

I read on through a few more pages of mundane items before I hit another short, account that begged me to pause.

> *June 19th, 1996: They found her. Even when dead, she's stealing all the attention.*

I flicked over the pages, one after another, but I could find no other reference to Laura Birkett, or her murder.

I would need to investigate this further. Never mind being Columbo, I would have to be Poirot and Miss Marple too. Was it Miss Scarlett, in the library, with the lead piping? Or would it be more likely, Mrs Sarah Taylor, in the dark alley, with the kitchen knife? I didn't know where the fuck to start but I knew that I had to. Everything I had come to know was a lie.

111

Present Day

I was somewhere in the limbo between being sleep and being awake. Road noise filtering in, people talking, a dog barking. But for everything I could hear, I couldn't see anything at all. The bedroom was filled with an inky blackness that vibrated as though it were alive, morphing shape in the confusion of the hour. I tried to flip on my side, to switch on the bedside light but I couldn't. My hands were tied. Thin coarse rope bit into the bones of my wrist, any movement unleashing pain. I couldn't roll. I couldn't twist.

I was trapped.

There was a movement. A sound.

My eyes gradually became accustomed to the light – shapes loomed out of the darkness, the wardrobe, the dressing table, the chest of drawers. Everything present. Everything correct.

But there was something else.

The noise of nocturnal life beyond the walls ebbed away and I became aware of another sound. Closer. Inside the room. I held my breath. But I could still hear the rise and fall of a ribcage.

It wasn't mine.

Another movement. Another sound.

A footfall.

I felt weight upon the bed. Pressure on the mattress that made me roll to one side. Not enough to turn fully, but enough that the rope gripped onto my wrist, ripping out hairs, cutting into skin.

'Who's there?' My hollow voice barely registered.

'Sshhhh.'

The response was female, but malevolent, barely human.

Snapping my arms back and forth, I tried to break free, hoping the rope would give before my wrists did. But the pain was intense, debilitating.

I could see the shape of a figure – a small figure – perched at the side of the bed. The figure leaned in, flicking on the lamp that I couldn't reach, the light blinding me.

It was Sarah.

Dressed in black trousers and a black hoodie, she gazed down at helpless little old me and smiled.

'I wish you hadn't taken my diaries, Will.' Her voice surprisingly calm, yet sinister.

I wanted to respond. I wanted to ask her if she'd killed Laura Birkett, if Dan was the father of Jessie, if she was responsible for Dan's whereabouts. I wanted to ask so much, but fear had stolen the breath from my lungs. I could also see what she was holding in her hand.

A knife.

Without another word, she placed the tip of the blade against my naked chest, applying pressure to break the skin. A little blood trickled from the nick. I wanted to scream, wanted to call for help but the air just wouldn't gather in my lungs, terrified of the blade edging its way toward my heart.

Then she lifted her arms high, both hands gripping the black handle of the long kitchen knife, to thrust it down, right up to the hilt into my ribcage. A silent scream in the night.

*

Like the rapid surge of electrocution firing through my limbs, I bucked out of my slumber.

My hands reached for the knife, for the hole, for the hands gripping the blade. But there was nothing but the cloth of my t-shirt. A patted my chest, examined my fingers in the dim light, looking for blood. But there was no blood. No blade. No Sarah.

A fine sheen of sweat covered my body, fusing my clothes to my flesh. I was still on the sofa. I must have fallen asleep when I shifted to the living room from the kitchen, trying to conduct my

364

amateur investigation through the power of social media in relative comfort. I'd fired out some messages before I'd fallen asleep – before the nightmare – with a hope of learning more.

A glance at my phone told me it was just before 5am. Too late to go upstairs to bed, but too early for me to start harassing people about what they knew. Tea, toast and a shower, not necessarily in that order, was the only option until the hour was more acceptable.

I was about to head to the kitchen when I noticed a message symbol on the top left of my smartphone screen. I didn't need to wait; I had a reply.

112

Present Day

Anything you ever wanted to know was available on the internet. There were also things you never ever wanted to know but couldn't un-see once viewed. I'd never been one for trawling over websites, looking through the intricate details of a celebrity's life or some political incident or a conspiracy theory. I think I had a normal amount of curiosity in everyday things and didn't go looking for things that didn't interest me at all, whereas some people might have a healthy amount of curiosity about the unknown, dwelling over websites and social media, looking for something to be interested in. I knew what I liked, and I liked what I knew.

What I wasn't familiar with was a clear route around the various social media sites. I had Facebook, with a hundred or so friends, mostly people I'd gone to school with, and a few contacts I made through work. It was nice to get a dozen or so birthday messages every year and tagged in some old photos when someone recognised my obscured bonce from a grainy picture taken back in the 80s. It was nice, but not necessary.

What I was able to work out was that both Sarah and Jon had blocked me, and I was no longer able to gain anything valuable from their accounts. But I'm a quick study and I knew that Sarah had an abandoned Instagram account with about three pictures uploaded to it. In the depths of the night, I had created my own, new Instagram account and went hunting, finding Sarah's quickly. Across the top banner, which included a circular picture of a beach, it stated the accounts activity and interaction: 3 posts, 5 followers, 22 following.

The three posts were of three different beaches under three different filters. There were only a couple of likes and comments on one of the posts. One of the comments was made by a *@bizzylizzy68*. I checked out the profile and found it belonged to a nurse who worked in Bristol. There hadn't been any activity on the account in about eighteen months, but I had her name and location, and checked her out on Facebook.

The Facebook account, however, was bang up to date. She was, Elizabeth Berry, a fifty-two-year-old staff nurse at Southmead Hospital and had loads of activity happening on her social media. A lot of the account was open to the public. I scrolled through her extensive collection of pictures, looking for some clues.

It took a while, but I found what I was looking for.

There was a photograph – in fact, a photograph of a photograph – that had been uploaded almost ten years previously. It was a group picture of what could have been a bunch of nurses on a night out. Bizzy Lizzy was front and centre, twenty or so years younger than she was now but her features hadn't altered much, just her hairstyle. There were two other familiar faces in the crowd. One, I had only seen for the first time on a news website a few hours earlier: a murder victim I'll never get to know. The other was a face, until recently, I had seen every day for the past twenty years and I knew only too well.

Laura Birkett was standing next to Lizzy, both had broad, toothy smiles and booze-sparkled eyes.

Sarah was at the edge of the group – not only in the photograph – but socially too. She was doing her fake smile. When a person gave a genuine smile, their whole face would respond, mouth, cheeks, eyes, but when a smile was fake, only the mouth would respond. Sarah had one of the worse fake smiles ever. A genuine smile would have her eyes narrowed down to a squint. In the photo her eyes were round and fixed.

This was not a happy night for her.

I noticed that the photo of a photo also had its date stamp cropped out, but the edge was still visible. I couldn't make it out so checked some of the comments. There were a few.

Most were about it being a great night, good times, and all the usual nostalgic kind of comments. But there were a couple in a tribute to Laura Birkett.

367

She probably never got to see the photo.

I was seeing all this at an ungodly hour but, undeterred, I sent a message to Lizzy, asking her some specific questions, wrapped around an apology for the lateness of the hour.

I trawled through a few more pictures and tried to make other connections from the comments but hit too many dead ends and secured accounts. It was probably wise that I didn't start messaging random strangers in the wee hours. I was fighting two battles as it was; one with my limited knowledge of social media, the other was with exhaustion. The combination of exhaustion and the new information I was receiving, had obviously brewed itself into the nightmare.

*

When I'd shuddered awake; the nightmare scenario running through my circuitry, snatching away the much-needed rest my body craved. I wasn't sure how long I'd managed to sleep, but it was long enough for the game to change.

Lizzy's reply was already sitting in my inbox.

I'd queried Lizzy under the pretence that I was researching a book about unsolved murders and that her name had popped up as someone who knew Laura Birkett. I strongly assured her that I wasn't seeking to glamourize the case, that her information would only form the basis of a narrative piece about Laura. I also asked if I could have a better copy of the image to use in the book, showing the victim as a sociable outgoing girl, but that I would blur out the surrounding faces. I also said that my source had mentioned Sarah and I wanted to know her relationship with Laura.

I took a shot and hoped for the best.

I think I got as much as I was going to get from the reply.

Hello Will Taylor,

This is quite a surprising contact, but I honestly don't mind doing something that honours Laura's memory and helps to keep her case in the public eye.

She was a lovely, bubbly girl, had lots of friends and was very popular with most of the group. She was only in Southmead for about four months but made friends quickly and had the makings of a very good nurse. The picture you speak of is of the last night Laura was seen alive. We didn't know she was missing until a few days after. It's a very bitter-sweet photo for all who knew her. As for Sarah, I didn't think her and Laura hit it off too well. Sarah was one of the designated drivers that night, but she didn't take Laura home. Laura lived in the centre of Bristol and often walked home, even when we warned her not to.

Also, don't read too much into this but I don't think Sarah Gardener is the best person to seek information from, not in relation to Laura.

I hope this helps. There's nothing more I can really tell you. I hope whatever you're working on is published, and if it is, please let me know so I can buy a copy to see my contribution.

Regards

Stay safe.

Liz Berry

In a separate message was an attached full image of the photo, the date stamp included. The digital date read *1.12am 31/05/96.*

That was the morning before Sarah's diary entry. Nobody else knew she was missing. But Sarah did.

113

Present Day

I had replayed all the possible scenarios and options over and over in my head, wondering if I should take my findings to the police. Should I go and tell officers Brooks and Delgado that I'd solved a murder case from twenty-odd years ago? No. Why not? Because it was weak. There was no evidence of a motive. There was only evidence of a dislike for a colleague and that was only a comment in the diary of a young nurse. It was ridiculous.

I continued reading through the next few diaries but couldn't find anything sinister. There was no smoking gun, but this murder business had me thinking all sorts.

I came up with a plan. It was very poor, at best, but it was all I had.

I checked my watch; the hour was reasonable. I texted Sarah one question. I asked if she killed Laura Birkett and then placed my phone on the table.

I got up to make another mug of tea but didn't get very far.

My phone started vibrating. It was Sarah.

'Are you crazy?' No greeting. No build up. Sarah was already at 1000mph when I hit the green accept icon on the phone.

'It's a simple question. Did you kill her?' I remained calm. Nothing upset Sarah more during an argument than serenity from my end.

'Because I didn't like the girl, you think I killed her. Is that what you're saying?'

'Yeah,' I said.

'If I killed everyone I didn't like there would be a trail of bodies behind me – including you. You really are a pathetic little man.' The rage had dropped to a more level-headed condescending tone.

'But did you do it?'

'Fuck you, Will. Fuck you and your deranged little game. Why don't you go and fuck your ragged old bitch whore?'

371

'You mean Tina, Jessie's grandmother?' I dropped that bomb and wondered how it would land.

There was a moment of silence before a calmer, even more condescending and sarcastic Sarah picked up the mantle. 'If you had been more of a man, I wouldn't have to fuck other guys to get what I wanted. You weren't up to the job.'

It was my turn to pause, to reflect over the harshness of her words. I had dropped my bomb and she had countered with a stealth weapon she often wielded when losing. Mine was barely on target. Hers landed with precision.

'Is Jessie Dan's child?'

'How should I know? I never did a test.'

I didn't need a test to know how I felt for the little girl I raised as my own. She was my daughter. Maybe not my flesh and blood, but she was my heart and soul.

'How very convenient for you,' I said, eventually. 'Have you killed anyone else on your travels?'

'Fuck you, Will. You're just like your mother. You can't see the world around you for all the drink you've put in you. The pair of you loved booze more than you loved anything else. So much so, that you had to be surrounded by it while you worked. Good riddance to her and good riddance to you.'

'And what about your mother?' I asked.

'What about my mother? She's gone, and so will you be. When can I have my diaries back?'

'When I'm done with them.'

'Well, I'm done with you, and your little bitch. I'll be round later to pick them up.'

'Don't trouble yourself. I'll bring them to you: Arthur Gwillam's bench, at 7pm, tomorrow evening.'

'Fuck you!'

The call was ended.

I had a little over twenty-four hours to digest the best part of the remaining diaries. I couldn't hold on to them forever, Sarah wouldn't allow it. Sarah didn't allow many things.

114

Present Day

Twenty-four hours passed without incident.

The evening held the warmth of the day, making the crazy situation the whole world was in seem a bit more bearable. The brave and foolhardy ventured out, forgetting about the pandemic and death and fear which laid behind many a door, so they may enjoy the evening.

I observed the haven as I had done a million times before. The darkening blue water speckled with orange and purple, heralding the end of the day, reflecting the sky it could only beg to touch. The sun descending behind the houses, shadows lengthening, silhouettes forming.

As agreed, I was sitting on the bench at the far end of The Rath, the Arthur Gwillam bench – we called it – due to the plaque in dedication to a man many people would only know because of the plaque. Because of the bench. I knew Arthur Gwillam. I served him from behind the bar of The Manchester Club during the early 90s. The large, ruddy faced, ex-Navy man would spend a Sunday morning at the fruit machine with his drinking buddy, Alan. The pair of them would drink Creamflow and talk the languages of sarcasm and banter. Harsh words exchanged without malice or regret. Occasionally, Alan's son would join them for a pint. I remembered him from school, a skinny kid with glasses back in those Central School days. He was very different by the time I served him pints of Guinness nearly a decade after the school closed its doors. We chatted about school days. Another lost memory. Another lost connection. I heard he writes books, now. Good luck to him.

'Let's walk!'

I hadn't heard Sarah approach. Her footfalls must have been lost in the gusts racing off the haven. She passed the bench.

'Sarah…' I called after her, but she was yards ahead, striding down the steep grass bank I had fallen down just a few days earlier.

She glanced back, beckoning for me to follow.

I picked up the shoebox and trailed after her.

She hit the bottom at full stride and took the dogleg down to the old railway line path. The rails were long gone but those with a long memory would never forget their existence.

I followed on but couldn't match her pace. My leg, still tender from my spill, every footfall felt like a hammer blow to the knee cap. I'd been fine on the flat, but the slope had woken up the problem.

Sarah wasn't on the path, but I could see her head bobbing down on the rubble beach alongside Ward's Yard, the derelict pier jutting out into the chunk of the haven named Scotch Bay.

'Sarah, stop, please,' I yelled the instruction, frustrated by her insistence, and the pain from my knee.

She stopped walking, turned and walked cautiously back toward me.

'He did it.'

'Who?' I wasn't getting her.

'Jon did it. He did it all. He killed them all.' Tears appeared on her cheeks.

'What?' I hadn't expected that, it made sense in some crazy way, but her admission wasn't convincing. 'How do you figure that?'

'I was there, I saw it all. I saw him bash Rob's head in. I saw him stab Tom. I saw him stab Dan – our Dan – I saw it all with my own eyes.'

'What about Laura Birkett?'

'Yes, yes, her too. He stabbed her,' she rambled, through tears.

'What about my mother?'

'What, your mother?'

I could see the cogs ticking over. 'Yes, my mother. Did he kill her too?'

'Yes, yes he did, he pushed her, he said.'

'And your mother, did he kill her too?'

The veil of tears came off. Somewhere deep in her deluded mind, she was piecing together my throwaway comments, creating a reality where she could see I knew all the angles. She knew I had read her diaries thoroughly. She knew I could read between the lines of her lies. The cast iron façade that she had built out of her scribblings now toppled down like a house made of rice paper in a force nine gale.

'My... mother? Yes... yes...' She didn't finish what she was trying to say. I could see the questions rolling over in her head.

'I saw that you'd written about my mother dying. *"Good riddance to the drunken old bitch,"* is what you actually wrote, didn't you?'

'Yes, I did,' her mind refocused for an instant. 'You weren't sorry to see her dead, don't say that you weren't. You had motive like everyone who knew her. You could have killed her.'

'Yeah, but I didn't.'

'I know, Jon did.' The façade was being rebuilt, badly.

'No, he didn't. You did. You killed her and you wrote it in your diary.' I held up the shoebox, taunting her with it.

'Writing that I was pleased she was dead is not evidence that I killed her. You're not the police. You're not a lawyer, Will.'

She was right, I was none of things. I was an unemployed barman with a borderline drink problem caused by a dysfunctional relationship with a mother who never wanted me. But while I could have sat in the pit of my own self-loathing and drunk myself into oblivion during the lockdown, I chose to reread the pivotal diary instead. There had been something bothering me about it, and I wanted to be clear in my own mind. 'My mother was found dead on St Valentine's Day, 2000. You wrote your good riddance entry on February 2nd – twelve days earlier. How do you explain that?'

Whatever cogs had been spinning were now at a halt because of the spanner I had just hurled into them.

'Jon...?' she offered.

'Jon was bragging about flying out to see his brother in New Zealand when we were talking at the Millennium party. He was out of the country through all of February. You can't blame him for that one.'

I could see the machine in her head explode under the pressure of failure. I wondered how far I could push her.

'Why did you kill them? The boys – my mother, your mother – that girl Laura: why did you do it?'

It was too much for her. I could see her eyes darting across the sky behind me, looking for answers that weren't there, looking for excuses for why she was the way she was. Her sorrowful face was bathed in the orange glow of the setting sun. A very different sun was setting also. The sun that had warmed her lies was heading for the horizon, never to return.

'Why Rob? What had Rob done?' I tried to get her to admit to them one at a time. It might've worked. It might not.

She took a deep breath.

'Do you remember what started the fight on that night?' her question lucid, controlled.

Of course, I did. 'Jon was having a blow job behind his girlfriend's back. I wasn't having that. Jennifer deserved better.'

'I was the one giving him the blow job,' she said.

We'd never known who the mystery girl was. I had often wondered but, in the grand scheme of how the rest of that night turned out, it was an insignificant detail. But now, with new light on the case and new impetus from the police, what was once insignificant was now vital.

'Why did you kill Rob?'

'I didn't mean to. He found out about me and Jon and was going to tell everyone. I tried to convince him not to say anything.' I could tell she wasn't lying. It made a vast change for her to be truthful for once. 'On that night, I'd followed you and saw you go into Tina's house. I was hurt, angry and confused. I didn't know what I was doing. I bumped into Rob, and we were talking, and I told him that it was me, sucking off Jon.'

'What happened next?' I kept pushing.

'He said he wanted some of that action and wouldn't say a word if I did the same for him.'

'And?'

I could see the shame on her face. It was probably the first time in twenty years that I'd seen some genuine emotion in her expression.

'And we went for a walk to find somewhere quiet. But on the way, Jon rocked up full of apologies and got drawn into the conversation. They both wanted me to suck them off. I didn't know what to do.'

'You could have said "No" and gone home,' I offered.

'And they would have talked…'

'And so, what? It wouldn't have mattered. You'd have been honest, and it would have been forgotten about it, eventually.'

'Eventually? Do you know how long *eventually* is when you're sixteen and you're fat and you're ugly and your self-esteem is so low you have to scrape it up with the rest of the dogshit? It would have taken years to be forgiven and *never* forgotten.' She was almost breathless with hurt and frustration. Nobody could know how the world looked from a teenager's perspective, not even other teenagers. Those formative years, on the threshold of adulthood, are a unique forging of character that is hard to un-forge. Standing on that beach, in the failing light, I could see clearly Sarah's traits could not be made malleable, not even under the fires of Hell. Hell was where she seemed to live.

'Why did you kill him and not Jon?'

'It was an accident. I hit him with a rock. He fell and hit his head. Jon knew they were in the wrong and helped me hide the body. It happened on Ward's Yard – the loch-bridge to the Mine Depot was closed and Jon carried the body over it. We dumped it in a hole in the floor in one of the main buildings and then covered it over the next day.'

378

I could see if that wasn't the truth, it was at least the remembered version of the truth – the version her mind had recorded as the fact regardless of how correct.

'What about Tom? Why did you kill him? Was he asking for blow jobs? Oh no, that's right, you were fucking him. Explain your way out of that one.'

'For fuck's sake, Will!' Her anger leeched into the twilight. The veil of sorrow replaced with the armour of rage. 'He was recording our sex and making tapes, to sell. He was fucking deranged!'

'You'd know what deranged is, wouldn't you?'

She picked up a rock and threw it. It missed.

'Why kill him? Why not expose him?' I asked.

'What? Your friend the porn-king?' she spat the words with a bitterness that had become all too familiar. 'Do you know he was bisexual? He used to love the porn for the cock as much as he liked it for the pussy. It used to thrill him to see you getting a hard-on when watching his latest offerings. He was sick in the head!'

She was trying to play the victim card, but I'd already seen her hand. We, who knew Tom well, knew he was bi. Nothing she could say about his sexuality was going to prejudice an opinion of the weird friend we remembered for his porn collection.

'Just remember, you put yourself on his cock. You made that situation happen. You knew what he was like, and you opened yourself up it-'

'Are you saying I asked for that? Like some girl wearing a short skirt is asking to be raped, is that what you believe?' She desperately tried to clamber to the moral high ground.

'No, that's not what I'm saying – and that's not the same thing at all – you knew what he was like, and you still put yourself into his bed anyway. If you play with fire, eventually you're going to get burned. You poured the petrol on yourself and sparked the match.'

'He filmed me!' She threw another rock.

Holding up the truth in the form of a battered shoebox, I tapped the top. 'You wrote it into your diary that you suggested it –

that you wanted to be filmed and liked the thought of boys and men wanking furiously over your image on videotape.'

Every excuse she could possibly think of were undone by her diaries. I knew it. And she knew it.

'Do you really want to know why I killed him?' She asked.

'Yeah, but give a convincing reason this time.'

'Because I thought he killed you.' The emotion spilled out with the words. 'I thought you were dead, that our actions – mine and his – were responsible. I didn't think I would ever forgive myself if you died, and I knew I wouldn't forgive Tom. I took him to the Mine Depot to show him the dump site of Rob and told him we should put you in there. But then he kept asking about how I knew where Rob was and why I never told.'

'I bet that was an interesting tale.' I interjected but she never acknowledged what I had said.

'He went on and on. Panicking. Calling me an ugly bitch and all sorts. I had a knife on me. He wouldn't shut up. He kept going on and on about you and Rob and how I was a stupid ugly fat bitch…' Her eyes fogged over as her own recollection must have revealed the truth behind her web of lies.

'And so, you stabbed him?' I asked.

'He wouldn't shut up. He told me how he saw me and I…'

'Murdered him. Like you did Rob. Bravo, Sarah. Bra-fucking-vo.'

Her expression switched from vague to rage. She bent down and started hurling anything fist-sized from the surface of the beach. Not aiming, just throwing.

I took a few steps back but, in the dimness of dusk, I didn't see a large, jagged boulder behind me. I went down, hard. My damaged knee giving way completely, the shoebox flew away from me, landing in the space between us.

She was prepared. The years of exercise had made her far more nimble than I. She was on her feet while I was sprawling in agony. Grabbing the box, she ran to a safe distance, away from where I couldn't crawl to. In her pocket she had a can of lighter fluid and a book of matches. Emptying the contents of the can onto the box, Sarah made a bonfire from the scribbled portions of her life. Burning the evidence – burning her version of the truth.

Fighting against the pain, I was able to get onto my one good leg, but I was not going to make much progress across the debris filled beach. The remnants of a deluded girl's memory went up in flames next to the remnants of a breaker's yard. All I could do was watch.

'It's over now,' she said, calmly. 'There's nothing left to defend.'

She started to make her way toward me, slowly, carefully.

'Why Dan?' I was stalling for time while fighting against the pain.

'Does it matter?'

Getting closer.

'Of course, it matters.'

'You couldn't give me a baby, Dan could. And if I got pregnant – which I did – and Jessie was born, he'd have known he was the father.' Closer still. 'I needed to bond you to me, for life.'

'We were already bonded as friends. And how do you know I couldn't give you a baby? How did you know one time with Dan was going to get you pregnant? We weren't an item then. Having babies wasn't on the agenda.'

She stopped less than a breath from me: her eyes cool, calm, in control once again. 'I needed a deeper bond with you and a baby would do that. I tried to get pregnant by you before, that night of the fight with Tom, but it didn't happen.'

'You were fucking Tom too. He could have gotten you pregnant.'

'I wore condoms with him. I didn't with you.'

'One time doesn't make me infertile.'

She paused to measure her reply. 'I heard Tina talking – years ago – when Kayleigh was born – that she thought she couldn't get pregnant again. But she did when she met her new partner. I knew who

381

her old partner was. It was you. You can't have children. I thought I might get lucky, but I didn't.'

I wasn't sure if this was another of her games. It was hard to know where the truth stopped, and the lies started. Why would anyone go to such lengths to have someone in their life?

We stood in the silence as the reality of our lives was open to the elements. The whip of the wind, the cry of a gull, the distant sound of a siren: somehow the world seemed so much smaller in that moment.

'Anyway,' she said. 'Maybe it's better we didn't have children together.'

'What are you talking about?' I braved the question.

'Do you know why your mother disliked me – disliked my mother – do you know?'

'My mother hated everyone except the men buying her drinks and sharing her bed. What's your point?'

'You just made it for me. You know how our birthdays are just two weeks apart?'

I nodded. (Sorry, Officer Delgado, I had no words for the benefit of the tape).

The sirens were getting ever nearer.

'Both our mother's shared their beds with men. Sometimes the same men. Even the same Danish fisherman.' An evil, comfortless grin spread across the face I no longer knew. 'Have you ever wondered why we have the same colour eyes?'

We did have the same colour eyes. The same rare shade of jade. I'd never thought of a reason why before. Why would I?

All the walls that held my childhood stigma exploded outwards. My mind contorted with twisted words spoken so calmly. All I knew evaporated, lifted effortlessly into the ether.

Could it be true? Was Sarah my half-sister? A pair of bastards brought together by the demented desires of the female sibling.

I was trying to put the pieces together, but I was helpless. All that I had come to know was shattered. The squawking gulls offered no help. Maybe the police would.

Sarah's head snapped up to her right, up to the top of The Rath. The sirens that could be heard were killed as the vehicles stopped on the road, but the blue lights remained on, illuminating their arrival.

'Did you call them?'

I barely heard what she said. I saw a flash of orange. The last murmur of the sun reflected on cold steel. She had a knife.

She looked down at me, and then up at the approaching officers. I looked for salvation but all I could see was the knife in her hand and the hatred in her eyes. I knew what was going to happen next. The cool orange reflection disappeared up to the handle and was replaced with a spray of warm red blood. It was done.

Epilogue

The reverend spoke words of God and love and loss to the scattered crowd. Three lives remembered in one memorial. Many faces, aged by time, by grief, bowed in a requiem to those young lives taken so needlessly. The clear azure canopy reflected in the haven's deep channel was a fitting tribute to the bodies which could be committed to the soil now that the black clouds of the unknown had been ushered away on the winds of truth.

But would anyone even know the whole truth?

Brooks and Delgado stood at a distance. Social distancing had been relaxed but not so much that they could rub shoulders with the mourners. There was a time and place for togetherness, and this was one such time. However, the officer's presence was purely out of respect for the families of the deceased.

When the reverend stopped talking, a member of each family stepped forward to pay tribute to their lost loved one. A brother, a sister, a mother: united in grief. Heartfelt and loving, the sentiment brought tears to all who knew the three young men. Separated by evil, reunited by love.

With the memorial over, Brooks and Delgado bid farewell to the immediate families and left to continue their investigation. For while the bodies had been laid to rest, the hearts and minds of those closest to the dead would never rest. Justice, if any could be sought, would be a respite, but nothing more.

*

The turnout was good. The boys would have been happy with it. Rob would have made some speech about the people being united in the face of sorrow and adversity, although there wasn't an adversity to identify. Dan would have been making inappropriate jokes about death and keeping us entertained, reacting to all that he saw. And Tom, well he would have thought about making a porno in a graveyard, or a chapel of rest, or in the back of a hearse. The activist, the comedian, and the pervert: my friends for life, gone forever.

I stood, gripping Tina's hand tightly as the reverend said his final words. We bowed our heads and spoke the Lord's Prayer in unison. The crowd was made up from a lot of old school friends who lived at the edge of our friendship group. Some faces that I'd not seen in years, others I saw every time I stepped into Tesco. Life was funny like that.

Brooks and Delgado were there too. Their faces were familiar, but not in a good way.

I could see another familiar face from across the crowd now. It was one I hadn't seen in decades.

Tina wiped her tears, rubbing my shoulder in solidarity for the tears I had also shed. Kayleigh stood to the side, her husband and kids with her. Charlotte and her family were unable to fly from Australia under the essential travel only guidelines.

There were other faces missing: some dead, some unable to attend. Jon was currently on remand for his involvement in hiding the bodies.

Yes. Plural.

He admitted to helping Sarah, covering up her crimes, being present when Rob was murdered, and helping her move Dan. She had him over a barrel. She always had. We always thought that he disliked her. But he just hated being in her pocket. She had information that tied him to the one crime and that was all the leverage she needed. When the house in Vicary Street was searched, a box was discovered in the attic containing – for want of a better word – trophies. The stone that had been used to smash Rob's skull was preserved in a rag that happened to be Jon's t-shirt on that night. It was covered in both Rob's and Jon's blood. I only knew this because Jon had told it to a visitor – possibly his brother – and it had been leaked on to social media. How true it was would be seen in court. Either way, Jon was looking to take whatever the justice system threw at him. Also, the knife Sarah used against Tom was in the box, complete with his blood and hers.

Of course, Sarah was missing too. She wasn't languishing at her majesty's pleasure. I would never know if the knife she had brought was to kill me or to kill herself. I guess she made an instant decision when she saw the police presence gathering at the end of The Rath. Maybe she didn't stab me for the benefit of Jessie. So that there was at least one parental unit left for her to mourn with.

Jessie didn't attend the memorial. She was away, in Cardiff, getting on with her life. I never told her the truth about her potential other dad. I would never say anything, and Tina had sworn not to speak of it too. As far as we knew, we were the only people to know and, until such time as a DNA test was done, there was no way to confirm it anyway. Jessie was still my daughter, and I was still her father.

The other question over DNA lay with Sarah's eleventh-hour admission. Were we half siblings? I'd never want to know. It could have been a last-minute attempt to fuck over my life, and most probably was. The stain of it would blight my life, forever. Somehow, I would have to live with the knowing and not knowing.

At least the road was open from here on in. Now there was nothing in my way. Tina and I were an item. No shame. No hiding. We didn't know what would happen next and we were taking it a day at a time. So far, so good. We may made not have had the best start, but we had as good a chance as anyone else in this crazy world.

As I looked over the crowd, I could see the face from the past seeking me out. I strolled over, meeting them halfway. They had company.

'Hi, Will, how have you been?'

'I've been better, but I've also been worse. How are you, Jennifer?' The old infatuation was long gone. My heart belonged to Tina and couldn't see any other woman in any other way anymore. What I had been looking for, I had found thirty-four years ago but just didn't know it. Jennifer was still beautiful and looked younger than her fifty years. Life had been good to her. My fiftieth birthday had passed without fuss or celebration, but I imagined hers would have been very different.

'I've been good. Still buying and selling property and living in England, now.'

'Nice,' I said, genuinely. 'I'm glad it's all worked out for you.'

'Oh, by the way, this is my son, Jack,' she said.

We couldn't shake hands because of the restrictions, but we did nod and greet each other. The boy looked about Jessie's age. I'd never met him before but here was a familiarity about him; something I recognised in his manner and his features. Maybe it was Jennifer's spirit, maybe it was Jennifer's looks. I didn't know what it was. But there was one thing I did notice, and it was something of a rarity. His eyes were the same shade of green as mine.

The End.

Author's Afterthought

Thank you for taking the time to read this book. Out of all the books I've written, this was the most difficult to execute. I'd never written a book in the first person before, but to go from first person to third person in different chapters brought a challenge all its own. Also, the thirty-plus year time frame of the book, with the same characters, was no easy task either. And speaking of the characters, I didn't want them to be likeable, I wanted them to be flawed, awkward, and sometimes, not very nice. Writing a character without flaws is no-no in fiction writing, so writing a bunch of damaged individuals was surprisingly rewarding, and hopefully, adds to making this book a far more memorable read. If you did enjoy this book, would you be so kind as to review or rate it on Amazon and/or Goodreads and recommend to your friends. Thank you.

Acknowledgements

I'm very fortunate to have a great support network around me; made up of friends, family, and readers. I'd like to thank my two Beta Readers – Lauren Greenway and Audrey Curtis for their input in the developmental stage of the story. And I'd like to give extra thanks to Lauren Greenway for being – despite being my long-suffering partner – my number one proof-reader too. She generally has to endure my books twice before I publish them.

I'd also like to give special thanks to Darrel Walters for donating the stunning image gracing the cover of this book. I think we can all agree it sets the tone of what lies ahead.